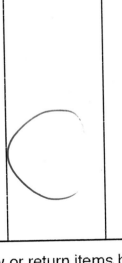

H I T

Please renew or return items by due date

www.hertfordshire.gov.uk/libraries

Renewals and enquiries: 0300 123 4049

Textphone for hearing or
speech impaired users: 01992 555 506

**There's a lot going on at Hertfordshire
Libraries! Scan the QR code to find out
more . . .**

L32 06.23

Hertfordshire

535 601 16 7

D1419584

KILL
FOR ME
KILL
FOR YOU

STEVE CAVANAGH

KILL FOR ME KILL FOR YOU

HEADLINE

Copyright © 2023 Steve Cavanagh

The right of Steve Cavanagh to be identified as the Author of
the Work has been asserted by him in accordance with the
Copyright, Designs and Patents Act 1988.

First published in Great Britain in 2023 by
HEADLINE PUBLISHING GROUP

1

Apart from any use permitted under UK copyright law, this publication may only
be reproduced, stored, or transmitted, in any form, or by any means, with prior
permission in writing of the publishers or, in the case of reprographic production, in
accordance with the terms of licenses issued by the Copyright Licensing Agency.

All characters in this publication are fictitious and any resemblance
to real persons, living or dead, is purely coincidental

Cataloguing in Publication Data is available from the British Library

Hardback ISBN 978 1 0354 0815 3
Trade paperback ISBN 978 1 0354 0816 0

Typeset in 12.76/16.82 pt Adobe Garamond Pro by Jouve (UK), Milton Keynes

Printed and bound in Great Britain by Clays Ltd, Elcograf S.p.A.

Headline's policy is to use papers that are natural, renewable and recyclable
products and made from wood grown in well-managed forests and other
controlled sources. The logging and manufacturing processes are expected to
conform to the environmental regulations of the country of origin.

HEADLINE PUBLISHING GROUP
An Hachette UK Company
Carmelite House
50 Victoria Embankment
London EC4Y 0DZ

www.headline.co.uk
www.hachette.co.uk

For Marie and Tom.

'*Stronger than lover's love, is lover's hate. Incurable, in each, the wounds they make.*'

– Euripides

'*Revenge, the sweetest morsel to the mouth that ever was cooked in hell.*'

– Walter Scott, *The Heart of Midlothian*

I

Amanda

Amanda White lifted the lid from the electric baby-bottle steriliser and stared inside at the .22 caliber revolver. It looked like the gun was sweating, its steel frame and barrel beaded with balls of hot condensation, the steam rising gently from the base. Turning away, she found her soft leather gloves, put them on and carefully lifted the weapon clear.

The gun had to be clean today. No fingerprints. No traces of her DNA. Last night she had the idea of using the steriliser to remove any prior trace of her from the weapon. It seemed fitting, somehow, that one of Jess's things should have a part in this. She was surprised that the steriliser still worked. It hadn't been used since Jess's first birthday, when she'd switched her on to sippy cups. She and her husband, Luis, had decided to keep the steriliser, though, in case Jess ever had a baby brother or sister down the line.

None of that could happen now.

The heat from the steriliser had begun to peel away the duct tape wrapped round the butt of the gun. It still felt alien in her hand. All of those days she'd driven out to the woods to practise shooting tin cans hadn't mattered. She still wasn't used to handling the weapon. She was a New York liberal. Anti-guns. A law-abiding taxpayer. Perhaps she was none of those things any more. Death changes you.

When that death was your six-year-old girl and, a week later, your husband, there was more to it than mere grief. That kind of death didn't ride alone. It brought more dark horsemen with it – unemployment, debt, addiction and pain that at times was too great to bear. Amanda's life had imploded in loss.

She put the revolver on the dining table, dried it with kitchen towels and loaded it with five expectant rounds of ammunition.

She only needed one of those rounds to end her suffering. It was an easy shot. Her arm would rise, the barrel level with the top of the man's head, and then – pull the trigger. She checked the clock. Six thirty in the a.m. He would be leaving his apartment soon. She needed to get ready.

At seven fifteen Amanda passed through the art deco entrance to the 96th Street subway station on the Upper West Side. A light rain was just beginning to fall. A man with dark hair, wearing a black overcoat, swiped his MTA card at the turnstile. Amanda waited a beat, pulled the hood of her sweatshirt over her ball cap. Five more people passed through the gate before Amanda slid her card over the sensor and turned left for the platform designated Downtown & Brooklyn.

She skipped down two flights of stairs. Before she reached the bottom, she saw the man in the overcoat again. Side view. He had a dark beard, which he kept neat. AirPods in his ears and a thick scarf round his neck, tucked into the folds of the coat. Like the other twenty or so people on the platform, he had his head down, gazing at his cell phone.

Time check. Seven nineteen. They had just missed the #1 train, an express to South Ferry that only stopped at Times Square, Penn Station, 14th Street and Chambers Street. If he'd taken the express, he would've had to get off at Chambers Street, then change onto the #2 or #3 for Flatbush to make his stop at Wall Street.

Amanda kept him in her eyeline, but moved behind him to his eight o'clock. Not directly behind him, because he might pick up her reflection in the train window as she moved. Her face was mostly covered, by the cap and scarf, but she couldn't take the chance he might spot her – recognize her.

Like he had last time.

At seven twenty-one, the #2 rolled in on a blast of ice-fresh September wind. The train slowed, stopped. Amanda moved forward. A voice on the PA system announced the train's arrival. There were now maybe a hundred people spread out on the platform. Rush hour on the subway. People going about their lives, getting through the journey, thoughts of their jobs already heavy in their minds.

Not for Amanda. Not any more.

The train doors slid open and commuters poured out. Amanda had to brush past a teenager in a school uniform and a construction worker with his hard hat clipped to his shoulder bag. They both said something as Amanda pushed in. She didn't care. She couldn't risk the man in the overcoat making it onto the train without her, leaving her stranded on the platform. That had happened before too.

She moved forward. He was five feet ahead. The departing passengers had left room in the car, but not much. There were two of the prized orange seats left. As usual, he made for them, and managed to get one this time. Amanda turned her back on him, took hold of a pole in the centre of the car and let it fill up. Let the embarking passengers jostle her up the car a little until she was close enough to reach out and touch him. She kept her back to his seat row.

The doors closed. Bodies crushed together all around her. Yet, she had enough room to turn. And she did. A half turn. There were two people standing side by side in front of the seated man in the overcoat. Their backs were to each other. An arm's width between them. The man in the overcoat started manspreading. The woman seated to his right gave him a dirty look and then swiftly returned her attention to the laptop balanced on her knees. The young man to his left was playing a video game on his phone. They ignored the man. Or tried to.

Amanda unlocked her cell phone, selected the first of the pre-programmed timers and hit *start* just as the train began to move.

The timer ticked down from one minute thirteen seconds – the average time between train doors closing at 96th Street and the doors opening again at 86th Street.

When she still had a job, she'd been a manager in a retirement home, having worked her way up from caregiver to the person who ran the joint for the company. She had found that if she had something to accomplish, she would only do it if she sat down and wrote out a plan. Step by step. This is how she got her degree at night school. This is how she got her promotions to supervisor, deputy manager and then manager. This is how she planned one of her paintings or sketches, which she worked on late into the night. This is how she planned the murder she was about to commit.

Amanda took another glance in the man's direction. She wasn't concerned he'd spot her from behind or even in a side view when they were this close. He wouldn't be able to see her face in any of the windows unless he stood up. She wore sneakers, a pair of baggy black sweatpants, a puffy coat and a hooded sweatshirt beneath it. As covered up as she could get without standing out.

There were three stops on this train that gave her the opportunity she needed. It had to be timed perfectly. The shot coming just as the doors opened. Her aim concealed by the mass of bodies around her. Then she would scream, like others surely would, drop the gun and run like crazy off the train. A gunshot on a crowded rail car would cause a panic, a stampede to get to safety. She would be one woman in a mass of people getting out of there, up the stairs and straight out of the station, her head down in the crowd, and no one would be able to identify her. Not eyewitnesses, not security cameras. She would hide, perfectly, in plain sight.

The next stop would be 86th Street. Ten seconds left on the timer. Ten seconds until the doors opened.

Amanda tilted her head slightly, side to side, checking who was getting off. She didn't want to be exposed. She needed bodies between her and the target. It looked like the pair between her and the man were staying on board.

The train slowed and stopped. A dozen people got off and a dozen more got on. A man in a business suit and raincoat carrying a half-folded golf umbrella got on and stood beside Amanda, but with his back to her. The doors closed, the train started to move and she hit the second timer.

One minute twenty-two seconds until doors would open on 79th Street. The longest average travel time of the three stops to Times Square. It was just one minute fifteen between 79th and 72nd, but 79th had better exits. No point in trying to estimate the average journey time from 72nd to Times Square, as the train frequently slowed to let other trains through because the stop was so busy.

She'd planned for this, in detail.

Now was the time.

The counter read fifty-one seconds.

Amanda took a breath, let it out slowly and put her hand in her coat pocket. Took hold of the revolver. Her gloves were thin leather, but even so it was a delicate maneouvre to snake her finger through the trigger guard without the leather catching.

The two passengers beside her still had their backs to one another, preserving the gap between them. She could see the top of the target's head, pointed down – his focus centered on his cell phone.

The train slowed down.

Fifteen seconds until the train doors opened.

Fifteen seconds until she pulled the trigger.

The *clickety-clack* rhythm of the wheels on the rails slowed down a beat as the train reduced speed.

They emerged from the tunnel. The carriage suddenly lit up. She glanced out of the window. The platform looked busy. Some people to her right made their way through the mass of bodies toward the door.

A screech of steel on steel as the brakes kicked in harder.

Eight seconds.

Click-clack

She turned towards the target.

Five seconds.

Click—clack.

She took a deep breath. Held it.

Three seconds.

Click———clack.

Amanda drew the hammer back on the pistol in her pocket until she heard it . . .

The man's head shot up. He stared straight at her.

'You,' he said, rising to his feet.

Amanda tried to pull the gun, but hesitated. He'd seen her. He'd spoken to her. And that would draw attention. If she shot him now, people might see her do it. Since she'd lost her family, Amanda sometimes went days without another person speaking to her. This man, Wallace Crone, was the last person she wanted to speak to her. And his voice, addressing her, was like being shaken out of a long dream. The train driver hit the brakes hard, throwing her off balance.

That moment's hesitation was long enough to give Crone the advantage, and ruin her chance. He stood, grabbed her by the lapels and shouted, 'Help! Police, help!'

He pushed forward and the back of Amanda's head hit one of the upright poles.

'Get off me,' she said.

His face was right up close to hers. She could smell the coffee on his breath. He gritted his teeth, called out again.

'Help me! Someone call a cop!' he said.

Amanda managed to pull the gun. Held it low, out of his line of sight.

'What's the problem here?' cried a voice. It sounded deep, authoritative. A man. A cop. Transport police. She could hear him moving toward them.

She dropped the gun, unnoticed, into the half-open golf umbrella of the businessman beside her. He promptly moved away, his eyes wide at the scene in front of him – not knowing whether to intervene and on whose behalf.

Amanda's balance left her, and she fell backwards. Crone on top of her.

She saw the cop standing over them, pulling at Crone's arm, asking what the hell was going on.

Crone let go, but as he got up, he said something else. Something she'd heard him say a hundred times. But now, as those words broke the silence of her loss and her loneliness, they sounded as hollow as old bones.

She didn't believe those words when she'd first heard them. She didn't believe them now.

'I didn't kill your daughter.'

2

Ruth

Ruth Gelman poured the remains of the bottle of Pinot Grigio into her glass and instantly regretted it. Scott sat across the dining table from her, his wine glass empty for the past half hour of their Friday-night meal. He'd watched her pour the wine, tipping the bottle upside down until she'd taken the final drop. But he didn't complain. The disapproving look was more than enough.

'I've had a rough day,' said Ruth, by way of apology.

'It's fine,' he said. 'I don't want to get loaded before the game anyway.'

Ruth noticed he hadn't asked her about her day. He never did on these Fridays. Ruth pushed her plate away. She'd barely touched the salmon, and the asparagus lay whole on the side. Even as she had prepared the meal, the thought of sitting down to eat it was far from her mind. She didn't want to eat tonight. No appetite. Only a thirst. When the notion to drink hit Ruth, she didn't want food. Food was antithetical. It didn't help her get to that serene space after the fifth glass. Scott was going out tonight. He went out every other Friday with the guys. Poker. Bowling. Pool. Sometimes they dropped the pretense and just hit a bar.

'Poker?' she asked.

He nodded, said, 'At Gordon's place.'

'How is he?'

'Poor bastard has been hitting the bottle all week.'

Gordon was one of Scott's oldest friends. A fellow Manhattan lawyer whose life was disintegrating. His wife, Alison, had kicked him out last week after she found messages on his phone from another woman. Gordon had been having an affair, and now he was paying the price.

'How are Alison and the kids?' asked Ruth.

'She won't talk to him. You should message her and find out,' said Scott.

'So you can tell Gordon? I don't think so. Alison and I were never close. If she reached out to me, that would be different, but I'm not fishing for information for Gordon. He's your friend. I don't want to get involved. And hey, don't tell me Jack will be there.'

Rolling his eyes at the mention of Jack, Scott said, 'I don't think so. Last I heard he was still on vacation in Atlantic City.'

That was one good thing, at least. Jack was an old friend of Scott's that he just couldn't shake, or more likely he didn't want to. No matter how much Ruth pressed him. They had been friends in high school, and, while Scott had risen, Jack had fallen. Drugs, gambling, online fraud. If it was bad and illegal, then Jack was into it.

'Well, if Jack's not there, at least you won't be high when you come home,' said Ruth.

Scott sighed, rose from the table with his plate and carried it to the sink. He rinsed it and put it in the dishwasher then came back over.

'Not hungry, huh?' he said.

There was more in that question, and she knew it. They'd been trying for a baby for a few months now. At thirty-nine Ruth thought she couldn't put it off for much longer. She wanted kids, truly. But, ideally, she wanted to be in a more stable position in the real-estate firm before making that jump. She didn't want to be reliant on Scott and his income from corporate law.

'What time will you be home?' asked Ruth.

'Don't wait up. The state that Gordon's in, I'd expect it to be a late one. He'll want to get wasted and forget his troubles – at least for one night.'

She nodded. He took her plate, scraped the food into the trash. He still hadn't asked her what was wrong. It had not been anything in particular that had got to her that day. Just the stress of being a Manhattan realtor. Traversing the city, meeting potential buyers and moving those sales. Competition was fierce and she'd lost a client during the week. Nothing unusual about it, but it hurt just the same. If she unburdened her troubles on Scott, he would feel guilty going out with his friends. He would still go out, of course, and that might hurt Ruth more. They'd been married five years and nothing much had changed since they'd moved in together. Scott still had his squash games twice a week, still went out with the guys every other Friday like it was holy writ, but since he'd insisted that Ruth stop her birth control pills he'd begun to give her dirty looks when she opened a bottle of wine.

If she opened a second bottle, she could expect to wake up the next morning to find an article waiting for her, hot from Scott's printer, beside a bowl of granola on the breakfast bar. It was invariably some study on the links between female infertility and alcohol consumption. Ruth hardly ever went out with friends. She'd always been a little light in that department. Had been since she'd left high school. Ruth was never great at keeping friends. Always too busy with something. She had people she could call up, but never did. Letting old friendships slide and not making new ones was a failing. Something she recognized. A promise to call school buddies and meet new people regularly appeared on her half-assed New Year's list of resolutions. A drink after work, on occasion, with some of the partners in her firm was all that she had by way of a social life.

Scott had worked in the district attorney's office as a prosecutor the first year they met. It was always going to be a temporary thing. Putting in some time to gain criminal law experience – give a little back to the community. His last six months in post had been a series of interviews with white-shoe law firms from old money whose business now stretched across the globe. He took a position as a litigator. This was not a nine-to-five job. At first it didn't bother Ruth – a realtor needed to do some evening appointments too. But, with Scott's friends and social life, Ruth sometimes wondered where she fitted in to his plans other than as the little woman who would one day bear his children.

Ruth took a fresh bottle of wine from the fridge, filled her glass and moved into the lounge. She sat down on the plush, soft couch and began channel hopping. Scott's arms folded round her shoulders and she felt his breath on her neck. First, his stubble grazed her cheek and then she felt his soft lips in that sweet spot just below her ear. He stepped over the back of the couch, sat beside her and they kissed. He held her then, for a time, and said, 'I'm sorry.'

'I'm sorry too,' said Ruth.

'No need for you to be sorry. You're not the one being an asshole,' he said. He smiled, paused and added, 'For a change.'

Ruth giggled, grabbed a cushion and hit him on the head with it in mock offence.

'I'm *never* the asshole in this relationship.'

'Of course not. Look, you want me to grab a glass and join you? I could blow off the guys for one night?'

'No, it's fine. I know you need your buddies. We can always do something tomorrow?'

'We could go for a meal then catch a movie. My treat.'

'That's a date. Now go have fun.'

He held her tightly before letting go and getting up off the couch.

This was what Ruth had always wanted. To feel safe and secure in a lover's arms. Her mother and father had split up when she was just seven. Ruth had no idea her parents' marriage was even in trouble. Everything was fine and then it wasn't. One minute they were all in matching PJs opening presents under the Christmas tree – the next she was seeing Dad every other weekend. Her eyes flicked to the wedding photo on the console table. Scott carrying her to the wedding car. Confetti and the blurred images of friends and family in soft focus framed their image. They both looked so happy. A layer of dust sat on the picture. In a way, Ruth found that dust comforting. They weren't a new couple, still getting to know one another, still wondering what the other was really thinking.

Scott gave her love. But, more than that, he gave her safety and security.

And it was those feelings that Ruth prized most of all. That this wasn't just a long but ultimately doomed relationship. They were stable. Solid. They had dust on their wedding picture.

'Okay, I'm out of here. I love you,' he said from the hallway.

'I love you too,' Ruth said. She thought about looking up an article on the effects of alcohol on sperm, printing it out and leaving it for Scott to find in the morning, as a joke, of course. She decided against it. She listened to his boots on the parquet floor of the hallway, the click of the deadlock sliding free, the brief blare of noise from a passing car and then a deep, resonant slam as the front door of their brownstone shut.

She took a long drink from her glass, set it down, went through to the kitchen. Standing on a chair, she retrieved a shallow, rectangular tin can from the top of the cupboard, brought it down and opened it on the counter. Rolled a joint, stood at the back door overlooking the small garden. You couldn't really call it a garden. A six-by-eight patch of grass, but it added half a mil to the list price of the house. She held the joint in her lips to light it. She didn't make a habit of smoking pot. Last time she'd lit up was Tuesday, just three days ago. She'd come out to the garden, while Scott was in bed, to watch the Tribute in Light – two spires of spotlights projected into the sky from the top of Battery Parking Garage in tribute to the lost lives from September eleventh. Like a lot of New Yorkers, that anniversary was hard, and she needed something to take the edge off.

The pot helped with her anxiety, and she thought one joint wouldn't hurt. She wasn't pregnant. The trash bag in their bathroom was filling up with negative pregnancy tests. With just a little more time, some more high-value clients on her roster, then she would feel better about taking the time off to start their family. She sometimes looked at little bootees and newborn outfits in the window of mother-and-baby stores and those things only gave her a feeling of excitement and warmth. Ruth took another hit from the joint. It was mild stuff, bought long ago. She remembered her second date with Scott. They met briefly at a party. One of Ruth's old friends had invited him. They got talking and he'd asked for her number. For a low-intensity second date, he'd brought her to another party at one of his friend's apartments in Brooklyn. They'd made small talk, standard second-date stuff, finding out more about one another, then Ruth had spotted some people with a bong in the kitchen. She'd taken a hit, and instantly regretted it. While Ruth had tried roll-ups, she'd never taken a hit before and it produced an instant coughing fit. Scott took her up to the building's roof terrace. She could still remember the sky from that night. Only a few clouds, thin and wispy against a deep, blue-black sky and more stars than she'd ever seen before.

'Take deep breaths,' said Scott.

Ruth inhaled, and while her throat and lungs no longer burned, the intake of oxygen had provoked a strong feeling of nausea.

'I think I'm going to throw up,' said Ruth. 'I'm so, so sorry. This is a horrible date.'

'It's fine,' said Scott. 'Normally, my dates wait until they see me naked before vomiting.'

Ruth laughed and her head spun. She stumbled into Scott, her palm landing on his solid chest to steady herself. He had a good build; he was just being self-deprecating.

Gazing up into his face, Ruth said, 'We're on a rooftop in New York, I'm a little high, and we're very close. Aren't you gonna give me a cheesy line right now and try for a kiss?'

'You want a cheesy line?'

'The cheesier, the better.'

'I think your father is a thief,' said Scott, 'because he obviously stole some of these stars and put them in your eyes.'

'Oh my God, that's soooo cheeeesssy,' said Ruth. And they both laughed.

'What did you tell me you do for a living?' she asked.

'I told you, I'm a prosecutor.'

'Well, you should arrest yourself or something, because that was baaaaddd,' she said, and raised her chin towards him, softly closing her eyes.

'I think I should get you home,' said Scott.

Within a half hour, a cab pulled up outside Ruth's apartment building. They got out of the taxi and Scott joined her on the sidewalk.

'Do you want to come up?' asked Ruth.

'I do, but not tonight. I think you need some coffee.'

Ruth remembered the feeling of disappointment. She'd let herself down, and now Scott didn't want to see her again.

'If you didn't want to come up to my place, why did you come with me in the cab?' she asked.

He leaned in towards her, said, 'I wanted to make sure you were safe.'

For the first time, Ruth felt a flood of familiar and long-gone feelings. Feelings of comfort and security.

'There's an ice-cream parlor two blocks over. I'll see you there tomorrow at one? My treat. They've got rum raisin.'

Ruth giggled, said, 'Now I think you're really trying to make me puke.'

With the memory of that night curling a smile into the corner of her mouth, Ruth stubbed out the joint. When the time came for Ruth and Scott to have a kid, it would be just fine. Her baby's parents would always be together. Her child would never have to go through what Ruth had endured. Scott and Ruth were rock steady.

Back in the lounge, she brought the bottle of wine with her and found an old movie on TCM. It was just starting. She settled in for the night. Finished the second bottle and then went to bed.

Ruth woke from a bad dream in darkness. The clock on the nightstand showed it was 11:45 p.m. She reached behind with her left hand. No one on the other side of the bed. Just cold sheets. Shaking her head, she sat up. The time between turning off the movie and going to bed seemed a little hazy, but she remembered she had a glass of water by her bed. She drank, tried to force the remnants of the dream from her mind. Moments ago, she had been in her boss's office, being fired for losing a property-developer client and she didn't care to get back to that nightmare. It had not been the first time she'd had that dream.

She sat up fully in the bed and reached for her phone. It wasn't by the bedside. She must've left it downstairs on the couch. She finished the water. The glass hit the nightstand with an almighty crash. The sound of glass exploding onto a hard floor.

Ruth sat up straight, touched the base of the bedside lamp to turn it on.

Her empty glass was intact. Perfect.

She heard glass being crunched underfoot. Cracking. The skittering of glass across tile. It was coming from downstairs.

Silence.

Glass being crushed.

Silence.

Crunching glass.

The small hairs on the back of her neck prickled. Her skin rose in goosebumps, the fear rising on her flesh, but then she heard something, a voice perhaps, downstairs.

Scott.

Scott was downstairs, drunk, and he'd dropped a glass or plate.

It had happened before. More than once. Especially when he was out with deadbeat pal, Jack. Maybe Jack had returned from Atlantic City, and he'd been giving Scott coke all night.

Ruth threw off the covers, tied up her dark brown hair and went downstairs in her night things. A vest and silk shorts. She hit the light switch on the landing, then took the last set of stairs to the first floor.

She started calling out Scott before she reached the bottom of the stairs.

'You frightened the hell out of . . .'

The kitchen light wasn't on. From the light on the stairs she saw broken glass on the kitchen floor. She reached inside, feeling for the switch. Flipped it.

The kitchen floor was covered with glass. She looked around, then saw that a pane had been smashed in the back door. The small one just above the door handle. The rest of the panes in the grid were intact. Then, in one of those panes, Ruth caught a reflection. A man, tall, dark clothing. Fierce blue eyes, a long narrow nose and square jaw.

He was right behind her.

An arm clamped around her throat and a hand stifled her scream. There was something in that hand. Something soft. It smelled bad. A chemical odor.

Ruth fell to the floor, her knees giving way.

Her vision swam, and then she heard his voice. Deep, crackling in a long, thick throat. Raspy and broken and utterly, utterly terrifying.

'Hello there, sweetheart . . .'

And the darkness took her.

3
Amanda

Amanda had been waiting for her lawyer for almost three hours on the first floor of the Manhattan Criminal Court Building on Center Street. She'd been arrested on the train two weeks ago, and somehow managed to make bail even though she'd been arraigned on charges of harassment and contempt of court.

The bench outside the courtroom was unforgiving oak and her back was beginning to get sore. A steady flow of people had entered the courtroom, alone or with loved ones, and some had come out again and some hadn't. She guessed some of the folks who had not emerged from court with their tearful relatives had gone straight to Rikers Island, or the Tombs next door. Amanda knew she could be one of those headed to prison before the day was out. The public defender, Gail Sweet, had told her as much on the phone last week. She would do her best for Amanda, but she also advised, 'Pack a toothbrush, just in case.'

'Mrs. White?' said a voice.

The lady standing above her was in her fifties, wearing a bright blood-red blouse over a pale blue business suit. She had a perm, an armful of files and a large bag overflowing with charging cables, pens and rolled up pieces of paper.

Amanda nodded.

'I'm Gail Sweet,' she said.

They talked for a half hour, then Gail left to talk to the prosecutor. She came back with a deal. One that Amanda didn't want. There was no doubting it was a good deal in the circumstances, and she had little choice but to agree. Only thing to do now was get it approved by the judge.

The judge was a white guy in his early sixties, pasty and looked as though he was covered in a fine powder – as if someone had found him in an old drawer and hadn't properly dusted him off before setting him down in the judge's chair for the day.

'Mrs. White, please step forward,' said the judge.

Amanda moved a little closer to the bench, Gail in step with her.

The judge's voice was low, monotone and dead to any emotion. He asked her if she had entered into the plea agreement of her own free will and that she was pleading guilty because she was guilty, and not for any other reason. She said yes.

'This charge arises on foot of a restraining order placing you in contempt of court if you should come within five hundred feet of Mr. Wallace Crone's building or his place of work, or if you come within fifty feet of him in any public place without lawful excuse. You breached that order on September 14th and you accept that breach. The District Attorney's office is withdrawing the assault charge on foot of your cross-complaint that Mr. Crone assaulted *you* on the subway. Both assault complaints are now withdrawn. I agree to place you on probation for a period of one year. You will keep your appointments with your probation officer and you will attend trauma counseling. Don't think that this court is blind to your suffering, Mrs. White. You're forty-one years old and that's no time to start a criminal career. You must stop this obsession with Mr. Crone. In the eyes of the law, he is innocent of your daughter's murder. I hope you keep to these terms and I approve the plea agreement.'

And that was it. Amanda left the building with the contact details for Probation. She had to make an appointment to meet her probation officer and attend court-ordered trauma counseling. She hadn't expected to walk back out of the courthouse that day. Pity. That's what it was. The prosecutor and the judge had taken pity on her because of Jess. Amanda's life story was now one of terrible loss.

It wasn't always this way. Her story used to be different – filled with hope and dreams. She thought, back then, that she and Luis, and Jess, could write their own future.

Jess had loved stories.

'Tell me a story,' Jess said, every night as she was tucked up in bed. Kids develop a night-time routine. For Jess, it was jammies, night-time toilet, brush her teeth and then story time with Luis. But the most important part of her nighttime routine was locating Sparkles. Right before she went to sleep, if Sparkles wasn't in bed with her, she would call out, 'Where's Sparkles? Where's Sparkles?' and a hunt through their apartment would begin. Jess didn't want for toys. Her room was filled with plushies, dolls and even a little playhouse for her burgeoning collection of Sylvanian Families. Sparkles, however, was her very favorite. It was a little white, fluffy unicorn with a purple, sparkly horn on its head. Jess had called it Sparkles. It looked cheap and didn't have enough stuffing to fill it out so it was always floppy. Jess had won it from an arcade grab machine during a summer trip to Coney Island when she was four. It was her first try on the machine. While Luis was gushing praise for Jess because she had won, Jess had waved away his words.

'I didn't win. Sparkles just wanted to come home with me,' she'd said that day.

Usually, Amanda would call for Luis and he read the bedtime story as Amanda cleaned up after dinner, or joined the hunt for Sparkles because Jess could not sleep one wink without that toy beside her. But, one night, Amanda had stayed. Curled up on the floor of Jess's little box room. Jess, blonde curls falling over her pillow, held Sparkles tightly under one arm.

Amanda had watched Luis perch on the edge of the bed and pick up one of Jess's storybooks. The cover was a picture of a little girl in a rowing boat on a stormy sea.

'This one? Again?' asked Luis.

Jess nodded, turned to Sparkles and then with a flick of her wrist Sparkles nodded too.

'Okay, then,' said Luis.

Amanda listened as Luis read the tale of a young girl who lived on a small island. Everything she could ever want was right there – all the fruit, fish and vegetables she could ever want – and her entire family was loving and protective. But the little girl was fascinated by the sea. Her parents wouldn't let her go out on the boats with the fishermen. Said it was too dangerous. One night, the girl went out on the boat when her parents were asleep. Soon the sea got rough, and the boat got turned round. Without the light of the moon, the little girl couldn't see which direction the island lay.

'She was very afraid,' said Luis. 'It was dark and cold, and she wished she had never disobeyed her parents and taken the boat out on the water.'

Amanda recalled Jess's eyes. They were large and intensely blue, lit by her bedside lamp and locked on every word from Luis.

'Then, suddenly, she saw a light. Someone had lit a fire on the beach. The little girl rowed and rowed and rowed, with all her might. She battled over waves as big as mountains, and eventually she got back to her little island and there, standing on the beach by the fire, were her mother and father. The little girl never went out to sea ever again.'

'Wow,' said Amanda. 'That's a pretty scary story. You okay, Jess?'

'I'm fine,' said Jess. 'Sparkles got a little scared, but I knew the girl would be okay.'

'Goodnight, Jess. Goodnight, Sparkles,' said Amanda, and she kissed Jess goodnight then followed Luis to the kitchen.

'You're a pretty good storyteller,' said Amanda.

'I've had practice,' said Luis as he uncorked a cheap bottle of red.

'You two are quite the artists,' he said, and nodded towards the two canvases drying on her easel. One was Amanda's latest work. Almost finished. An impressionist landscape of the East River. The other was by Jess. Amanda loved to paint, but more than that she loved to watch Jess paint. From a young age she loved getting her little chubby fingers into the oils, and spreading them on an old canvas, giggling with delight at the bright colors.

'Another day or two that picture will be finished. Just a few more pieces and I'll have enough for another showing,' said Amanda.

She had a real talent and had even sold some pieces at her debut exhibition in a little gallery in Soho.

'I still prefer Jess's,' said Luis with a smile. 'Say, I'll take Jess to the park in the morning. I had a meeting with a new client set up, but they pulled it last minute. It will give you time to work.'

That night stood out in Amanda's mind because it was fun and warm and filled with love for her husband and her daughter. But she didn't know at the time it would be the last night.

Luis had woken her with a kiss that morning. A kiss she'd had a thousand times. Luis always rose early and had an orange for breakfast. Without fail. She could smell the citrus from his hands, and it made his lips even sweeter. Luis had grown up in rural Mexico. When he was a kid, he'd picked a fresh Navelina orange off the trees on the way to school. The habit had stuck with him, even after his parents moved to Juarez. Amanda's in-laws didn't care for her. She wasn't Catholic, and they had not come to the wedding. Luis was planning on taking Jess to meet them in California once his digital recruitment business calmed down in the summer.

He gave her a tray with eggs, toast and coffee, kissed her once more and said he and Jess were hitting the park and would be back later.

The last kiss.

Three hours later, her hands covered in paint, she got the call from Luis. Frantic. Only snatches of sentences were audible. He was breathing so hard he couldn't speak.

At the lake . . . Jess ran on ahead . . . ice cream . . . saw her . . . talking to a man with dark hair . . . He took Jess's hand . . . I ran . . . ran . . . ran . . . police . . .

The amber alert went up fast. NYPD were quick too. The detectives, Andrew Farrow and Karen Hernandez, held her hand, calmed Luis down from blind panic. Farrow did most of the talking. He was a tall, thin man. He didn't really *wear* a suit; it was more like he haunted it. Still, he had a deep voice and something in his eyes that let Amanda know he understood what she was going through. Farrow had sat in rooms like this before, with parents going through the same or worse, and told them so. Their little apartment was filled with police officers, but those detectives were the only thing that stopped Amanda from going insane. Farrow told her he would bring Jess home. He told Luis he would bring Jess home.

And he did.

Three days later.

In a little white coffin.

Jess was six years old when she was murdered. Her body was found naked, discarded in a dumpster in Queens. That was the twenty-fifth of April. The day Amanda's life changed. When they told Amanda and Luis that they'd found their daughter, Amanda couldn't speak. She wailed, and Luis just sat there – numb. Saying nothing. He didn't try to comfort her. Didn't put an arm round her. He blamed himself. He'd had his daughter in sight, then turned his back for two seconds.

Luis took his own life a week later. He'd found Amanda's sleeping pills, left the apartment and bought a bottle of vodka. He checked into a motel, and never checked out.

They were buried together. Amanda didn't make the funeral – she'd been admitted and sedated in Gracie Square Hospital. While she was under sedation, Luis's parents flew in from Juarez, buried their son and granddaughter and flew home.

Three weeks later, Amanda was discharged to a program. The first of many that she quit. She had tried. Two different grief counselors, a psychologist and a psychiatrist. The drugs made her sleepy, and the talking made it all worse. Amanda didn't think of losing her daughter and husband as a traumatic life *change* – it was her life *ending*.

Her parents were both deceased, and she had no other family, so it fell on others to try to comfort her. Friends from work, fellow burgeoning artists, old school pals – they all came to see her. Some took it in shifts. But it always ended the same. They sat on her couch and tried to talk, and held her as she cried, and then fell silent.

They didn't know what to say. They began to doubt every word, wondering if they here helping their friend or making her worse. Some came with food parcels, lasagnes and casseroles she could reheat, but never did. Amanda stopped taking their calls, for their sake. Still the food deliveries came – brown bags from Wholefoods, or fruit baskets. Amanda hated the fruit baskets. When they arrived, she threw out the oranges immediately – the smell of them made a painful hole in her chest. The only thing that did occasionally lift her spirits were letters from long-term residents of the care home – men and women Amanda had cared for, and who'd watched her rise through the ranks to manager. Those letters, in old spidery handwriting, lifted her heart – but only for a few moments. Letters were okay, because she could be alone to read them. Calls from worried friends were too hard.

Now, the only calls Amanda took were from Farrow, updating her on the investigation.

Farrow and Hernandez had found a man on security-camera footage that was taken outside the park. He had walked along Park Avenue holding a little girl's hand just minutes after Jess went missing. From time to time, the girl would seem to struggle against the man's grip. The cops believed the girl was Jess. Same blue shorts, white sneakers and unicorn tee. They got into a black SUV, with stolen plates, but NYPD lost track of it on security footage once it left the island and drove into Brooklyn.

The man looked like someone on their books. A man with a past. His name was Wallace Crone, thirty years old. A stockbroker for a large firm on Wall Street, who at the age of twenty-one was arrested for the sexual assault of a girl aged thirteen. He had a great attorney, paid for by his wealthy parents, and he got off with a fine and probation on a plea deal that reduced the charge to supplying alcohol to a minor. At twenty-five he'd been found in possession of indecent images of children. Another fine, more probation, but this time he had to become a registered sex offender. In any other world that meant he would lose his job – but not when his father owned the company.

Some people, those with money and the ear of power, never pay for their crimes the way ordinary people do. Farrow had told Amanda that Wallace Crone was their man. He'd been arrested and questioned about another child's murder long before Jess had been killed – a little girl aged nine who'd died some years ago. Farrow had been the detective on that case and built up quite the file on Wallace Crone. He shared his views on Crone freely and often when he dropped by to see how she was coping and update her on the case. Crone was one of the more dangerous sexual predators Farrow had ever encountered.

'Believe it or not, the ones who get caught early and released are the really dangerous ones. Crone had been caught for rape and illegal images. That's two strikes. He knew the next time he got caught there would be no way he could be saved, no matter how many lawyers his father hired for him. So he made sure he didn't leave witnesses. That's why we never found Emily alive.'

'Emily? Was that the nine-year old?' she asked.

Farrow nodded, said, 'Emily Dryer. Her father had been a family friend to the Crones. Wallace Crone's father, Henry Crone, had a mansion on Park Avenue and the Dryers stayed there from time to time. Their little girl, Emily, liked to swim in the pool in the basement of the mansion house. Wallace Crone was said to be friendly with Emily. Overly friendly. He swam with her, read to her, they played hide and seek together. Emily's father said Wallace Crone was like an uncle to her. He didn't know Wallace was a sex offender. We did. When she disappeared, he immediately became a suspect, given his history.'

He took a sip of coffee, leaned forward on Amanda's couch and stared at the floor.

'There was nothing to connect him to her disappearance other than they knew each other.'

'You said she was murdered.'

Farrow nodded, said, 'We hauled Crone in and sweated him and got nothing. I know he killed that girl. I saw it in his eyes. He hasn't changed. Monsters like that don't, but what they do is make sure they don't get caught. They no longer leave their victims alive. We found Emily's body in a dumpster.'

Amanda swore, stood up and began pacing the room.

'But Jess's case is different to Emily's, right? There's the security camera footage. You can get him this time.'

'Right, I just hope it's enough.'

This was the first time they had something solid on Crone. Video evidence. They raided his apartment, his office, his holiday home in Aspen. No forensic evidence linking him to Jess nor the vehicle they'd seen on camera. Still, they were so sure it was him on the video footage that they arrested and charged him.

For all of thirty-five days it looked like Jess and Luis would get justice. On that last day, Crone's lawyers had the charges dismissed on a pre-trial motion. There wasn't even a jury, just a judge. The assistant district attorney had his hands full against a veritable army of Wall Street lawyers saying the footage wasn't clear enough – and of course Crone was relying on an alibi from his father. After the hearing, Farrow didn't call Amanda – he went to see her.

They sat in her apartment and both of them cried for Jess and Luis.

That was the last time Amanda had shed a tear.

'What do we do now?' asked Amanda finally.

'There's nothing we can do but wait until he tries to take another child,' said Farrow.

'But you can't watch him twenty-four seven,' she said.

'No, I can't. No one can. One thing I'm sure of is that he'll do it again. And this time we won't let him get away,' said Farrow.

'I'll watch him,' said Amanda. 'I'm not going to let this happen to another child.'

'Amanda, I don't think that's a good idea,' said Farrow.

She reassured him she wouldn't let him see her. She would keep an eye on him from a distance. And so, for months, Amanda watched Wallace Crone. She built up files on him. Photographs, news articles, memos on his routine, his garbage, his social life, his work . . .

While Amanda built information at the rate of an obsessive, she had no skill for covert surveillance. Not at first. Crone spotted her a few times and reported her to the police. Farrow managed to smooth things over until Crone applied for a restraining order, which he got in a heartbeat. Amanda didn't have money for a lawyer. Instead, she got wise. She read everything she could about surveillance, watched hours of YouTube videos and seemed to be able to keep up her vigil for most of the day without detection. She knew his routine, inside out. She planned her surveillance, made notes, got better. Just as she'd planned out every major life goal. She knew what she wanted and prepared to succeed.

His travel to work, where he ate, his gym, his appointments, his predilection for young call girls. She'd called Farrow about that one. She noted everything in detail. She would watch a girl, much too young to be out on her own late at night, arrive at Crone's building and wait in the lobby. Sometimes he went out with them to a local Italian restaurant, or a bar, then back to his place. Most of the time he just buzzed them up to his apartment. If he didn't occasionally go out with them somewhere then Amanda wouldn't have known they were going to his apartment. She had no way of getting a view into his window. One of those girls might go up there and never come back down again.

She didn't go back to her job. At first, the care home directors were sympathetic, and then, as the months went on, their sympathy ran out. Amanda was fired, with a small severance payment. The bills and the overdue rent mounted up in envelopes that she stuffed into the kitchen drawers unopened. She only cared about one thing. Saving another family from what she'd gone through and getting justice for her little girl.

Then, sitting in her Volvo across the street from Crone's building one night in August, watching him leave arm in arm with the dark-haired Asian girl, there was a knock on Amanda's window.

Farrow. He got into the passenger seat. It took him a little time. He bent slowly at the waist, putting in one foot, then lowering himself further, then another foot. The last foot coming in made him bite down as he let out a grunt.

'How's your back?' asked Amanda.

'How do you think? Never mind my back – I just got a call from a pal at the precinct. Said they had a report of you outside this building in breach of your restraining order. The sergeant there is a good man, and he called me. I need you to go home, Amanda. I'm sorry. I feel I started you on this whole thing and that was wrong of me. I made a mistake. Don't throw your life away on this scumbag.'

Amanda lit a cigarette, cracked the window and said, 'My life is over anyway. I don't care if they send me to jail. I'll get out, and I'll come right back.'

He sighed, said, 'I didn't want to have to tell you this, but they iced Jess's case this week.'

'Iced? Does that mean closed?'

'Pretty much. There are no alternative suspects, and no new evidence against Crone. His lawyers have been leaning on the commissioner, who leaned on my captain who told me to bury it. Amanda, he's not going to pay for this crime. And he's too smart to take a risk with all this heat on him. The only thing we can do is let it go.'

'Let it go? He murdered my daughter!'

'And maybe others too, but he won't see a day in prison for any of it. You have to come to terms with that.'

'You know that girl he's with tonight is probably under-age, and she's working as an escort.'

'We know, and vice knows. There's a bigger operation in the background. They want to save hundreds of young girls and destroy the whole operation. They're not going to blow it to book Crone for soliciting so a friendly judge can give him a smack on the wrist, even if it is his third time in court. Go *home*.'

Amanda had agreed to leave that night, and not come back. She also agreed to take some time out of the city on a vacation. Clear her head. That's when she bought a gun on the dark web and drove upstate to the woods to learn how to use it.

If the law wasn't going to make Crone pay, Amanda had only one choice. It was all clear in her mind. She was going to kill him. Or herself. Better that he went first. The subway shooting had been her best plan. And it had failed.

Now, standing on the sidewalk in Centre Street, fresh from her latest court hearing, Amanda hung her head. She realized she couldn't beat the system. Couldn't get close enough to kill the man who'd taken her child.

She walked in the cold for hours, feeling the bite of the wind on her cheeks. She let herself wander back in the general direction of home. In the 7-Eleven across the street from her building she bought a bottle of vodka, then refilled her prescription for sleeping pills from the CVS beside it. The sun had gone down, and afternoon had passed into evening. The day would soon end.

Amanda just wanted the pain to stop.

She emptied her mailbox in the lobby of her building, more out of habit than anything else. Tucked the pile of mail under her arms and went upstairs to her empty apartment. She dropped the mail on the table, filled a glass – half vodka, half Pepsi, and poured out the whole bottle of sleeping pills on the counter. She took two in her mouth, washed them down. If she was going to take the whole bottle, she would need to swallow more than two at a time. Otherwise her throat would begin to close. Amanda had never been good at swallowing pills. If she still had the gun, she wouldn't have this problem.

She glanced idly at the mail. On top of the stack was an envelope with the name of a law firm stamped on the outside. If her landlord was trying to evict her, he wouldn't need to take her to court. If she could manage the pills she would be leaving the apartment tomorrow wearing a body bag.

She ripped the envelope open, read the letter.

It wasn't from her landlord.

The letter fell from her fingers, swooped and tumbled through the air to land at her feet. She stomped on it, once, returned to the counter and began scooping up the pills in her palm and pouring them back into the bottle.

Taking her drink with her, she then sat down at her laptop. First thing she saw was an email telling her there was a new article on Crone. Amanda had set up an alert on his name so she could keep up to date with police investigations. She clicked on the link: a press report on her case today detailing her guilty plea. She shook her head, then logged into her bank account.

Four hundred and twelve dollars.

That was all she had left. Luis hadn't had life insurance.

Amanda had nothing left now. No family. No justice. No job. She just needed a little more time.

Two things were keeping her alive.

She didn't want another mother to go through what she was going through. No family should be ripped apart by this evil ever again. The second thing keeping her breathing was hate. New and refuelled by the letter from Wallace Crone's lawyers.

He was suing Amanda for harassment. His lawyers wanted five hundred thousand dollars in damages. Suing *her*. For the damage and emotional trauma *she* had caused *him*. Her heart wanted to explode. She wanted to cry, but she couldn't. She had lost the ability to cry. It was all tied up inside. Instead of tears, she let out a barking laugh. If it wasn't so sick, it would be funny.

But it wasn't funny. There was no way Amanda would let him take any more.

She got up and went to Jess's bedroom. It was exactly as it had been on that last night, with Luis reading the story to them both. Amanda took hold of Sparkles, and lay down on the bed.

When Luis's parents had buried Jess and Luis, they hadn't known to put Sparkles in Jess's coffin, and for a few days after she'd learned this, Amanda was so sick with grief that she threw up almost constantly. The thought of her murdered child, unable to rest even in death without her toy.

Where's Sparkles?

Where's Sparkles?

She took hold of Sparkles now, held it tightly. There was a smell on the toy that reminded her of Jess. It reminded her of happier times, but even her memories of great days with her little girl were now sharp with loss. And she couldn't take it any more.

There had to be a way to kill Wallace Crone.

And she was going to find it.

4
Ruth

Mount Sinai hospital had been home to Ruth for three days before they let the detectives talk to her. She had woken in her hallway, in horrific pain, her stomach and legs covered in her own blood. Weak and hysterical, she had crawled to the house phone on the hall table and dialed 911 before she passed out.

She didn't wake again for a long time. She slept. And her dreams took her back to that hallway.

She stood in her night things, gazing into the pane of glass in her kitchen window, staring at the reflection of the man who had come to kill her.

Hello, sweetheart . . .

Ruth woke suddenly, her eyes wide open, mouth gaping. Like she'd come up for air from the depths of a dark ocean.

She could still see the man's face. His eyes. His voice echoed in her mind.

She looked around, found herself in a dimly lit hospital room. There was an IV on the back of her hand. When she started to sit up, she felt a tightness across her stomach and chest. The pain in her left leg was sharper still. Then the wave came. It started low down in her stomach — a cold fire, and quickly it spread over her body causing every limb to tremble. Her breathing stuttered. Unable to take a deep breath, she gulped shallow mouthfuls and moaned until finally she had pumped enough air into her lungs to scream.

A nurse banged the door open, and as soon as she saw Ruth she approached very slowly, her hands up, telling her it was okay – she was safe now in the hospital.

That it was all over.

Even then, in the midst of panic, Ruth knew this would never be over.

Two more nurses came in, but Ruth couldn't hear what they were saying. For a second, she wondered why, then realized she was still screaming.

'She's going into shock,' said one of the nurses and took hold of Ruth's arm. Ruth felt the butterfly needle pulling at her skin, then she felt suddenly dizzy, and then, sleep came.

And the blue-eyed man came with it.

When she next woke, it took some time to open her eyes. Her eyelids weighed five hundred pounds, her limbs wouldn't obey her and she heard herself talking but couldn't understand a word. Her fingers drifted to her face, and she felt a tube in her nose, helping her breathe.

Then she turned her head, with great effort, and Scott was sitting on a chair beside her bed. He was holding her hand, and whispering to her softly, telling her to lie still. She tried to lift her head, but it was too heavy. Unable to do anything else, she lay quietly and gazed at her husband. Black, hard stubble on his face and dark rings beneath his pale blue eyes. He caressed her hand, kissed it and a tear fell upon her skin.

'What happened? There was a man . . .' she began, and felt the wave rising in her chest again.

'He's gone. It's all over. You're going to be okay,' he said, and repeated it until Ruth began to calm and then she cried. He got up on the bed and held her and together they wept until Ruth drifted off to sleep again.

*

'Ruth, my name is Dr. Mosley. How are you feeling?' said the man in the white coat standing beside her bed. He had a soft face, round cheeks and a shaven head. A handsome man with gentle music in his voice.

'My chest, stomach. It feels tight. My leg hurts. The left one,' said Ruth.

He came closer and nodded to Scott.

'I've already spoken to your husband, but I need to know if you feel well enough to speak to the police. They have been very keen to talk to you. How would you feel if I let them in for five minutes?'

'Okay, I guess,' said Ruth. Her voice sounded scratchy. Her throat was still dry and sore, no matter how many glasses of cool water she sipped through a straw. Scott had wiped her lips with an ice cube, combed her chestnut hair and washed her face. She felt better, but she had questions. She'd tried to ask Scott what had happened, but he'd just said she was okay now. That it was over. Part of her didn't want to know – was afraid to find out.

'What happened to me?' she asked.

Scott rose from his seat, his hand outstretched, as if he didn't want Mosley to say anything. She was too weak to start an argument, but Mosley didn't get into it with Scott – simply gave him a look, like he was admonishing a foolish child.

'Ruth, you were admitted in the early hours of Saturday morning, the fifteenth, with multiple stab wounds and lacerations,' said the doctor. Ruth closed her eyes, took Scott's hand and squeezed it as hard as she could. 'After you called 911, paramedics broke into your home and brought you here. You had lost a lot of blood. The stab wounds were deep, but we were able to repair a lot of the damage. You have been through a terrifying attack. As far as we know, you were not sexually assaulted. We will need to talk in more detail about your injuries, but not immediately. What is important right now is that you talk to the police. Do you think you can do that?'

Ruth nodded, opened her eyes and said, 'Thank you. I'll do my best.'

Mosley smiled then turned and opened the door to Ruth's hospital room. Two people came inside. One man, one woman. One tall, one short. Both wore black suits and woollen overcoats. The tall one introduced himself as Detective Andrew Farrow, and his partner was Detective Karen Hernandez. The smaller one had a tattoo of a bird on the back of her hand, the same hand that held a pen. She sat and opened a notebook, ready to take notes. Farrow approached the bed. He walked stiffly, as if in pain, and swept a lock of blond hair from his eyes as he looked down upon her. He was still a young man. Early forties, maybe.

'Mrs. Gelman, do you mind if I call you Ruth?' he asked.

She shook her head. 'Ruth is fine.'

'Thank you. I've stood by a lot of beds in a lot of hospitals. Each time it's different. A lot of people can't talk about what happened to them. If you are able to answer some of our questions, it would be a big help. If you need to stop for a while, my partner and I can go kick back, drink coffee and eat donuts.'

Then he leaned over a little, and whispered, 'One of the perks of being a cop.' He winked. 'So please don't feel under pressure to talk for too long. I just want to ask a few questions now, and then we'll let you rest.'

Ruth nodded. Farrow seemed to wince a little as he straightened up, his hand reaching for his lower back.

'I want to ask you about the attack. We have it recorded as occurring on Friday, September fourteenth. Your 911 call came in just before midnight. What do you remember about that night?' he said.

She licked her dry lips, and remembered Scott going out and leaving her alone in the apartment. Watching a movie. Wine. Then bed, then it was all a little hazy until . . .

'I woke up late that night. I heard a noise downstairs. Glass breaking. I thought it was Scott at first. I went downstairs and I saw the back door had been broken. The window I mean. Then I saw a reflection . . .'

Farrow nodded but didn't say anything.

'A man was standing behind me. He had blue eyes; I know that. They were really clear and bright. He had high cheekbones. They sat out, sharply. And a square jaw. Dark hair. He grabbed me, put something over my mouth and I blacked out. Whatever it was had a strong, chemical smell. I remember waking up, and he was gone. There was blood everywhere. I crawled to the table in the hall and I got the phone, but I don't remember much about that.'

Nodding, Farrow said, 'I know this is hard, but it's important. Can you remember anything else about him? Any facial scars? Birthmarks? That kind of thing?'

Ruth thought hard, her jaw trembling, her gaze rigidly fixed on the ceiling.

'No, I don't think so.'

'Could you describe his clothing?'

'It was dark, black. I don't know what kind.'

'Did he speak or threaten you before he grabbed you?'

Ruth gasped at the memory.

'He did say something.'

Farrow looked to Hernandez. They exchanged a glance before he turned back to Ruth.

'What did he say, Ruth?'

'He-he said, "*Hi there, sweetheart.*" Or something like that . . . God.'

Her free hand covered her mouth, and Scott took her by the shoulders, held her, as if he were bracing her for an earthquake.

'Do you remember what time you went downstairs?'

Ruth shook her head.

'Do you think you would be able to recognize this man if you saw him again?'

She nodded.

'Thank you, Ruth. We will need to do a further interview when you're feeling a little better. Is there anything else you can tell us now?'

She shook her head again, sobbing into her palm.

'Have you found this guy?' asked Scott.

His tone shook the room. Farrow straightened up to his full height, which was at least three inches over Scott.

'We have collected what evidence we can from your home, Mr. Gelman—'

'Have you found him yet?' said Scott, cutting off Farrow.

Hernandez closed her notebook, stood and placed her pen in her inside pocket then buttoned her coat.

'Every available resource is dedicated to catching this perpetrator,' said Hernandez. 'Ruth is lucky to be alive. Two other women weren't so lucky. This man is our top priority. Every cop in the city is on alert. You have our word we won't rest until we catch him.'

'Two women?' said Ruth, removing her hand from her face.

'Yes, ma'am,' said Farrow. 'I know this is hard, but we will need to talk again soon. If anything else comes to mind in the meantime, I've given your husband my card.'

And, with that, Farrow and Hernandez turned to leave.

Ruth sat up and winced, biting her lip with pain as she tried to move.

'Wait, why did he let me live?' she asked.

Farrow and Hernandez slowed at the door. Hernandez opened it, nodded at her partner.

Turning back to Ruth, Farrow said, 'We're working on this. That's all I can tell you for now.'

'Don't bullshit us. You know a lot more about this asshole than you're saying,' said Scott.

'We don't have a lot to go on. No forensics at the crime scenes. Now we have a description, that'll really help. We'll be in touch,' said Farrow.

5

Farrow

'That description fits a lot of people,' said Hernandez.

Farrow nodded as they entered the basement parking lot of the hospital.

'But she said she'd recognize him if she saw him again. That's a start. Once we have a suspect, we can show her some mugshots. At least we know he doesn't like them to watch him as he works,' said Farrow. 'That's something we didn't know before. He knocks them out before he starts cutting.'

'And that's useful how?'

'He needs chemicals. Chloroform. Maybe we can trace it? When we get back to the precinct, we'll call the coroner, see if he can test for the presence of chloroform in the bodies of the first two victims. Say, do you remember where we parked?'

Hernandez pointed to the far corner. 'Somewhere over there.'

Farrow let her lead the way. His back was playing up more than usual. It slowed him down, and he got progressively worse as the day went on. He didn't try to match her pace – he just plodded slowly behind. Hernandez had long black hair, which she wore in tight curls, and it bounced with every step. He followed her while she pressed the key fob and listened for the sound of the car unlocking.

An encouraging *thunk* sounded up ahead, accompanied by a flash of headlights.

'Here it is,' she said.

'Some detectives we are. Can't even find the damn car.'

'Don't beat yourself up about this. We'll get the bastard,' she said.

Farrow said nothing. He followed her to the car in silence. Lowered himself gently into the passenger seat. Gritted his teeth against the pain.

'Take a pill,' said Hernandez.

'I had one this morning.'

'Shift will be over in four hours. Take the damn pill, man.'

'I'll take one on the way home,' he said. He heard Hernandez taking a breath. She started to say something, then stopped abruptly when she saw the look on his face. They had been partners for many years now. After a while, it had become something like a good marriage. The meds helped Farrow's back pain, but they also dulled his brain. For most cops, they wouldn't think twice. If they're in pain, and the pills ease that burden, they'll pop them all day long. Not so with Farrow. He carried his cases with him. All those victims were right there on his back. And if he popped codeine or oxy, he sacrificed his edge. The drowsiness and lethargy took away that razor-sharp mind.

The man not only worked to help the victims of this city – he suffered for them. By choice. He took a breath, raised his eyes to the ceiling. Farrow was thinking, and Hernandez knew the signs and understood it was better not to interrupt him. If he didn't have some quiet thinking time, Farrow would become irritable. No words passed between them – she just knew something was working on him and he would let it out when he was ready. It didn't take long.

'We need to know why he didn't finish it. First two victims had multiple stab wounds, but the fatal blow was to the carotid artery. He didn't get that far with Ruth Gelman. Why not?' said Farrow, putting on his seat belt.

The motor started with some effort, and Hernandez sucked air through her teeth as she put the car in gear and rolled out of the space.

'Maybe he just couldn't go through with it this time?' said Hernandez.

'Oh, I don't think so. Two women dead and a third attacked – this guy's not stopping any time soon. Something happened to make him stop,' said Farrow.

Their car wound through the lot, up the ramp and stopped at the barrier. Hernandez swiped their ticket and exited. Cops always had their parking validated. Another perk.

'It's a miracle she survived anyway. Maybe he thought he'd done enough?'

'Not this guy. Not someone this meticulous. He would make sure. So why didn't he this time? What's special about Ruth Gelman?'

'Maybe nothing. Maybe something else happened. Could be we never find out. So, where to now, chief?'

'The precinct. I want to know how we did door-to-door.'

The precinct house used to be a small museum before it was donated to the city at the end of the nineteenth century. Since then, central heating had been fitted, maybe two coats of paint and some alterations to make the building more secure, but that was about it. The detective bureau was on the second floor, spread across two large rooms, with six desks in each room for twenty detectives. Desk hopping was a natural part of the job. One that Farrow hated. He had managed to claim a desk by never cleaning it, leaving all his shit sitting proudly atop. No one said a word to Farrow. He was too long in the job and just too damn tall to argue with.

Sitting on Farrow's chair when he arrived was a stack of reports. A Post-It note was stuck on top with a phone number for patrolman Tony Gale.

Farrow picked up the desk phone, threw the reports on the floor and was about to call Gale when the patrolman walked into the detective bureau.

'Desk sergeant said you just got back. How's your vic?' said Gale, a ten-year veteran officer with a hatred for police politics and arms that had won him the NYPD Golden Gloves tournament two years in a row.

'Not good. She can't give us anything more than a basic description. She'll live, but she's pretty shaken up. You about to tell me I can just file away all these reports without reading them?'

'Top three reports are statements from neighbors across the street. One of them remembered last night all too well. Her husband had a suspected cardiac arrest and she called the paramedics.'

'That's it,' said Farrow.

Hernandez nodded, said, 'The sirens. Flashing lights. They must've spooked the perp. Jesus, Ruth Gelman has no idea how lucky she is.'

'I'm not sure she would see it that way,' said Farrow. 'Did any of them see anything? Anyone fleeing the scene?'

'One old lady saw a tall guy dressed all in black running down the street. That's all we got.'

Farrow thanked Gale and promised him a beer at the end of the week. He said he'd believe that when he saw it, and left.

'What do you think?' asked Farrow.

'We've got a man in black, a decent description, but not much else. Mr. Gelman is going to be hard work too. I didn't warm to him,' said Hernandez.

'We have to cut him some slack. I've seen that kind of reaction before. The wife is attacked and the husband goes into full testosterone mode. It's primal – they feel the need to protect their woman and they feel guilty they weren't there to stop it in the first place. Poor guy.'

'That's some sexist, toxic-masculinity-type bullshit,' said Hernandez. 'I think he's just an asshole. Kind of controling too. I got that vibe. I don't like the guy.'

'If we arrested everyone you don't like, they'd need to build two more prisons on Rikers Island. Let's get to work on the chloroform.'

6

Amanda

From the passenger seat of the car, Amanda looked up at the first-floor windows of the redbrick building on 43rd Street. The glass was blacked out with thick paper that had yellowed with time, as if it had been painted with grease.

'You sure this is the place?' she asked.

Farrow put the car into park, said, 'This is the place. Second floor. I know it's scary, but you just have to give it a chance.'

'Give what a chance? I've spoken to counselors before. It doesn't help.'

'Look, this is part of the court order. There's no getting out of this. You've got to go so you may as well try to make the best of it.'

Amanda looked back at the building. There was a street level shop. They sold used musical instruments and a sign said they also did repairs. The store was closed. She couldn't tell if there was light on the floor above because of the paper on the windows. The door beside the entrance to the music shop had a red buzzer.

'I don't feel well enough. Can't I skip just this one last time?'

'You've put it off for long enough. You were supposed to start counseling before the end of September, it's now November. Your PO should've breached you a month ago. She only relented because I called her and told her I'd be bringing your ass to this place myself,' he said.

'I'm sorry. Look, I know you've gone beyond the call here. It's just . . .'

'It's just what?'

She fell silent for a moment. 'I'm not ready to deal with this.'

Farrow leaned over with some effort, wincing as he stretched his back, popped open the passenger door, said, 'Just go in and be a fly on the wall tonight. For now, let's not breach the damn court order.'

Amanda nodded. Farrow was only looking out for her and she knew it. She thanked him, gave him a mock salute and got out of the car. Hit the buzzer on the door. Waited for ten seconds. Pressed the buzzer again. The thought of going inside filled her guts with dread. She looked around the street. It was almost eight in the evening and the city was still alive with tourists, New Yorkers and traffic. There was a pizza parlor across the street, beside a Wendy's. A lot of the stores on this street were pop-up tourist traps selling 'I ♥ NY' hoodies, ball caps, postcards and miniature figurines of the Statue of Liberty.

Farrow was still parked by the curb. Waiting. She knew he wouldn't leave until she was inside, but it didn't look like there was anyone in the building.

Amanda turned away from the door just as it opened.

'Can I help you?' said a voice.

Amanda stopped and swung around nervously.

The man standing in the doorway was in his thirties, wearing a burgundy sweater and skinny jeans. He had a thick mop of brown hair that curled over his forehead, onto his coke-bottle glasses.

'I was looking for the parents T and B group?' said Amanda.

'Parental Trauma and Bereavement is right upstairs. It's my group. Hi, I'm Matt,' said the man, extending a hand.

Amanda huddled into her black wool overcoat, pulled off a glove, shook his hand and said, 'Hi, I'm Amanda.'

'I've been expecting you. It's cold – please come inside.'

She turned, waved at Farrow, who honked and pulled away.

Amanda followed Matt up two flights of creaking, uneven wooden stairs, and into a large room. A single halo of light from a bare bulb hung over a group of people seated in a circle. There were boxes, stacks of chairs and large odd-shaped items covered in white sheets behind them. A photocopier sat in the corner. Matt asked her for ID and she handed over a driver's license. He copied it, said he needed it for his files, then handed it back. Amanda's eyes adjusted to the gloom and she saw that this was a storage area for the store downstairs. She made out the shapes of drum kits, double basses and guitars lining the four walls. Just beyond the group was a table with a coffee maker and plastic cups.

There were six or seven people in the group, most of them making small talk. Ordinary-looking women and men, all dressed in sweaters and overshirts, bulky coats resting on the backs of their chairs.

Only a few seats were left in the circle.

'Before we go over there, would you like to choose a name?' said Matt.

'I'm sorry?' said Amanda.

He spoke quietly, a passive look on his face. 'This is a closed group, Amanda. And there are two simple rules. Number one, we don't use our real names. Number two, we don't give away details, places or names that might allow other group members to identify you. A lot of people here have been through horrific experiences and in order to be able to share them they want anonymity. We talk about our emotions here. Some people don't want to share if they think their fellow group members will go home and google them. You know what I mean?'

Amanda nodded. If she had to participate in the group, she hadn't planned on revealing anything about her past for that very reason. Keeping things anonymous made sense.

'Call me Wendy,' she said.

'We already have a Wendy,' said Matt, pointing to a small, thin woman with bright blonde hair swept up in a baseball cap and ponytail.

She wore blue jeans and a bulky navy sweater in a way that made her look as though she was trying to hide her wiry frame. Her cheekbones stood out proudly on her face, and her skin looked like it hadn't felt the sun in a long time. It was difficult to pinpoint an age. Older than Amanda, but hard to tell by how much. There was a haunted look about Wendy. But when Amanda cast her gaze around the rest of the circle, she caught the same look in some of the other faces too.

'I suppose it doesn't really matter what I'm called here. How about Jane?'

Matt nodded, said, 'Jane is fine. Help yourself to coffee and take a seat.'

Amanda sat down in a chair beside a large woman with curly hair and a bubble-gum-pink cardigan who introduced herself as Betty. She had a set of rosary beads entwined in her thick, round fingers. Betty smiled at her, painfully, then the moment she looked away the smile dropped from her face as if it was tied to an anvil that had just fallen off the side of a cliff.

Some of the group were already in conversation. Two or three were talking basketball. The rest of them were discussing the mayoral elections and the news of a woman attacked in her home that had been doing the rounds on the local TV channels. That kind of story always got people talking. The thought that New Yorkers might not be safe in their own homes had people scared.

Amanda didn't join in any of the conversations. Betty chimed in here and there with a comment or two. The only other person who sat silently was Wendy. She had tucked one leg beneath the other and turned away from the two men beside her, who were discussing last night's game.

Matt stepped into the center of the circle of chairs and called for quiet before sitting down next to Amanda. She noticed his cologne for the first time. Rose and vanilla, maybe Calvin Klein. She hadn't noticed it earlier and it made her wonder if he'd sneaked into a bathroom to put some on for her benefit.

'Thank you all for coming out, folks. I know it's a cold one out there and snow is due. We have a new member in the group tonight. Everyone, this is Jane,' he said, and threw out his hands towards her as if she was about to walk through a set of sparkling drapes onto the stage of a crummy daytime TV game show.

Everyone mumbled a hello. Everyone except Wendy, who was staring into her coffee cup. Amanda nodded in acknowledgement, but said nothing more.

Matt folded his arms, crossed his legs and leaned back in his chair. His eyes still on Amanda. No one said anything. The silence began to build in her ears, like a pan of water slowly starting to bubble. She glanced up from the floor, feeling heat rising to her cheeks. People were staring at her. Smiling. Friendly. Expectant.

All except Wendy, who couldn't seem to bring herself to look.

Was she supposed to say something? Was that it? Amanda hadn't planned on saying anything in the first session. She'd hoped she could keep her head down and just get through it. She didn't want to talk about Luis or Jess. Talking only made things worse.

With every passing second, she felt more eyes on her, trying to see into her heart – trying to look upon her pain. She kept that to herself. It was her grief. Her loss. Her pain. And she wanted it hot and private. So she could use it. Make it her secret weapon. It was the nerve ending that would eventually make her pull that trigger in Crone's face.

She had to stop this. Now.

'I'm not ready for this. Not yet,' she said.

Betty nodded her head, said, 'You're stronger than you think, honey,' and reached over, patted Amanda's knee.

'It's all so raw,' said Amanda.

She clamped her lips shut, hugged her sides and began rocking back and forth in the cold air that surrounded her statement.

'You can get through this, Jane. With help and support, and knowing that there are others just like you who have dealt with that pain and continue to fight it every day. That's what we do here. We're fight-ers,' said Matt.

Amanda's eyes flicked forward. She'd sensed movement opposite her, and, sure enough, it was Wendy. She rolled her eyes at Matt, dramatically, then shook her head.

'Wendy, perhaps you might like to share something for our new member. Show them how it's done?' said Matt.

Wendy reached into her pocket, drew out a soft pack of Lucky Strikes, shook it until one stood up, which she then took between her thin lips.

'There's no smoking in here, Wendy – you know that,' said Matt as Wendy lit up and inhaled.

'I'm not ready to talk tonight,' said Wendy.

'I don't mind talking,' said Betty, raising her hand, the cheap ros-ary beads jangling. Matt nodded, somewhat reluctantly. The rest of the group shifted in their seats, some exhaled loudly. Amanda got the impression they were readying themselves for a long night of listening to Betty and they'd been down this road more than once before.

'I know some of you must've looked up my case, and I don't blame you. I'm not judging. When my boy was shot in the street, I swore I wanted to kill the one responsible. My boy never hurt nobody. Six-teen years old and his whole life ahead of him. And to think this punk pulled a gun and shot him in the street for what? The ten bucks he had in his wallet? It nearly killed me too. But then I went to the trial, and I heard about this kid's life. The beatings, the poverty, the abuse . . . He was treated just as bad as a half-crazed dog. If you treat a human being like that, well, what d'you expect? I went to see him in prison with my pastor, after he was sentenced. And I stood in the same room with him and the district attorney, and Pastor Joe, and I opened my arms . . .'

To emphasize her point, Betty closed her eyes and stretched out her arms as if she was waiting for a hug. There were a few more sighs, and some barking from the plastic chairs skidding on the floor as two people took the opportunity to get up and get a coffee refill.

'. . . And I said to this young man, I believe in the Lord Jesus Christ . . .' continued Betty. She then paused, took a sharp intake of breath, as if she was steeling herself – getting ready to reveal some miracle. 'I am of his church, and his people, and I forgive you for your wicked sin against my family,' said Betty. 'And you know what he did? This punk kid? He cried. And we hugged. I found it in my heart to forgive him that day. I felt *the Lord* that day. He was right there in that room with us.'

Betty nodded, sniffed back a tear, fumbled with the rosary beads. There were some murmurs of approval among the other members of the group.

Wendy noisily blew a plume of smoke into the air, and Amanda followed its trail as it kissed the ceiling light and whirled around it.

'I wish you wouldn't smoke in here,' said Matt.

'Why?' said Wendy. '*The Lord* isn't dragging his ass into *this* room, that's for damn sure,' she said.

'Wendy, please,' said Matt.

She shook her head, looked at Betty and said, 'I heard your story before. We all heard it before. It's good you've gotten some peace, but some of us don't want to forgive. Can't forgive. And that doesn't make us bad people. It's just the way it is. Some bastards don't deserve forgiveness. Ever.'

Matt launched into a long placatory diatribe about forgiveness, why no one was judging anyone's reaction to grief in this room. He was placating both Wendy and Betty, and making sure the session didn't turn into a fight. Amanda sat quietly and listened, watched Wendy light up another smoke.

She was beginning to like Wendy.

Some of the other members gave a brief rundown of where they were in their 'personal journey' as Matt called it. As each of them began to talk, they prefaced their stories by giving a macabre introduction.

'Hi, I'm Lucy. Lost my husband and little girl in a car wreck . . .'

'John here, my son was killed in a bar fight . . .'

'Terry, my daughter, was in the North Tower on 9/11 . . .'

And so on. Amanda imagined that it would almost be better for them to wear name badges saying stabbing, terrorism, hate crime, drunk driver . . .

Their lives were defined by the children who had been taken from them.

'There's meaning in every life,' said Matt. 'Your children were loved. And their love is still here – right here, with us, in this very room. That's enough for tonight. See you all next week.'

The circle of people broke slowly, with some staying in the seats to talk, and others making a last visit to the coffee station before hitting the street. Amanda beat it out of there fast. She heard the front door slamming shut just as she began to descend the stairs. She went outside, looked right, and then left. To her left, the slight but unmistakable figure of Wendy walked away leaving trails of smoke in her wake.

Amanda tucked her hands into her pockets and strolled after her. She didn't get far. There was a bar on the corner, and Wendy flicked the butt of her cigarette into the traffic and ducked inside. Slowing her pace, Amanda gazed through the window. Wendy sat at the bar, a cold Miller in front of her already, and no one else within ten feet. It didn't look like the kind of place you'd arrange to meet someone. It was a dive bar with heavy-metal music and stains on the carpet – visible even from the street. As she reached the crosswalk, Amanda stopped to wait for the light.

She could feel that familiar itch.

'Fuck it,' said Amanda, and she went inside. There was a stool beside Wendy. She stood beside it and said, 'Do you mind if I sit here? I could use a drink.'

Wendy looked slightly uncomfortable without a cigarette in her lips. It looked as though her face had nothing to do without it. Yet it was expressive enough to tell Amanda that Wendy recognized her.

'You're the new girl, Jane. The one Matt embarrassed,' she said.

'Thanks for reminding me. Is this seat taken?'

Glancing at the seat, and then Amanda's face, Wendy hesitated before answering, 'You can take it as long as I see a driver's license.'

'A driver's license?' asked Amanda. 'What? Do you work here? I know I don't look a day over sixteen, but, trust me, I'm way past thirty. Anyway, I thought this whole group thing was supposed to be anonymous. Matt told me about the rules.'

'We're not in the group any more. You see a set of rules above this here bar? It's nothing to do with your age, honey. I just want to make sure you're not a journalist. Some of them infiltrate groups like this, trying to worm a story out of a victim. It happens. It almost happened to me and now I'm *extra* careful. So, what'll it be?' said Wendy.

Amanda drew out her driver's license from her purse, slapped it on the counter.

Wendy took it, studied it and then entered Amanda's name into the Google app on her phone.

'No, don't do that,' said Amanda.

'You afraid I'm going to find out you work for the *New York Post* or . . .'

Amanda took her ID, put it in the back pocket of her jeans, looked away. She didn't want to risk seeing some of those search results. The photos of her, Luis and Jess. Especially that one taken last year during their hike upstate. Jess's cheeks were rosy red from the cold and she looked so full of life and happiness.

'Oh, fuck. I'm sorry,' said Wendy. 'I had to check. I didn't mean to—'

'It's fine,' whispered Amanda. If she'd spoken any louder, Wendy would've heard her voice tremble and threaten to break.

'How about I buy you a drink?' said Wendy.

Amanda nodded, said, 'Vodka tonic,' and took the seat at the bar beside Wendy, who ordered from the bartender. The two women sat in silence for a time, although it didn't feel awkward to Amanda. It was as if Wendy knew the woman beside her needed a moment to beat down the pain.

The bartender placed Amanda's drink on a beer mat and slipped away.

'You said something in the group that I found interesting,' said Amanda. 'You said something about forgiveness. That sometimes people don't deserve it.'

'That's right,' said Wendy, 'but let's not go there yet. Neither of us are drunk enough for that conversation.'

Wendy raised her beer bottle, Amanda took her drink and as they clinked glasses Wendy said, 'I say we get good and drunk first. Then we can talk all you want.'

7
Ruth

Early evening turned to night, but it was difficult for Ruth to tell. There was no clock on the wall. She asked Scott what time it was and he checked his phone. Her windowless private room in the hospital was kind of a bunker. Scott stayed with her after the police left, but they didn't talk. She ate a little soup, but it made her feel queasy. Probably the painkillers. She dozed on and off, for how long she couldn't tell. It was hard to focus after her meds.

'What time is it?' she asked.

Only Scott hadn't heard her. His head was turned to one side on the green leather chair, and his chest was moving slowly in the rhythms of sleep.

Ruth dug her fists into the bed by her sides, and slowly pushed herself into an upright position. It messed up the pillows behind her, making it uncomfortable. With her right hand she reached down to the side bars of the bed, looking for the bed control. She had remembered one of the nurses using it earlier to elevate her head for the soup, before slowly letting the bed recline so Ruth could sleep.

Her fingers alone couldn't locate it, so she leaned over to see where it had gone. It felt as if someone had inserted a fishing hook into her stomach and had begun to tug on it as soon as she leaned over. No sign of the bed control, but she saw something else that struck her with biting surprise. Suspended from the bed was a bag half filled with a dark orange liquid. There were flecks of red in that bag too, as if someone had dripped a red pen into it. A line ran from the bag up and under the bed covers. She sat up straight, felt between her legs. A catheter. That was the uncomfortable feeling she had registered earlier on.

'What are you doing? Lie down – you'll break your stitches,' said Scott, getting to his feet.

'I'm fine. I was just looking for the bed control,' she said.

Scott lifted the corners of the covers, found the white plastic bed control and adjusted the head of the bed so Ruth could sit up a little more comfortably. Gently, and without being told, he placed his arm under hers, held her up while he fought with the pillows, then carefully lowered her onto them.

'That's better,' she said.

'You don't need to worry any more. I'm here. I'm . . . I'm never going to leave you again,' said Scott.

Forcing a smile, Ruth felt another wave of fear coming over her. She blinked, and her eyelashes spilled a tear on her cheek.

'It wasn't your fault,' she said.

And they held each other. She was glad to have him close, feel his arms around her.

He couldn't have known anything bad was going to happen to her. Scott had proven himself to Ruth over and over again. Even when at first she'd had doubts about him.

They had been dating for almost a year. A week away from their first anniversary and Scott had booked a table at her favorite restaurant in Chinatown. A small mom-and-pop place with cheap tables and rickety chairs that did noodles and pork bao buns and not much else. They had both arrived at around seven, in their suits, straight from the office. The restaurant only had twelve tables, and the last one by the window was reserved for Scott.

'You look great,' he said.

He always complimented her. Never failed. They looked through the menu and ordered. The meal was on Scott – he'd made that clear. Even though Ruth earned a lot more, he'd insisted.

Scott fidgeted with his chopsticks and napkin. 'I wanted to talk to you about something,' he said.

Ruth had felt a nervous swirling sensation in her stomach at those words. Her relationship with Scott had been better than she could have imagined. He had booked a table – there was something clearly working on his mind. He was getting up the nerve to tell her it was all over. Ruth could feel it coming.

'I quit my job today,' he said.

'You what?'

'Yeah, don't worry. I'm sorry,' he said, and scratched his head. 'I'm fucking this up, aren't I?'

'I don't know what's going on. Have I done something or said something that you didn't like?' asked Ruth.

He seemed to stop focusing on himself, reached out both hands and took Ruth's palms in his.

'Jesus, no. No, of course not. This isn't about you. Well, it kind of is.'

'You're right,' said Ruth nervously. 'You really are fucking this up.'

They both smiled. Laughed awkwardly.

'Did I ever tell you why I became a prosecutor?'

She shook her head.

'I was the smallest kid in my high-school year. It was only in late teens that whatever messed up growth hormone in my body that hadn't been functioning suddenly kicked into gear. Doesn't matter. What matters is I was bullied in school pretty relentlessly.'

'God, I'm sorry,' said Ruth.

'It affected me for a long time after school. That's why I moved to the city, went to college here. I just couldn't face my home town. Look, I'm not explaining myself very well. Whenever I put a bad guy away, particularly somebody who is violent – I get a little piece of me back. Does that make sense?'

Ruth paused for a second, then nodded, not fully understanding.

'It's like this: when you're bullied, you don't have any power. There's nothing you can do about it. When I told my parents about what was happening, my dad just said I should man up – fight back. But I never did. I couldn't.'

Ruth squeezed his hands.

'I got a lot out of my job. It was cathartic, you know? Like I was finally fighting back.'

'So why did you quit today? What's going on?'

Before he spoke, Scott took a breath, released Ruth's hands.

'I quit because I had an interview last week at the second-largest law firm in the city and they're offering me a position as a senior litigator. It's five times what I make now.'

'Holy shit, that's amazing!'

'Thank you. I wouldn't have done it without you.'

'What do you mean?'

'I want the best for you. That means I need a good salary. A signing bonus will help toward a deposit for a house in the city. For us. For our family.'

Scott got up from the table, stood to one side and went down on one knee. From his jacket, he brought out a small jewelry box, popped the lid and said, 'Will you marry me?'

Ruth said yes. Right there. In front of the whole restaurant who then broke out into spontaneous applause. A real New York moment.

Scott had given up something important to him. Something that really mattered. And he'd done it all for her. Ruth had no doubts any more. This was her man.

He would make sure she was taken care of. That she was safe.

And Scott would never, ever leave her.

She knew it that day.

She knew it now, with the man in her arms, leaning over her

hospital bed. She was lucky to have him. He would see her through this nightmare.

'Mind if I have a minute?' said a voice.

Scott stepped back and Ruth saw Dr. Mosley at the door. A chart in his hands, but no smile on his face. Not this time.

'Sure, sure, everything all right?' said Scott.

'It's fine. I just need to have a talk with Ruth about the surgery that she has undergone, if that's okay?' said Mosley.

'Maybe we could do that in the morning?' asked Scott.

'Do you feel up to it Ruth?' asked Mosley, ignoring Scott.

'I don't see how it can be that bad. I'm alive, and that's all thanks to you,' she said.

Mosley closed the door, giving them some privacy. He approached the bed, folded back the covers. Ruth was wearing a hospital gown. Mosley took hold of the bottom of the gown and asked if he could take a look. Ruth nodded.

She watched as he methodically rolled up the gown, almost to her neck. Ruth saw a network of bandages and gauze covering her entire upper body.

Mosley began to palpate her stomach. Pressing on it lightly, here and there, and asking about pain. When he was done, he rolled the gown back down and thanked Ruth.

'You're going to be all right,' said Mosley. 'Stitches look to be holding together nicely. Now, we have some things to talk about.'

'Is that really necessary? Right now?' asked Scott.

He was protecting her, but he had no reason to be so protective unless he already knew what the doctor was going to say.

'You know about it already, don't you?' said Ruth.

Closing his eyes, and pursing his lips, Scott nodded.

'Then tell me, Doctor,' said Ruth.

Mosley sat down on the edge of the bed. He spoke in the way good doctors do – plainly, and with genuine empathy.

'When you were brought in, your injuries were severe and life threatening. You had multiple stab wounds to your abdomen and chest, and lacerations to your thigh. We had to operate to stop the internal hemorrhaging.'

Ruth nodded, unable to speak. The room seemed to darken and shrink, until there was only Mosley and his voice.

'There is no right way to say this,' said Mosley, his tone changing, a deeper, more resonant timbre to his voice. As if he was coating each word in honey, trying to soften the sharp edges, knowing that what he was about to say would hurt.

'I'm afraid there was some damage we were not able to repair. One of the abdominal stab wounds was very deep.'

Her eyelids fluttered, her mouth opened, but there were no words and no breath to give them life.

'There was significant uterine damage. I'm sorry to tell you that because of this it's unlikely, maybe even dangerous, for you to conceive and carry a child naturally through a pregnancy.'

She felt Scott squeezing her hand, stroking it. Then felt his lips on her fingers. She felt as if something had been taken from her. Something precious that she hadn't even known she'd had. Not until it was gone. A cruel robbery. Her future.

She began to cry and thought that she might never stop.

8

Amanda

The bar didn't close until two a.m., but the doorman started his shift at ten and he threw Amanda and Wendy out at eleven. Even though the management thought the women had enjoyed more than enough alcohol for one evening, neither Amanda nor Wendy could be persuaded and they adjourned to Wendy's apartment off Broadway for a nightcap.

They fell into the elevator, giggling and cold. It was a nice building. Much grander than Amanda's. The apartment was bigger too. A large kitchen with room for a full-sized dining table. The five-seater couch in the lounge area had been separated from the kitchen by a floor-to-ceiling bookcase. There was even a view of the skyline.

Amanda flopped down onto the couch. She was feeling tired, but good. Wendy was a riot. There was a strange freedom enjoyed by her new friend, and Amanda found it just as intoxicating as the liquor. She had smiled tonight. And even laughed. It had been a long time since she'd done either of those things. She talked to Farrow, but always about Jess, Luis and Crone. It wasn't a real conversation. Not like tonight.

Wendy returned from the kitchen with a pair of Bloody Marys, a large stick of celery in each tall glass.

'Dinner is served,' said Wendy, sitting beside her.

Amanda hadn't realized how hungry she was until the first bite of celery. She devoured it quickly, not tasting the vodka amongst the tomato and pepper.

'I had fun tonight,' said Amanda. 'Thank you. I don't remember the last time I . . .'

'How long has it been? Since . . . you know?'

Amanda swallowed a mouthful of the drink, said, 'Six months since I lost them.'

Wendy nodded. 'I remember the first six months. And the next. It's only the first two years that are the hardest,' she said with a smile.

Amanda spat out a laugh. 'How long has it been for you?' she asked.

'Three years, eleven months, twelve days,' said Wendy.

'And it's easier?' asked Amanda.

Wendy stood, looked out the window at the city lights.

'It becomes different. More distant, I guess. The pain changes. It dulls. It's always there, but it doesn't always rip your heart out, you know?'

Amanda didn't know, but she nodded anyway. 'What happened to you?' she asked.

Still with her eyes on the view, Wendy said, 'My daughter didn't come home from school one day. She was fifteen, used to the subways. I called the school. They said she'd left with the rest of her class. She wasn't the type to run away. She'd been having some problems, but wouldn't open up to me. Couple of weeks before she disappeared, I had found her in the bathroom, cutting her forearm with a razor. We talked about it, but she said it was just a thing. Nothing specific. Teenager anxiety. She even agreed to go talk to a counselor.

'When she didn't come home that day, I called all her friends. Her cell phone was off. Then I called the police that night. They weren't interested at first. Kids that age sometimes wander, but they nearly always come back. Some don't. Rebecca never came home.'

Amanda gazed at Wendy's reflection in the window. With the

backlighting, she could see her clearly, the sky outside somewhat obscured by the bright glow on the glass. She focused on Wendy's expression. A blank, deadened look. Just for a moment, Amanda wasn't sure if she saw rain running down the windowpane, or if Wendy was crying. She got up, put a hand on her shoulder.

'What happened?' asked Amanda.

Wendy sniffed and wiped her cheeks with her sleeve.

'I called the police again. This time they put out an alert. I searched her room, found a journal I'd never seen before. It was in her handwriting. She said in the journal she was having an affair with her music teacher – Mr. Quinn. He told her to keep it quiet, that he would hurt her, or me, if she told anyone. That's what the journal said. She was scared. My poor baby. The cops hauled him in and he denied everything. It's a Catholic school, and they have the best lawyers. Her father took off when she was young, and I raised her on my own – best I could. I never expected this. I never expected to ID her body. They found her in an abandoned lot. She'd been strangled. The police had the journal, but without Rebecca there was no case against Quinn without some corroborating evidence. The DA said maybe it wasn't a diary but fiction – a teenage fantasy.'

'Jesus.'

'I know what she wrote was the truth. It was so detailed. She even mentioned a birthmark he has on the inside of his thigh, near the groin. I thought that would be enough. How could she know that if he wasn't raping her? The cops wanted to nail him, but the DA said there wasn't enough to get past reasonable doubt. Quinn never even went to trial. He killed my little girl, and he's still in that fucking school. Still teaching young girls, if you can believe that?'

'That's horrific. How can they do that?'

'They have power. They have the city councilors in their pockets all the way up to the mayor. That's why. And they don't care about those young girls. I've been wondering, for the past three years, when the next teenage girl is going to get Quinn's treatment and what he might do if she threatens to tell someone? So that's why I don't buy into Betty's forgiveness. There is no forgiveness for scum like him. He deserves to fucking d—'

She stopped short of using the word. Hung her head.

'I'm sorry,' said Wendy. 'You don't need to hear my problems.'

Amanda stepped closer to Wendy and did something she hadn't done in months. She put both her arms around another human being, and Wendy reciprocated. Amanda felt like crying again. Only it felt different. Because for once she didn't want to cry for those that she had lost. She wanted to cry for Wendy. For some time, the two women held each other and took whatever warmth and human decency they could from that embrace.

Not long after, they finished their drinks in silence. Then Wendy said, 'You can crash on the couch if you like?'

Amanda felt far too tired and loaded to brave the subway, and she was short on cab fare.

'Thank you, I will. That's really kind. I just need to use the bathroom,' said Amanda. She put her empty glass on the kitchen counter, made her way along the hallway.

She put her hand on the door handle of the first room on the left, and heard Wendy calling out from the kitchen.

'*Don't* go into that room, it's ahm . . . it's a little messy in there. Bathroom is *second* on the left.'

Amanda clung to the sides of the small wooden dingy. Another wave was coming. Tall and black against the turbulent night sky, like a mountain roaring toward her out of the deafening storm. Cold sea water splashed over the side of the little boat, soaking her already wet clothes. The boat rose on the wave, higher and higher. The wind, rain and water lashing her hair to her cheeks, stinging them. As the boat reached the crest of the wave, and tilted over, she found that she could see all around her for miles. A beam of moonlight had broken the clouds and she saw the towering waves beyond and then, in the distance, she glimpsed a light. Land.

A small fire burning on a beach. Two people stood in the light of the flames. A man. Tall and lean, and beside him a little girl with blonde hair. No matter how hard she tried to get to that beach, the dark waves threw her back, and then Amanda knew what would happen next. She had seen this before. Lived this before. Dreamed this dream before.

The boat capsized and Amanda fell into the icy sea. The shock took her breath, the cold ink-black water flooded into her mouth and . . .

She opened her eyes, gasping for air. The back of her neck ached, and her head too. She could see the city through a large window, and she remembered where she was. Amanda sat up on Wendy's couch, stretching her shoulders. The time on her iPhone read seven twenty a.m.

Shit. She'd missed Crone's morning commute.

Her head hadn't hurt like this in a long time. She got up slowly, put on her boots and made her way to the kitchen. Found water.

She often had that same dream. It started not long after she was hospitalized following Luis's suicide. She'd told one of the counselors about it, and they said it was her subconscious working through her trauma. Recurring nightmares are common in those with PTSD. They can diminish, with time and treatment. Amanda didn't want that. She liked the dream. She knew, one day, she could get through that storm to the little bonfire. She knew she would get to that beach once Crone was dead. His death would take her to the light. It would take her to Luis and Jess.

The headache started beating a pulse in her head. It was getting worse.

Wendy should have some Advil around here somewhere.

Nothing in the kitchen cabinets, which she opened and closed soundlessly – reluctant to wake her host. There was a hallway off the kitchen. Three doors. Two on the left. One at the end of the hallway, slightly ajar. It was dark in that room. Drapes drawn. Amanda made her way down the hall, peeked into the gloom at the far end. She could just make out the soles of Wendy's feet at the bottom of the bed, the sheets crumpled and spilled to the floor. Wendy snored softly.

Last night she had used the bathroom. There was a cabinet built into the mirror – there might be some painkillers in there. Then she remembered something Wendy had said at the end of the evening. She'd told Amanda where the bathroom was, but she also seemed pretty adamant Amanda shouldn't go into the other room because it was messy.

Amanda knew the feeling. After Jess and Luis died, it was a good two months before she even tried to clean the apartment. And, yes, it was still embarrassing. She didn't want to embarrass Wendy, even though Amanda of all people would understand. The events at the end of the night came back to her a little clearer. And she remembered at the time thinking Wendy was making a lame excuse to keep Amanda out of that room. Now, Amanda couldn't help but feel curious about why Wendy would lie about it.

Amanda tried the door closest to the kitchen, and it opened quietly.

It wasn't a bathroom.

And it sure as hell wasn't messy.

A second bedroom that Wendy had converted into an office.

A desk and chair in one corner, some plastic storage boxes stacked neatly in the opposite corner. The drapes were open. Amanda began to back out of the room and stopped. Wendy had seen Amanda's driver's license in the bar – had insisted upon it. She knew all about Amanda. And Amanda could not resist taking a closer look at what Wendy was so keen to hide.

She listened, heard the faint sound of snoring from Wendy's bedroom, and then moved slowly into the office. There was a corkboard above the desk with documents and sticky notes nailed to it with dozens of little red pins. Amanda crept forward, scanned the board.

There were newspaper articles on Saint Patrick's High School. Funding for a new science block, their new scheme on truancy and one on their new pastoral-care scheme. Maybe twenty or more articles, some looked to be from the school's website. There were photos of the school in some of the news articles with staff pictured at the front gates, shaking hands with bishops, businessmen and other men in slick suits. There were two photographs that weren't from the newspapers. They were glossy photoprint paper, but in black and white, and enlarged so that the image was grainy. A man, in his late forties maybe, with dark hair. One was taken as he was getting into a car outside the school. Another, from further away, as he got out of the same car parked outside a house. The pictures were a little fuzzy, but it was clearly the same guy.

Beneath the photos lay a map of Manhattan, with handwritten annotations too small for Amanda to read unless she got in real close. There was one more article, small and rectangular, hanging off the bottom of the cork board.

She suddenly felt uncomfortable.

It was a photo of a young girl. Teenager. Blonde hair in pigtails, smiling with a pair of orthodontic braces in her hand. She looked happy and her teeth looked perfect. It was the kind of photo a mom took of her daughter the first day she got her braces removed. Wendy's daughter had been a beautiful girl and would've grown into a greater beauty had she not met an evil man along the way.

There was something underneath the photo. Another printout from the web. She placed a finger at the bottom of the picture and tilted it so she could see what lay beneath.

It was a death notice in the local newspaper. For a fifteen-year-old girl.

Amanda left the room and held her breath as she softly closed the door and tip-toed to the next one. This door was the bathroom. But there was no medicine cabinet, never mind a bottle of painkillers. Instead she used the toilet, washed her face and hands, took a pea of toothpaste and ran it around her teeth and gums with her finger. Spat.

She opened the bathroom door. This time she wasn't concerned about the noise. She heard Wendy stirring.

'I'm going to take off, Wendy,' called Amanda. 'Thanks for last night. It was fun,' she said, and she meant it.

'No problem. Just shut the front door on the way out, would ya?'

'Sure thing,' said Amanda, gathering her purse. She put on her coat and was on the way to the front door when Wendy appeared from the hallway, running her fingers through her thin blonde hair as if she was trying to wrestle it into shape.

'I couldn't let you go just like that,' said Wendy.

Amanda halted, unsure.

Wendy gave her a hug, and Amanda felt that warmth once again. A warmth she had sorely missed.

'I'll call before the next group meeting. Maybe we could get Chinese food or go see a movie?' said Wendy.

'Sure,' said Amanda, recalling that they had indeed exchanged numbers the night before, drunk and proclaiming each other new best friends.

Amanda left Wendy's apartment, called the elevator and rode down to the first floor. By the time she stepped outside Wendy's building, her mind was already racing. She looked back up at the tower of glass, and wondered if she should tell her new best friend what she had seen in that room. She knew Wendy's real name now. And she knew they were more alike than Wendy could possibly imagine.

9
Ruth

Ruth stood naked in front of the full-length mirror in the hotel bedroom and let her fingers follow the pink line that ran horizontally along the bottom of her stomach. It was the longest and thinnest scar, but the one that had remained resolutely bright and keloid. The others were a mix of jagged little curves and some thick pink bumps. Mostly on her stomach, some on her left side, one on her thigh and some on her chest.

She counted them.

All seventeen of them.

The long one, lowest on her stomach, was the scar Dr. Mosley had made when he'd opened her up. Same for the one on her side to repair the lung. Somehow, she didn't mind those scars. They were kinder. They were the ones that had kept her alive. She took a band from the dresser and put up her thick brown hair. It was getting too long. There was no way she could face going to the salon. She couldn't face a lot of things.

She had not returned to work since leaving the hospital. She had not left the hotel room. Not even once. And so the days had rolled into one long miasma of time, marked only by the weekends when Scott got a break from work on Sundays. She guessed it was around a month since she'd left the hospital – maybe more. The 9/11 anniversary had been on the Tuesday, and the attack had happened that Friday, September fourteenth. When Farrow and Hernandez came to her hotel room to take her full statement, they kept repeating that date, September fourteenth, and then calling it *the night in question* or sometimes *the date of the incident*. She supposed it was to make it clear exactly when this had happened for any prosecutor or cop reading it, but it had a strange effect on Ruth.

Some dates in the calendar become haunted by their events – like 9/11. It has significance for the whole country, but she knew it held a cold place in the hearts of those who'd lost loved ones that day. They would look at the towers of light in the sky from Battery Park not just with the deadening sense of loss shared by the city, and the country, but with their own personal grief gnawing behind their eyes.

Nine/eleven would now have an additional significance for Ruth. It would mark three days until her next dark anniversary. There would be no Tribute in Light on that date. She knew September fourteenth would have no light at all.

Ruth shook her head. Who was she kidding?

So far, every day had been September fourteenth. She couldn't get that man's face out of her head. And he was there every night in her dreams. Ruth knew the dreams had significance. As if her brain was reminding her of the events that had almost killed her, so that she would never forget the face of her attacker, and never put herself in that danger again.

She checked the date on her phone. Ruth had been meaning to check the date for days. This evening was the first time she felt brave enough. It was nearly November. Six weeks had gone by since September fourteenth, but it didn't feel that way.

All of her scars were still raw. Not just those on her skin.

She heard the shower stop, and quickly put on her bathrobe. She still couldn't wear underwear – the waistband grated against her scars. She got into bed and grabbed the TV remote.

Scott emerged from the bathroom in a cloud of steam, wearing only a towel. His hair was still soaking wet, along with his short beard. Ruth wasn't sure about the beard. It was a change, but she had more on her mind and couldn't bring herself to object. It felt rough on her cheek when he kissed her, itching on the back of her neck when he held her during the night after she had woken screaming.

She wondered if he would bring it up again tonight.

Scott wanted to go home. Go back to the house with her. She'd worked hard to buy that house with Scott. It was supposed to be their dream home. The house they'd grow old in, the house that they'd bring their baby home to, the house where Ruth would draw lines on the door frame above their child's head to mark their height on their birthday, same as her mother had done.

Now it was the house where she'd almost been murdered. And her future, their future, had been stabbed to death in the hallway.

There would be no baby for this house. No pencil marks on the door frame. No sound of small feet on the parquet floor. The house had changed. It wasn't safe now. It had no future. It was a grave for all the children she would never have.

And yet part of Ruth didn't want to let this monster have her house. She had decorated every room, chosen the floor, oiled it twice a week, picked out every painting and every piece of furniture. The monster shouldn't be able to take her house too.

He had taken too much already.

'You want to watch *Jeopardy*?' asked Scott.

'Okay,' said Ruth, finding the right channel. The volume was way down, and she turned it up a few notches.

'Are there any snacks left?' asked Scott, opening the mini fridge.

'Not many. I got hungry this afternoon. There might be some pretzels,' said Ruth.

He closed the fridge, knelt and opened the little cupboard beside it.

'Nope, looks like you went through the pretzels too, honey.'

'Sorry,' said Ruth.

'It's okay. I'll go get us some in a second,' he said.

'But you'll miss the show,' said Ruth. She didn't want anything. She still felt a little sick from the snacks she had eaten for lunch.

'It's fine. I'll go to the vending machine at the end of the hallway.'

'There's a vending machine?' said Ruth.

'Yeah, we passed it when we checked in.'

Ruth had not left the room since they'd checked in. Nor had she let anyone in. The maid left fresh towels on a tray outside the room, as per Ruth's note. Ruth left the used ones outside the door each morning. Twice a week she asked for fresh bedding. Scott didn't like her changing the sheets. She said it was light work. She was fine.

Ruth was far from fine. She thought back to the day they'd checked in here, at the Paramount Hotel. Having to pass strangers on the street as she moved from the car to the hotel, then the lobby, and all of those people just standing and sitting around. There was nothing untoward about them – just guests and tourists going about their business. And yet the thought of it made her skin crawl. She remembered the vending machine now. They'd got out of the elevator, walked down a long hallway, turned left and found themselves in another chamber, with elevators at one end and the vending machine, then straight through, past four doors, to their room at the far end.

She looked at Scott, handsome, well built. Strong. She felt much better when he was with her. He had to work during the day, and his boss was understanding after the attack – letting him have some time off. He'd returned fulltime now. Some nights Scott wouldn't get back to the hotel until past seven or eight. Those were the worst times. She wanted him with her before it got dark.

He toweled his hair, shaking droplets of water everywhere. She heard the hollow patter of those drops falling on the stack of pill boxes piled up on the dresser. Another new addition to her life. Ruth now had to take pills every day. Two in the morning – anti-depressants, to fight off the demons. One pill in the afternoon, a mild anti-psychotic, and one at night to help her sleep.

'I'll go to the machine in a second. What would you like?' he said.

Ruth thought about the vending machine. In the hallway. Forty, maybe fifty feet from their room. The hallways would be quiet. Not like the morning rush down to breakfast. Room service and Scott bringing in pizza or Chinese food was all that Ruth was eating these days.

The vending machine was just outside. She could keep the door open with her novel. Be able to see the light from the room.

Forty feet.

A minute at the vending machine. Tops.

Ruth got up and put on her loose, high-waisted sweatpants – the ones Scott bought for her at Macy's so she could have something comfortable to wear leaving the hospital. She put on one of Scott's T-shirts, then the white toweling bath slippers.

'Do you have some ones?' she asked. 'I'll go to the machine.'

Scott stopped rubbing the top of his head with the towel, looked at Ruth. He smiled, then tried to hide it. He knew it was a big thing for her. Her first steps outside of the comfort of this room in two weeks. Important. Very important. But he shouldn't play it that way. If he built it up too much, Ruth might lose her nerve. All these thoughts played out on his face like a movie screen. After five years of marriage, Ruth knew how to read him.

'Sure, in my jeans,' he said.

Ruth found his jeans in the bottom of the wardrobe, fished in the pockets and found twelve bucks in singles. She turned to the door.

Her book. She almost forgot. She retrieved the Patricia Highsmith novel from the bed, stood in front of the door. Money in one hand. Folded. Book in the other.

Ruth knew every grain of wood in that door. The dark swirls in the oak veneer just below the peephole. The evacuation notice pinned above that, framed in gold-painted plastic. The selection of door signs that hung on the handle.

She had studied that door like a prisoner looks at the door of their cell. Only Ruth didn't want freedom. She didn't want to step beyond. She loved the door, how solid it felt. And she hated it.

Ruth took a breath. Let it out slowly. Then she opened the door, took two steps forward and peered out. No one in the hallway. She turned, placed her book at the base of the frame, so the door couldn't close, then quickly straightened up and turned round, fixing her eyes on the hallway, fearful in case the situation had changed.

There was no one.

The patterned carpet was richer here. Deeper. Her toweling slippers sank into it. Another breath in.

Out.

She stepped forward, knowing that at some point Scott would probably come to the door and watch her through the gap. That made her nervous, but also slightly braver. He wouldn't let anything happen to her.

Ruth kept moving forward, slowly, picking up the sounds of TVs as she passed one door, then another. She developed a rhythm. Breath in, step, let it out, another step. Her hands were rigid by her side, tensed, her fists clenched. Dollar bills in one fist, the other she felt her nails sticking into the palm.

She reached the end of the hallway, slowly glanced left at the elevator bank around the corner. No one there. Just ahead and two feet to the right, stood a vending machine. It had water, soda, candy bars, potato chips and nuts. She stood still and listened. Distant voices, the muted thump of a drawer slamming, a door closing, the ghostly echoes of someone shouting, the music from a TV commercial.

Once she reached the vending machine, Ruth began to feed it with one-dollar bills. All the snacks were on display behind the glass, held upright by coils of black plastic that spun them into freefall when she made a selection. Ruth typed in the codes for her favorites and Scott's. She inserted another dollar and selected orange Fanta and it landed with a clang in the bottom drawer. There was a collection of items there now behind an aluminum flap. She hit the coin return, listened to the rattle of dimes and quarters hitting the change slot. As she bent down to retrieve her change, the ceiling light hit the glass of the vending machine.

She saw something. Something that froze her body stiff.

In the glass she saw her reflection. And the distorted face of a man. Standing behind her.

Her mouth was open, sucking in air in a great gasp. And then she couldn't let it out. The oxygen turned to cement in her chest. Her eyes were wide, staring, her body unable to move, her voice strangled in total panic.

Suddenly, the lizard part of her brain took over. The back brain. For Ruth, it started with shaking, as the fear pounded through every blood vessel, getting her heart rate up, screaming at her to *move*.

She jumped up, and half turned. Her chest opened and she let out a shriek that quickly filled the hallway in a long high-pitched scream.

As she turned, she saw the old man step away from her. He was in his eighties, wearing a brown cardigan and slippers. He raised his walking frame as he stumbled backwards, surprise written large on his face.

There was only the old man. No attacker with sharp features and electric-blue eyes.

She felt strong hands grab her, and she shrieked again, clawing at them. But then she focused her eyes and saw that it was Scott. He was getting further away from her, as if he was falling into the ceiling – but then she realized he wasn't the one moving. She collapsed and the hallway carpet started swimming around her.

Within minutes, there were people all around. She recognized one of the receptionists who'd checked them into the hotel. The blonde with the big red lips that barely moved as she spoke.

Ruth could smell something foul and powerful. Smelling salts.

She'd felt quite faint, but the salts brought her round. Helped her focus.

'There was someone behind me. I'm so sorry, I just panicked.'

'It was just Mr. Perkins,' said Scott, pointing behind him to the sheepish-looking elderly guy in the cardigan. Someone had brought him a chair. There were more people around her. Hotel staff, other guests. Her head hurt and there was a terrible taste in her mouth. She apologized to the elderly man.

'Don't worry, honey. I move slow and quiet with this walker. I didn't mean to startle you.'

'I didn't mean to frighten you,' said Ruth.

Ruth had never felt so small. And yet Mr. Perkins somehow made her feel okay about things. She was frightened. And that was all right.

She had Scott to protect her. That was all that mattered.

10

Amanda

Amanda could think of nothing else for three days.

On the third day it proved too much. She packed her cheap laptop into her backpack and set off from her apartment. There was a Starbucks one block away. In Manhattan, like most major cities, Starbucks doesn't seem to be more than one block away no matter where you are. Amanda walked past it, and down the steps to the subway. She rode five stops, got off at Grand Central, and made her way to the street. She found a Starbucks on Lexington, half a block from the train station.

Nursing a coffee, she took a bench seat facing the window and searched the web on their Wi-Fi. She didn't find what she was looking for on the first try. The second search, with more refined terms, got a lot of hits. On the fifth page of the search results, she found what she was looking for.

It was from *USA Today*. The date matched the timeline Wendy had given to her. Over three years ago. The dates and the names matched too.

Fifteen-year-old Rebecca Cotton was found dead in a vacant lot by a member of the public last night. She had been reported missing by her mother two days before.

Rebecca's mother, Naomi Cotton, said, 'My daughter was raped by her teacher. He threatened her, told her to keep it quiet and before she could tell the truth he strangled her. I know it. That man killed my baby.'

The school issued a statement to say that they were sorry to hear of the tragic death of one of their students, and that Mr. Frank Quinn denies all the allegations made by the late Rebecca Cotton. An NYPD spokesperson refused to comment on the case.

A service for Rebecca Cotton will take place at . . .

The three photographs accompanying the piece were interesting. One of the school; one of the man she'd seen in the photos in Wendy's office, again, not a great picture; and one of Rebecca.

Naomi was still Wendy in Amanda's mind. She wanted to keep that name in her head in case she accidentally called her Naomi. That wouldn't do. Not yet, anyway. For now, Amanda went through search after search, and found similar articles from the *New York Daily News*, *Metro New York*, the *Queens Chronicle* and more. She noticed there was no mention of the story in *Catholic New York*. Most of the articles were much alike. There wasn't much in the way of new information either about Naomi, Quinn or Rebecca.

The last hit she got proved interesting.

Bereaved Mother of Teen Arrested for Facebook Post.

The article from the *New York Post* gave the history of what had happened with Rebecca and said that Naomi had posted on the Saint Patrick's Facebook page, saying Quinn was a pedophile and a murderer and should be shot. She wasn't charged by police, but agreed to refrain from making similar posts on social media. Amanda bookmarked this page and made a mental note to print it out later along with the rest. The picture of Quinn was a little clearer and in color. He had a handsome face. One that she would remember.

The time in the corner of her screen read one oh five in the afternoon. She pulled the ball cap low on her head, put on a pair of shades and looked up from her laptop.

She scanned the street. There was construction work going on at the corner, and the workers were sharing their coffee and doughnuts with a homeless man who looked as though he hadn't eaten anything in a long time. Women in long coats and boots walked quickly by, their scarves trailing in the wind. Men in suits with umbrellas and iPads tucked beneath their arms. Steam rose from the vents in the street and yellow taxis honked their horns like they were talking to each other.

Any time now . . .

And there he was. Wallace Crone in a dark suit, black coat, AirPods in his ears, a bag over his shoulder. He exited Grand Central and used the crosswalk. Amanda watched as he entered the building directly opposite her. He was running late. He normally made it there at one ten. It was almost one twenty now. Amanda knew he came here every week, same time, same day, but so far she could only make an educated guess at what he was doing in the building. There were more than sixty tenants.

The once-a-week visits ruled out a lot of those businesses. It wasn't work for Crone, because he sometimes arrived in his gym gear, and would go for a run afterwards. She doubted he needed to visit a medical doctor once a week. A psychiatrist's appointment was the most likely. He came from wealth. His father was a Wall Street legend, and Crone worked in Daddy's firm. He'd graduated from Harvard Law with honors. His criminal record was never a problem, because his father didn't let it become a problem.

She figured the weekly session in the shrink's chair was something that Crone's father had insisted upon. If his son was regularly seeing a psychiatrist, it might curb his tendencies.

Amanda felt sick every time she saw Crone walking freely around the city while her daughter and husband lay in their early graves.

Amanda had loved walking these streets with Luis and Jess. The year before, in the summer, they had walked ten blocks on this very street. About a half mile. A big walk for a five-year-old in ninety-degree heat. Jess hadn't complained, but her little face had turned red under her sun hat and she said she was thirsty. For the last two blocks, Luis had grabbed Jess by the waist, hoisted her up onto his shoulders. When they arrived at Mary Arnold's, one of the oldest toy stores in the city, Jess drank most of her juice before they went inside.

Jess had loved Mary Arnold's toy store. So had Luis. As Jess was pulling Amanda towards the back of the store, where they kept Silly Putty, Luis pointed out the old Fisher Price toys – too babyish for Jess then.

'I had that phone,' said Luis, pointing to a white rotary phone with a face and wheels on its base. It had a red receiver and eyes that wobbled when you turned the wheels.

'I think I had that one too,' said Amanda.

Jess tugged at Amanda's hand.

'The Silly Putty is this way, Mommy,' she said.

They spent an hour in the store. Jess left with her putty, some comic books and a pair of cheap mini sunglasses for a doll that Jess hoped would fit Sparkles. Stepping back into the sunshine on the Upper East Side, shopping bags full of toys, Jess turned and looked up at them both. Then she'd wrapped her little arms round their legs and said, 'You're the best mommy and daddy in the whole world.'

Luis and Amanda had locked eyes. She'd never seen him so happy.

That night, as Jess slept, Amanda and Luis ate dinner in front of the TV, watched SNL in each other's arms and went to bed tired and happy.

It was the most perfect day.

There were no more days for Jess and Luis.

And yet Crone's days were laid out in front of him.

She could not let this go. She would never let this go.

Amanda closed the laptop, took out her phone and typed out a text to Wendy.

Want to grab coffee or a drink?

She'd had an idea. A crazy idea.

And it just might work.

II

Ruth

Detective Farrow sat on the desk chair in Ruth's room at the Paramount Hotel. His partner, Karen Hernandez, remained standing. Sweat stuck Farrow's hair to his forehead and Hernandez couldn't seem to raise her chin off her chest for more than a moment. Scott sat beside Ruth on the bed. One hand in Ruth's, the other around her shoulders. Scott had taken the call from Detective Farrow the day before to arrange the meeting.

Ruth had already made a full statement from the hotel room. And she'd worked with a sketch artist who sat with her for an hour in the room afterwards, drawing a composite sketch. That was the last she'd heard from the police until yesterday.

Today was the fourteenth of November. Two months, exactly, since the attack.

'So how have things been?' asked Farrow.

'Not good,' said Ruth. 'I get nightmares. I haven't had a good night's sleep since . . . well, since I woke up in the hospital. I'm anxious all the time.'

'That's understandable. And have you been seeing any doctors lately?' asked Farrow.

Ruth knew what the detective really meant. He'd used the word 'doctors' when he really meant 'shrink'.

'Not really. I haven't been able to see anyone regularly. I had one appointment – he put me on some meds,' she said.

'I can give you a few recommendations,' said Farrow.

'No, it's fine. I know a couple of therapists. I sold them their apartments. I don't want to see anyone at the moment. It's all so raw. Until you catch this guy, I just feel exposed. I don't leave this room, really.'

Farrow's eyebrows knotted together and he asked, 'You haven't been out of this room since you checked out of the hospital? How long has it been . . .?'

'Around six weeks,' said Scott.

'Six we— Look, Ruth, I really think you should see someone. We're concerned about you. There is a process every victim goes through – there's stages to it. It can be conquered, you know? With the right help.'

'I'm fine,' said Ruth, drawing her closed lips into a trembling smile.

'If you could leave some contacts, or email them to me, we can take a look,' said Scott.

'Good, great. I'll do that,' said Farrow, sitting up straighter in the chair. As he did so, he winced slightly, reached round and held his back.

'We wanted to give you an update on the case. It's taken a while, but we have the forensic results. I'm afraid it's not good news. We were unable to find any forensic material that might have come from the perpetrator.'

Ruth felt Scott's fingers tighten around her own.

Farrow said nothing more. He just sat there with his big eyes gazing at Ruth.

'What about fingerprints? Or security-camera footage, things like that?' asked Scott.

Hernandez was already shaking her head.

'I'm afraid not. There are some cameras in the area. I'm afraid we didn't catch anything useful on them. What we've found is that the attack comes after a protracted period of surveillance. The first victim reported a tall man in a hood following her home from work. That report came in five weeks before that particular victim was attacked. It's likely he knew where the cameras were on the block and how to avoid them,' said Hernandez.

'What do you have on this guy?' said Scott, his voice rising.

Farrow rubbed the stubble on his chin, then folded his arms.

He looked at Scott and said, 'We've had a more detailed analysis done of our first two victims, and we found traces of chloroform, so we know for sure now that these attacks are connected and we are building a profile of this perpetrator. We have a description, and we have the composite sketch, thanks to Ruth working with our sketch artist. We're talking to our media department about releasing the sketch to the public. We know he stalks his victims; Ruth has heard his voice too. We are asking the public to be vigilant.'

Scott let go of Ruth's hand. He stood up fast, before she could pull him back down.

'You haven't released the sketch yet? Why wouldn't you do that straight away?'

'Well, there's pros and cons. The sketch is good, but it could be a likeness for a lot of people, you know? We release it and we get flooded with calls. Pretty much all of them are going to be false leads and right now we don't have the manpower to go chasing five hundred guys who look a little like the man in the sketch.'

'So get more cops on this. Do you even have a suspect yet?' said Scott.

Farrow looked at Hernandez. She slid her hands into the front pockets of her jeans and stared at him for a second before she turned her attention back to the carpet.

'No, we do not have a suspect yet,' said Farrow.

'But he's out there now,' said Ruth.

'I know he is. And when he makes a mistake we're going to catch him. We figured out that there was a paramedic call to someone on your block around the time of the attack that night. It was those sirens that spooked him, made him run. Next time maybe he won't be so lucky.'

'Next time? You mean you hope he makes a mistake or gets caught when he tries to kill someone else? That's not good enough,' said Ruth.

Hernandez must've felt she had to come to Farrow's defense. She stepped forward and said, 'We canvassed the neighborhood – that's how we found out about the ambulance. We've checked security footage and went over every inch of your house and the grounds. There's no trace of the prowler.'

As soon as she'd spoken that final word, Farrow shot her a look.

'The prowler? Is that what you call him?' asked Scott.

'No, that's what some of the papers call him,' said Farrow. He didn't tell them that Hernandez and some of the other cops at the precinct now had another name for the perp. They'd started calling him Mr. Blue-eyes.

'So that's it? Go home, see a psychiatrist, pray he doesn't come back for me and just try to forget about all this? Is that what you're saying to me?' said Ruth, tears in her eyes.

'We'll get this guy, but we have to be realistic. Even if you ID him, identification evidence on its own probably won't be enough to get a conviction beyond all reasonable doubt. That's just the way the law works. I'm sorry. We are doing everything possible to find this man. Look, we are concerned about you, Ruth. You haven't left this room in almost two months and I think you should—'

She cut him off. 'I should what? See a shrink? I don't need a shrink. You think I don't want to go outside? Do you think I don't want to go back to my life? My job?'

Farrow stayed quiet, and simply nodded as she spoke.

'I want this to be over, Detective,' she said. 'The truth is I'm scared. I'm fucking terrified. He's somewhere out there, right now.

Do you have any idea how that makes me feel? I don't want to be afraid any more. I want you to catch the man who tried to kill me. That's what I want. That's *all* I want from you. No amount of counseling or medication is going to ease that fear until he's behind bars.'

12

Farrow

Hernandez pulled out of the Paramount Hotel parking lot and joined the throng of New York traffic. Neither she nor Farrow had spoken since they'd left the hotel room. There was little they could say.

'Fuck this guy,' said Hernandez, breaking the silence.

'Which guy? The prowler?'

'Yeah, I'm sorry I dropped that name in there.'

'Mr. Blue-eyes would've sounded a *lot* worse, I think.'

'I just can't believe we don't have a forensic hit yet. Literally nothing.'

Farrow nodded, said, 'I think if there was a trace, our people would've found it. This is not a fuck-up in the tech department. Mr. Blue-eyes is very careful, but, even at that, it's incredible that he's not given us a single fiber yet. How does he work so clean? It's not a controlled crime scene. He kills at the victim's home, so it's unfamiliar territory. He doesn't know what the hell he'll be facing inside. And yet he's never so much as dropped a single hair off his goddamned head.'

'Maybe he cleans up?' said Hernandez, then leaned on the horn as a cab stopped dead in the lane ahead to pick up a passenger.

'How could he clean himself? There's blood everywhere. He must be covered in spatter.'

'Hazmat suit?'

'Doesn't fit the description given by Ruth.'

'You could hardly call it a description. Maybe that's why he knocks them out with the chloroform, so he can get changed into a suit before he starts to work?'

'That sounds plausible,' said Farrow. 'Unfortunately, those suits are sold all over the US, and I'm sure there's a black market for them too, just like the chloroform. I've seen those suits used in meth cook houses. We're not going to trace him that way.'

Hernandez swore, smacked the wheel.

'What is it?' he asked.

'Mrs. Gelman, that's what it is. She seems so helpless. I just hope she gets better.'

'Ruth Gelman is never going to recover. Not fully. Imagine that, being at home, your safe space, and a monster breaks in, mutilates you with a knife . . . I mean, how could you even function again?'

'I'd function,' said Hernandez. 'I'd find the motherfucker and I'd put a bullet between his legs. Then I'd go to work on him.'

'Not everyone is a psycho like you, Karen.'

'Don't knock the psychos. We can be useful.'

'Would you really do that? If you found the guy, and you knew he was guilty, but you couldn't prove it? You'd take him out?' said Farrow.

Hernandez sighed, pulled into the next lane to get around a cab and hit the accelerator.

'Is that an on-the-record question?' she asked.

'You're not talking to Internal Affairs, here. Come on, we're partners. You can tell me.'

'Then, off the record, hypothetically, yeah. If I was sure it was the guy and we couldn't prosecute him, there's no chance I'm going to let him go and do that to somebody else.'

'So you're saying if we found Mr. Blue-eyes, but we couldn't make a case against him you would put him down?'

'Damn right I'd put him down. With a smile on my face while I squeezed the trigger.'

They fell silent for a time, and the sounds of the city buffeted the car as they rolled east.

'What about you?' asked Hernandez.

'What about me? You want to know if I'd do it?'

'Sure.'

Farrow gazed out the window. On the sidewalk, two homeless guys were fighting over a cardboard box. Each of them had an end, and they were ripping it apart in the process. With each rip, their remonstrations and anger grew.

'Are you talking about Mr. Blue-eyes here? Or are you really talking about Wallace Crone?'

'Either one,' said Hernandez.

'I've already asked myself that question,' he said. 'I still don't know the answer.'

13
Amanda

They were two cocktails down, working their way through the menu with a Negroni in the shaker, when Amanda started to move the conversation around.

'You know he's suing me for harassment, right?'

'The guy who killed your daughter, Crone?' asked Wendy.

'Yeah, son of a bitch.'

Wendy hit the outdoor heater again and lit up a cigarette. The bar was on the rooftop of the Pod 39 hotel on 39th Street. It was cold, but the heater was surprisingly powerful. Amanda had to take off her coat at the table.

'That's awful. Why is he suing you? What did you do? Something bad, I hope.'

'I was following him. Watching his movements, where he ate, where he slept and who with? At first, I thought I might find out something. Something that could help with Jess's case, you know? But I never did. Then I had another idea.'

'What was that?'

'If I wasn't going to find something to take him off the street, the next best thing was to find a way to take him out.'

Wendy said nothing. She took a moment to appraise Amanda.

And she felt Wendy's gaze as she sipped the last remnants of the cock-tail from her glass.

'Take him out? You mean . . .'

Amanda nodded.

'You serious about that?' asked Wendy.

'I had a plan. I was going to do it on a crowded subway.'

'Jesus, you *are* serious,' said Wendy, leaning forward.

Amanda nodded and lit a cigarette. She used the time to study Wendy who sat, composed, engaged. Amanda had to judge this very carefully. Take it slowly.

'This is just between us, right?' asked Amanda.

Wendy's eyebrows flicked upwards, just for a second, then settled back down. She was either nervous or intrigued by what direction the conversation might take.

'Absolutely,' said Wendy.

'Like, just between us, have you ever thought about it?' asked Amanda.

Wendy took a drag on her cigarette, absently tapped the butt with her thumb, sending a cascade of ash onto the brick-paved floor. Her eyes roamed the sky, then shot back to Amanda as she spoke.

'Do you mean have I ever thought about killing the man who raped and murdered my daughter?' said Wendy flatly.

At first Amanda didn't know how to respond. Wendy's tone was difficult to read.

'Don't tell me you haven't thought about it,' said Amanda.

Wendy surveyed the skyline again, taking a deep breath and hook-ing a lock of blonde hair behind her ear. The lights from the windows of the building opposite were reflected in those brown eyes. It reminded Amanda of Jess. She would take her to see the Christmas tree at Rockefeller Plaza. All those beautiful lights dancing in her wide eyes. Amanda took another drag on her smoke and admired the view. Black monolith buildings towered against a brushstroke of

rose-colored clouds. The silence grew while they smoked their cigarettes and Wendy rolled that question around in her head.

Then Wendy's smile fell away as she focused her attention on
Amanda.

'You saw my office that night you spent in my apartment. I'd asked
you not to go in there,' said Wendy.

It was a statement. Not a question. If she denied it, she would be
chipping away at the very layers of trust she was trying so hard to
build.

'I'm sorry. I couldn't remember which door was the bathroom. I
just stumbled in and I couldn't resist taking a look. I apologize for
that, but it's okay, I'm not going to tell anyone what I saw in there,'
said Amanda.

'And what did you see?' asked Wendy. There was a new sharpness
in her tone.

Amanda knew she had to be careful; this was all so finely balanced. Either she would make a friend of Wendy for life, or Wendy
would storm off and never speak to her again. Either was possible.
Amanda decided she would not regret this if she just told the truth.

'At first I wasn't sure,' said Amanda, 'but when I saw the cork
board it made sense. It fit with what you'd told me the night before.
Remember? You'd told me about your daughter. And Quinn. And in
the group session you said some of us can't forgive the people who
killed our children. That's *exactly* how I feel. And I knew then what I
was looking at. The map, the photos, the articles – you've been watching Quinn. Maybe you've been planning how to kill him?'

Wendy said nothing. Her eyes locked on Amanda's. And they
stayed that way for a time.

The waiter brought their drinks over, and both women thanked
him. A slice of orange sat atop the Negronis. Amanda fished it out
from her drink, wrapped it in her napkin and dropped it in the ash-
tray. Even the smell of the fruit made her throat tighten. It brought
images and smells of Luis and his breakfast oranges. It was a little

stab of grief that she wasn't expecting. Mourning is sometimes a dull ache that won't leave, and other times it's like pricking your finger on a needle hidden in a shopping bag. Amanda forced herself to take a sip. All the while, Wendy regarded her inquisitively – carefully weighing her next words.

'We're just talking here, right?' asked Wendy.

Amanda nodded.

'I've thought about killing Quinn. It's just a thought, right? A revenge fantasy. That's not a crime,' said Wendy.

'Imagining your revenge isn't a crime. I've done a lot of thinking. Too much, maybe. *You've* done a lot of thinking. Planning too. Just like I have.'

Wendy took a long drink from her Negroni, put the glass gently back on the table, smacked her lips and said, 'How far did you get with the subway plan?'

Amanda noticed Wendy had ignored the implied question and had fired back one of her own. She reminded herself not to pressure Wendy – she had to be patient. But she still had to lead the way. She had to let Wendy know that she trusted her enough to tell her the truth.

'I was there, on the subway car, the gun in my pocket. I was all set to do it and the son of a bitch must've sensed me or something. I don't know. He looked up, right at me and spoke. After he'd drawn attention to me, I couldn't do it. People were looking. They would've seen me pull the trigger. I would've been caught right away. So I stopped. He called for the cops – they arrested me. It was just luck that I managed to hide the gun otherwise my ass would be in jail right now, instead of court-ordered counseling and probation.'

Wendy sat forward, said, 'I had no idea you'd gone that far.'

'I would've gone a lot farther if he hadn't noticed me first,' said Amanda.

Wendy shook her head, took half the cocktail down in one swallow. She looked to the side for a moment, thinking.

'Fuck, I've imagined myself in that position. Tell me, hypothetically, if he hadn't seen you, would you really have pulled that trigger?' asked Wendy.

Amanda had asked herself that same question, over and over again, late at night, lying awake in her bed with Jess's toy, Sparkles, next to her. She always had the same answer. Found a strange comfort in that knowledge.

'Yes,' she said.

Wendy nodded. 'I believe you.'

'It's a weird thing – justice. It feels personal, you know? Like it's something I should have as a right. When Jess was murdered, it . . . it felt like my whole world just turned upside down. Jess shouldn't have died. Luis shouldn't have died. You go through your entire life thinking about what's going to happen next – when are we going to get a bigger apartment? What's Jess going to be like when she's older? Will she be popular in school? God, I'd even thought about how I would feel watching her get ready on her wedding day . . . and then everything is just *gone*. It's not right. And when the man who killed your daughter gets away with it – that's not right *either* . . .'

Wendy nodded as Amanda continued.

'None of this was supposed to happen – the world is so far off kilter that the only thing I can think about is putting it back on track. Setting things straight. None of this will bring back Jess or Luis, I know that. But it might stop the fucking world from spinning out of control.'

'I know how you feel,' said Wendy. 'When I told you it gets easier – I lied. I feel exactly the same way as I did the day they found Rebecca's body. Grieving is a process, right? That's what Matt and all the rest of the counselors tell you. But what they don't tell you is that you can't start the process when your kid's murderer is still walking around a free man. At least I can't.'

Wendy's words seemed to echo somewhere deep inside Amanda's chest. She didn't just hear Wendy, she felt her.

'Same for me,' said Amanda. 'I know the grief is there. It's waiting.

Getting bigger every day, but it won't come to me. I can't cry over Jess any more. I can't process it until things are put right. Every day that goes by, I feel worse.'

'It doesn't have to be this way – we could just walk up to these fuckers and bam! Put two in their heads in the middle of Fifth Avenue. Sometimes I think that's what I should do,' said Wendy.

'I've thought the same. But then I'd go to jail. Crone's family would get the justice denied to my daughter. I'd be paying for that murder all my life. I don't see how that's fair.'

Wendy nodded, said, 'That's *not* fair.'

'What if . . .' said Amanda, then she paused, swallowed, pushed a fresh cigarette from the pack. She was working up the courage, taking her time. The silence became uncomfortable, and Amanda told herself to just spit it out. 'What if we helped each other? What if I helped you kill Quinn? And then you helped me kill Crone?'

Wendy let that question hang in the night air for a time, before she grabbed hold of it.

'If something happened to Quinn, with my public vendetta against him, the cops would be all over me in a heartbeat, unless . . .' said Wendy, pausing to ignite her Zippo and offering it to Amanda.

'Unless what?' asked Amanda, urging her on as she brought the cigarette to the flame and inhaled.

'Unless I wasn't the one who killed him. And I had a cast-iron alibi,' said Wendy.

Amanda blew out smoke. This was what had been in her mind for days – the two of them working together, but not quite like this. Amanda had intended to share the burden – put their minds together. This was a plan she hadn't anticipated.

'Do you ever watch old movies?' asked Wendy.

'Sure, sometimes,' said Amanda. 'What, like black-and-white movies? Humphrey Bogart, Audrey Hepburn?'

'I was thinking about Hitchcock movies. *Strangers on a Train*?' said Wendy.

'Yes, I saw it. A long time ago,' said Amanda.

'It's the set-up that is so fascinating,' said Wendy. 'Two strangers meet on a train, by accident. They get to talking and we find out one of them wants to kill his father, and the other has secret fantasies about killing his wife. The point is both of them have a good reason to kill somebody. But if the husband kills the ex-wife, he's automatically a suspect. Same with the son if he tried to kill his father. Then one of them has the idea . . .'

'They swap murders,' said Amanda, smiling and nodding.

'Right. That way each of them can set up the perfect alibi, and they can't be tied to the crime. There's no connection between the two men.'

Hearing that out loud sent a shiver of excitement over Amanda's skin.

'Jesus, that's a great idea,' said Amanda.

Never before had Amanda wished real harm to anyone – not until evil had taken her life apart. That's what Amanda felt – that Crone had an evil inside of him. How else could you kill a child? It had to be evil. And that kind of sickness must be stopped. For the sake of the child he'd killed, and the children who were now in danger. She wanted to kill him so badly it had taken over her life. That had isolated her even further. She never spoke to friends, ex-colleagues – anyone, really, apart from Farrow. And here was someone fired with the same kind of hate that was keeping her alive.

Both women stubbed out their cigarettes.

Amanda didn't want to be the first to say it aloud. To state it plainly. That would be like shifting tectonic plates beneath the earth – it would inevitably result in a volcanic eruption. Once she spoke, there would be no going back.

'We could do that for real. We could swap murders,' said Amanda. 'What are the chances of the two of us meeting? The group is supposed to be anonymous, so there's no connection between us.'

'We're strangers in therapy,' said Wendy with a smile. 'But let's be clear about this. We're talking about wiping out the scum that killed our children. If Quinn gets hit by a truck on Fifth Avenue, the cops will be up my ass for a week. They'll think I had something to do with it. Same with you if something happened to Crone. The only way to do this is to make sure we have a solid alibi. I'll kill Crone for you, while you're somewhere far away, with dozens of alibi witnesses . . .'

Amanda cut her off, 'And I'll kill Quinn while you're somewhere else, with your alibi witnesses. No one knows we're friends. I want justice for my poor girl, and my husband. And I'll get it or die trying.'

Wendy slumped in her chair, as if she had been struck. She blew out her cheeks then downed the rest of her Negroni. Sitting there for a moment, her eyes wandered. Amanda could see her working through the idea. Thinking of all the angles. All the possible ways this might go wrong. Eventually, Wendy sat up, leaned forward.

'It will work,' said Wendy.

'I know it will,' said Amanda.

Wendy held out her hand, said, 'Let's keep talking. Fuck the Wendy shit. You know my name is Naomi, so let's go with that. We could do this, but we'll need to do it right. Tell me everything you know about Wallace Crone.'

'Are we still just talking?' asked Amanda.

Wendy pulled her seat closer, lowered her voice. 'What do you think?' she said.

14
Scott

Scott hadn't set foot in the district attorney's offices since the day he'd left. Before Scott went to law school, he'd bummed around in various jobs, gone traveling, then got work in the court office. It was there that he saw lawyers in thousand-dollar suits and decided he wanted a piece of the action. He worked hard, graduated law school and hit the bar exam out of the park. He clerked for a judge for a while before securing a position in the DA's office. That's when the initial attraction of money fell away. Within a week of being in the DA's office, Scott knew he wasn't like the other assistant district attorneys who were putting in their time in the saddle so they could make enough connections to leap into a mid six-figure salary in a big firm. For Scott, this was a calling. He was putting things right – for society.

And for his younger self, the part of him that still knew fear even when just thinking about a locker room or a quiet school hallway. If it wasn't for wanting to have a better life with Ruth, Scott would still be in this office putting bad guys away.

He occasionally played racquetball with one of the assistant DAs from his time there, but even that guy had now left his post. There were some career prosecutors who he'd recognize if he saw them again, but they were never overly friendly. He knew them enough to pass the time of day – that was it.

The place hadn't changed much, even if the personnel had. Still the same tiled floor, still the same old leather furniture in the small reception office, still the same smell of damp in the air. This was an old building, and the pipes groaned late at night with the effort of heating it.

'Mr. Rush will see you now,' said the receptionist.

Scott followed the receptionist down an oak-paneled hallway to the last office. She knocked, opened the door and said, 'I have Scott Gelman for you,' then left.

The man in the green leather chair, behind a wide mahogany desk piled with files, was David O. Rush, the assistant district attorney in charge of Ruth's case. His office was plain, painted an industrial beige, with a few watercolors of cattle and castles scattered around.

'Mr. Gelman, good to meet you,' said Rush, coming forward with a smile and an open palm, ready for a manly shake.

'Please, Scott is fine.'

'David. Likewise,' he said, pumping Scott's arm in a media-trained handshake. Rush looked about the same age as Scott. He was a small man with an air of unearned authority and an ill-fitting suit that came straight off the rack.

'Nice to meet you too,' said Scott, letting go of the man's hand.

'You used to work here, right?' said David.

'Sure did, a long time ago. Thanks for taking this meeting. I'm glad we could set it up.'

'Is Ruth with you?' asked David.

'No,' said Scott, closing the office door behind him. 'She couldn't make it. She can't leave . . . I mean, she wasn't feeling up to it.'

David nodded, explained how sorry he was then offered Scott a seat at the other side of the desk while he returned to his green leather office chair.

'So, what can I do for you? I understand Detective Farrow spoke to you and your wife three days ago.'

'That's why I'm here,' said Scott, before clearing his throat. 'I wasn't happy about the way Farrow left it. Look, I get it. Overworked cop. And getting a conviction in a case like this isn't easy on ID evidence alone. I understand that, but it just felt like Farrow and Hernandez never even tried, you know?'

David pulled his face into something that was supposed to look sympathetic. Scott couldn't help notice that when he said Farrow and Hernandez hadn't put in any effort David rested an ankle on his other knee. Then he began to swivel his chair, side to side.

'I've known Farrow for almost ten years. He's a dedicated officer – married to the job. There's blue in his veins. His father was a cop twenty plus years. Farrow is one of those pricks who calls me at four in the morning because the lab is taking too long to get him some results. Not that he's on shift at that time either – he just doesn't sleep. If I'd done something wrong, the one man I wouldn't want coming after me is Farrow.'

'So he's dedicated, but maybe he thought he couldn't get anything from Ruth's case and moved on too fast, without properly looking into suspects.'

'He talked to me about Ruth's case. I reviewed the file. The description probably matches ten thousand people in this district alone. Even if she pointed him out in a line-up, the defense counsel would rip her apart because she only saw the attacker for what . . . half a second? And, even then, she only saw a reflection in a pane of glass. A mirror image. It's not a good ID case.'

'She saw his eyes. She saw his face. But the important thing is she told Farrow she would recognize the man if she saw him again.'

'Scott, come on. You used to work here. We don't have a suspect. And, even if we find the guy, without some other piece of corroborating evidence it's going nowhere. I'm sorry. I'd really love to nail this son of a bitch – believe me.'

'So even if you catch this guy, and Ruth identifies him, that's not good enough? Unless he flat out confesses, there's no way Ruth is going to get justice, is that what you're telling me?'

Rush stood up, signaling the meeting was over, and said, 'I'm terribly sorry for what happened to your wife, but I have to look at the evidence, dispassionately. You know what it's like. There's just no case here.'

At first Scott didn't move. He stayed in his seat, leaned forward to rest his elbows on his knees and looked at the floor.

'I'm sorry, Scott.'

'So am I. I never should've left her alone that ni . . .' Scott didn't finish his sentence. He couldn't. He balled his hands into tight fists, then shook his head, breathed in and out in short staccato bursts, and then, once he'd calmed – one long exhale. He was winding himself down, before he really blew.

He got up, shook Rush's hand. He was worried he might lose it in front of him. He wanted out of that office, right now.

'Look, Scott, I want to help. We'll put out the sketch on the local news, a few of the newspapers and the website. See if it shakes anything loose?'

'Thank you.'

In five minutes, Scott was in Foley Square, headed for the subway. He stopped at a hot-food stand and bought coffee. He needed to get back to work. His firm would only tolerate so much time off, then it would become a problem. Yet he couldn't face the office. Not yet. He sipped his coffee and wandered for a while, letting his feet take him away from the courthouses in case another lawyer from his firm caught him loitering.

There was a tightness in his chest he couldn't shake. For the first time since the twelfth grade, he felt completely powerless. Scott had grown up in Hartford, Connecticut. An upper middle-class neighborhood and a good school. But a school filled with some bad kids all the same. Scott was small in those years. He was a late bloomer, according to his mother. His height had made him stand out, and his skinny arms were the talk of his class. He'd had to put up with insult after insult and he'd never done anything about it – until one day. His senior year, he cracked at the group of jocks who were giving him their usual treatment in the locker room. He stood up to them, said they were a bunch of pussies.

The beating he got that day, naked, in the shower, left him quivering. He didn't know if it was the cold, or the beating, but he couldn't stop shaking for days. That's when he ditched his set of dumbbells and joined a gym, used some of his savings for a personal training session. All through college in New York, if Scott wasn't studying, or in class, or out partying, he was in the gym putting in the hours.

The work had paid off. He looked like an athlete now. And he'd shot up in height his last teenage years. His shoulders widened, his arms had grown thick with muscle. What drove him was that feeling he'd had while lying on cold white tiles in his high-school shower block. He'd felt powerless. Utterly weak. Sending bad people to prison had given him a sense of fulfilment, even of revenge. But, somehow, the part of Scott that had been beaten down on that shower room floor never got back up again – no matter what he did.

That feeling of helplessness was always part of him.

And that feeling had returned in force now. This time he knew he couldn't shake it by torturing himself in the gym, and he was no longer a prosecutor so he couldn't heal vicariously by punishing other bad men. He would have to deal with it some other way. And hide it as best he could from Ruth.

Scott tossed the coffee and headed back to Foley Square and the subway. He wandered the streets, head down, not really looking where he was going. His mind elsewhere. As he passed the people in the street, he couldn't help but study some of the men. The killer who'd attacked Ruth was loose.

The man who had almost murdered his wife.

Scott wanted a family, a perfect family. He was never so far away from achieving that dream, and a man had taken it from him. The killer could be any man in this city. And he was free to walk around while Ruth stayed in a hotel room like a prisoner.

And there was nothing he could do about it.

15
Ruth

A week after the visit from the police, Ruth stepped into the hotel elevator with Scott. She gripped his hand tightly. It was seven in the evening, and they were dressed for dinner. There was no one else in the elevator, and it rode smoothly to the lobby.

The elevator slowed, stopped.

Ruth breathed out, rolled her shoulders.

Scott said, 'You can do this.'

Ruth nodded.

The doors opened on the lobby.

Scott stepped forward. Ruth didn't move. He turned back toward her.

She held his gaze, fighting back the tears and that familiar panic that had begun to twist in her belly like a corkscrew. It felt as though the heels of her shoes were cemented to the floor.

'It's okay, honey. I'm here. Come on, let's eat,' he said.

There were three people waiting for them to exit so they could take the elevator. A young couple and a toddler. The man looked around Scott's age. The woman was a little younger than Ruth. She was getting up from a kneeling position, still holding her child's hand.

'Just wait for the nice lady,' said the woman to her little son. He was trying to get through the doors to the lift, but she was holding him back.

Ruth closed her eyes and took a step. Then another. She was in the lobby; the family had passed her. She heard the rollers on the doors as they closed. Above that sound, a melody played on the hotel's PA system. A piano. Something soft, slow and jazzy. She could barely hear it over the sound of her pulse thumping in her ears.

She felt Scott's hand gently tugging her forward and she opened her eyes.

The hotel lobby was dimly lit with a range of muted lamps and a huge glass chandelier that hung over the mosaic tiled floor. There were people all around. Young, old, black, white, Asian, some tall and some short. Men and women.

Strangers.

Gooseflesh covered her skin.

'None of these people know you. No one is watching us. We're safe. I promise,' said Scott.

She held on to Scott tighter, and walked with him as he turned right. Together they made their way along a carpeted hallway. A tall man wearing a black leather jacket was coming the other way.

'It's okay,' said Scott.

And it was. With every step, Ruth reminded herself that she was safe. No one was going to harm her. Not while Scott was here.

Yet her hands wouldn't stop shaking. That feeling of being watched, like a cold blade on the back of her neck.

At the end of the hallway, a young greeter brought them into the restaurant and settled them at a table in the corner, just as Scott had requested. Ruth sat with her back to the wall, the whole restaurant in front of her. There was a decent crowd, but still a few empty tables. It was a good restaurant for a hotel. Great food served well at the Paramount earned them a loyal clientele. White linen tablecloths, subdued lighting, candles and silver and all manned by staff who were warm and efficient. The waiter poured water for them both while Scott scanned the wine list.

'None for me, please, but you go ahead and order whatever you'd like,' said Ruth.

'Not even one glass with dinner?' asked Scott. 'It might help you relax.'

Ruth shook her head. The last time she'd had a drink was that night. And she never wanted to touch it again. Besides, she felt it might interfere with her meds. So far, they were holding her upright and she didn't want to test that.

Scott closed the wine list, said, 'I'll just have a glass of the Malbec, please.'

The waiter thanked him and left them with dinner menus and a promise that someone would be along to explain the specials.

'You're doing great,' said Scott. 'And did I mention that you look amazing?'

She'd spent time on her hazel brown hair, curling it at the bottom so that it caressed her bare shoulders. The dress had been ordered online and delivered to the hotel. It was her size, but it felt a little big on her. Even though she hadn't been exercising, she hadn't really been eating either. This would be her first real dinner since . . .

September fourteenth.

The night of the incident as Farrow called it.

It would be Thanksgiving in two days' time. More than two months since the attack. Those thoughts came frequently now. Her life was suddenly divided between the woman she had been before that night, and the woman she was now. It was a line. A life before, and not much of a life after. This life felt a lot like death. Or a punishment that was just as bad. She was afraid of everything – people, noises, being on her own. Because she knew the man who did this to her was still out there, somewhere.

Another waiter appeared, told them all about the specials and left them to think.

'How are you feeling?' asked Scott.

'My head is a little clearer,' said Ruth. 'At first, I just wanted every-thing to go back to the way it was. To reset. Now I know that can't happen. I don't think there is a normal any more. Not for me.'

Scott nodded, said, 'I know.' But she could tell by the wrinkles in his brow, his eyes darting to the left and then back to her that he didn't know. Not really. Not that he hadn't been trying, and he had looked after her so well, but he would never fully understand.

'It's like someone I love is dead, but I can't grieve for them. Not properly. And so the pain just goes on. I'm sorry. I shouldn't be talk-ing about this now. This is supposed to be a special night.'

He reached out, placed his hand delicately on top of her slender fingers.

'I think we could get close to normal. Look at us now. We're out in public, about to enjoy a fine meal. This is what normal people do. We have to grab these moments. There will be more of them. We can take it slow, bit by bit. Maybe we can come back here for Thanksgiving on Thursday?'

Ruth resisted the urge to tell Scott not to put any pressure on her.

'We could still have a great life,' he said.

Her lips curled into a smile, but it couldn't wipe away the strain of sadness and fear preserved in her eyes. She had seen it in the mirror. An anxious dread, frozen in her pale brown eyes like a mosquito imprisoned for all time in a bead of amber.

Scott talked about some of his friends – Gordon and his continu-ing marital difficulties. Ruth knew he was attempting a normal conversation. She nodded along, and then he changed the topic to the office. This was what ordinary couples talked about, and it all seemed so frivolous. Scott sighed, and looked at the menu, perhaps sensing Ruth wasn't taking anything in. He was trying. And it made Ruth want to try too, but it was so hard.

Ruth already knew she couldn't eat. Even looking at the food on the menu made her feel a little sick. She put her elbows on the table and rested her chin on interlocked fingers. It stopped them shaking.

If she could never be rid of this fear, at least she could pretend not to be afraid. For Scott, as much as for her.

Families with young children had dressed up for the night – boys wearing their little neck ties and girls in pretty dresses. A group of women in the corner were the loudest, clinking glasses before throwing back their coiffured heads in fake laughter. There were some couples, two groups of men who were almost as loud as the women and a man seated alone.

Ruth's heartbeat began to quicken.

He sat four tables away.

He had dark hair in a side parting, a black turtleneck sweater beneath his charcoal sport coat. His arm moved in a sawing motion, cutting a slice of rare steak, which he plopped into his red mouth. The pale skin on his cheeks accentuated his wet, bloody red lips. Cheekbones jutted out like an overhanging rock and below them a square jaw. Setting it all off was a pair of terrible blue eyes that never left his plate.

The man raised his head, looked directly at Ruth, then stabbed his knife into the steak and began to cut.

A waitress approached his table, carrying a glass of red wine on a tray. She placed a napkin on the table, and put the wine glass on top of it.

Ruth leaned forward. The background noise dimmed with a lull in conversation at the tables.

The man looked up at the waitress, winked at her, said, 'Thank you, *sweetheart*.'

That voice – it was . . .

She couldn't say it. She couldn't think it. Ruth suddenly had to use the bathroom – her bladder was about to let go and she could feel her pulse throbbing in the large vein in her temples. She rose, her head spinning, stumbled, righted herself.

'I-I need the ladies' room,' she said.

Scott got up, said, 'They're behind you. Come on, I'll go with you.'

Ruth backed away from the table, her eyes locked on the stranger.

Because he wasn't a stranger. Ruth had felt something crush her stomach and steal her breath when she saw those eyes. She imagined it was the same feeling an antelope had when it saw a pair of lion's eyes in the long grass. Something deep and old in her brain, passed down through generations, and it yelled to her loud and clear – there is *danger* here.

Scott took her arm, she turned and saw the sign for the bathrooms. There was an alcove just a few feet away, leading to a short hallway. Two doors on the left. Ladies at the end.

'Are you okay?'

Ruth nodded, but couldn't speak, her chest heaving air into her lungs. Scott let go of her arm when they reached the ladies' room, but Ruth grabbed hold of him, shoved the door open and moved quickly inside.

The bathroom was well lit, and the white tile on the floor and walls made it all the brighter, a stark contrast to the dim hallway outside. A bank of mirrors above the sinks on the left, a row of stalls on the right. Five of them, all with their doors open. No one else in the bathroom.

'Give me a second. Please wait in here,' she said.

Ruth made for the nearest stall, swung round and locked the door, panting, her hands pressed against the door as if she was desperately trying to hold it firm against a battering ram. Head down.

That's when she heard a single, faint *drip*. Liquid hitting tile. She focused on the ground, watched another of her tears fall toward the white tile between her feet.

Drip.

She hadn't even realized she was crying. Not until she wiped her face, felt the wet lines on her cheeks.

She had recognized him straight away. She had never been more certain of anything in her life, and it scared the hell out of her. He'd seen her too. He'd looked straight at her as he'd plunged that knife into the meat.

And then the phrase he'd spoken to the waitress. Ruth was sure he'd said that so that *Ruth* could hear it.

He'd found her. He'd come for her. To kill the only person alive who could possibly identify him.

She sat down on the toilet seat just in time. She couldn't have held on much longer. Breathing was becoming more difficult, as if someone had their hands around her throat, or – worse still – a rag covering her mouth. There was not enough oxygen in this whole hotel for her – she needed air, or she would choke and die.

And then she remembered something her counselor had told her.

She was in control of her body. All of it. Her breathing, her heart rate, everything.

Shutting her eyes, Ruth began the breathing exercises she'd learned. A big breath in – hold it for five – exhale and repeat. She rolled her shoulders, tensed her core.

It was no good. Panic flooded her veins, and two words resounded in her head like a siren in a tunnel.

It's him. It's him. It's him . . .

'Ruth, are you okay?' asked Scott.

The exercises weren't working. She hid her face in her hands. She knew she had to get the hell out of the restaurant. Get away fast, and it took everything she had to stand, and compose herself to be able to think and move.

She left the bathroom stall, saw Scott leaning against the sinks opposite, and took his hand.

'You okay?' asked Scott.

'W-w-we have to leave, r-r-right now. There's a man sitting at a table alone on his own. Come and see.'

Scott took her hand, and they walked out of the bathroom to the end of the hallway, until the man came into view.

'There,' she said, pointing.

The man was finishing his steak, chewing the last morsel. He was the only diner sitting alone. Scott turned back to Ruth, a puzzled look on his face.

'He's not familiar,' said Scott.

Ruth pointed again and the two words that screamed inside her mind now spilled from her lips – and she had never said anything with as much certainty and conviction as she did now.

'That's *him*. That's the man who attacked me,' she said.

16

Amanda

Amanda passed the entrance to the musical instrument store, and pressed the buzzer for the separate entrance to the upstairs space for her support group. Her phone started to ring.

She thought it might be Wendy, or Naomi, as she insisted upon being referred to now.

It wasn't Naomi. The screen said *Farrow*. He'd already called her earlier that day to remind her to go to tonight's meeting. She picked up.

'Tell me you're on 43rd Street right now and headed for your session,' he said.

'Believe it or not that's exactly where I am,' she said, with some pride.

The door opened and Matt greeted her.

'Hi, Matt,' she said, then into the phone, 'Do you want to say hi to the counselor?'

'That's not necessary. I'm just glad you're going through with it. If you need me, you know how to reach me. Hang in there. You're doing great.'

Amanda made her way upstairs, past the coffee station and looked out over some of the assembled group. Betty was there, and a few others.

No sign of Naomi.

She checked her watch. It was almost eight. Amanda grabbed coffee and made sure to take a seat with another empty one beside it. She put her coat on that chair to keep it for Naomi.

It was only three days since they'd had their night out on the rooftop bar of Pod 39, and they'd made it a late one. They had sunk a lot of cocktails, a lot of beer and ended up in an all-night pizzeria with the rest of the drunks and addicts who only seemed to venture out in Manhattan during the small hours of the morning.

Even after they'd finished a large pepperoni pizza, Amanda still felt buzzed from the conversation and the booze. Naomi wouldn't shut up, asking questions about Crone. His routine, his background, the case against him, whether the police were really sure it had been him who had murdered Amanda's daughter. She'd wanted to know how he lived, where he worked, his social life. Every last detail.

It was all they had talked about that night. Right until the end when Naomi drained the last of her vanilla Coke, threw down a pizza crust and said, 'I can't believe we're really talking about this. That's something I had not expected at the start of the night. You know, you can be quite persuasive.'

'I need this,' said Amanda. 'I haven't thought about anything else for months.'

'Do you think you could do it? You think you could kill Quinn?' asked Naomi.

Amanda knew she could kill someone. There was no doubting the strength of that desire – but it was aimed at a specific target. The man who had murdered her little girl. She knew Crone wasn't the only monster. There were more like him. And Quinn sounded just as bad. Could she kill someone *like* Crone? She didn't know if it was the alcohol or the company, or both, but the answer came quickly.

'Sure I could.'

Naomi nodded, but she didn't look convinced.

Amanda saw the doubt on Naomi's face straight away and latched on to it. Amanda drained her soda, put down the cup and said, 'Let's make a promise. We're not going to forget this night, what we've talked about. We could do this for real. Together. Like real sisters.'

And, with that, Amanda extended a shaky hand. Naomi smiled, took it, and Amanda was surprised by the strength of her friend's grip.

'I promise I won't back out,' said Amanda. 'Now you.'

'I promise,' said Naomi, and relaxed her grip. Amanda did not. She held firm.

'Nah, nah, nah, you gotta do this for real. Promise me you won't back out. Say it.'

'I *promise* I won't back out,' said Naomi.

Neither of them spoke another word. They stood up from the table, moved out onto the street, turned and embraced one another. There were no words required. The strength in their arms, as they held each other, said it all.

In the three days since, they hadn't spoken, and the more time elapsed the more embarrassed Amanda felt about that night. Those three days had passed quickly in Amanda's new routine. She met with her probation officer as requested, started taking some pills, cleaned the apartment and made an effort to stay in at night. With Crone suing her for harassment, she had to cut back on surveillance. He was more alert in the evenings, so she stayed at home. In the morning, when the city heaved with cars and people in rush hour, Amanda observed him from afar on his daily commute. It was easier to hide during the day.

If Amanda wasn't focused on getting Crone, there was nothing else to occupy her mind. There was only her loss. Unending. An empty void that threatened to consume her. When she saw him, it fired her rage. Her anger at the injustice was a real feeling. It electrified her senses, made her feel alive. It made her feel there was something worth living for – even if it was just the simple act of willing his murder. To imagine his death was *something*. Without that – there was *nothing*.

The fact that Naomi had not reached out to her since that night led her to believe Naomi was embarrassed by their conversation. It had seemed like a great idea at the time, but now Amanda could see that it was probably just a fantasy for Naomi – just the alcohol talking. It's easy to imagine what you could do to someone when you've got a bellyful of strong liquor. Maybe it was for the best. Amanda wasn't so sure she could kill a man she didn't know – even if he was a monster.

Now, it didn't look as if she'd have that problem. Naomi had gone quiet, and Amanda resigned herself to the fact that she'd have to kill Crone on her own, when the time was right.

Amanda had sent Naomi a text that morning to ask if she was going to group tonight and got a simple thumbs-up emoji in response.

She checked her watch. It was five minutes past the hour. Matt was about to begin the session. She took out her phone to text Naomi and found a new message from her, waiting to be read.

Are you at the group session?

Amanda texted back.

Yeah, I saved you a seat.

A reply slammed back fast.

Sorry, can't make it. Something has come up. I'll call you tomorrow x

Amanda sighed, put her phone away. She hoped she hadn't ruined what could've been a good friendship with Naomi. The thought was soon lost as Matt opened the meeting, and introduced someone new to the group. The rest of the parents looked at Betty. Amanda could tell she was psyched, ready to tell her redemption story to a new listener.

Amanda left the group at nine, went home and spent another restless night in bed. The dream again – cast adrift on a raging black sea, a bonfire on the beach in the distance.

Two figures on that beach holding hands in the firelight.

Luis and Jess.

The dream ended with the boat capsizing again.

Amanda knew she would never beat those waves.

She would never get to that beach.

Her alarm woke her at six a.m. Time to go and put in a shift watching Crone. She showered, dressed and made it out the door with the thoughts of her first coffee of the day.

A half hour later, Amanda blew a cloud of vapor off the top of her latte. The little deli on the corner of 96th Street was always busy this time of the morning. Guys in khaki pants and sweaters getting hot sandwiches, women in business suits and heels getting croissants and fruit, and the little tables outside were regularly full, with standing room only around the heater. This morning, the heater wasn't working, so she had some space.

She watched the 96th Street station entrance, keeping an eye out for Crone. She was looking forward to seeing him. Anticipating the bitter sight of him, walking free. It was something to fill the nothing. Until she could figure out a way to kill him.

People walked by, some went into the station and some kept on going.

Amanda took another sip of her latte to keep out the cold, then checked the clock on the Miller Lite banner in the deli window.

Seven twenty-five.

That couldn't be right.

She had been watching the entrance to the 96th Street station diligently. And Crone had not entered the station. He was never this late. Amanda thought she was being stupid. That there was obviously a reason she'd missed him. Maybe she hadn't been paying attention and he'd slipped by.

That had almost happened yesterday. She'd stood in the same spot. Same coffee, from the same deli. And just caught sight of him with his back to her as he disappeared inside.

'Fuck this,' said Amanda.

She made her way past the station, one more time. It was seven thirty. No sign of him. She must have missed him in the crowd. It was his appointment day today. She could go to Starbucks this afternoon, watch from the window. She wouldn't miss him from that vantage point. She needed her fix. Needed to feel the hate. Needed to know that some day she would wipe him from the face of the earth.

Amanda went home, put on the news for the first time in weeks and sat in front of the TV for a few mindless hours. Time moved on, but some things stayed the same: Celebrities got caught up in sex scandals, kids were shot in school, the president was still making an ass of himself at press conferences or whenever he happened to open his mouth – the world was still in conflict. The difference was that Amanda felt as if she wasn't a part of it any longer.

She checked her watch, put on her coat and took the subway.

There was one seat left at the window in her Starbucks. It was coming up to one p.m. Amanda held her black coffee in her hands as she gazed across the street.

One ten p.m. and no sign of Crone.

At one thirty she knew he was a no-show for his regular appointment. It was two days until Thanksgiving, and she wondered if he'd taken off on a plane somewhere for the holidays. She got off the stool, still thinking about Crone, when her phone began to vibrate. She made for the door as she took out her cell. The caller ID read – *Naomi.*

'Hi,' said Amanda, answering the call.

'How's the coffee?' said Naomi.

Amanda froze, turned and saw Naomi at the back of the coffee shop waving from the couch. At first, Amanda couldn't figure out why Naomi was there. Then she remembered she'd told her about this place on their night out, and how it gave a perfect view of Crone going into that building.

She approached Naomi, they hugged and Amanda took a seat

beside her on the couch. No awkwardness, no embarrassment between them. That made her glad, because perhaps Naomi could be something in her life too. A real person, a friend – another distraction from the void. There were people occupying the table opposite, but far enough away so they didn't need to whisper.

'You know you could have just called and said you wanted to meet,' said Amanda.

'I'm not good on the phone. Besides, I've got something to tell you and I wanted to do it face to face.'

Amanda felt her cheeks flush with embarrassment. 'Look, I know our conversation maybe went a little too far the other night. I want us to be friends. To trust each other. Maybe I got carried away, but I'm not crazy.'

Naomi cut off Amanda, said, 'You're definitely not crazy, because it's going to work.'

'What's going to work?'

'Swapping murders,' said Naomi.

'Really? When I didn't hear from you, I just figured you got cold feet.'

Naomi took hold of Amanda's hand, and whispered softly, 'I meant it. I hope you meant it too. I damn well believed you meant it. You made me promise, remember? That's why I came here. To tell you in person. Crone didn't show up for work today. He won't show for his appointment this afternoon. He won't be in work tomorrow either. And his lawsuit against you will disappear.'

Amanda's grip tightened on Naomi's fingers.

'What are you talking about?' asked Amanda.

'I killed him last night. While you were in the group meeting. I've kept my promise. Now it's your turn.'

17
Ruth

'How do you know that's him?' asked Scott.

Ruth clamped her mouth shut. Her teeth ground together, squeaking. She was trying desperately not to cry. Not here, standing in the alcove, looking out over the restaurant. She wanted to scream and run as fast as she could. Every instinct told her to get away, get as far from the man as possible.

'Because I *know* it's him. I'd know that face anywhere. I see it every goddamned night before I go to sleep and it's right there, waiting for me in the morning, those eyes staring at me as soon as I wake up. I'll never forget him. I was *there*, Scott, remember? Unlike you,' said Ruth, and instantly regretted it. One thing she'd been careful not to do was blame Scott for the attack. Sure, he wasn't home when it had happened, but the man, the prowler, would've known that too. Scott wasn't responsible. He couldn't be with her twenty-four hours a day. They both had lives and careers.

At least they used to.

Her last words had wounded him. He took them like a bullet to the chest. His head sank low, and she watched his right hand curl into a fist.

'I'm *sorry*,' he said, a little too loud.

'I can't be here. He's found me,' said Ruth.

The waiter suddenly appeared beside them and asked, 'Is every-thing all right, folks?'

Ruth knew Scott's voice had carried through the restaurant, and maybe hers too – a couple of diners turned and looked towards them.

'I'm not feeling well. We're sorry, but we have to leave,' said Ruth.

'Oh, I'm terribly sorry. Is there anything I can do?' the waiter said.

'No, it's fine. We just need to go,' said Scott.

'No problem. Please do come back and visit us. I'll charge the wine to your room as you'd arranged,' said the waiter, then moved quickly on to the next table, who were signaling to him for more water.

Ruth made sure to keep Scott between her and the killer with electric-blue eyes. As they moved to the door, Ruth began to feel faint. She couldn't pass out now. She had to get out of there. By sheer force of will, she put one foot in front of the other, and took Scott's arm.

He whispered to her that she was safe, that he was here, and every-thing was going to be okay. She wanted that to be true, desperately. Just before they reached the door, Ruth glanced back, craning her neck behind Scott's shoulder.

The man at the table was watching them leave, a half-smile on his face. His eyes seemed full of secret knowledge as he picked up his steak knife. Pink juices were still on the blade as he slid it between his lips, licking the tip of the knife clean – his blue eyes fixed on Ruth.

Ruth quickly turned away, picked up the pace and practically dragged Scott down the corridor to the elevators. She couldn't breathe, and tears ran down her face, smearing her make-up. It was all she could do not to stand in the middle of the floor and scream for help.

'Get me to the room, please,' said Ruth.

They waited in the lobby for the elevator. There were no other guests in line. They would have it to themselves.

'We have to call the cops,' said Ruth.

'No,' said Scott. 'What's the point? They don't want to know. Even if we told them you'd IDed the guy they wouldn't believe us. There's nothing else to link him to the crime. There's literally nothing they can do. They're useless.'

The elevator arrived, and they rode it to their floor. Ruth's fingers began to hurt – Scott was holding her hand too tightly. He wasn't looking at her, just watching the floor numbers rise on the digital display. The doors opened and he moved fast to their room, opened the door and led them inside.

Ruth didn't breathe out until the door closed behind them and she grabbed the desk chair and jammed it under the door handle. When she turned round, Scott was standing in the middle of the room with his hands on top of his head.

She started to speak, but Scott cut her off.

'Give me a minute, I'm thinking,' he said.

Ruth closed her lips tightly. Scott was riled up. She hadn't seen him like this in a long time. In the beginning of their relationship, possibly their fourth date, some random asshole had grabbed Ruth's ass in a club. She'd felt the hand, and swung around fast to remonstrate with the guy, but before she could open her mouth she'd seen a fist flash in front of her, and the creep's face rocked back before he disappeared into a heap on the floor.

Scott had a temper.

'What are you going to do?' asked Ruth.

'If the cops won't do anything, then I'm going to go and see what this asshole wants. Why the fuck is he here? In this hotel?'

'Don't go near him. He's dangerous,' said Ruth.

'He's a tough guy when he's got a woman alone and a knife in his hand. Look, I just want to know who he is. Are you *sure*—'

He didn't finish the sentence. He got his answer in her widening eyes before she even spoke.

'You sound like Farrow. I'm telling you that's the man who attacked me, and he's in our hotel, Scott.'

'Okay, I believe you, honey. I'm sorry. I didn't mean to—'

'I'll *never* be able to forget the face of the man who did this to me.'

'Then let me try to find out a few things. It might help. Maybe we get enough on him to call the cops? Look, I have to try to do something at least.'

'Please be careful, Scott. I just couldn't bear it if something happened to you. Don't go near him,' said Ruth.

'I won't. I just want to see where he goes, what he's doing. Why don't you take one of your pills? You're shaking.'

She sat down on the bed, her heart and mind racing. Scott fetched her sleeping pill, an anti-anxiety pill and a glass of water. Ruth swallowed them, and Scott sat down by her side. For a time, he said nothing. He stroked her hair and waited while she calmed.

'Don't go out there. He's been looking for me. I don't know how he found us, but it doesn't matter. He's a monster. What if you got hurt? What would I do? Who would protect me?' said Ruth.

'It's fine. He won't even see me. I'm just going to take a look. See what he's up to and then I'll be back. I love you, and I won't let anyone hurt you ever again. I promise.'

Ruth's eyelids felt heavy. Her breathing slowed. The drugs were beginning to kick in. She held Scott's arm tighter and tighter, as if he was a life raft, but the drugs were too strong, and she felt her grip loosening. She lay down on the bed and was soon fast asleep.

18

Amanda

'This is a joke, right?' said Amanda.

'Do I look like I'm joking?' asked Naomi. She sat forward, her elbows on the table, her face set in pure determination.

Amanda thought of the parting embrace that night in the pizza parlor. The drunken promise. It wasn't just talk.

This was real.

'What did you do?' asked Amanda.

'I sure as hell didn't try to cap him in a crowded subway car. That was never going to work. No, I found his weak spot and used it. The call girls . . .'

'What?'

'I followed him back to his building last night, watched him go up to his floor, then I took the elevator up there and waited. It didn't take long. The girl left, a petite blonde, ridiculously young. I went in straight after, wearing a red wig, short black leather skirt, halter top and boots. Doormen don't ask hookers questions. It's above their pay grade. I went to his door and knocked. He opened it straight away, probably thinking it was the girl who'd just left – like she'd forgotten something and had come back to get it.'

Amanda studied Naomi's face, taking in every word, every expression. She wasn't just listening to a story – she was living it.

'Soon as the door opened, I shot him with pepper spray,' she said, reaching for her bag. She removed a small, thin aerosol can encased in a black, plastic hood with a finger grip down one side.

'I emptied the whole can into his fucking face. Point blank range,' said Naomi, and put the cannister back in her bag. 'I closed the door, then I went to the kitchen, took the biggest knife I could find. When I came back, he was still in the hallway, rolling around on the floor, screaming. I got scared then. I thought someone would hear him.'

Amanda began to feel a dull pain in her jaw. She sat up straight, opened and closed her mouth – she'd been clenching her teeth tighter than an industrial press.

'But no one came. That's a huge apartment, and I'm guessing it's grade-A insulated for his own damn reasons. I stood over him with the knife in my hand. He was on his front, his hands over his face. I'd made a mistake. I'd sprayed too much. My eyes started to water – I could taste the damn stuff. I couldn't focus, and my throat started to burn. I knelt down beside him so I couldn't miss, raised the knife over my head.'

She stopped talking, swallowed. It seemed to be getting harder to get the words out.

'I thought about my darling Rebecca, and I thought about your Jess. And that's all I needed to jam that knife into his back. Right behind his neck. He stopped moving then. And the screaming stopped. I took the knife out, had to pull really hard. It was stuck in there good. All the way to the hilt. There was a lot of blood when the knife came out. I turned him over, stuck it in his throat. Then I left.'

'But there's a whole security-camera system in his building. They would've seen you.'

'No, they saw a woman in a red wig who doesn't look like you, who is taller than you, wearing a dark coat, a mini skirt, boots and gloves. The doorman didn't even give me a second look – I swear. There was a lot of action in Crone's apartment. That doorman was paid to look the other way. He did exactly that when he saw what he thought was another hooker. He wouldn't recognize me, but, even if he could, the main thing is he wouldn't recognize *you*.'

'Me?'

'You were at the group session last night. With witnesses. When the cops look back at the security tape, they'll see Crone letting me into his apartment, and me leaving on my own, in disguise. The time of death will coincide with my visit. You have a solid alibi for when the cops come calling. I don't need one because I have no connection to Wallace Crone, and no one would recognize me. I'm telling you – it went down perfectly.'

'Jesus Christ,' said Amanda, her fingers shaking as she raised them to her lips. 'He's really dead?'

'He's really, really fucking dead,' said Naomi.

'Have the cops . . . I mean, fuck . . . The cops will be looking for me.'

'Of course, soon as someone finds Crone's body. His maid will probably see it tomorrow when she does her house call. So don't be surprised if the cops come see you then.'

Amanda felt a lurch in her stomach. The nausea was stepping up.

'That's why you've gotta return the favor tonight . . .'

'Wait, wait, wait – what? Tonight?' said Amanda.

Naomi leaned back, gave Amanda a stern look.

Amanda felt it all the way down to her shoes.

'It's happening,' said Naomi. 'And you're not going to let me down, Amanda. I did it for you. For Jess. And Luis. You've gotta do it for me and Rebecca. You talked me into this. You made me promise. And I kept my promise. Now it's your turn.'

Amanda swallowed, and thought about Crone's absence from the 96th Street station, and the fact that he hadn't shown up this afternoon either. He hadn't done any of those things because he was dead. Amanda inhaled, shut her eyes and thought that the air itself smelled sweeter.

He was gone.

He couldn't hurt anyone else, and he'd died in pain. A friend had done this for her and, even though her hands wouldn't stop shaking, there was a strange peace that fell upon her. Suddenly, she felt free. Terrified and yet free of a demon that had haunted her thoughts every second, for months. It didn't matter that she hadn't been there to watch him die. It didn't matter that she'd not been the one to kill him. What mattered was that he was dead. That was a gift. Could she deny that gift to the one who'd given so much to her?

'I can feel it,' said Amanda.

'You can feel what?'

'His death. Jesus, I'm so relieved and at the same time I'm really fucking scared.'

'You should feel good. There's one less monster in this world. Tonight, you make it two. But I won't lie – this is going to be more difficult than Crone.'

Amanda was coming around. Instead of processing Crone's death, she now had to think. Naomi had avenged the murder of Amanda's daughter. The man who had tortured and killed her six-year-old girl. And that was a release. But she knew it came with a price.

'Why does it have to be tonight?'

'It must be tonight, because I just hung my ass out for you. I've risked a life sentence. We're in this together now, in blood. My hands are dirty, and I won't rest easy until you have blood on your hands too. Then I'll know you won't go to the cops. Then I'll trust you again. You're going to kill the man who raped and murdered my baby girl. The longer you wait, the harder it will be to do it. Also, you're not on the police radar right now.'

Amanda felt the world tilting. Now it was as if the entire coffee shop was slowly beginning to rotate. That drunken plan hatched in the hotel bar the other night. It wasn't just the booze talking. This was really happening. And now Amanda had to kill a complete stranger.

'Wait, stop. I'm not ready for this,' she said.

'You were ready the last time we discussed it. I'm all in. And you're up.'

Amanda needed more time. To get it all straight in her mind. A few nights ago, in a bar, she had tossed a snowball up a frozen hill and now it was rolling back down, twenty feet high, and it was going to crush her.

'I need to take some time. I wasn't expecting this . . .'

'You don't have time. It's simple. All you have to do is pull a trigger.'

'I don't have a gun. Not any more. I ditched it just before the cops caught me on the subway.'

Naomi's head sank to the table. She swore, thought for a moment, then looked at Amanda.

'All right, then we do it my way. But it has to be tonight.'

'Why the hell does it have to be tonight? I don't get it.'

'Because Quinn has to be dead before they find Crone's body. It might take another day, tops, for his maid to find him. But know this, once Crone's body is found, the cops will be all over *you*. They'll bring you in, sweat you for as long as they can and when they do let you go they are gonna be watching your ass twenty-four seven for a long time. Our plan falls to shit if the cops tail you to Quinn's house next week and arrest you before you can kill him. Come on – you're not thinking straight.'

That was for sure.

'Okay, wait a minute. What if we wait until the cops talk to me about Crone's murder, establish my alibi and leave me alone.'

'No,' said Naomi, a little louder than she'd meant. A few heads from nearby tables glanced over at the two women, stared, then went back to their own business.

'They'll be on you for a long time. Crone's father is one of the richest men in this city. Powerful men like that will make sure the police do a thorough job. The police could be on you for months before they give up. No, you have to do this before you come under investigation.

I'm at another group tonight. My child-bereavement session. I'm there at nine for an hour. That's your window. Now, tell me how you feel?'

'What?'

'He's dead. Tell me how that feels.'

Amanda straightened in her chair, said, 'I honestly don't know what to feel. Kind of happy, kind of empty. Free. Like someone just hit a reset button on part of my life.'

'And I want that too. More than anything. You can give that to me. These men are a cancer. This is the right thing to do. Quinn raped and killed my daughter. And pedophiles don't just stop. They can't be cured. He'll do it again. You know it's only a matter of time before he rapes a girl, and if she tries to scream or tell someone then he'll kill her. That's what happens. You know it, and I know it.'

Amanda nodded, because Naomi was telling the truth. While she had been investigating Crone, Amanda had read every article and book she could find on child killers and serial killers. The scenario Naomi had just laid out was all too familiar. It followed what Farrow had told her about how these perverts turned into killers. It had happened before. Many times.

'It felt good killing that prick Crone,' said Naomi, tears forming in her eyes as she gazed out of the window, unseeing, her internal vision replaying the memory perfectly. 'He whined and screamed and I swear to Jesus on the cross that I felt Rebecca beside me, willing me to stab that evil son of a bitch. End him. I walked out of that building feeling better than I have in years. And part of that was that I had a friend. I had you. And you were going to do the same for me.'

Amanda hung her head. She understood what had to happen. She knew Naomi was right, and yet she couldn't think. Couldn't focus. For the longest time, she had only felt one thing – hate for the man who'd killed her daughter. Now that it was gone, she couldn't adjust. Not yet. And she was afraid of what she had to do now, even though she knew it was the right thing.

'I'm not sure I can do it. I'm scared,' said Amanda.

Naomi said, 'You've got to be brave, girl. You can do this. How badly did you want Crone dead?'

'Oh, fuck, more than anything. I wanted that man to suffer for what he did. It's all I've been thinking about for *months*.'

'I've been feeling that way for *years*. You can do this. He's exactly like Crone. Maybe even worse. I know you can do it.'

Raising her trembling fingers to her lips, Amanda nodded. She had no choice now.

Naomi reached out, took her hand.

'I'm asking you, please. Do this for me. Like I did this for you. You're stronger than you think. I know you can do it. You've just got to take Jess with you. Luis too. Put them right there beside you, in your mind. And your heart. There are monsters in this world and laws don't apply to them. We have to do what we did thousands of years ago when we lived in caves. If a wolf came to the mouth of the cave, the first ones attacking it were the women, defending their children. Our children are gone . . .'

A tear fell onto Naomi's cheek. She wiped it away with the back of her hand, sniffed and said, 'We were too late to save our kids. The only thing we can do now is kill the wolf.'

19
Scott

Scott didn't leave the hotel room until Ruth was fast asleep. It didn't take long. Ten minutes from the time she'd swallowed her sleeping pill. She wouldn't wake for hours.

He walked into the lobby at speed, with purpose, down the hallway to the restaurant. Before he reached the entrance, he slowed. Stopped. Took out his cell phone and stood in the open doorway.

The man with the blue eyes was examining the check while he sipped from a coffee cup.

'Can I help you, sir?' said a voice.

It was the greeter at the doorway.

'Oh, yeah, my wife took ill before we could have our meal. I had a glass of wine and put that on my room, but I didn't sign the check for a tip. Could you get it for me?'

'Certainly, sir. What's your room number?'

Scott advanced into the restaurant with the greeter who spoke to one of the waiters, then told him they would retrieve the check. Scott gave them the room number, thanked them and waited by the electronic register. The waiter returned in under a minute. The man with blue eyes was still at his table.

'I've found it. We've automatically added a twelve-and-a-half percent gratuity. Is that satisfactory, sir?'

'That's fine. I just wanted to make sure I hadn't forgotten the tip.'

'All taken care of,' said the waiter.

Scott nodded and stepped outside the restaurant, buttoning his blazer, and heading back to the lobby. In the middle was a large round table, with a glass veneer and a huge vase filled with exotic flowers in the center. Scattered around the table were stacks of complimentary newspapers for the guests. Scott picked up a copy of *The New York Times*, found a chair that faced the bank of elevators and settled in.

He didn't have to wait long.

The man with blue eyes walked past Scott, glanced at the papers on the table and pressed the button to call the elevator.

Scott folded his paper under his arm, got up and casually stood just a little behind the man. Scott didn't pay too much attention to fashion, but he knew the man wore handmade shoes. He had big feet. Size thirteen, at least. A tall, lean individual. The suit fitted him perfectly and Scott expected it was bespoke too. A woolen mix the color of charcoal. His dark hair was parted, and his skin was very pale.

Ping.

The elevator doors opened, Scott gritted his teeth, followed the man inside. The man pressed the button for the twelfth floor and looked at Scott.

'Twelve is fine,' said Scott.

The man nodded and cupped his hands in front of him, spread out his legs a little. He maintained a wide stance, his back straight. Scott had seen some partners at the firm who were ex-military stand in the same way.

His eyes. It was as if there was a forty-watt bulb behind each orb, lighting them for the world to admire. And while they were arresting, Scott found them cold. A killer's eyes. It was risky getting into the elevator with him. The killer must know what Scott looked like. He'd watched their house before he attacked Ruth.

Scott swallowed down the fear rising in his stomach.

The doors closed. Scott moved further back into the elevator.

'You here on business?' asked Scott.

The man half turned, said, 'Something like that.'

He was from New York. Scott could tell by the accent.

'You sound like a New Yorker,' said Scott.

The man smiled, revealing a row of small, white teeth, but he didn't say any more.

The elevator slowed, stopped.

The doors parted.

Before they were fully open, the man stepped forward then turned to say, 'I hope your wife feels better soon. She looks like a real sweetheart.'

The comment rocked Scott back on his heels. How did he know? He must've been watching them, in the restaurant. He didn't bring it up when they were standing in the elevator, like a normal person would have if they'd been genuinely concerned. He had been watching them, and now he was giving Scott a parting shot. Scott could've sworn there was a trace of a smile on the man's face as he spoke.

And that word.

Sweetheart.

The same thing he'd said to Ruth during the attack. Ruth was dead right. It *was* him.

Cocky son of a bitch – saying that to the husband of his victim.

Scott moved forward out of the elevator. Looked right. No sign. Looked left. The man was fifteen feet ahead of Scott, moving down the hallway, passing by the first rooms along there.

Scott skipped ahead, a couple of steps, just to narrow the distance between them. The man swung his arms as he walked. Casual. Unafraid. Like he owned the place. He took long, confident strides and Scott found himself walking much faster than normal just to keep up with him.

He could feel his cheeks burning. A wash of adrenaline was scalding his skin, firing his muscles, curling his fists. As his body fizzed with chemicals, his mind began to boil with questions. How dare he come to this hotel? This sick motherfucker – it was a game to him. He said he wasn't here on business exactly – it was *something like that*? What did that mean? Why does someone who lives in the city take a hotel room?

Unless it was to stay close to someone else.

And then Scott almost came to a stop. A thought hit him like a ten-pound hammer. *He came here for Ruth. He wants to kill her.*

Of course the prowler would want to finish off Ruth. She's the only victim who'd managed to survive. And the only victim, the only person in the world, who could identify him as the prowler. He was there to kill her.

Scott quickened his pace. He imagined the man in front of him waiting outside their house. Watching as Scott left that night, then going round back and breaking a window. Getting inside. And waiting for Ruth in the dark.

Scott was suddenly aware that his breath was ragged. A patch of sweat stuck the back of his shirt to his skin, and he was shaking.

The hallway had dim, mellow lighting, with a wall lamp every ten feet or so, and every fifty feet a ceiling light in the shape of a large hanging dome. Scott began to glance at the doors as they passed. Rooms 1242, 1243, 1244 passed quickly by. There were coming up on a left turn. Only two more doors before the hallway broke left.

This man had destroyed his wife. Ruined any hope of Ruth carrying his baby. And when this had happened, Scott hadn't been there. He'd left Ruth alone. He should've been there. He could've stopped it.

The man began to slow, just a little, and he dipped his right hand into his pants pocket. He stopped in front of the last door on the left before the hallway turn. Room 1248.

Scott's vision narrowed. He moved faster, but everything around him seemed to slow down.

The man drew his key card from his pocket, raised it toward the sensor lock on the door. He placed his other hand on the handle.

There was a beep as the door unlocked and he pushed the handle down.

The man paused, perhaps sensing movement.

Room 1246 must've been celebrating something. On a tray outside stood two wine glasses, a silver ice bucket and an empty wine bottle. As he passed, Scott bent low, swept up the bottle by the neck.

Then he swung it at the man's head as hard as he could.

20

Amanda

Amanda spent two hours with Naomi, going over Quinn's routine and the layout of the back of his house. Naomi had a plan. One that would work. One that Naomi had carefully choreographed by staking out Quinn's house, watching his movements.

'I don't have a gun either,' said Naomi. 'If you're going to kill someone bigger and stronger than you without a gun, or poison, you need a weapon that will deliver massive damage. You need to take them by surprise . . .'

That was hours ago. Amanda sat now in her car, parked three blocks away from Quinn's house. She drank some more coffee. It was two hours old, and thoroughly chilled. She didn't care. She needed the caffeine hit.

In fact, she needed a hit of something stronger than caffeine – but she knew she couldn't risk it. A Jack on the rocks would help calm her nerves. But it might be her undoing. Instead she lit a cigarette.

The streetlights were on and no one was on the sidewalk. Too cold tonight. A fog shrouded the moon, as if it was hiding behind a thin silk veil. Cars lined both sides of the street for the next four blocks. She had already driven past the front of Quinn's home. A three-story brick townhouse in one of the oldest parts of Greenwich Village. She had made the run twice. Once to check out the house – see if lights were on and whether the neighbors were home. On that run, she saw drapes were drawn, dimming the lamp that burned inside Quinn's home. A low, warm light. He was probably watching TV.

The second drive-by was to check for foot traffic. It was a quiet residential area. High-class real estate. However Quinn was paying for this place, it wasn't with a teacher's salary. Maybe he came from old New York money.

As Amanda followed her route, around ten miles per hour, she saw someone looking right at her. A man's face reflected in the side mirror of his car. He was parked on the right, sitting in the driver's seat of a dark-colored Chevy Escalade. She saw his face only for a second, reflected in some kind of internal light in the car – maybe a cell phone.

She drove on, checked her rearview.

The man watched her car move on up the street. The Escalade was parked around fifty feet from Quinn's front door, on the opposite side of the street.

Amanda wasn't too concerned about the guy. Probably a neighbor, checking his cell phone before he got out of the car and went home. Amanda wasn't going in the front anyway – she was just making sure there wasn't a cop car right outside the house.

She drove three blocks before she found a parking space. It was nine thirty, and Naomi would be at her support group. She had another half hour before Naomi was on the street again and her alibi useless.

Thirty minutes to kill a man.

Amanda took another sip of coffee, threw the cigarette butt in the street and thought about Wallace Crone. Naomi had taken him out. Put him out of this world with a cold blade. Amanda was beyond the initial shock of this news.

She had imagined this moment many times. There was an odd sense of peace. As if something had been given back to her. The world, struck from its course, was slowly righting itself.

Once she'd gotten over the bombshell of Naomi's actions, she was thankful. Truly thankful. She sat in the car, thinking of her girl. Her husband. And for the first time in months, she felt hot tears on her cheeks. Her grief had been contained by a dam of hatred and fury and now there was nothing to hold it back.

She wiped her face and knew then that there was no way she could deny this to another person. Especially not a mother. And a mother who had given her this very same release.

There was a job to be done. She would do this one thing for Naomi. She would kill another monster, and then part of this nightmare would be over. But it wasn't just for Naomi. It was also for Naomi's daughter. Just as Naomi had killed Crone for Jess and Luis.

She looked at the picture of Frank Quinn from the news article she'd printed out. He was tall, but well-built all the same. Good-looking. Quinn looked physically powerful. She would need to be quick, and pray the plan worked.

Amanda put on a pair of gloves, got out of the car, closed the door and locked it. She headed south along the street for three blocks, then saw the alley on her right.

Naomi's instructions were just hours old. They had gone over and over this. She remembered Naomi's plan word for word.

It's an old block. There's a gated alley, but the gate is never locked. You go in through the back yard. Quinn doesn't have a gun permit. He's not armed. There are no dogs in the house, but two houses further up the street there's a German shepherd. It mostly stays indoors. Approach from the south and you'll be unlikely to set the dog barking.

Naomi had scouted the property very well. She had planned this meticulously. All Amanda had to do was follow Naomi's instructions.

There's no way to get to him from the front. You have to get over the backyard wall from the alley. The wall is eight feet high. There's a dumpster on the corner that you can use to climb over it.

Amanda saw the dumpster at the corner of the alley, just like Naomi said. She opened the lid. It was full of glass. If she moved it, it would make a lot of noise, like dragging a box of bells across rough concrete. She left it and found the gate to the alley unlocked, just as Naomi had said. Counting the houses from the rear, she moved north and stopped when she got to the rear of Quinn's house. Amanda put her shoulder blades against the wall opposite, and ran at Quinn's backyard wall. She leapt, got her hands on top of it, dragged herself up, but banged her right knee hard against the brick. Scrambling, she crawled up on top and swung her legs over. Her boots hit the grass. She stayed low, watched the house.

No lights on in any of the windows at the rear. Amanda pushed upwards into a crouch, but couldn't help a low moan as her knee clicked, sending a shockwave of pain through the joint. The right knee – same one that she'd banged against the wall. She looked at it now, saw her jeans had been ripped over the kneecap.

It wouldn't take her weight at first. She thought it could collapse at any moment.

Fuck.

Tentatively, she took a step, testing the joint. The throbbing blazed when she tried to use it. There were two options now. Keep going or haul herself back over the wall and call Naomi, tell her that something had gone wrong.

The tool shed was just ahead of her.

She thought for a moment.

It could still work.

Hobbling now, she reached the shed. It had an old padlock securing the slide bar in the locked position. Just as Naomi had said.

The lock on the tool shed is a single bolt, padlocked. The frame is rusted, the screws too. The wood is old. That tool shed has probably been there since the seventies. There's only a couple hundred coats of varnish holding the thing together. A screwdriver should deal with the bolt.

The bar was set into the wood with eight screws. All rusted. Amanda took the screwdriver from her pocket. She had brought the wrong type. A flathead would've been easier. She managed to work it between the bar and the wood and then pulled. The screws came out of the wood with a dry crack. The bar fell to the lawn, the sound dulled on the grass.

The door opened outwards. The little side window for the shed was covered in cobwebs, but the worktable was clean. Tools hung on nails, planks of wood were stacked on the floor. Even monsters have hobbies.

Like I said, if you don't have a gun, you're gonna need something else – something heavy duty to take this guy out. He's big and very strong. A knife won't do it. Not like Crone. Inside the tool shed you'll see an axe. I saw it from the shed window. It'll still be there. Take it. That's what you use. One good swing is all you'll need . . .

Amanda found the axe on the top shelf, lifted it down.

You'll only get one chance at this. You have to make it count. If he's not down after that then you get out of there because he'll kill you. If you do what I tell you, then you'll have all the time in the world to make that swing. Take these burner phones . . .

Amanda took the first burner phone from her pocket, switched it on and placed it on the worktop. Then left the tool shed with the door ajar.

Now was the time.

Up until this point she could call it off. Just walk away.

In a few seconds, it would be too late.

She hesitated, the axe heavy in her hands. But it wasn't just the axe that weighed her down. She was about to attack a man. A real person. She would be ending their life in a bloody, horrific murder.

She stood there, motionless, frozen in place by her innate humanity. It takes a lot to kill someone. Human beings in crisis cannot think straight; their instinct to preserve life gets sidelined in the sea of their desperation. In the absence of a psychological disorder or crisis or the impairment to rational thinking brought about by drugs or alcohol, it is very hard to kill another living, breathing member of the human race. She knew all these things. She'd thought about them a lot.

Amanda's dream came back to her. The same one she had almost every night since she'd got out of the hospital.

Adrift in a stormy sea, in a small boat.

Luis and Jess beside the fire burning on the beach, guiding her home, yet impossible to reach. With Crone dead, Amanda felt those seas calming. There was one final storm to get through, and then she could step onto sand and enjoy that welcoming fire.

She looked down at the axe.

She had rationalized Crone's death many times. She'd come to believe that killing him was not an act of murder: it was an act of mercy – she was saving the lives of his future victims. Another parent wouldn't have to feel her pain, her loss. She told herself now that it was the same with Quinn.

Amanda closed her eyes. She remembered that day on the subway. Right before Crone had glanced up at her. She could smell the other people surrounding her in the carriage – their perfume, aftershave and sweat, and the faint odor of hot motor oil and grease that pervaded the subway. She could feel the vibration from the brakes beneath her feet. The sweat on her hands in those gloves. Her fist wrapped round the butt of the gun. She saw herself, no longer in memory, but the fantasy of what could have happened, as she pulled the gun from her coat, and pointed it at Crone's head, and pulled the trigger, hearing the blast . . .

Her eyes snapped open. The sound of her imaginary gunfire still in her ears. In Amanda's mind, she was not going to kill a man named Quinn who had raped and murdered a girl she had never met. No, Amanda was killing Crone tonight.

She swung the axe at the kitchen window of the house, and it broke through with more noise than she'd been expecting. Glass exploded around her, but most of it fell into the house. Amanda took the axe and limped behind the tool shed, hunkered down and waited.

She glanced up at the house when she saw a beam of light hit the lawn.

The kitchen lights.

She took out the second cell phone. Another burner. Switched it on.

A voice in the dark, mumbling, indistinct. The crunch of boots on glass.

Amanda held tightly to the axe, but she couldn't stop her hands shaking.

The back door opened. Amanda took out the second burner phone, hit dial on the only pre-programmed number. She heard him coming closer, step by step.

Amanda stood, her back to the shed, her knee screaming.

The shed door whined open. Quinn must've seen the light from the burner phone in the tool shed and had come to investigate.

When he comes to the tool shed, he'll want to find out what the hell is going on. He'll see the phone ringing and he'll step toward it. You come around from the back of the tool shed and hit him from behind. Go for his neck or the back of his head. That's all it'll take. Be careful. You fuck up this part and you are in a lot of trouble . . .

Amanda whipped around the shed, the axe raised over her left shoulder. Quinn was ahead and to the right, standing in the doorway of the shed, gazing into it. Just as she turned around to the front of the shed, she saw his exposed back. He wore sweatpants, sneakers and a tee. It was him all right. The same man she'd seen in the photos – no doubt. He held a baseball bat in front of him.

This was her chance. Back turned. Wide open.

She was going to kill the wolf.

Amanda took a breath. Held it.

She gritted her teeth.

Tensed her muscles.

Her grip tightened on the axe haft.

One step forward and she would be in range.

One swing.

Instead of Quinn's neck – she visualized Crone's.

Imagined the sharp, heavy steel head biting into his flesh.

Amanda took one step forward.

Hesitated.

The axe trembled in her hands.

Her whole body shook.

She breathed out.

And let the axe fall . . . by her side.

She took a step back, emptied her lungs.

This wasn't the man who'd killed her daughter, no matter how much she wanted him to be. This was a stranger. A life.

She couldn't do it. Her heart wouldn't let her.

Even though this man was a monster, she couldn't kill him in cold blood.

Amanda blinked. Her mind had wandered in indecision.

Her vision snapped back into reality.

The man called Quinn had turned. He was still in the tool shed, his face in shadow. But now she could see the light from the kitchen reflecting in his feral eyes.

Twin moons that blazed at her from the darkness.

'I'm sorry, I've made a mistake,' said Amanda, stepping back, her left palm raised toward him.

He moved forward, out of the dark shed. His voice was soft, yet it carried a sinister hiss.

'You're damn right you made a mistake,' said Quinn, moving forward in step with Amanda's retreat.

This man wasn't frightened of her. Amanda felt like someone who had stumbled through the jungle and suddenly come upon a jaguar. Quinn's eyes were so large and unnerving they looked as though they had no lids. They didn't move. They were fixed upon Amanda. His mouth, large and wide, drew into a grin exposing sharp, yellowed teeth.

Amanda suddenly became hyper aware of her surroundings. She was a long way from the back gate and her knee was biting her painfully with every step.

'Who sent you?' he asked.

'I'm s-sorry. I-I-I made a m-mistake. I'll go,' said Amanda.

'You're not going anywhere,' he said, and at once he was moving with tremendous speed toward her, the baseball bat curling in his right hand.

Amanda hurled herself backwards as fast as she could, instinctively holding the axe in front of her.

The baseball bat *cracked* into the axe haft, tearing it from her grasp as both bat and axe then cartwheeled through the night air.

Amanda flinched at the impact. Before she could open her eyes, she felt her throat close and she was falling. She landed on her back, the lawn unforgiving.

Quinn landed on top of her, both hands round her neck.

Amanda couldn't breathe. Couldn't move.

He was so heavy. Sitting on her chest. His eyes bulging, mouth cracked wide in violent delight, veins standing out on his muscular arms as he squeezed her throat.

'Go to sleep now . . .' he hissed.

'Go to *sleeeeep* . . .'

21

Scott

The sound of an empty, heavy bottle crashing into a human skull was a dull, echoey *thunk*. The bottle didn't break, but the man let out a muffled grunt as he fell into the room and onto the floor.

He landed face down, and immediately got his arms beneath him, to push himself upwards, his legs bending, trying to scramble forward and up into a standing position.

Scott was faster.

The door had hit the opposite wall with a bang and was now swinging shut. Scott was already halfway into the room, and he ducked inside and kicked the door shut behind him.

The man began to shout as he got to his knees.

'What the fuck is this?'

Raising the bottle over his head, Scott heaved it forward and down. This time it exploded as it hit the top of the man's skull. Scott still had hold of the neck of the bottle, which was still intact. The man fell forward, rolled to the side, gripping the top of his head.

In that moment, Scott was not the successful Manhattan lawyer, married, with a big house and a huge salary. He was the boy, naked and bleeding on the floor of the shower after the jocks had kicked the shit out of him. Scott felt like his heart was tearing clean through his chest. He was angry and afraid and filled with a rage that he could not control. There was no thought. Only action. As if his body was taking over.

He knelt, straddling the man.

'You hurt my wife,' said Scott.

The man didn't respond. His eyes were shut tight, his hands on top of his head.

And then, suddenly, his eyes popped open and his right hand flew upwards and a fist cracked into the side of Scott's face, sending his head reeling back on his shoulders. His vision swam and another fierce blow landed on his chin, slamming his mouth closed, rattling his jaw like an old windowpane in a tornado.

Another punch. This one caught Scott in the throat. The man beneath him was going wild, kicking and bucking and punching. Scott began to panic. He'd made a mistake. He'd provoked a killer. This man would beat him unconscious and then he'd kill Ruth.

Scott still had hold of the neck of the bottle. He reversed his grip, the mouth of the bottle close to his thumb, the jagged remnants of glass now a dagger.

His vision grew hazier with every punch. Scott raised the bottle, then stabbed down. Into the man's face.

Still the killer fought back.

Scott raised the bottle, stabbed down again. This time he heard glass cracking.

Up and down again, harder this time. Scott closed his eyes.

Again.

Again.

Again.

Scott gulped fresh air. It felt as thick as soup. He brought his hands to his throat and coughed. The killer's blow had almost shattered his wind pipe. He rolled off the man onto his back, his chest pumping, and let his lungs fill up.

He lay there for what must have been a few minutes, the man beside him had not moved in all that time.

Scott got to his feet and looked down at him. The neck of the bottle was still covered in gold foil. It was tinged red. His face was cut and bloody, and only one perfect blue eye stared up at the ceiling. The other eye was gone. In its place were four inches of wine bottle that stood upright, like a chimney, from his eye socket.

As Scott stumbled backwards, his calves caught the bed and he flopped down on top of it, in a sitting position. He saw himself then in the mirror. The man's blood had soaked Scott's jacket, shirt and the waist of his pants. Blood leaked from that ruptured eye socket and spread across the carpet.

It was on the soles of Scott's shoes.

Fuck, think.

There had been some noise, but not a huge amount. He listened, couldn't hear a sound. No pounding footsteps in the hallway, no urgent, panicked voices from the next room on the phone to reception to tell them of a disturbance.

Nothing.

Scott moved to the bathroom, switched on the light. Gazed in horror at his image in the mirror.

He'd been an assistant district attorney for years before he took the litigation job in the city. He'd got to know the NYPD, and how they think. How they catch people. He knew what the police would look for, and so far he'd been stupid.

Time to work smart.

He stripped, put his cell phone and wallet on the floor, and dropped his bloody clothes in the tub. A fast shower. He didn't use a towel – better to air dry while he looked through the man's closet.

Two suits, a pair of black jeans, some plain black T-shirts and an overcoat. There were no shoes.

Scott put on the T-shirt, pants. They were too long for him and he turned up the legs with a couple of folds.

He moved quickly to the body. The pool of blood beneath the man's head had widened, but so far hadn't reached beyond his shoulders. The man's shoes were not stained, but they were two sizes too big. Scott took the man's last three pairs of socks, put them all on then put on the shoes and the overcoat. He put his own wallet and cell in the coat.

One last thing. He glanced around the floor, careful not to step in the blood.

There, beneath the console table.

The man's key card.

Scott crawled up to it and reached over the blood stains to retrieve the card. He washed the blood spots off it in the bathroom sink, then put it in his pocket. He had to walk over the bed to get to the door without stepping in blood, but he made it.

Even though he'd just showered, Scott was sweating in the overcoat. He swiped a hand through his still wet hair, keeping it away from his face, then tentatively opened the door. Glanced up and to the left, then right.

He breathed out. A huge sigh.

There was a security camera fifteen feet to the left of the door, on the ceiling, pointing back down the corridor. His attack on the man would not have been caught by the cameras. They might pick him up following the man, but they wouldn't have seen Scott lifting the bottle. The camera was after room 1246. That gave him a shot.

Scott turned right out the door, to where the hallway dog-legged to the left. There were no cameras in this short hallway and door leading to the stairs. The stairwell was concrete with painted iron stair rails. It was a long way down, but there were no cameras. At the bottom of the stairs there were two exits. Left and right. One for the lobby on the left, and one for the basement parking lot. Scott went right, through the parking lot, up the ramp and out onto the street.

His teeth rattled. His body was still full of adrenaline and fear. But at least he was now thinking straight. And he knew what he had to do next.

He had to do some shopping.

22

Amanda

'Go to sleeeeep . . .'

Panic had taken Amanda.

Her boot heels dug into the earth, legs flailing. Her hands pulled desperately at Quinn's wrists and all of it useless. He was so heavy, and his hands around her throat drove the back of Amanda's neck into the lawn. A tremendous pressure built in her head. She felt like her eyeballs were going to pop right out of her skull. Even the skin on her cheeks burned – as if the tiny blood vessels in her face were rupturing under the strain.

Her sight darkened.

She only had moments before she blacked out – never to wake.

With huge effort, she managed to turn her head slightly. Her right arm snaked out, feeling along the grass.

Feeling for the axe.

She twisted, just enough to see it lying three feet away from her reach.

It may as well have been in the next state.

She knew then she would die. She could not get this man off her, and her limbs began to feel like lead.

Amanda accomplished everything through planning.

She'd had little time to plan for tonight.

But finally, through the shock and fear and utter terror gripping her body and mind, some primal survival instinct kicked in.

Amanda's right hand dived into the pocket of her jacket. Her gloves felt around until they landed on something hard.

In the next second, something warm splashed on her face,

Quinn's grip on her throat relaxed and his head swiveled down to gaze at the shaft of the screwdriver that poked through his bicep.

He let go of her, and Amanda's mouth opened wide as she took huge gasps of air, flooding her lungs. Quinn's mouth was open too, in a scream. Amanda had driven the screwdriver through the back of his arm. He rolled off Amanda and she was able to get to her knees.

She coughed and breathed and got to her feet.

Quinn was already on his knees, getting up, his right arm hanging useless by his side. He stood between Amanda and the back gate. As soon as she'd stood, she'd felt the burning pain in her knee.

She wouldn't be quick enough to get past this man. Spinning on her good knee, she took off toward the house.

Heavy feet began moving quickly behind her.

She wasn't going to get to the back door either.

Amanda pivoted, her knee now a howl of agony, and she limped and hopped toward the open door of the tool shed. She leapt at the last moment, grabbing the handle on the inside of the door, pulling it shut behind her.

A second later, a loud bang shook the door as the axe smashed into it.

Amanda stood, her knee singing in agony as she pulled on the handle, keeping the door shut as Quinn bellowed and pulled from the other side. He got it open an inch.

Another inch.

He was strong, even with one hand. Amanda hauled harder on the handle, wedging her feet at the door and leaning back.

He let go and the door slammed shut.

Then another slam as a panel split at the top right-hand corner and

Amanda saw the axe head poking through the wood. It wobbled, left and right, as Quinn worked it free, then it disappeared, and re-appeared again with a *thunk*, this time in the center of the door.

He'd be able to reach through and grab her with one more good hit.

Amanda looked around the tool shed. There were hacksaws, screwdrivers, two vices and in the corner exactly what she was look-ing for.

A ballpeen hammer.

The wood squeaked as Quinn withdrew the axe to wind up for another blow. Amanda reached for the hammer. It was still a good two feet away. She'd have to let go of the door to reach it.

Slam.

A hole the size of a head now appeared in the center of the door, and the axe slid free this time.

The sound of police sirens came to her. Still in the distance. But getting closer.

Amanda knew what she had to do. Tears and sweat covered her face. She wiped them away from her eyes. This had to be timed per-fectly. Or she would end up dead.

Slam.

The axe stuck in the wooden door this time. She watched the blade wriggle, then, as it came free, she let go of the door, grabbed the ham-mer and took hold of the door handle again.

Slam.

The axe hit the central beam of the door and stayed there. Soon as she saw the blade being twisted, in an attempt to free it from the tim-ber, she threw all her weight at the door.

As the door opened, the axe, still buried in the wood, was wrenched from Quinn's grip. He turned toward her just as the hammer cracked into the side of his head. He went down without a sound.

The sirens were getting louder.

Quinn lay on his back, a thick stream of blood pouring from the side of his head. His right arm was soaked in his own blood, which looked as black as oil against the night sky.

He shook his head, sending blood cascading from the wound. He turned quickly away from her and began to get to his feet.

Amanda dropped the hammer, pulled the axe free from the door.

She held the bottom of the axe handle in her left hand, her right up toward the head.

When she looked back at her attacker, Quinn was standing still. He raised his right arm and with his free hand pulled the screwdriver out of his bicep with a spitting, venomous hiss from his throat.

'I'm going to put this in your belly,' he said, brandishing the screwdriver as he rushed for her, a maniacal, crazed, murderous look on his bloody face.

She couldn't run.

There was no other way out. No choice.

She could fight back or die.

She raised her arms, allowing the axe to arc, and as it did so she let her right hand slide down the shaft. Using the momentum of the swing for power, she pulled, guiding the weapon, twisting at the hips, using all her strength.

The axe buried itself in the center of Quinn's chest, knocking him from his feet. He landed on his back. His legs and arms spasmed and then he lay still. His dead eyes stared at the night. Amanda didn't stick around for another blow.

The job was done.

She grabbed the hammer, limped to the back gate and struck the lock twice before it broke off, allowing her back into the cool darkness of the alley. Dropping the hammer, Amanda stumbled away quickly, the sirens growing louder all the time.

When she reached the end of the alleyway, she stood up straight, headed back toward her car. She limped along the blocks until she saw her car parked up ahead.

And the car parked behind it.

A black Escalade. Facing away from her and parked on the other side of the street, right behind her Saab. She could see the outline of a figure in the driver's seat.

Amanda stopped in the middle of the sidewalk. The sirens also ceased, just as abruptly. She guessed the cops had arrived at Quinn's home.

Amanda glanced around the street. There were ample places to park. A good thirty feet of open space behind the Escalade. Her old Saab was maybe twenty feet from the entrance to an apartment building, just up ahead from where she'd parked. There were spaces outside the building. No reason for someone to park so close to her car. It was the same Escalade she'd seen earlier, close to Quinn's house.

Amanda turned and walked back the way she'd come. She didn't like the look of that car, but had no idea who might be inside. Maybe a friend of Naomi's? Someone to make sure Amanda went through with the job. Or maybe someone who was watching over Quinn. Or maybe just a regular member of Joe Public, going about their business. Either way, it didn't matter. Amanda didn't want to take the chance that the driver would recognize her as someone who had driven past Quinn's house, twice.

She was four blocks from the subway. Amanda raised her trembling hands, pulled up the collar of her coat and walked away. Checking the time on her cell, she saw it was just past ten o'clock.

As she turned the corner, she heard, behind her, the sound of a heavy car door slamming shut.

23
Scott

That electric panic stayed with Scott the whole time he was shopping. He doubted he would ever calm down. It felt very much like a current, low level, passing through his body, making it shake, allowing him only shallow breaths.

Scott knew that most of what he needed to get away with murder could be bought over the counter in a Target. He was walking to the store around the corner. Thinking with every step. Thinking helped. It always had. No matter what kind of situation Scott was in, if he thought about it, he could see a way through. He was a rationalist with a blinding temper. The logical part of his brain always saved his ass.

First thing he needed was a backpack. He chose the largest, not the cheapest. Eight-gallon capacity. Sixty bucks. He had one-hundred sixty dollars in cash and needed to keep fifty for cab fare. No way did he want any of these purchases showing up on his bank account.

Next on his list was a roll of trash bags, a carton of disposable latex gloves and two three-gallon bottles of strong bleach. A hooded sweater, jeans, underwear, socks and sneakers.

He put all of it in the backpack, paid in cash. The lady at the register didn't bat an eyelid at his purchases. They were innocent enough.

Ten minutes later, he was climbing the hotel stairs and took a break halfway. The twelfth floor was a long way up. When he pushed the door open into the hallway on that floor, he was covered in sweat and breathing hard. After checking there was no one else around, he moved the *Do Not Disturb* sign so the card reader could recognize the key card. The beep let him in, and he made sure the sign was secure before he closed the door.

There was a smell from the dead man on the floor. Blood, mostly, but Scott guessed his bowels and bladder had emptied too.

Scott opened the carton of gloves and put on a pair before he did anything else. No need to spread his fingerprints and DNA any further around the crime scene. Bending down, he checked the man's hip pocket, found a wallet.

Five hundred-dollar bills, a stack of credit cards and a New York State driver's license.

Patrick Travers.

The name meant nothing to Scott. He memorized the address, took the cash and left the cards before throwing the wallet on the bloody floor. Scott stepped over the body, put his backpack on the bed and got to work.

His bloodstained clothes went from the tub into a trash bag. He popped the cap on one of the bottles of bleach and scattered some over the shower tray. He then ran the shower to make sure no trace of him could be found. The rest of that bottle went on the carpet and then Travers. He made sure to soak the bottle protruding from Travers's eye socket. There would be a lot of trace DNA and fingerprints on it. He knew the bleach would do the job of eradicating trace evidence. There wasn't enough to cover Travers, so Scott opened the second bottle.

When he thought he'd covered every surface his skin had touched, Scott went into the bathroom, got out of the dead man's clothes, put them in the trash bag along with the bloody clothes and dressed in his new clothing from Target. Tying the trash bag tightly, Scott then stuffed it into his backpack. It just about fitted.

Scott checked his own pockets. He had his cell and his wallet. Didn't want to leave those behind. He glanced at Travers's empty wallet on the floor.

With any luck, the NYPD would think this was a robbery.

It didn't matter. As long as he hadn't left any forensic evidence behind, it would be okay. Scott was happy with the clean-up. He opened the door, left the *Do Not Disturb* sign in place and let it close behind him as he made for the stairs.

Two floors up.

Scott was in the hallway, headed to his room when he suddenly realized he didn't know what to tell Ruth.

He couldn't tell her the truth. Not yet, anyway.

The thought of Ruth living in fear of this man for the rest of her life wasn't an option either. He would have to tell her at some stage. For her sake. So that she knew her nightmare was over – that this man could never hurt her or anyone else again.

She was fragile. Right now, never more so. If he walked into their room and told her straight up he'd just killed the man who'd attacked her, and that they needed to get away for a while until it all blew over – that might be too much for Ruth to bear. She would crack. He could be doing her more damage.

No, he decided now was not the right time. He would have to wait. At least until he was certain the cops weren't going to catch him. Ruth had to be in a better state of mind too. She had to be away from this city – somewhere far away where she knew no one, and no one knew them. If it all turned to shit, and a warrant went out for Scott's arrest, he could at least get in touch with his old buddy, Jack. If it was illegal, Jack was plugged into it somewhere or he knew a guy who knew a guy. His old high-school pal could hook him and Ruth up with fake IDs and get them a plane ticket out of the country.

That was the back-up plan.

He shook his head, trying to clear his mind. He had more pressing things to consider. Like getting the fuck out of this hotel as soon as possible.

He used his key card to open the door to their hotel room. Ruth was in bed, asleep, but she stirred as the door closed behind him.

And then she screamed.

Scott dumped his bag on the floor, flicked on the bedside lamp and sat down on the bed beside her. He took hold of her shoulders and whispered softly to her that she was okay. She was in a hotel. She was safe. He was right there with her.

Her eyes were wide open, her chest heaving, and as she looked around the room and oriented herself she seemed to calm a little. But only for a second. Memories of the restaurant clearly flooded back into her mind as she reached out and grabbed his arms.

'What happened? Where did you go? Did you find anything out about the man in the restaurant?'

'Relax – it's okay. I followed him around a little and then I came back up. I managed to find out his name, though. I overheard him on the phone.'

'Where's your jacket? Are those new? What . . .'

'It's okay, I tailed the man around town, and got wet in the rain. Luckily I had my sweats bag downstairs in the hotel gym locker.'

Ruth looked first at the bag on the floor, then glanced out of the window. It looked like a clear night, but Scott thought it would be hard for her to tell in the dark from a lofty hotel window that didn't open. It's not like she had been outside.

'Does the name Patrick Travers mean anything to you?'

Ruth looked to the side, her eyes moving rapidly as if she was scrolling through a Rolodex in her head.

'No, I never heard the name.'

'Definitely not a client?'

'Definitely not. I don't know the name. God, should we tell Detective Farrow?'

'No, like he said, honey, there's nothing they can do. We'd just be wasting our time.'

She grabbed him then, held him tight, and he held her. They sat motionless together, clinging on to one another.

For the first time since September fourteenth, the night Scott got the call from the police telling him his wife had been attacked, he knew everything would be all right. If they got out of there now, everything would be just fine. He could feel it.

'We need to pack up and get out of this hotel. I don't like the fact that he's here. It's not safe. We need to go. We should go right now, okay?'

She let go of him, nodded, with tears in her eyes. And a smile. It almost made Scott break down. Over the past ninety minutes, he'd wanted some kind of release, and this almost unmanned him. He didn't regret killing Patrick Travers. Not now. Not after seeing her face. His death – his deserved death – had given them back some hope and the promise of a life still to come.

Behind Ruth were two large suitcases and two smaller ones.

'Let's pack,' said Scott.

It didn't take long to throw their belongings into the suitcases. Ruth dressed hurriedly in jeans, boots and a sweater.

'Where are we going to go?' she asked.

Scott checked his watch; it was almost ten.

'Let's start by getting out of the city. We can go anywhere, but for now let's just leave. I want to go someplace no one will follow us, and no one would think to look. It's okay now, honey. We're going to be just fine. We'll take a cab to Grand Central and jump on a train.'

24

Amanda

Amanda swiped her MTA card at the turnstile in Christopher Street subway station and made for the platform. As she turned the corner, she glanced over her shoulder.

There were a few people behind her. A mother and teenage daughter. An elderly man with a cane. And a man who jogged through the entrance, looking around. He was thirty feet away, at least. She estimated he was over six feet tall and he looked well built. Sandy brown hair. His head turned from side to side, and stopped when he saw Amanda. Then he moved towards her, quickly.

Amanda gritted her teeth against the protests from her knee, and moved down the stairs quickly to the platform. A train was just pulling in. She could hear the screech of brakes, and then the doors rolling open. Amanda reached the platform, moved swiftly onto the train and made for the back of the carriage. There were a handful of people seated already. She dared not look behind her.

The warning signal sounded, and within a few seconds the doors closed. The train started to move just as the man reached the platform. Amanda ducked down in her seat, making herself small, but never letting the man from her sight.

She didn't recognize him. Yet she was sure he was the same man who'd been in the black Escalade outside Quinn's house. The same

Escalade that had parked behind her car and the same man who'd got out of that car and followed her.

And she had no idea who he might be.

A cop? Personal security for Quinn?

It didn't matter. She wasn't going back for her car any time soon. She looked around the carriage and noticed some of the people there were giving her attention. Their stares quickly shifted as she met each gaze. It was then she realized she was panting – out of breath – but more than that. She touched her face. Her hand came away wet. There were spots of drying blood on her cheek. She wiped them away with spit.

Amanda leaned back in the seat, biting down as she stretched out her injured knee. By the time the train rolled into Times Square her breathing hadn't eased. She was jacked up on adrenaline. And this wasn't going to pass any time soon.

Not wanting to draw attention, she changed trains, got on the #7 to Grand Central. It was a good place to lose herself. At Grand Central, she got off the train, went up the escalator and into the main concourse. The warm marble halls always reminded her of Christmas time. The painted stars above her head, the vast glistening chandeliers, the solid brass four-faced clock that sits atop the center of the information booth. There were people around the booth, waiting, checking their cell phones. Every New Yorker knew the clock. The phrase, 'meet you at the clock' only ever meant this one.

Ahead was the escalator to the Metlife Building, and 45th Street beyond. She stood on the right, gazed up as she ascended.

A couple got on the escalator to her right, coming down onto the concourse. They were about her age – a man and a woman. The woman had soft, chestnut hair and wide, fearful eyes. Those eyes were so round, so watchful, that they reminded her of the opal faces of the clock she'd just passed. She had linked arms with her partner.

As they passed each other on the escalator, Amanda glanced at the woman. She stared back, and then both women quickly looked away.

In that half a second, Amanda knew comfort. Here was someone else, just as afraid and uncertain. The angst and trepidation poured from her eyes. And in that moment when their gaze had met, Amanda didn't feel alone. In a city of eight and a half million, loneliness is common. Most people were alone. Alone as they traveled through the belly of the city in packed subway cars. Alone as they weaved through the brick and steel canyons of Manhattan on sidewalks thick with strangers. Alone as they lay in bed at night with their problems and their pain.

Just then, Amanda knew the companionship found in the fear and loneliness of others.

She reached the top of the escalator, paused, turned and watched to see if the man from the Escalade was following her. She waited for a minute. No sign of him.

Making her way through the lobby of the Metlife Building, and then into the cold night air on 45th Street, Amanda's shoulders dropped, the tension easing down a notch.

She took out her cell phone. Called Naomi.

No answer. She didn't want to leave a message either. Maybe it was better that they didn't talk tonight. She just wanted to get home. And she knew when she got into the apartment and closed the door the weight of what she'd done tonight would hit her like a freight train.

It was two thirty in the morning when Amanda got back to her apartment. She threw her keys on the kitchen table and went immediately to the bathroom.

She vomited once, and her body wanted more but there was nothing left in her stomach. Her throat raw, a vile taste in her mouth, Amanda ran hot water into the tub, stripped her clothes off and put them in a trash bag, along with her coat. She hadn't looked too closely, but she guessed there would be blood spatter on them. Definitely the gloves. Those clothes would need to find their way into a random dumpster later that day. She managed to lever herself into the water mostly using her arms. It was hot. Much hotter than was comfortable, but her skin would soon get used to it. She needed the heat.

Her knee looked like a football. There was a cut across it that stung like hell, but it wasn't deep and had already closed. It didn't look bad compared to the purple and black bruising forming over the knee cap. Amanda kneaded the muscles and tendons in her knee, and then her shin, which had begun to ache because she was dragging that leg. Her neck was still red, tender, and she knew there would be some livid bruising on it tomorrow. She could cover that with thick foundation.

It had all gone to shit last night, and she knew she was lucky to be alive. That phrase formed in her mind.

You're *lucky* to be alive.

It wasn't her conscious mind speaking. This was her internal thought process, which couldn't really be categorized as conscious or unconscious, because when that thought occurred she found it to be true – to her great surprise.

I am *lucky to be alive.*

Just a few days ago, Amanda had no strong feelings on being alive at all. If she was breathing, then it was with the sole intent to make Wallace Crone stop breathing.

Now he was dead.

And another monster was dead too.

She knew it was the right thing to have done. On some level. Amanda was coming around to the view that what was legal and what was right were often two different things. Her father had been a union organizer, and a civil rights protester. This meant he had an arrest record longer than a Jersey longshoreman with a drinking problem. And he was proud of it too. She'd watched him being hauled off picket lines and protest marches by the NYPD more than enough times.

What would he have to say about what she'd just done?

Amanda knew the answer. He would say she'd made a terrible

mistake. And that, yes, she'd been forced to defend herself against a killer, but . . .

Amanda knew she should never have climbed that wall. Should never have gotten herself into that situation where she'd had to fight for her life.

She thought of bathing Jess in this same bathtub. Filling it with suds, listening to her squeals of delight as she splashed and played with her little yellow boat that sat still and unused now on the windowsill.

Amanda slid down and let her head go under the water. It was quiet beneath the surface. And warm. The opposite of being thrown into an icy sea at the end of her recurring dream. For Amanda, being beneath the water was like going into a different world. Or seeing the old one through a different lens – a view altered and soothed by calm, swirling water.

She came back up for air, stretched out her knee, which was beginning to feel a little better. With her arms on the sides of the tub, and a towel behind her head, Amanda allowed herself to drift off to sleep.

When she next opened her eyes, the sun was threatening the sky with an angry red haze and the water in the tub was almost cold. She had not dreamed of being in that boat on that roaring black sea, so far away from the fire on the beach.

Today was Wednesday, Thanksgiving Eve. This time last year she was already up, prepping the food for the next day, making potato salad and corn fritters.

She wouldn't be doing any of that today. She hadn't even bought a turkey for tomorrow. The thought of it made her feel sick.

She stood, took out the bath plug and turned on the shower to get the heat back into her body.

She found bandages and surgical tape in the medicine cabinet and strapped up her knee. It wasn't as sore as it had been last night, and the strapping helped stabilize it. Last thing she needed was a trip to the emergency room after falling down a set of stairs because her knee had given way.

Her stomach felt better too. She was hungry. She dressed in blue jeans and a black turtleneck sweater to hide the bruising, then made her way to the deli on the corner of 96th Street. She'd become quite fond of their breakfast wraps, and the coffee was always good. She took her meal outside and found an empty table under the awning. Amanda sat down and began to eat her roll.

She tried Naomi's cell phone. It went straight to voicemail.

Glancing behind her, at the Miller Time sign, she saw it was seven oh nine. Maybe Naomi wasn't up yet. There was no reason for Amanda to be here now other than breakfast sandwiches and hot coffee, and the realization of this gave her a sensation of warmth. Suddenly, a little bit of life was slowly returning to her. She was feeling something other than pain, loneliness and rage. There was life out there, after all.

She finished her roll, screwed up the wrapper and glanced around, looking for a trash can.

Her gaze flashed over the 96th Street subway entrance, and something in the back of her mind registered an alarm. She focused on the subway entrance, looked around and . . .

There he was.

Wearing his overcoat, backpack, AirPods. Walking into the station like he did six days a week.

No, it couldn't be him.

At first, Amanda couldn't process the image across the street. She got up from her table, spilling the coffee, leaving the wrapper to the winds. She didn't look left to cross the street, and only an angry car horn saved her from being hit. She stepped back, let the car pass then jogged across. As her legs began to pick up speed, pain stabbed at her knee, but she ignored it, pushed on. She swiped her MTA card at the turnstile, swung left for Downtown & Brooklyn, the #1, #2 and #3 trains, gripping the rail, sliding her hands down it to ease her knee as she hobbled deeper, down one flight. Then the next.

As she reached the platform, she heard the familiar swish of train doors closing. Amanda stumbled on the last three stairs, bit her lip to mask the jolt it gave her knee, but managed to stay upright. She needed a closer look. She needed to know. Maybe this was a mistake. She'd only seen him from a distance. One good look was all she needed. Amanda knew this man's face better than she could remember the face of her little girl.

There was no one on the platform. Through the train window she saw him sitting down in the train car, facing the platform. His cell phone in his hand.

Amanda approached the window just as the train began to pull away.

Wallace Crone's head lifted, and he stared at her. Only for a second. The train was moving, but it was all the time she needed.

Crone was alive.

Naomi lied.

25

Ruth

The cab dropped them off at 45th Street. They took their luggage and entered the Metlife Building. They went through the lobby and onto the escalators, which led down to the main concourse at Grand Central. Ruth clung to Scott, her arm looped under his.

A stone of solid fear sat in her gut. She hated being outside. Every damn second robbed her of breath. She was smart, intelligent. One part of her brain told her this was not right – this was an illness. There was no need to be afraid. She wasn't going to be attacked in public, not with her husband beside her.

And yet she knew it was right to be fearful. A killer was stalking her. He'd come to her hotel. The man who'd put a knife in her flesh knew who she was, and to protect himself it made sense to finish the job.

You're not paranoid if there's a good reason to be afraid.

It reminded her of a time when she was twelve. Her parents had split that year and neither of them could agree who would take Ruth for the summer. Turned out, neither of them could look after her so she spent that summer break at her grandparents' rickety house on the lake. It was a colonial painted house with creaking floorboards, a wrap-around porch and screechy doors. When the wind picked up at night, and rattled the windows, she was sure it was a vampire tapping on the windowpane and seeking an invitation inside. Ruth felt alone, unloved and lost. Her fear and loneliness turned those tree branches into the nails of a vampire at her window. But it was more than that. Back then, at nighttime, every dark corner held a ghost or a scary face. Scott had taken all her fears away when she'd met him.

Until the blue-eyed man came calling on her on September fourteenth.

The fear that she had experienced in her grandparents' house was with her now. Except she wasn't twelve. She wasn't in their old spooky house. Her parents were gone. She was a grown woman, afraid of every face in the shadows, every dark corner and what might be lurking there. It wasn't youth trauma and childish imagination fueling that fear now. He was real. The danger was real.

The monster was real.

She looked around, unable to think of anything else other than the blue-eyed man she'd seen at dinner. Patrick Travers. The monster had a name now. She looked behind in case he was following but there was no one there.

When she turned back, she saw someone on the adjacent escalator. The one beside theirs that ran in the opposite direction, going up toward 45th Street. It was only a woman. It wasn't him. She took a few quick breaths.

Once they reached the bottom of the escalator Scott said, 'We have to be quick. Our train is leaving.'

As they got to the ticket office, the clerk told them they'd just missed it. She noticed Scott was out of breath, even though they hadn't exactly been running.

'It's fine, we'll take the ferry,' said Scott.

Another cab, and then a short wait until they boarded the ferry across the river. Ruth sat up top, huddled into her coat against the cold, rocking gently back and forth with Scott rubbing her back. The near freezing temperature kept the rest of the passengers below in the heated cabin. Scott said he needed some air.

He got up from the bench beside her as the ferry sailed through Buttermilk Channel, between Governor's Island and Pier 12. The lights from the island shone on the black water like neon ghosts. She felt better. Calmer. The fresh smell from the water, the wind in her hair, the isolation on the deck, the gentle rock of the boat – it all helped. She was still shaking, but she didn't know if it was from the anxiety of being outside or the cold. They would dock at Red Hook in five minutes, and the fear of passing through the crowds grew on her, but Ruth closed her eyes and fought it down. She'd watched the small group of passengers carefully as they'd boarded. The man was not following them. Of that, she felt sure.

Scott leaned on the rail, looking out at the island. She saw his shoulders heaving as his gaze lowered to the water. The noise from the wind and the engine made it difficult to hear, but she thought he was sobbing.

He'd been through a traumatic experience too. Nothing like the horror she'd endured, but Ruth knew she sometimes didn't appreciate the effect all this was having on Scott. He had been a rock since the attack, but it was taking its toll. Sometimes she caught him staring at her, in something like pity.

Or guilt, perhaps.

Even though there was no one else on the deck, she didn't like being apart from Scott. Not like this. Not out in the open.

She got up and moved towards him. She stopped in her tracks when he heaved his guts over the side, a long trail of brown spit hanging from his lips in the wind. He wiped it away with the back of his hand, sank his torso over the rail and kept his head down. She took another few steps, placed her hand on his back.

'You okay?' she asked.

He swung round, startled, and then he softened.

'Sea sickness. I'm okay, honey. And look at you. You're doing great. See, it's not so bad being outside.'

She nodded, gazed out at the water. 'I know he's not on this boat.

Travers, I mean. I know he's looking for me. I just . . .' The panic began rising, her chest felt tight, sweat broke out on her top lip. 'Oh, Scott, what are we going to do?'

He took her in his arms, but she resisted at first. Then she felt the strength of him. Solid. Sure. Her protector.

'Let's get somewhere safe first. Then we can talk. It's going to be okay,' said Scott.

26

Amanda

Banging shut her apartment door, Amanda limped to the kitchen cupboard, threw it open, grabbed the bottle of vodka and took a hit from it – straight.

The burn felt good.

She needed it. She couldn't think straight. Naomi had lied to her about killing Crone, and seeing him on that train, alive and well, it hurt in a way Amanda had never known. She knew pain. It had been an animal that had lived with her for months now. And yet this, this betrayal, was a different kind of creature whose claws tore at her flesh in a whole new way.

She had been given release – the knowledge that Crone was dead – and she had believed it. Every word of it. More than that, she'd felt it. And when she'd seen him that peace had been cruelly ripped away.

Now that she'd had a taste of what it would be like if Crone was dead, she knew she wanted that, needed that, now more than ever. She had to calm those raging seas in her dreams. Amanda closed her eyes, enjoying, just for a moment, the memory of the stillness that had come with news of Crone's death. She promised herself then that she would kill him. She would do it herself. She had to.

But not yet.

She put the bottle of vodka on the table, went through to her bedroom and found the pages from the web she had printed out. It was the article she'd found while researching Naomi, sitting in that Starbucks while she'd waited for Crone to make his appointment. It was from the *New York Post*. She'd printed it at home because it was the one article with the largest, clearest picture of Quinn. Still only half his face, the other in shadow.

The picture looked like him. No doubt, that was the man she had killed last night.

She went to her laptop, typed in the search terms again. This time focusing on Naomi.

Nothing.

Not one relevant hit.

She clicked on her favorites bar in the browser. She'd bookmarked the relevant sites. The top one was the picture of Quinn alongside the article in *USA Today*. She clicked on the bookmarked link.

The results sucked the air out of her lungs.

Error 404 'Page Not Found'.

She clicked through the rest of the bookmarks for the *New York Daily News*, then *Metro New York*, *The Queens Chronicle*, and the *New York Post*.

Same error message for every single one.

Shaking her head, Amanda typed in a fresh search for 'news' and found all of the websites for those publications were up and running. She did a fresh search on Naomi, Quinn and the school.

Zero relevant hits.

Then something hit Amanda. She picked up the article she'd printed and examined the URL at the top of the printout.

https://www.usetoday.com/ny/frankquinn/naomi . . .

She didn't need to read any further. It wasn't USATODAY, it was USETODAY. One letter had been changed.

The web articles were fake.

All of them. And now they'd been deleted.

Amanda had taken an afternoon course on how to create a website for her art. It was easy these days. You could do it in a couple of hours. Anyone could.

Naomi had laid a careful, convincing trap for Amanda. One that had almost gotten her killed, and had made her take a life just to stay alive.

She bounded off her bed. Her knee reminded her it wasn't working properly by sending a squealing hot jolt of pain through her joint and dumping her on the floor.

Amanda got up carefully, made her way to the kitchen and found a box of Advil. She washed the pills down with more cheap vodka, grabbed her keys and left, headed for the subway.

All the way to Naomi's apartment, she tried to reach her on the phone. It didn't even ring. Either it had been switched off, or had no signal. When she got to Naomi's building, she found the front door slightly ajar. It was almost nine, and people would've been rushing out of the building for the last two hours, on their way to work. The last person out must not have closed it properly. This was the first piece of luck she'd had that morning. She got out of the elevator on Naomi's floor and pounded on her apartment door.

No answer.

Amanda listened at the door and heard nothing from the outside. Only the thumping of her own heart.

The closest apartment to Naomi's was down the hallway, maybe twenty feet away. Naomi's was the corner apartment, and that meant a little space from the neighbors. She figured anyone who could afford to live in the building needed a good salary to pay for it. Maybe even two salaries.

Chances were that Naomi's closest neighbors were not in the building, having already left for work.

The hallway curved before revealing the rest of the apartments. On the wall, before it turned into a longer hallway, a red firehose was mounted to the wall. Below the firehose reel sat two large fire extinguishers. Amanda approached, lifted one of the extinguishers and tested it for weight.

It felt heavy enough.

She went back to Naomi's apartment, held the extinguisher by the handle with one hand, her other on the base, and she swung it like a battering ram at the spot just below the door handle.

The first hit shot the extinguisher out of her hands and it fell to the floor with a loud metallic *thunk*. Her left wrist felt as if someone had tried to tear it off. She shook it, then picked up the extinguisher before it rolled away. Stood back. Took a run at the door. The base of the extinguisher struck the door an inch below the handle, and the frame gave a loud crack. One more. This time the door opened.

She went inside, dropped the extinguisher. When it hit the floor, there was another loud *clang*. She looked down, confused. The extinguisher should've landed quietly on the apartment carpet.

But the carpet was gone.

Amanda moved quickly through the apartment. Lounge, kitchen, bathroom, bedroom, second bedroom.

There was nothing but a toilet and a tub.

No pictures on the walls, no furniture, no bed, no desks, no corkboard with photos of Quinn, no carpeting, no drapes, no blinds, not even a lightbulb.

It was as if Naomi had never been here. Amanda returned to the front door of the apartment, double checked to make sure this was the right place.

And it was.

Amanda shuddered. Naomi had lied about everything. She had tricked Amanda into killing someone and she had no idea why.

Before panic robbed her of her senses, Amanda ran out of the apartment, and into the elevator. As the lift descended, she tried to think. She had to understand what had just happened.

Crone would have to wait.

Amanda had put herself at huge risk. One that might get her a life sentence. There were questions that had to be answered.

Who was Naomi?

The second question put a lump in her throat – who was the man Amanda had murdered last night?

27

Ruth

Scott got them a cab from Red Hook ferry port to Jamaica Station, and then a train to Huntington, Long Island. Ruth never let go of Scott's arm while they moved from the station to the train, and then disembarked at Huntington station.

'Where are we going?' she asked as they stood on the platform.

'We'll get a train to Port Jefferson. With everyone heading home for Thanksgiving, they've put on a late-night crossing – we'll take the midnight ferry to Bridgeport and another train to Hartford,' said Scott, hefting his backpack onto his shoulder.

'Why are we going to Hartford?'

'Because I lived there for a while with my parents before they moved to Florida. I know the place, and it's far enough out of the way that no one will ever look for us there.'

Ruth felt a chill at the thought of someone looking for them.

There were a dozen people on the platform, all walking in the same direction towards the main concourse. Ruth noticed that Scott kept his head down, hiding his face under his baseball cap.

'If we were going to Hartford, couldn't we have gotten another train from Grand Central?' asked Ruth.

'Yeah, but we would've had to wait for hours. I want to keep moving. And I like the ferry across the Long Island Sound. We should just make the last crossing. It's really peaceful at night.'

They had coffee and sandwiches in Starbucks in the train station while they waited for their train to Port Jefferson. Scott opened his laptop and started working. He sat across the table from Ruth, so she couldn't see what he was looking at, just the glare from the screen illuminating his stern face. Ruth took only a few mouthfuls of the sandwich. She was hungry, but her stomach was all tied up with anxiety.

She noticed Scott hadn't touched his food either. Sweat polished his forehead even though it wasn't warm in the Starbucks. Scott stood, looked around the coffee shop. Ruth tensed and followed Scott's eyeline around the room. There was a young couple on the other side of the shop, very much in love, laughing and taking pictures of themselves with their phones. One barista behind the counter.

'Honey, I need to use the bathroom,' he said.

Ruth bit her lip, gripped the edge of the table with both hands.

'I'll only be a minute, tops. I promise. There's no chance Travers knows where we are. You're safe here, okay?'

At first, Ruth couldn't speak. Her mouth had become cinderblock dry. She took a sip of coffee, and tremulously set the cup back down on the table.

'Are you sure?' she asked.

He leaned over, put his hands on her shoulders, said, 'I'm sure. He couldn't have followed us. I'll only be a minute.'

Up close, she could see the strain on his face. A little tremor in the muscles at the corner of his left eye and his skin had turned the pale color of fresh bone.

'Are you feeling all right? You don't look well,' she said.

'I-I'm fine. Still just a little nauseous from the boat is all. I'll be quick.'

'Please,' said Ruth, pleading with her eyes not to be left alone.

'It's okay, honey. You'll be fine. I'll just be a minute,' he said, wiping sweat from his face.

She nodded, and watched him disappear into the bathroom. Ruth told herself she was safe. There were no windows in the Starbucks, and they were seated all the way at the back. She would be fine for just a minute, but it didn't stop the sole of her shoe hammering against the floor as she gripped the table with both hands.

She looked at the young couple who were laughing and kissing again. Somehow it made her feel better. She turned Scott's laptop round, just to see what he was doing. Anything to keep her mind from running into bad thoughts. Thoughts that would take over, send her into a frenzy.

He was checking the local news. Two tabs were open. Both on breaking news in New York. Ruth had avoided the news since the attack. She didn't want to know about people being stabbed, or shot, or murdered. It was all too much. She turned the laptop back round to face where Scott had been seated, and willed him to return – fast.

When Scott came back to his seat, his hair was wet, and he looked a little more composed.

'I'm going to book an Airbnb, okay?'

Ruth nodded, and Scott continued to tap away on his laptop.

The train to Port Jefferson didn't take long, and they got another cab to the ferry. The streets of this Long Island town were short, dark and largely deserted. It was such a transition from Manhattan where everyone walked or took the subway. No one walked around here. Everyone drove. They got their tickets for the last sailing, and Scott suggested they take themselves to the top deck again. The air was soothing. Cold as all hell, but at least there were only a handful of people who embarked and all of them sat below in the warmth.

As the ferry made its crossing of the Long Island Sound the lights from Port Jefferson disappeared behind them leaving only the glare from the occasional buoy and, in the distance, the dim glow of life from Bridgeport. The ferry had more passengers than Ruth had expected. It was Thanksgiving in two days' time, and people were traveling home for the holidays.

Scott looked over the barrier then turned round and winked at Ruth with a smile. He stood there, leaning against the painted white rail, framed by the dark waters behind.

She loved him in that moment. The stress of this had been starting to show. She reminded herself he was doing this for her. To protect her, to make her feel safe. He was agitated as hell and worried about both of them, but he was trying to make her smile in spite of it all – trying to turn this into a fun trip. And for a heartbeat it felt like that. Just for a second, they weren't running away from a monster – they were running away from themselves and all the pain of these last weeks.

Ruth looked down at her feet, willing her own smile to appear. And, when it did, she lifted her head to Scott.

Only he had his back to her.

And he was no longer wearing his new backpack. It wasn't by his feet. It wasn't in front of him.

For a second, she wondered what had happened to it.

Then she heard a faint splash.

28

Farrow

By the time their NYPD pool car pulled up at the brownstone, the forensics technicians were packing up their equipment at the rear door of their van.

Hernandez killed the engine and got out of the Crown Vic at the same time as Farrow. Even though his feet touched the blacktop in concert with Hernandez, it took Farrow a lot longer to straighten up. His lower lumbar disc problem that had been steadily getting worse was now almost unmanageable. There were good days and bad days. Of late, mostly bad days. He waited until the pain passed. His first movements were slow, but he knew he would loosen up when he started to move around.

Karen Hernandez was already yammering with the forensics tech by the time Farrow took his first step onto the sidewalk. A black-and-white and another unmarked squad car were parked along the curb outside the house. Silently, the flashing berries and cherries from the top of the patrol car sent blue and red light around the street. There was no ambulance, and no sign of the medical examiner yet. At any murder scene in New York, the medical examiner was the one who arrived in the most expensive car. Mercedes or BMW, sometimes an Audi.

With no expensive German engineering in sight, Farrow thought it likely he'd beaten the ME to the punch. He took another couple of steps and felt the burning in his back just as a mild distraction, and the pain in his right leg had gone. The longer he stood, the easier it would get.

He heard heavy metallic doors slam, and saw the forensic techs making their way to the front of the vehicle, the rear doors now closed. Hernandez came back to give him an update.

'Who was the tech on scene?' asked Farrow.

'Belucci,' said Hernandez.

'Good. He's thorough. Did they get anything?'

'Not much, by the looks of things. We won't know until they get lab results back.'

'I won't get my hopes up. Let's go inside.'

There was a patrolman in uniform standing at the front door of the brownstone with a clipboard in his hand. Hernandez and Farrow ducked under the tape, made their way up the steps and showed their ID to the officer. He entered their names in the scene log and said, 'Statler and Waldorf are out back.'

Hernandez rolled her eyes, and the patrolman stifled a smile.

Farrow and Hernandez entered the home. A neat hallway, with a shoe rack and an umbrella stand. There was only a pair of boots and a pair of sneakers on the rack. Both pairs belonged to a male they guessed, by their size and color.

They passed by a lounge on the right. A TV sat silently in front of a leather couch. On the left they found a kitchen diner. A row of copper pots and pans hung from a ceiling fixture above a kitchen island with a built-in hob. It looked like an expensive kitchen, with double ovens and lots of cupboard space and a wall taken up with shelves of cookbooks. Yet the décor and the books had a decidedly male slant. A row of kitchen knives displayed on the wall, clinging to a magnetic strip.

'Somebody sure liked to cook,' said Hernandez as they made their way toward the open back door. Stopped.

Broken glass lay on the floor from the busted kitchen window. Carefully, they stepped over it.

'Look familiar?' said Hernandez.

Farrow wasn't sure yet. Mr. Blue-eyes entered his victim's homes from the rear, breaking a window in the kitchen to gain access. This time, one of the windows above the washbasin was broken. Ragged shards of glass still clung to the frame. The window beside it remained closed and intact.

'Doesn't look like they climbed through the window,' said Farrow. 'The glass wasn't broken for access to the property.'

Opening the back door, Farrow let Hernandez go first, then followed.

The yard was large. Maybe the largest Farrow had seen in Manhattan. A lawn of fifty feet or more, thirty feet wide, with rose bushes on the left-hand side. A brick wall at the rear. A small tool shed sat on the right, on the lawn.

That's where they found Statler and Waldorf, standing outside the shed. Not their real names of course. Detectives Donnelly and Carter of the 86th Precinct were well known to most cops in the city. They'd started their beat when Reagan was president. Two old white-haired guys who'd been busting each other's balls, and everyone else's, for getting on for forty years.

'Look what we got here, Saint Jude and his apostle,' said Donnelly.

Farrow nodded. He'd picked up that nickname some years ago, and in truth he didn't mind it.

'Watch yourself, Carter. The *real* police are here,' said Donnelly.

'If they're the *real* cops, then I should've retired ten years ago,' said Carter.

'You did retire ten years ago. They just forgot to tell you,' said Donnelly.

'You want to fill us in?' asked Hernandez.

'You asking me out on a date, young lady?' said Donnelly.

'I would, but the old folks' home wants you back in bed by eleven,' said Hernandez.

The two old men laughed heartily, and at that moment Farrow saw that the yellow police-evidence markers on the lawn highlighted a pool of blood. It was still wet and looked black in the darkness.

'Don't worry,' said Farrow. 'We're not muscling in on your case. We have a call out on any home invasion assaults or homicides. Your dispatcher gave us the heads-up when you called in the scene. Does this look like our guy?'

The old men nodded at one another. The pissing contest was over.

'Don't think so. Looks like a bad domestic,' said Donnelly. 'Neighbors called when they heard shouting out back. Sounded like a man and a woman having a fight, so one of 'em said. The vic is male.'

A male didn't fit their profile, but it wasn't unheard of for a suspect to change up their victim selection. Either because they wanted a change, or to throw the cops off the scent.

'Was the vic stabbed? Do you have the weapon?' asked Hernandez.

'Oh, we got the weapon, all right,' said Carter, giving a throaty laugh, filled with phlegm. 'The perp left it in his chest. A fire axe. Or looks like one. We'll get a better look at it when the doctors separate it from his ribcage.'

'Jesus,' said Hernandez. 'That's one hell of a domestic.'

Farrow stepped over the pool of blood and glanced at the tool shed. It looked as though somebody had taken the axe to the outside of the door before they'd buried it in the homeowner's chest. The bolt on the shed was lying on the lawn. It had been ripped away. Farrow stepped inside the shed, looked around at the neatly arranged tools. It was a lot tidier than Farrow's garage, except they both shared a problem with cobwebs. Every tool had its place. Neatly and intelligently arranged. A diligent craftsman had put this shed together. There was a spot on the wall, two thick nails, two feet apart – a perfect place to hang an axe.

A crime-scene marker sat beside a cell phone on the worktop.

He stepped out of the shed.

'So how did this go down?' asked Farrow.

'Lover's tiff. She comes at him with the axe because he cheated, stole her money, whatever. There's a baseball bat on the lawn. Maybe he threatened her first? Doesn't matter. She kills him then she breaks for the border, goes out the back gate into the alley,' said Statler.

Farrow and Hernandez made their way to the back gate. It was open. The bolt, secured with a padlock, had been broken from the wood. It lay on the path beside a hammer, all delineated with crime-scene markers.

'What do you think?' asked Farrow.

'It's not Mr. Blue-eyes, but I don't buy a domestic. Not yet,' said Hernandez.

'Me either. But those two won't look past their own noses on a case. And they work slow. Look at them,' said Farrow.

Leaning to one side, Hernandez watched the two men. They were holding folded notebooks, using them to lean on as they each filled out a document.

'They're filling out their overtime forms. That's their priority,' she said.

'This feels a million miles from a domestic. Maybe we can give them a steer.'

They walked back to Statler and Waldorf, who were now finishing their forms. Ready to leave.

'Any sign of a disturbance in the house?' asked Farrow.

'Zip,' said Donnelly.

'Fair enough. Let me know if forensics come back with anything. It doesn't look like our guy, but I can't rule it out yet. There are a few things making me think this isn't a domestic, though,' said Farrow.

'What things?' asked Carter.

'The broken door on the tool shed, the broken lock on the back gate, the broken window. If the female, let's assume for now it was a female, had a fight with her partner, why break the locks? Why not just use the key? Or go out the front door? And why break the window?'

'Who knows. People don't think clearly when they've just planted an axe in their lover's chest. Fingers crossed we'll know exactly what happened by morning,' said Donnelly.

'By morning? That's Thanksgiving Eve. You figuring on an early holiday miracle?' asked Hernandez.

'No, little lady,' said Donnelly. 'When the paramedics took away the vic, he still had a pulse. This guy ain't dead. If he makes it, he can just tell us what happened.'

29

Amanda

The world had turned for Amanda.

Again.

She sat on her couch. It was now ten thirty in the morning. She needed to sleep, could feel her body becoming sluggish, but her mind was racing far too much to even contemplate getting under her sheets.

This was not how life was supposed to be. Growing up, all she'd wanted to do was paint. To capture a moment, a feeling on a canvas, gave her the greatest pleasure. She'd hoped, one day, that this would be her way of making a living. In her thirties, she'd wanted a husband and a family of her own. And for a while she'd had that security. She'd had her job that paid the bills – her art for the evenings, which might some day pay those bills.

Bringing baby Jess home from the hospital three days before Christmas, she'd known this was how life was supposed to be. She'd found her path. Her happy place. Luis had decorated the tree, cleaned the apartment, made a nest for his new daughter and the woman he loved, and Amanda had never felt so full of hope.

For those six amazing years, her life was filled with possibility and peace.

Wallace Crone had taken everything from her. Destroyed the life she had and the life that was to come. Her past and her future, gone.

She couldn't work. Couldn't paint. Couldn't cry. She couldn't even mourn her husband and little girl. There was only anger and pain.

She knew she had to turn on the TV. She knew the local news would carry the story of the man she'd murdered. And yet she couldn't do it.

What if they named him? What if they gave her guilt a *name*? Made it a real human being instead of an anonymous man who'd fought for his life.

Images crashed into her mind. Unbidden and unwanted. Quinn's arm pierced by the screwdriver, and the sound made by the blade as it bit into his chest and stayed there. Moonlight reflected in the small pool of blood forming on his chest. These were new demons that she knew would haunt her memories.

She told herself that she didn't have a choice. He would've killed her.

That thought didn't dissipate the anger she felt for Naomi who'd put her in that situation.

Something happened then. Something that hadn't happened in a long time.

Amanda cried.

She wasn't crying for herself but for the man she'd killed.

She thought about calling Farrow. Telling him what she'd done. Naomi was a member of her counseling group, sure, but no one else knew that they'd talked privately. Bar a few irrelevant text messages and a printout from a fake web page, there was no evidence that any of their conversations had ever happened. And there was certainly nothing to back up a story about swapping murders – anyone could've created a fake web page. If she told Farrow the truth, things were only going to go one way – it would buy her a ticket for a life sentence without parole. Naomi had disappeared. The cops wouldn't believe Amanda. Neither would a jury.

She had been led to this. Naomi's plan had been to manipulate Amanda into murdering this man. Turned out she'd not needed much persuasion. Now, she needed to know why this had happened. Why had this man been a target? She had to face it. Had to turn on the TV. The only way to find out about Naomi was to find out about the man she'd murdered.

Amanda wiped her eyes, went into the living room and turned on the TV.

News was a river in America. Ever flowing, constantly changing and presented as if the viewer's life depended on them hearing these stories right now. The newscasters were trailing a statement from the president to be made later that day. The press loved to make him out to be an idiot, and in fairness he often gave them a helping hand.

It didn't take long for the news station to go to a local affiliate for New York. Today was Blackout Wednesday, and the NYPD would have their hands full of drunks home for the holidays and out to party before Thanksgiving tomorrow. Amanda put her index finger in her mouth, bit down on it. Just enough to hurt. She needed to be sharp. The lead story was on a fatal stabbing on the Upper East Side, then . . .

'*In other news a fifty-five-year-old man from Greenwich Village is in a critical condition in a nearby hospital today after suffering life-threatening injuries during a brutal home invasion . . .*'

She shook her head. That wasn't the story. Amanda closed her eyes, breathed out slow while she waited for the news to cover her killing.

'*. . . Neighbors called the police around eight thirty last night when they heard what sounded like a disturbance coming from his back yard . . .*'

Amanda's eyes flashed open. Held on the newscaster's face.

'*. . . Police and paramedics found the homeowner lying on his lawn with an axe buried in his chest. His condition in hospital remains critical. In other news, the New York Fire Department . . .*'

Thoughts flew around Amanda's head as the afternoon sun sent bright sprites of sunlight dancing around her walls. He was alive. And for that she felt saved. Saved from the shame and guilt of having taken a life, even in self defense. But, if he lived, he could describe his attacker. Identify her.

She knew if the man recovered one of the first things to happen would be an interview with the cops at his hospital bedside. Maybe within the day, or tomorrow.

The cops had her mugshot. And her DNA. All of it stored following her arrest for breaching the restraining order on Crone. In the fight with the man, she might have left some DNA behind. It was possible. It had all become so brutal and messy and she'd cut her knee. They may not even need DNA. All it would take would be the man to pick her out from a six-pack of mugshots. It wouldn't take long for them to come for her.

Maybe forty-eight hours. Maybe seventy-two with it being the holidays. Three days. Tops. That's how long it would take for the cops to track her down.

Naomi had used Amanda. Used her pain. And for that she wanted answers. She wanted payback. She couldn't let this go. She would put Crone aside for now, track down Naomi. She was done with being a victim. She wasn't going to let Naomi get away with this.

She had to fight back.

She had to find Naomi before the cops found Amanda.

It might not help much, but if she told the police she'd been manipulated – pressured into this – it might just make a difference. That and the fact that she'd tried to walk away and he hadn't let her. She'd had to fight.

Amanda changed the strapping on her knee, took more painkillers, grabbed her coat and headed out.

Killing Wallace Crone would have to wait.

The clock was ticking.

And she had to find out the truth.

30

Ruth

She woke at dawn.

There was no blackout blind on the bedroom window. Just thin drapes. The sun on her face brought her gently awake. Ruth turned over, spread out an arm and found Scott's side of the bed empty and cold.

She sat up. Looked around.

She was in someone else's apartment, the Airbnb Scott had booked in Hartford. They'd gotten in late and Ruth, tired and emotional, had gone straight to bed. Last she'd seen of Scott the night before was him lying down beside her, still dressed. Just keeping her company until she fell asleep. Scott had said he wanted to unpack, would watch TV later. She could tell he was too wired to sleep.

Her watch read six twenty a.m. It was Thanksgiving tomorrow. They'd already apologized to Scott's parents, and Ruth was the excuse why they couldn't be with them in Florida. He'd told them they'd decided to stay home for the holidays, that they'd made no plans for Thanksgiving this year. It didn't feel like Ruth had a lot to be thankful for.

She wondered if Scott had come to bed at all last night. The thought made her uneasy. She got up, yawned and stretched and felt the familiar pull from her scars. It was always the same first thing in the morning. Irritated by the heat and the cotton, they itched and stung after she'd been lying in a warm bed.

Ruth wore one of Scott's T-shirts, which doubled as a nightgown. She pulled open the drapes and looked out at the street below. The apartment sat on the top floor of a three-story building. The building was what Scott called a 'perfect six', the old style of middle-class apartments built over a hundred years ago: two apartments on each floor with three-story bow fronts on each side of the oblong building. Scott's parents used to live in a perfect six when they'd first got married. These historic apartments on Park Terrace overlooked the park, hence the name, but behind them was an area of the city crumbling into decay. This part of Hartford was called Frog Hollow. The Park River used to flow close to the houses and the land was part marsh and part swamp until Samuel Colt started making guns there, and with it came other businesses – the first to make bicycles and sewing machines in the country.

Frog Hollow grew up around the factories, and as they closed their doors so did the neighborhood.

Still, Ruth thought the view pleasant. Almost peaceful.

She found Scott in the kitchen watching the news on a small flatscreen television that sat on the counter, beneath the cupboards.

'I'm starving,' said Ruth as she put her arms around him.

He said nothing. Scott felt like a tightly wound spring. Hard, cold and ready to explode. The tension radiating from him gave her a jolt, like a shock of static.

She recoiled, said, 'Are you okay?'

'I'm fine. I'll go out in a minute and get some groceries.'

His voice sounded dead. Monotone.

His gaze never left the TV. The president was due back from his golf trip to make some kind of statement, probably something stupid, judging by the man, thought Ruth.

Ruth went back to the bedroom, found her case, threw it on the bed and popped the lid. She picked out jeans, sweater and underwear.

She showered, dressed and dried her hair. When she returned to the kitchen twenty minutes later, Scott still hadn't moved. The news channel was still speculating on the president's upcoming speech.

Then the female news anchor interrupted an interview, cutting them off to take up the full screen.

'*Some breaking news now on our top story – Murder on the Upper East Side. Sources in the NYPD have confirmed to our reporter that a senior advisor to the Mayor of New York City was found dead in his hotel room at the Paramount last night . . .*'

Her mouth fell open, her eyes locked on the screen.

Her mind was making calculations. Connections.

A man murdered in their hotel *last night*.

Scott had gone out to follow a man. The man she had identified as her attacker. She had slept for a time and didn't know how long he'd been gone. When he'd come back, he was wearing cheap clothes. The kind he would never wear. And they had to suddenly leave the hotel – where they'd been staying since she'd left the hospital. He had come back to the room that night not just with new clothes but with a new backpack. That backpack had not made it to this apartment. She knew on the ferry it had gone over the side into the dark waters of the channel. That's why they had taken a circuitous route, including a long ferry crossing to Hartford instead of getting a direct train from Grand Central. She guessed he had blood-covered clothing that he had to dispose of.

'. . . *the victim was brutally murdered* . . .' said the TV reporter, standing outside the Paramount Hotel.

Ruth's voice barely rose above a whisper, 'What did you do last night?'

The shock and fear hit him immediately. Not at the news that a man had been killed, thought Ruth. No, Scott was worried that she'd put two and two together. She could see it registering on his face. He glanced at the TV, and the banner headline.

Scott said nothing. He just stared at the screen like it was the headlight from an overnight freight train thundering toward him and he was trapped in that beam, unable to move – completely frozen.

Ruth's thoughts could not be contained – they spilled out of her mouth – given voice as if they had a will of their own.

'The news says there was a man murdered in our hotel last night. You changed your clothes when you were out. You were gone a long time. And I know you dumped that new bag in the river. You . . . you . . .'

She didn't finish the sentence. It was too heavy to say it out loud. She didn't need to. Scott hung his head, took hold of the kitchen counter as his knees gave way. He crumpled to the floor. It was almost as if his body had suddenly taken on the physical weight of what he'd done.

'I didn't mean to kill him,' he said. 'I just lost it and I hit him. And then he fought back. I had no choice. I thought he was going to kill me, and then he would come for you. I had no . . .'

His last words died as he cupped a hand across his mouth, his eyes squeezed shut. Tears tumbled over his fingers.

Ruth's breath quickened; her chest tightened.

'Are the cops looking for us?' she asked.

Scott sniffed, said, 'I don't know. I don't think so. I cleaned up the scene pretty good . . .'

Her back straightened as she blew out the air in her lungs. It felt hot. Toxic. When she drew another breath, it felt cool. Like inhaling the morning mist that floated on a calm mountain.

She approached Scott, knelt and raised his chin with her forefinger. Her shoulders no longer ached with tension. As she drew her hand away from his face she stopped, gazed at her fingers as if they belonged to someone else – they were still. No tremors. Her thoughts, always clouded with fear, suddenly felt calm – clear.

'You killed Travers. You killed the man who attacked me,' she said.

Through tears, Scott spoke. A long trail of saliva stretched between his lips, never breaking, but there with each word.

'I'm sorry. I fucked up.'

She leaned in close, wiped his lips with her thumb and then kissed him.

'You've *saved* us. You've *saved* me. He can't come after us. I don't have to be afraid. He's dead and I *love* you. I love you more than I can ever say.'

31
Amanda

There were two ways of tracking down Naomi.

Neither of them easy. The first was the most obvious. If Naomi wanted the man she had called Quinn dead, then there must be a connection. Maybe a close connection. And because of that she could not be the one to kill him.

Before he attacked Amanda, he'd asked who had sent her. Naomi had history with this man. The police would automatically think her a suspect. So maybe part of what Naomi had told her was probably true. Amanda thought this made sense. To find out the connection, she first had to find out the man's real identity. That would take her one step closer to Naomi.

She scanned her phone for all the news alerts she could find on the story. None of them revealed the identity of the man in ICU who'd had an axe removed from his chest. No point going to the hospital, either. There might be a cop posted on the ward to protect the man in case his attacker returned to finish the job, and if she went near the hospital she put herself at risk of an earlier arrest. Her arrest would come. She was certain of it. When the man woke, he would provide a description to the police, and then of course they'd probably find her DNA somewhere at that messy scene. It wasn't a question of *if* she was going to be arrested for attempted murder – it was *when*. And, once that moment came, she wanted to be ready with the truth. That someone else had put her up to this and forced her into that situation. Plus, she had wanted to leave, but the man had attacked her. It was self defense. That had to count for something, but it would count for nothing if she didn't have evidence to back it up. And yet she couldn't get too close to the man she had to investigate. Not at the hospital anyway.

No. She couldn't track him that way.

It was too dangerous.

There was an alternative. A second way to trace Naomi that didn't involve the man she had called Quinn.

Through Matt, and the counseling group. Naomi would have had to show Matt her ID maybe? Like Amanda had. He would know who she really is. He would have files. Records.

Amanda sat at a corner table in a deli on Lexington and 33rd, her grilled cheese half eaten and going cold in front of her as she watched the front door. Checking the time on her phone, she calculated Matt was running almost a half hour late. Not late enough to give her pause, although if he didn't show in the next five minutes she would beat it. It was almost one thirty in the afternoon. The city was busier than ever. Holiday traffic. Tomorrow, the cars would leave the city for Macy's Thanksgiving Day parade.

No new text messages from Matt. The last one said he would come meet her. Amanda had texted him to say she was very low, and having dark thoughts, and could he spare an hour to talk. He texted back saying he could, although this was unusual and he didn't normally see anyone out of the group hours. He said he would make an exception. This one time.

Amanda looked up from her phone as Matt walked into the deli. He wore a long, thick scarf, which he had wrapped around his neck half a dozen times, a fleece-lined denim jacket and jeans. He carried an umbrella, even though it wasn't raining. Matt was the type of guy who was prepared for most things.

She waved, and he waved back as he made his way through the rows of tables to the corner.

'How are you?' he asked.

'Not great. Thanks for seeing me,' she said.

He stretched out of his jacket, then unraveled his scarf. It was warm in the deli, and cold outside. His glasses had misted in the heat. He took them off and placed them on the table.

'Some people struggle to open up in a group. I understand that. But you've got to try. I'm supposed to give a report to your probation officer after eight sessions. It would be good to tell them that you participated.'

Amanda nodded, said, 'That's why I contacted you. I want to open up, but I'm having some problems with Wendy. She and I have been talking outside of the group. She, well, she can be a little scary some-times. Maybe it's just her bullshit, but I don't think I could go back to group if she's there.'

Just then the waitress arrived. Matt ordered a tuna sandwich on rye and Amanda took a coffee refill.

'Look, I don't encourage social contact between group members. That's a recipe for disaster. I've seen it before.'

'I'm sorry. I really didn't mean to step over the line. I didn't know there was a line.'

He nodded and waved his delicate fingers at her.

'Don't worry. It's fine. Wendy has an attitude. That's all it is. It can be intimidating at first, but I assure you it is a safe environment. I want you to feel comfortable sharing your thoughts and feelings.'

Amanda nodded, and smiled at him. He smiled back.

'So is there something in particular you wanted to talk about?' he asked. 'You sounded as if you were in a really bad place.'

'Yeah, I just feel very foolish. I know the group could be good for me, but it's Wendy . . .' Amanda paused, thought for a moment before finishing her sentence.

Matt wiped his glasses on his shirt, then put them on and leaned forward. He steepled his fingers, elbows on the table, head slightly cocked to one side.

'Well?' he said.

No choice. She didn't have time to mess around. Amanda came straight out with it.

'Wendy told me her real name was Naomi.'

She searched Matt's face. Gauging his reaction. His eyebrows lifted, just for half a second. He was a little surprised, but was he surprised that Wendy had shared her real name or that she'd given a false one? Amanda couldn't quite tell.

She said, 'I don't think that's her real name, either. I don't like being played for a fool. My little girl and my husband were taken from me. Anyone who would use that to exploit me shouldn't be in a group with others where they can do real damage. I don't trust her.'

He sat back, raised his hands, as if in surrender.

'Look, I don't know exactly what went on between you two. Anything that happens outside of group isn't really my concern. I can't control that, but if it starts to affect what happens in my sessions then I will have to do something about it.'

'So, what can you do?'

'Can you tell me what happened?'

'It's kind of personal, you know? I just need to know she's on the level. If not, I might need another group. Could you talk to her?'

'Sure. I'll call her and see what she has to say,' said Matt.

'When?' asked Amanda.

Matt paused, said, 'When will I call her?' He smiled, laughed nervously, then said, 'I suppose I'll call her after we finish talking.'

'Like right away? Couldn't you call her now?'

'I don't have her . . . I mean, my files are in the trunk of my car,' he said, gesturing over his shoulder with his thumb. 'I lead groups all over the city, so it's easier just to keep the records in the car. I'll call her when we're done here. I promise.'

The waitress arrived with his sandwich, and Matt unfolded his napkin, placed it on the table, looked around and said, 'I'm just going to the bathroom. Back in a sec.'

Amanda took a sip of coffee while she worked out her next move. She knew what it had to be. It made her more than a little uncomfortable, but there was no choice.

That clock was ticking.

The bathroom was in the basement, like a lot of restaurants in the city. Matt disappeared through a door labeled *restrooms*, and Amanda got up, walked round to Matt's side of the table and picked up his jacket. She heard the rattle of keys, fished in his pocket and found a large bunch of them on several interlocking keyrings. Attached to the bunch was a key fob for a BMW.

Across from her was a guy in a business suit with an iPad propped up on the table.

'Excuse me, I have to go outside and make a call. Would you mind watching our table for a moment? My friend is in the bathroom.'

'No problem,' said the man.

Amanda thanked him, jogged to the door and was soon out on the street, walking as fast as she could in the direction Matt had approached the deli. There were no lots around this area, at least none that she could think of. A line of parked cars stretched along the sidewalk. The last car at the end of the block was a silver BMW. She hit the fob. The lights flashed. Amanda opened the trunk.

Inside were three boxes containing neat rows of folders. The boxes were labeled according to the type of counseling – Couples – Addiction – Parental Trauma.

Amanda pulled the last box and started going through it. Within it she saw her file – Jane – thin and new. Her fingers walked through the tops of the files, separating them fast so she could see the names on each file.

There it was – Wendy. She lifted it, flicked it open.

She bypassed Matt's notes on the file. She didn't rate him as any kind of therapist, and his insights wouldn't amount to much. She remembered that when she had joined the group Matt had taken a Xerox of her driver's license for the file. She turned the pages. Found Wendy's.

Naomi Cotton. It had a date of birth, and an address.

Same address as the abandoned apartment.

Shit. She took a picture of it on her phone.

She looked through the rest of the file, disappointed, still hoping she might get something worthwhile.

Looked like Naomi had joined the group two weeks before Amanda. There was a phone number on the file, handwritten on the side, but it was the same number for the burner phone. The one that Naomi had no doubt discarded.

She had been hoping that Naomi's real name would be there. She was sure Naomi Cotton was a false name, and that this was a false ID. If it was, it was good. Very good.

She closed the file, put it back in the box, then slammed the trunk shut. By the time she got back to her table, Matt was already there. Her knee was burning with the effort. She put the keys in her coat pocket, took her seat and mouthed a thank-you to the guy in the suit.

'Everything okay?' asked Matt.

'Fine, sorry. I had to call my bank. Problems with my card. I haven't been working since . . .'

Matt nodded, said, 'Don't worry. This is on me.'

They talked little after that. Amanda making polite comments as Matt led the conversation to the healing properties of exercise, meditation and yoga. He paid the bill, stood up and grabbed his coat. Just as the coat moved, Amanda tossed his keys under the table.

Matt looked down, saw them and picked them up without question, probably thinking they'd just fallen out of his pocket. She thanked him, and he said he would get back to her once he'd got in touch with Wendy.

Amanda left the deli, headed for the subway and was glad to have some time to think.

She had come up short. But in some ways she knew more about Naomi now than before.

She knew Naomi was a false name. That she expected someone to try to trace her through the group. That she had only attended the sessions after Amanda had been sentenced to probation and assigned to that particular group. And Amanda knew Naomi was smart, maybe with money behind her to get a false ID that good, and she was careful. She also had the criminal contacts to get a false ID.

Naomi was perhaps more dangerous than Amanda had realized.

She turned the corner, headed downstairs into the Manhattan subway system. She liked to ride the trains sometimes. It helped her think. She swiped her MTA card, took the train for downtown, got on and found a seat.

As the doors closed, Amanda already knew her next move.

It was the only play she had left. The only question was whether there was still time.

Maybe Quinn was awake already? Maybe giving a description of Amanda to the cops right now? She had to find out the truth, before she wound up behind bars. She had to find out who Naomi was and why this had happened. She'd almost killed a man for her. Maybe a good man? Maybe an ex-husband? Maybe a loan shark? Maybe a blackmailer?

Maybe a relative?

The only thing Amanda knew for certain was that she had to know why she'd been manipulated into attacking the man Naomi called Quinn. She would need to tell a story in court. But, more than that, she wanted to know for herself. The thought that she might have attacked a totally innocent person made her feel sick. She had to know. For better or for worse.

She had to take this risk.

And it had to be done tonight.

32
Ruth

It took Scott an hour to calm down.

Ruth sat in the kitchen with him. He rocked back and forth on the kitchen floor, his arms wrapped round his frame. He had stopped crying now.

'How could I have done this?' he said. This was the third or fourth time he'd said it. And this time Ruth had to answer.

'You did the right thing,' she said.

He looked at her, the skin beneath his eyes red and puffy from the tears. He wanted to believe Ruth. He needed to. She could feel his desperation to draw some meaning, some justification from this terrible thing.

'The cops couldn't do anything. They would've let him go. He would've been free to kill more women. He was hunting us, Scott. What else was there to do? This was survival.'

He nodded. Sniffed. Let out a low moan.

'He tried to kill me. What you did was right. Never forget that.'

She helped him up and they held each other for a long time. Resting her chin on his shoulder, she was reminded of something long ago. Emotional touchstones in a life create powerful memories that can live large again with a smell, a word, or a feeling.

Ruth's mother had got stomach cancer in Ruth's senior year of high school. There had been a lot going on in that year, and Ruth had missed most of it. Her parents had divorced years before and her father had moved to Holland with his new wife. Ruth's mother, Beth, needed support and so Ruth accompanied her to the clinic for chemotherapy, for months. She sat up late, holding her mother's hair while she vomited into the toilet; wiped her mother's emaciated body with a cool cloth all night; made sure she got her meds; made light dinners and sometimes even spoon-fed her mom ice cream when she couldn't hold down anything else.

The morning of her senior prom, Ruth's mom tied a bright purple scarf round her head and drove them to the clinic. It was a big day for both of them. It had been a date marked in their calendar for a while, for two reasons – the prom, of course, and it happened to be the same day Beth's scan results were due. At the clinic, Ruth sat in a pine chair, covered in beige leather in an antiseptic hallway, swinging her legs and smiling at the nurses and patients who passed by. Her mom was in the consultation room, talking with the doctor. Ruth spent most of that half hour staring at the bell on the wall by the nurse's station. It was old. While everything in the hospital looked like new, this brass bell was covered in a dark layer of grime and dirt engrained into the brass. Discolored and out of place in the white-walled, white-tile hallway. A small hammer hung on a piece of string from the bracket holding the bell.

If her mom got bad news, Ruth had already decided that she couldn't leave her on her own that night. She would just miss the prom. Her mother was more important, and their time together now was precious.

Beth emerged from her oncologist's office. Ruth couldn't see her face yet. Couldn't gauge what the results were like because she couldn't yet read her expression. And then Beth turned, a blank look on her face. Ruth's grip on the armrests tightened. Beth didn't look at her, she just walked calmly toward the bell, took the hammer in her hand and smacked the dirt clean off the brass.

Rushing forward, Ruth took her mom in her arms, and they held one another while the bell pealed, and all the nurses, patients and doctors applauded and whooped. Cancer patients rang the bell when they got the *all clear*. It was the best sound Ruth had ever heard in her life, and the feeling she had then was indescribable. It wasn't just relief – it was love growing stronger, a blessed release from sickness and impending death. They held each other and cried with something more than joy.

As Ruth held Scott tightly in the kitchen of the little apartment in Hartford, she felt that extraordinary sense of elation and relief again. Only this time it was more powerful. She thought if she shut her eyes tightly enough, and listened, *really* listened, she might even hear a bell ringing softly in the distance. There would be no more long, dark days being haunted by a killer.

Ruth was in remission.

Cupping his face in her hands, she said, 'I know it's hard. But he brought this on himself. It was either him, or me. You did the right thing, so no more tears.'

He nodded, cleared his throat.

Ruth said, 'Why don't you make yourself some coffee? I'll go to the store and get us breakfast.'

He looked at her, astonished. And then his brows furrowed into doubt.

'Are you leaving me?'

'Don't be stupid. I'm going out on my own. Like I used to do. There's no reason to be afraid any more. You've given me my life back. I'm going to take it.'

33
Amanda

Three hours icing her knee gave her time to think.

Time to plan it all out.

She sat in front of the TV. Front door locked. Chair under the handle. Phone charging beside her.

There were various news bulletins mentioning the home invasion by the axe-wielding maniac, and press conferences on other violent crimes. And then, in the afternoon, they flashed up his picture.

It didn't give an occupation, just his age and his name.

Frank Quinn.

So that was his real name. But there was nothing about him online. She had checked.

The channel used a photo of Quinn that Amanda had not seen before in any of Naomi's fake online articles. He had brown hair. Strong, masculine features – a broad jaw, angular cheekbones. Gray-blue eyes.

Amanda needed more than that.

She would have to do it the hard way. That meant going out late. And in the full knowledge she might never come back. There was no other way to get the information she needed to trace Naomi. This man, Quinn, was her only link. She needed to get inside his house and learn everything she could about him.

Last chance to find Naomi.

And it had to be tonight, before the cops kicked down her door.

She put her pants back on, her knee feeling looser, and cooler. The ice had brought down the swelling from the morning's exertions. It still hurt like a son of a bitch, but nothing compared to the hurt Naomi would feel if Amanda ever got hold of her.

She ate little, dozed lightly and waited for dark.

She put on Doc Marten boots – black, of course – a dark hoody and a black leather jacket. Her hair was hidden under a beanie hat. In addition, she packed a small bag containing a flashlight, a flathead screwdriver with a long shaft, a pocketknife and a fresh pair of disposable latex gloves.

Riding the subway to Greenwich Village, she thought about the man who had tailed her last night. In the blinding light of Naomi's betrayal, she hadn't had time to think about him. Maybe he'd be waiting at her car, still parked a few blocks from Quinn's house? Maybe he'd spoken to the police? Maybe he'd told them that someone was in the area, acting suspiciously on the night of the murder and this was their car?

The more she thought about it, the more Amanda was convinced that the cops could be looking for her already. She had to find Naomi as fast as possible.

Her thoughts turned to tonight's job. She had been at the back of the property before. She knew what to expect, and she'd planned this. It wasn't going to be easy. But it had to be done. Her first twenty-four hours were up.

She left the subway station, walked to the street where she'd parked the night before. Her car was visible in the distance, no other vehicles around it. She looked for the dark-colored Escalade, and the big man who'd tailed her, but the street was quiet, the sidewalks clear as far as she could tell. Still, there were pools of darkness in between the streetlamps, and she tensed every time she had to step out of the light, her fingers locked around the pocketknife in her coat, anticipating a pair of big hands grabbing her from behind and dragging her deeper into the shadow – never to emerge again.

Still, she walked on, because she had no choice. On past the brownstone that belonged to Quinn, who now lay in a nearby hospital, still in a critical condition. No cops outside the property. The front door was covered in strips of blue-and-white NYPD crime-scene tape, and there was a notice pinned to the door – doubtless the notice prohibiting entry. The house looked to be in darkness. No lights on in any of the rooms facing the street. No sign of the Escalade.

She kept walking, performing a loop of the block. No cop cars anywhere. No cops on the street. There were some cars parked along both sides of the sidewalk like last night, but none of them were NYPD patrol cars, none were occupied and none were Escalades. She thought that neighbors might be on high alert, because of the attack last night, so she had to be even more careful than before. The pain in her knee was still there, but tolerable. If anything, those little jolts of dull pain that came with every step helped keep her alert.

Amanda turned the corner, walked to the alleyway that led to the back wall and yard of the brownstone. The same wall she had vaulted the previous night.

Except now she couldn't get down the alley.

It was sealed off with more police tape, crisscrossed along the entrance in such a way that there was no way to get past without ripping at least two or three strands.

She exhaled, turned round, checking the street. There were two people, two hundred yards further up, walking away with their backs turned to Amanda. She had come too far to turn back now. This was too important. No choice but to go on. She put on the gloves, took the pocketknife and cut the bottom strands of tape. Once they were loose, she crawled forward on her elbows, trying to save her injured knee. She stood on the other side of the police tape. There was no way to tape it back up. She hadn't brought anything with her. She just had to hope nobody noticed, or that if they did they'd think the tape had just come loose and no more.

It was a risk. A sign that all was not secure.

Her flashlight sent out a narrow beam. On and off. Just to make sure the dark alley was clear. That there was no one waiting in a dark recess to grab her as she walked past.

It was clear.

She made her way along, feeling one side of the wall with her fingers as she went. Then she reached the back wall she'd climbed over the night before. She gently pushed at the back gate. It had not been fitted with a new lock. It opened maybe six inches then hit something on the other side. It told her a lot. The fact that there had been an attack in the property twenty-four hours earlier and the lock on the back gate had not been repaired meant that there was no one else living in the house. If there had been, they would've bolted it shut for security.

Probably the cops had just placed something in front of the gate to stop it opening. That, and sealing off the alley was all they could do.

She pushed harder. The gate bowed at the top, which meant the obstruction was on the ground, low down at the bottom of the gate. She leaned up against the wood, then used her full weight, keeping the pressure coming from her good leg.

There was a grating sound. Metal against the concrete path. Not loud. But audible nonetheless. It was heavy going, but she soon had enough of a gap to slip through.

A garden bench on the path. That was it. She kept low and moved toward the house. There was no light coming from the rear windows.

She was surprised to find the house looked largely the same as when she'd left the night before. The tool shed door was still open, hanging on its hinges and swaying slightly in the gentle breeze. There was a dark stain, about the size of a small, circular kitchen table, on the grass. The rear window was still broken. A few shards remained in the yard beneath it. Amanda had thought the NYPD would at least have got someone to come out and replace the window or board it up.

Maybe that wasn't their problem.

She found herself looking back at the tool shed when she should've been concentrating on the house and possible points of entry.

There was something about the tool shed that stirred a lingering doubt in the back of her mind. She didn't know quite what it was. She thought maybe she had meant to do something in the tool shed, but she had forgotten . . .

Forgotten.

Amanda ran to the tool shed, peered inside.

The burner phone Naomi had given to her to lure Quinn into the shed. It was gone.

Amanda knew straight away she had forgotten to retrieve the phone before she'd left. Now the police had it.

She thought back to yesterday. As far as she could remember, she had not touched that phone without gloves. Naomi had given her the phones while still in their wrapping. It was a mistake to leave one behind. She still had the second burner phone in her apartment, in a bag with the clothes she'd worn last night. Soon as she got home, she had to dump that bag.

Amanda swore under her breath, shook her head. She needed to get her mind back on business. Otherwise she might make another mistake.

She tested the back door of the house and found it locked. There were four glass panels in the upper half of the painted wooden door. The smashed kitchen window was much too high for her to crawl through. It still had sharp edges of glass. Too noisy to break those pieces off to get inside. It was either try the door with the screwdriver or go home. She placed the flathead at the door jamb, just below the lock, and pushed and wriggled it, scraping the paint and the wood, trying to slip it between the door and the upright.

No luck. She would need a hammer and a chisel to get through it.

And it would be much too loud. She couldn't risk alerting the neighbors.

Amanda had never broken into a house before. She'd never imagined it would be this hard. She stood still for a few seconds, thinking through the problem. Gently got onto her knees, biting her lip as her left knee took her weight. She brought out her flashlight, cupped a hand over it, and held it close to the lock. She looked through and saw that the key was in the lock on the other side of the door.

She stood, killed the flashlight. Quinn had probably left the key in the door as he made his way outside last night. The cops, who had to make the property in some way secure, would more than likely have just closed this door, locked it and left the key in the lock.

If she could break the lower right pane of glass, she could reach in and unlock the door with the key.

But breaking it would alert the neighbors.

Amanda walked back to the tool shed, went inside, looked around. It was too dark to make things out clearly and she couldn't risk the flashlight.

Instead, she used her hands to feel around.

There was a stool beneath the workbench with a small cushion strapped onto it. With no time to waste, she cut away the straps with the pocketknife then found a roll of duct tape on a shelf.

Perfect.

Amanda returned to the back door. She put strips of duct tape on the pane, covering it. Then a single strip from the center, down tight over the frame, and extending to below the lock. Taking her time, she placed the cushion against the taped pane, and stabbed at it with the screwdriver, so that the head was jabbing at the edge of the glass, through the cushion. It sounded like ice being crushed in a cocktail shaker, but somehow muted, as if it was happening in another room close by. Not loud enough to be heard by any next-door neighbors unless they were in their own back yards.

Amanda pushed that thought away. Moved the cushion. Stabbed.

When she had manoeuvred the cushion all round the edges of the pane, she threw it back into the tool shed. Then, she pushed at the pane. It fell through onto the other side of the door, but the tape she'd placed across the center made sure it didn't fall to the floor. The broken glass was all still attached to the tape and remained in one piece. Careful to avoid the small shards surrounding the edge of the frame, she curled her arm through the door, and unlocked it.

The door opened. Soundlessly. No creaks. No alarms.

She was in.

Finally.

She gave herself ten minutes to search the property. She was looking for papers. ID. Mail. Credit-card statements. Anything that might give a clue to where she might find Naomi. She was certain Naomi had known Quinn – all that information she'd given Amanda about the layout of the back of the property. Either she'd been watching him for a long time, or she'd been in the house before.

No one wants a man dead like someone who knows him well.

Amanda didn't fully shut the door behind her in case she needed to make a quick exit. She moved fast through the home of her victim, her flashlight leading the way. She was careful not to let the beam hit the windows. The drapes were all closed, but she didn't know how thick they were and didn't want to advertise her presence.

Nothing of interest in any of the kitchen drawers. Some art on the walls, same as the living room. No photographs, though, nor any placed on the mantelpiece – no images of Quinn, nor his family nor loved ones. The dining room was a small office, with a laptop on the desk and a bookcase to match the one in the living room. No papers in the desk drawers, not even a notebook. The house was clean, minimal, with straight lines and white and black as a color palette.

Before she went upstairs, Amanda saw a console table in the hallway. She opened the drawer and hit paydirt.

Some utility bills and other assorted mail.

All in the name of Frank Quinn.

There were no pictures of him in the house. There was a thin veil of dust on the console table, but it had been disturbed. A thin line about eight inches long, with another smaller line behind it. Probably a picture frame. A picture of Quinn, she thought. More than likely the picture they'd used on TV.

Among the mail she found a birthday card. It was at the bottom of the pile and had once been white, but it had yellowed with age. The front image was a single lit birthday candle. She opened it to find more dust inside.

Happy birthday to the world's best son.
I love you so much, Frankie.
God bless,
Mom
X

She swallowed, noticed the sting of emotion welling up at the back of her throat. Quinn may have done many things to Naomi to make her plot his murder. Maybe he was an unfaithful lover? A crook who swindled her out of her money? Maybe even someone who physically hurt her or hurt or killed someone close to her? Or maybe he was an innocent, and Naomi wasn't acting out of vengeance but malice. At this moment, Amanda didn't know. She only knew Quinn was someone's son.

She knew there would be a price to pay for what she had done. Both emotional and legal. Who would believe she'd acted in self-defense when she had broken into the man's back yard and he'd found her holding his axe.

Amanda put the mail and the card back in the drawer, slowly pushed it shut. She closed her eyes, tried to reset, as if she was shutting her guilt away in that drawer to be dealt with later.

Right now, there was a job to be done.

There was nothing she could find on the internet about Frank Quinn. Not since the fake websites had been taken down. He certainly wasn't a teacher, and she could find no link between that name and a school, and, so far, nothing to reveal who this man really was, and the link between him and Naomi.

Amanda crept upstairs.

A single toothbrush in the bathroom.

There were three bedrooms, one of them empty apart from a spare double bed. The second bedroom was essentially a walk-in closet. Two wardrobes, a shoe locker and a chest of drawers. Just clothes: suits and shirts and a shelf of books.

The main bedroom had a double bed, and a nightstand. There were books piled up by the bed, mostly on history and some books on espionage and spy rings. Non-fiction. This sparked her curiosity briefly, but it wasn't relevant and she knew it.

The nightstand had a single drawer, quite deep. When she opened it, she found a metal lockbox inside. It was small, the kind of box an office might use to keep petty cash or important documents inside. It was painted gray, and the lock and construction of the box looked sturdy.

She picked up the keys on the nightstand, flicked through them until she found a small key that looked as though it might fit into the box. Amanda slotted the key into the lock . . . and then she heard a bang.

Something heavy, slamming. Then there were voices. And footsteps in the hallway.

The bang had come from the front door banging shut.

There were people downstairs in the house. She killed the flashlight.

Amanda held her breath, looked around the room. Under the bed. The only place she could hide. She got down on her knees, slowly, careful not to make any sound, and crawled beneath the bed, taking the lockbox with her.

34
Farrow

'What are we doing here? I thought we agreed this wasn't Mr. Blue-eyes,' said Hernandez, closing the front door to Quinn's property.

Farrow had gotten the keys from Statler and Waldorf. They didn't mind him taking another look around. Especially as the victim had yet to wake from the coma and identify a perp. Statler had told him he could even take the case for all they cared – one less unsolved on their pile was as good as a win.

'I know it's not our guy. But it's not a domestic, either,' said Farrow.

'Okay, since when is that our problem? Statler and Waldorf unloading a shitshow on us?'

'No, I haven't agreed to take it. Not yet.'

'Why would we take it? It's not like we don't have a full roster of cases. The lieutenant's not going to like this.'

'You leave her to me. Look, you know me by now.'

'That's exactly why we're having this conversation. We don't *need* another case.'

'If you were a relative of Quinn's, would you want the Muppets investigating this case?'

'That's the department's problem. Not ours, *Saint Jude*.'

Farrow leaned against the wall for a moment, found the light switch and flicked it on. For a second, both of them were blinded. In the Catholic Church Saint Jude was the patron saint of hopeless cases, and that's how Farrow earned his name, and a considerable reputation, because he closed cases that nobody else could, no matter how long it took. He took on cases from other cops when they'd hit a wall, and he cleared them.

'I'm not saying we take on every unsolved in Manhattan. You know that. But there are aspects of this case that don't make sense. Come on, admit it. And Statler and Waldorf don't care.'

'Not our problem, not our case,' she said.

'Come on, the locks are broken on the tool shed and the back gate. That's an intruder, not a domestic. This is the kind of shit—'

'*That will keep me up at night*,' said Hernandez, mimicking Farrow's voice.

Farrow stood, stretched his back, said, 'Am I that predictable?'

'I've heard that line before. Last year, in fact, with the ATM murder, and six months before that with the shooting in Central Park, and the year before that—'

'I get it. But we closed those cases, didn't we?'

'Okay, anything to help you get some shuteye,' she said sarcastically. 'Let's look around. But leave the case with Statler and Waldorf for now. Give them your notes. Maybe they'll change their approach?'

'And if they don't?'

'Then we'll work it. They'll be only too happy to hand it over.'

Together they went through the hallway to the living room, switched on the lights as they went. Farrow had at least been given a name for the victim – Frank Quinn. He was listed as the owner. There was a large flatscreen TV in the corner, some books arranged on a shelf and a single couch. Farrow followed Hernandez to the study, looked more closely at the bookcase as Hernandez went through the desk drawers.

'Nothing,' she said. 'This guy is a bit of a minimalist. A clean freak. What does he do for a living?'

'Statler couldn't find any family – no marriage or divorce records, no hits on birth certificates apart from Quinn's own, so he started searching for employee records. It says he's a self-employed consultant on his tax returns, and he's got a shit ton of money in the bank. No hint of what kind of consulting this guy does.'

'Whatever it is, it must pay well. This house is off the charts.'

They left the study and Hernandez checked the drawer of the console table in the hallway.

'Well, found some mail addressed to Frank Quinn. Nothing of interest,' she said, dropping the mail back in the drawer and closing it.

'Back yard again?' asked Hernandez.

Farrow cast his eyes up the stairs, sighed.

'Let's check upstairs first. Don't want to walk mud through the whole house. Check the bedrooms, then we'll hit the yard.'

35
Amanda

She heard the male voice in the hallway downstairs. He was discussing something with a female – something casual. Most of it she couldn't make out. A friendly argument, maybe.

'*Let's check upstairs first. Don't want to walk mud through the whole house. Check the bedrooms, then we'll hit the yard.*'

The male voice sounded familiar, but she couldn't quite place it.

She wondered who it might be, coming to a crime scene late at night. Her only guess would be the police – or a landlord maybe.

Heavy footsteps on the stairs made the small hairs at the back of her neck stand on end. They were coming up right now, a step near the top squeaking under their weight. The hallway light came on. The door to the master bedroom was open, but she couldn't see out into that hallway, just the triangle of light thrown onto the bedroom carpet.

More footsteps.

They were both upstairs now. She heard the creak of a door, a snap as a light came on, accompanied by the noise from a fan.

Bathroom. Had to be.

There was no conversation between the two of them now. The sound of a cabinet closing. Probably the bathroom cabinet. She'd noticed it when she'd stuck her head into the bathroom earlier, but hadn't bothered to check it once she'd seen the single toothbrush in the cup on the sink.

'He takes a lot of pills, this guy. Heavy-duty sleeping pills, by the looks of it,' the male voice said.

Now she knew where she had heard that baritone voice before. It was deep, and rich, but there was something soft in it. Something gentle.

Detective Farrow. Of course he was the one investigating this crime. That's why he was in the house.

Shit.

That meant they were searching the place. A feeling like a bucket of ice being thrown onto her back accompanied that thought. Amanda looked at the steel box in front of her. She had taken it with her when she'd crawled under the bed. The keys were still in it. She wondered then if she'd left the drawer of the nightstand open.

If she had, they would spend a bit of time in this room. They would look under the bed, Farrow and his partner. And Amanda would be out of time.

She thought about sliding out from under the bed, leveraging open the window and making a jump for it. This bedroom was at the front of the house. She was on the second floor. It would be a long drop to the hard sidewalk below. No way her injured knee could take it. It would just mean she would be arrested and charged with a busted knee.

She shut her eyes tightly, tried to think of a way out. No way to get into the hallway now without being noticed. She couldn't get to the stairs.

It was the window, or just stay where she was and pray.

Another creaking door. Another snap from a light switch. Closer now. They were in the guest bedroom. Not much in there.

Amanda let out her breath slowly, feeling her stomach tighten. She put her hands flat and placed her head down on the carpet. To the side. So she could see when someone came in. A thick layer of dust was now close to her nose and mouth. She wasn't unusually sensitive to dust, but there was a lot of it, and it brought a scratch to her throat. Pressing her lips tighter, she swallowed it down. If she coughed or sneezed now, it was all over.

A pair of large brown leather shoes came into the room. They were dirty from the street. Splashed here and there with muddy water. Farrow never looked as though he paid much attention to his dress, and she guessed he cleaned his shoes when he could no longer see the leather. The bed covers hung a little over the mattress, leaving her a gap of maybe eight inches from which to watch those inquisitive shoes.

Those shoes stood still for a time, sinking deep into the carpet. Farrow was a large man.

Then they turned and made their way to the nightstand.

Suddenly she was hyper aware of her entire body. Her legs, curled up and motionless, began to ache with the need to move. She knew she was imagining it, but the dull throb in her knee was not a product of her imagination. It was hurting, and there was nothing she could do but take the pain.

Don't move.

Don't breathe.

Take the pain.

She heard the soft brush of varnished wood on wood. He was either opening the drawer or closing it.

Those shoes didn't move. He was thinking.

She imagined the lockbox calling out to Farrow, whispering its location. Begging him to get down and look under the bed.

Her chest began to hurt. Holding her breath was not going to work. Slowly, she released the air from her lungs and started to breathe as lightly as possible. She could feel the pressure building with each shallow breath that brought her body off the floor, and brought it back down as she exhaled. She knew she was trembling, and her breath sounded like a bellows. She opened her mouth, hoping it would make the sound softer.

The shoes turned.

Farrow's feet pointed straight at her.

This was it.

He was going to bend down, lift the covers and peer under the bed. Every cop would look under a bed, wouldn't they?

She saw the leg of his blue suit pants riding up, his heels lifting from the ground as he crouched. The rattle of his bottle of painkillers in his coat pocket.

Amanda held her breath.

Four large fingers appeared, taking hold of the bottom of the bedsheets.

36

Farrow

'Hey, come look at this,' said Hernandez from the other room.

Farrow let go of the bedsheets, straightening up with a groan.

His pills were calling to him.

But not yet. He needed to think.

He gazed once again at the half-open drawer of the nightstand. There was nothing in the drawer. No reason to believe whatever had been in the drawer was of any significance. It was just that it hadn't been closed fully, and the rest of the house was so neat.

From the décor – charcoals, grays and blacks laid over a palette of white walls – it didn't much look like a woman lived in the property. Everything felt masculine. Even the dark, abstract paintings on the walls.

'What've you got?' said Farrow, coming out of the master bedroom.

Hernandez was in the adjacent bedroom.

'Check this out,' she said, pointing to another bookcase.

Farrow scanned the books. A lot of them were on counter espionage, biographies of ex-CIA and KGB agents, and how-to manuals on spy tradecraft and cyber warfare.

'There was a stack of books like that on the nightstand. You think this cat is up to no good?' asked Farrow.

'I don't know. Maybe he just gets off on that stuff?'

'Maybe,' said Farrow.

'There's nothing up here. Want to take another look out back? Or are we done?'

Farrow sighed, looked at the books again and took one off the shelf. It was supposedly written by an anonymous former member of the British secret service. The index to the book went through the various stages of identity theft, how to avoid it and how to do it.

'Maybe he's a crook? If he doesn't wake up soon, we should get someone out here to take a look at his computer,' said Farrow.

'There's no way a woman lives here. Maybe the guy has a girl-friend, but they don't live together. I agree we don't have a domestic. I don't know what it is. Could be he's a bad guy and this is a hit?'

'I don't know. Doesn't feel like a professional job. Hitmen don't kill victims with their own axe.'

Farrow shut the book, put it back on the shelf, said, 'Let's take one more look downstairs then get out of here. Kitchen first. Then the back yard.'

37

Amanda

She listened with tears in her eyes, as Farrow and his partner made their way downstairs and into the kitchen.

The breath leaving her body felt like a premature release. She inched forward, dragging her body with her arms and pushing with one leg.

She still had to get out before they noticed the back door had been broken again. She turned the key in the lock of the metal box until the lid popped gently open. Then she pushed it in front of her, clear of the bed and crawled out. Opened the lid.

Inside were five fat rolls of cash, each of them the same thickness as a soda can. She gasped when she saw that much money. She took one of the rolls, without thinking, and put it in the pocket of her coat. Then two more rolls. That left two behind. She didn't think this guy would need it. He had a big house, and he must've been rich to pay for it. He wouldn't miss this. She would need cash, because now that she'd come up empty-handed from her little midnight excursion she had nothing else to do but run. Leave her apartment, leave the city behind and just take off. Plus, who has rolls of cash in a lockbox? Maybe Quinn was a crook like Farrow had said?

Someone who might one day need this cash to go on the run

himself, or maybe it was just a little something Quinn was hiding from his tax return? Either way, she needed it now.

They would catch her eventually. She knew they would. Farrow was a smart guy, even if he didn't have time to shine his shoes.

Her knee screamed as she stood. She'd need a couple of steps to loosen it up.

Tiptoeing, she made her way to the top of the stairs.

These stairs creaked. At least one of them did. She'd heard it, when Farrow and Hernandez were coming up. Her heart was beating so hard and so fast she could feel it pounding in her ears.

It wouldn't take them long to search the kitchen. If they even bothered. They might go straight to the back yard. They'd see the broken pane. They'd know she had been, or was still in the house.

Which stair had creaked? She stared at them now, breathlessly.

No way to tell from looking at them. She couldn't remember. And she had no time to waste. Amanda threw her right leg over the banister and took hold of it in her gloved hands. Slowly, quietly, she slid down. As she got halfway, she caught a glimpse of Farrow, in his big black overcoat, going towards the back door. She got off the rail, tiptoed to the front door and took hold of the lock.

Started to turn it.

38

Farrow

Hernandez stood at the back door, staring at it. It took Farrow a moment to realize what she was looking at, then he saw the door was open an inch.

'Did Statler and Waldorf leave this door open?' he asked.

Hernandez beckoned for him to come closer, shaking her head.

One of the windowpanes, just above the lock, was missing. Although, not altogether missing. It was still largely intact, broken, yes, but held together with black duct tape and hanging down from the pane on another piece of tape.

Farrow exchanged a look with Hernandez, and they drew their weapons in tandem. Hernandez was first out of the back door, low, checking the corners of the yard. Farrow followed, watching her back, then they both approached the tool shed. One from one side, Farrow keeping an eye on the other.

No one in the back garden.

'The house – did we miss anything?' she asked.

Farrow's eyes fell. They roamed over his feet as he thought through his movements upstairs.

'Did we check under the beds?'

'Shit,' said Hernandez.

Farrow was already moving. He got to the kitchen first, lumbering through it, heavy-footed, his back protesting at the speed, gun raised, ready to aim and fire if need be. Through the hallway, up the stairs, his Glock trained overhead, watching the rail for any sign of a head or a weapon peeking over it, ignoring the strain caused by the movement.

Farrow covered her as Hernandez fell to her knees in the guest bedroom, looked under the bed. No one and nothing below it.

Master bedroom.

Same.

Except, there was a metal box. Like a document locker, on the other side of the bed. It was open, and a set of keys lay beside it. Farrow hadn't come around this side of the bed, nearest the window, so he couldn't be sure if it had been there minutes ago, or not.

He opened the lid and saw two thick rolls of cash bound tightly with an elastic band. The top bill was a fifty. Must have been thousands of dollars in each roll.

'Fuck, was that there before?' asked Hernandez.

'Maybe. If someone broke in to loot the place, why not take this? It's the jackpot. Unless they missed it too.'

He moved to the window, pulled the drapes, looked out on the street.

There was a single figure in the distance. Walking away. A quick pace. A female, he guessed, by their size and the way they walked.

She was limping. Yet, judging by the way she was moving, she had to get somewhere – or get away – fast.

'Woman on the street, limping away. Let's move!' said Farrow.

39

Amanda

Every step was agony.

Being wedged under that bed had sent her knee into spasm. Now that she had to move quickly, she was really feeling it. And yet she'd got out of that house. She wondered how much longer her luck could hold. She was extremely fortunate not to be in handcuffs.

She was almost at the end of the block. Another block to go before she reached her car.

'Hey, you! Stop! Police!'

The voice crying out behind her forced her to turn.

Farrow's partner, Hernandez, was sprinting toward her. Farrow came out of the front door after her. He moved with speed, but stiffly, as if there was a board strapped to one of his legs.

A hundred yards between Hernandez and her. And closing fast.

Amanda had the hood of her sweatshirt pulled up, and it was too far away for her to be recognized. She swung round and ran.

The pain was unbelievable, as if with every step on that bad knee a hot bolt was being driven into her flesh. She cried out with each step. But still she moved.

It wasn't a run, not really. A shambling, mechanical lurch, and then another one, and another.

And then her knee buckled, Amanda sprawled out on the

sidewalk. She got her good leg beneath her and fired up into a standing position.

Hernandez was fifty feet away.

She wasn't going to make it back to her car.

A black Escalade pulled up at the curb beside her. She took all her weight on one leg. She couldn't even put the other foot on the ground.

The passenger door of the Escalade opened.

A big man wearing a blue jacket and a white shirt sat behind the wheel. The same man who'd been watching the house last night. The same man who'd followed her to the subway.

'You just came from Frank Quinn's house. We're looking for the same woman. I can help you – get in quickly!'

Amanda's jaw fell open. The man had his hand out, beckoning her into the car.

'Hurry!' he said.

Hernandez was closing. Thirty feet. Farrow was behind her with his own faltering, staggering jog.

Who the hell was this guy?

'Get inside now!' he said.

No choice. Get into the car with this stranger or go to jail for attempted murder.

Amanda hopped to the car, gritting her teeth against the pain, then threw herself into the passenger seat and closed the door.

The engine roared as the man hit the gas.

She turned to look at him, but he was ignoring her. Watching the traffic, making sure he didn't crash into another vehicle as he made the turn at the intersection and then floored the accelerator.

'Who are you?' she said.

'My name is Billy Cameron. You're safe. It's okay. Let me get us out of here and I'll explain everything.'

40

Farrow

He saw an SUV stop beside the limping figure. He couldn't see much more than the roof of the vehicle because of the line of parked cars along the street, with only a few spaces in between them.

Farrow had already slowed to a fast walk; his back was going into meltdown. Hernandez clocked the vehicle too, and somehow put on a spurt. She didn't make it. At one moment, he thought she would, because at first the hooded limping woman didn't get into the car. She seemed to stall. Undecided.

Then she leapt inside, and the vehicle took off. Hernandez slowed down, stopped, bent over and put her hands on her knees to catch her breath. She stayed that way for a few seconds, then straightened up and walked back down the street toward Farrow.

'Did you get a license plate?' he asked.

Hernandez was still out of breath; she just shook her head.

'You think that was the person who broke in?' he asked.

'Maybe,' was all she could manage.

'Did you see the way she hesitated when the car pulled up? That wasn't a getaway car. She thought about it before she got in.'

'Farrow, let's hand this back to Statler and Waldorf. They're probably right. This was a domestic, and I'm guessing that was the perp.'

Farrow gazed down the street.

'I told you it's still their case. But this isn't a domestic. Say that *was* the perp. Why did she come back? It's not like it's full of her clothes or anything. There was still a lot of money in that lockbox, so it's not a robbery. Why come back to a crime scene? What the hell was she looking for?'

41

Ruth

Closing the front door behind her, Ruth clipped down the steps of the perfect six, and stood on the path. A chicken-wire fence spread around the building. It was old and had collapsed in parts, as if a giant had sat on it. She went through the opening. The park was in front of her. To the left, a long street. To the right, the street ended not far up. There were traffic lights and more cars that way. She took a moment to admire the park.

Lush green fields, willow and elm trees, a riot of birdsong in the early winter sunshine.

The apartments and houses on this street were in various stages of decay. Old couches and mattresses lay outside some of them, and the trash bags were piled high out front of every building. Ruth ignored the houses, focused on the park. She could smell the grass from across the street. This was her first time in Hartford, and her first morning of what felt like a new life. A light wind blew her brown hair across her cheek, and she felt a chill on her shoulder. Her top was still wet with Scott's tears.

Her phone buzzed in her pocket.

A text from Scott. And a missed call from him. She hadn't felt the vibration from that call. Too occupied with admiring the view. Drinking in the outside world, with no fear for the first time in forever.

Are you ok?

She texted back.

I'm fine.

She got a quick reply.

Please get me the newspapers. Nothing local. New York Post, the Times.

With each step she felt more confident. It was a beautiful morning and life felt full of possibilities. Good ones.

At the crossing, Ruth turned right and soon found herself in a small shopping district. A lot of the stores had signs written in Spanish. There were a few restaurants – seafood, tapas and one Italian. Cell-phone stores, dry cleaners, diners, fresh-fruit stalls.

The first supermarket she saw she went inside, took a basket and filled it with breakfast pastries, some cereal, eggs, milk and coffee. There was a magazine rack in the area just before the register, and a selection of newspapers laid out beneath them. She took a copy of the *Post*, and the *Times*. Had a quick skim through them, but found no mention of Travers. Maybe they would carry the story in a later edition, or the next day, surely. There was a long line at the registers. Always the same the day before Thanksgiving.

Today was Wednesday, the twenty-first of November. The night of the incident, as Detective Farrow called it, was September fourteenth. Over two months now since the attack. Had it really been that long?

The date of the attack no longer held such a place of fear and dread in her mind, nor in her heart.

Perhaps, with greater distance, September fourteenth might just be another day. It was over, thanks to Scott.

While she stood in line, she kept her head up, back straight, shoulders relaxed. The mere act of standing up, unafraid to meet the gaze of other shoppers, well, it was something special. The clerk at the register was a middle-aged man with graying hair. When it came to Ruth's turn, she put her items on the counter. He smiled at her.

She smiled back, couldn't help it.

'It's gonna be a beautiful day out there,' he said.

'You know what? It's already a beautiful day,' said Ruth.

She paid cash and left with her bag of groceries.

Stepping out into the late morning sun, Ruth felt like she had passed some milestone. She felt normal.

Smiling to herself, she realized the importance of that statement. Before the attack, she hadn't known how truly lucky she'd been. All the arguments, the petty little squabbles with Scott – none of that meant anything any more. The future had been altered. Doc Mosley had said she probably wouldn't be able to conceive again, naturally. She hadn't explored that further. Hadn't thought about it.

Passing a group of men on the sidewalk, she caught one of them checking her out. Yesterday that would have caused Ruth to shut down in panic. Today, she smiled back at the young man, and walked on, shopping in one hand, the other arm swinging by her side. Raising her chin to the blue sky, she took a long breath. A smile burst on her lips.

Just up ahead she saw a young woman with her son. A little boy of four or five. They were at a food stand. The woman counted out her dollars and gave them to the vendor, who wrapped a doughnut in a napkin, handed it to the kid.

Ruth knew what she wanted. There was a way to fix things. There were possibilities now. She would investigate IVF, or some other kind of treatment. Get a specialist opinion. And if none of it worked they could always adopt.

There was still a chance for a good life. And this time Ruth knew in her heart she would appreciate every damn second of it. She had been given a reprieve. Released from her prison of fear. And all thanks to the man she loved.

There was a Starbucks up ahead with its door open. As she passed, she smelled the coffee. It might be nice to walk back to the apartment while sipping a coffee. She stopped, went inside. There wasn't much of a line, but there seemed to be a lot of people scattered around the serving area, just waiting. The servers were slow. She ordered a drink and moved along to the end of the counter, then stood to one side with her back against the wall. The man who ordered after her came and stood beside her.

Just an ordinary guy. Waiting for his coffee.

No problem standing beside him. No fear. Ruth felt tears welling.

'Grande skinny latte for Ruth?' said a voice.

She took the coffee, thanked the barista, and quickly left the store. The coffee tasted good as she walked back to the apartment, passing men, women and children on the street. No panic attacks. The wind in her hair and on her skin was exquisite.

That latte was the best she'd ever tasted.

She got back to the apartment with a lightness in her step. Something like her old self. She closed the apartment door quietly, moved through the lounge to the kitchen.

The TV was still on, but there was no Scott. She thought he might be in the bathroom. Ruth put the grocery bag on the kitchen counter and listened to the toilet flush down the hallway. The bathroom door opened, and she heard Scott's footsteps on the solid wood floor as he moved through the living room, toward the kitchen.

A news report on New York was playing out. A man had been attacked in his own home last night, and there had been a number of stabbings, but then they moved on to the main story.

A banner headline ran across the bottom of the screen.

PATRICK TRAVERS MURDERED IN NY HOTEL ROOM.

Scott came in, his hair still wet from the shower and wearing fresh clothes. The channel flashed up a picture of Patrick Travers, and all the oxygen left Ruth's body. Seeing his face chilled her flesh. And yet it didn't have the same power. He was dead, and he could never hurt her again.

The news anchor began to read more on the story.

'We can confirm that the individual found murdered in his room at the Paramount Hotel last night has been identified as Patrick Travers.

The forty-three-year-old was the close campaign advisor to Mayor Anthony Toscano. We understand the mayor's office is preparing a statement and we'll bring that to you when we have it. Police are treating the incident as a homicide, and they've issued an appeal for witnesses. Anyone who was in the hotel last night who might have seen something should contact NYPD immediately. The news of Mr. Travers's murder is the latest in a long line of incidents that have plagued Anthony Toscano's re-election bid. Viewers may recall that two weeks ago The New York Times *revealed that Mayor Toscano was under investigation for awarding lucrative city contracts to businesses allegedly linked to organized crime, and, in particular, businesses owned wholly or partially by Jimmy 'the Hat' Fellini. Following* The New York Times *piece, Mayor Toscano issued a statement denying any personal relationship with the Fellini family. A few days after that statement of denial, these pictures emerged on social media . . .'*

The screen changed. The anchor was replaced by a photograph of three men at a beach bar. Each holding a drink, they were wearing tees and shorts. Two of them wore necklaces of flowers. One of them was Travers. More photos. The same three men, at night under a palm tree, the ocean behind them.

The image shifted back to the news anchor, with an over-the-shoulder-image in the corner of the screen, Patrick Travers, arm in arm with the mayor and another man. This time they were on the beach.

'These images were taken at an exclusive resort in Hawaii where Patrick Travers, Mayor Toscano and Jimmy Fellini were pictured socializing together . . .'

Scott said, 'The police will think Travers's murder was a mob hit. They won't come looking for us. Jesus, it's going to be all right, Ruth. Everything is going to be okay.'

The news anchor continued.

'The mayor issued the denial on November eighth of this year, saying he had no relationship with Fellini, but these pictures, which emerged

subsequently, contradict that statement. The photographs, which we have authenticated, clearly depict Mr. Fellini entertaining the mayor and Mr. Travers at a private resort during their week-long stay, this last picture taken the night before Mr. Travers and Mayor Toscano flew home from Hawaii on September fifteenth of this year . . .'

Ruth's coffee cup slipped through her fingers, hit the floor and splashed all over her shoes.

When she had been attacked in her home on September fourteenth, Travers was not in New York. He was in Hawaii with the mayor and a mob boss.

She'd pointed out the wrong man. Scott had murdered an *innocent* man.

Ruth felt Scott's strong hands taking hold of her arms.

42
Scott

He spun Ruth around, his guts churning, a hollow feeling in his chest, as if he'd been punched hard in the solar plexus, and he couldn't breathe.

There was fear and shock in her eyes.

He could feel her body trembling beneath his fingers. Tears already forming over her eyes. Her mouth opened, but no words came. Then, as if something was bubbling up inside her, something she couldn't control, something toxic, he let go and took a step back.

Not fast enough. She pushed him away, hard, as she bent double from a scream rushing out of her. The scream was a single word that emerged with such violence that he covered his ears. It was a sound he never wanted to hear again. Within it was loss, yearning and pain. Her gaze fluttered around the room fearfully. Scott knew she could no longer see him. Her mind had gone elsewhere and still she screamed . . .

'*Noooooooooooo!*'

'Ruth, Ruth, stop it!' he cried.

As the last echoes of her cry died on the walls, she reared up. Her eyes were wild, filled with terror.

He moved toward her, grabbed her, and held her as tightly as he could as she wailed into his chest.

And Scott felt the full force of what he'd done hit him anew. He hadn't killed a murderer. He hadn't killed a predator. It wasn't going to save Ruth's life. It was all for nothing. He had killed the wrong man.

His arms locked around Ruth, his fists balled into hammers, his jaw starting to ache from gritting his teeth together. He thought he could feel the anguish flooding back into his wife. She was shaking her head, holding him, willing it not to come. For a moment that morning, he'd watched her shed her anxiety, and go out, unafraid. She was becoming the woman he'd married again, but now it was all gone.

And, as much as he wanted to comfort her, he felt his anger rising. Not at Ruth, not exactly. But at himself.

He released her, suddenly, turned and began to hammer his fists into the kitchen cabinets. Lefts and rights. One of the cabinet doors broke in two, cutting him, and that felt good. The pain felt good. He deserved it, welcomed it, and started hitting them harder.

He threw another punch, slamming his bloody knuckles into the side of the cabinet. Panting and bleeding, he suddenly bent over, retching. He stood at the sink and vomited. Ran the faucet. Splashed water on his face and tried to catch his breath, both hands on either side of the basin in case another wave of nausea came. He thought of the corpse he'd left behind, the neck of the broken bottle buried in his face. That was an image that would stay with him like a scar, but he felt sure it would stay red and raw, and never fade.

'You told me it was him,' said Scott.

When Ruth spoke again, her voice was soft and low, 'I thought it was. I was sure. It looked almost exactly like him.'

'Almost?' he said, turning toward her.

'It was him. In my mind, it was him.'

'Jesus, Ruth,' he said.

'Look, he was probably a bad guy anyway. You saw the news. You did the right thing.'

'What? How can you say that?'

'Because when I thought he was dead, God almighty, I felt *good*. Going out this morning was like the best thing to ever happen to me. I wasn't afraid any more. Do you know what it's like being terrified all the time? It's killing me, Scott. The fear is literally killing me. And believing he was dead gave me a new life. And now it's gone. And the fear is back. Stronger than ever . . .'

The TV was still on, although both had ignored it for a time. The show cut away from a story on the Middle East to reveal some men in police uniform at a podium.

'We're interrupting that story to bring you live now to the NYPD press briefing on the murder of Patrick Travers. We understand the police have identified a suspect . . .'

43

Amanda

The man who'd introduced himself as Billy threw the wheel to the right round another corner, and took them onto 2nd Avenue.

'Are you all right?' he asked.

Amanda's chest was heaving. She didn't know what the hell was going on, and she wasn't sure she wanted to. Whatever happened, she was on her guard. The man glanced at her, then turned his eyes back to the road.

'It's okay. I don't think the cops are following us,' he said.

Her mind was so full of questions she didn't know where to start.

'Who are you?' she asked.

'My name is Billy, like I said. You're safe. I'm a friend. You don't know it yet, but I'm exactly like you. I'm looking for someone. Someone who tried to trick me. A woman. Blonde hair, skinny. Five six, maybe five seven. Late forties, early fifties. Smokes like the Marlboro Man and drinks too much. That sound like the person you're looking for?'

Amanda tried to swallow, felt a burning in her throat. A bead of sweat curled over her dry lips and burned like salt in a cut. She was still breathing hard, and she realized she had squished herself against the passenger door, staying as far away from the driver as she could. She didn't know who this man was, and she didn't want to get too close.

'I take it that's a *yes*,' he said.

'Are you a cop?' she asked.

'Do I look like a cop?' he asked, with a smile.

The smile seemed genuine. Amanda took a moment to look him over. He wore a blue sports coat, blue jeans and a button-down white shirt. He had a pinkie ring on his little finger. Gold, bright, but not ostentatious. His skin was lightly tanned, his teeth white and clean. He smelled good. He wore his brown hair short, gelled to make it look a little messy. Amanda thought he looked quite handsome for an older man, but not in roguish way. Not the kind of guy she would go for. Billy had soft brown eyes, and there was a kindness in them. The car was clean and an expensive high-spec model. It had a leather interior and smelled as if it had just rolled out of the showroom that day. Billy looked like a rich New Yorker who'd just dropped out of the sky to help her. In a way, he did kind of look like a cop – certainly his posture. Upright. Back straight. Not slouched behind the wheel with one wrist flopped on top. He held the wheel two-handed – at two o'clock and ten o'clock – like a driving instructor.

'Cops don't dress like you,' she said.

'I guess not. I'm a retired captain. United States Marine Corps. I'm looking for a woman I met online. The same one you're looking for, I'm guessing.'

Amanda sat up, shook her head. As she moved, she felt the bark of pain from her knee and winced.

'You need to get that knee looked at,' he said.

'Never mind about my knee. I need to know what the fuck is going on.'

She felt in her coat pocket, put her hand round the knife.

'The woman you're looking for lied to you. You trusted her and she betrayed you. And now you want answers. Well, we have a lot in common. I say we go find a diner. Somewhere crowded. Nice and public. Some place you feel safe. Then we'll talk. You don't know me and you've no reason to trust me. I get that. I know this is all super weird right now. Same for me, but I need to find this woman before she hurts someone else.'

Billy said no more. He hit the power button on the console in the center of the dash, bringing the radio to life. Amanda held the knife tight, her eyes never leaving Billy.

They drove on, just the sound of the stereo in the car, the volume low. A country-and-western song.

Amanda got her breathing under control, but kept a firm grip on the knife as Billy pulled up outside a diner on Second Avenue and 51st Street.

44
Ruth

There was a press conference starting on TV. Three cops. All male. Two detectives that neither Ruth nor Scott recognized. The third cop was in uniform. They were on a stage, with a table in front of them, facing the crowd. There were three chairs set at the table, and three microphones. One of the detectives stayed to the left of stage. The uniform and the other detective, a small man in a beige suit, took a seat at the table, each of them in front of a mic. The cop who stayed on his feet ushered a young woman to the table. She sat in the middle. A brunette with a haunted look. The cameras at the press conference flashed all over her. The skin below her eyes was red and swollen. She hung her head, shielding her face with her hair, trying to keep the cameras from blinding her.

The uniform began speaking.

'*Thank you for attending, ladies and gentlemen. Another senseless murder in our city and we need the help of all New Yorkers and anyone who was staying at the Paramount Hotel last night to come forward and speak to our officers. We are setting up a toll-free number dedicated to gathering as much information as we can to help solve this crime. My colleague from the press corps will give out that number at the end of this press conference. I'm joined on my right by Detective John Starkey, and on my left is Michelle Travers, Patrick's widow, who wants to send out a personal appeal for witnesses in this case. First, Detective Starkey will explain where we are so far in this developing investigation. John . . .'*

Starkey cleared his throat, leaned forward and spoke into the microphone.

'Thank you, Captain Roberts. Holidays can be a tough time for families, and there's one family that won't have a son and a husband at the Thanksgiving table tomorrow. This is a heinous crime, and we will catch the perpetrators. We can tell you that at approximately ten thirty last evening we were contacted by staff at the Paramount Hotel. A maid noticed a substance, a chemical of some kind, leaking from under the door to a guest's room. She knocked, got no answer, entered the room and discovered a body on the floor, covered in what smelled like bleach. She quickly realized the person was deceased. We can tell you that the victim in this case was Mr. Patrick Travers. A forty-three-year-old adviser to the mayor's office.'

The murder rate in New York is nothing compared to what it used to be, but most weeks there will be some shootings, stabbings, robberies, something that will result in the loss of life. The victims don't ordinarily get a press conference. But if you knock off someone from the Mayor's office you can expect the full force of the law marshalled and sent in your direction with all speed.

'Fuck,' said Scott, running his hands through his hair. He then linked his fingers together behind his neck, let his elbows fall together and cursed some more.

Ruth turned back to the TV.

The detective spoke in a throaty, hoarse voice – a voice that was no stranger to hard liquor and long cold nights.

'We do have some security-camera footage from last night, and we are keen to speak to this man. If you recognize him, or know who he is, please call the precinct or use the toll-free number, which we will give out at the conclusion of this briefing . . .'

The screen changed, and Scott moved towards it.

Footage from a security camera showed a hallway in the hotel with a man in the frame. It was Scott. But only from the back. The other image that flashed up was from the front, but he was looking away and his face wasn't visible to the camera.

Ruth would know her husband anywhere, but she wondered if anyone else might be able to ID Scott from this footage. Probably not, she thought.

'*If you recognize this individual, please contact NYPD immediately. This is our main suspect. All avenues of inquiry remain open, including possible links to organized crime. Now I'd like to ask Michelle to say a few words,*' said the detective.

The camera shifted, pulled in close to the grieving partner. She kept her head low, her hair covering most of her face. Only her eyes seemed visible. She had that look of a life derailed. Grief is an injury. Ruth knew that look.

'*Someone took my partner away last night. This is the toughest day of my life. I want whoever did this brought to justice. Patrick worked every day for this city. And now . . . now he's gone. Please help bring his killer to justice.*'

She spoke, despite the obvious strain in her voice, with a quiet dignity.

The camera zoomed in further, tracing every line on Michelle's face – the tracks of tears through her make-up, the puffiness around her eyes, the quivering strand of hair that hung in front of her face.

It was a stunt, a deliberate and callous one to gain sympathy for Travers. To get people to react and co-operate with the investigation. It hurt the woman to talk about her husband.

Ruth shook her head.

'They want us to feel sorry for her,' she said.

Scott threw Ruth a questioning look.

'I don't feel anything for her,' said Ruth. 'Is that wrong? I just don't. Now she knows what it feels like. Now she knows how I feel. Now she knows how the pain tastes . . .'

'What are you talking about? I killed this poor woman's husband. He wasn't the one who attacked you . . .'

'It doesn't matter,' said Ruth through a snarl. 'They should all suffer. Why should I have to go through this? Why me?'

Scott's mouth fell open.

'When we thought he was the prowler, you were relieved he was dead so that he couldn't hurt you again, so he couldn't hurt anyone else—' But he didn't get to finish the thought.

'Maybe,' she said, cutting him off. 'Maybe I wanted him to hurt the same way I do? Him and his family. That's fair.'

'But he's not the one who hurt you, Ruth. Don't you see that?'

A headache began at the back of her neck, spreading up, over her skull. She wanted the man who hurt her dead. That's all she wanted. And she didn't care about anything else. And if Scott had made a mistake and killed the wrong man – so what. Life is pain, and fear, and she wanted everyone to know what it felt like to be her, because otherwise it just wasn't fair. That was part of it. Maybe a big part. It helped. And in the knowledge of others suffering just as she suffered she didn't feel as afraid as before.

Scott shook his head, and they both looked back at the screen.

'*Thank you, Michelle,*' said Starkey. '*I will now hand you over to Dan Puccini, from media relations, who will give you that number and all the contact details for the precinct. He will answer any questions you have at this time. Thank you.*'

Starkey and Michelle got up, the detective holding her arm as they left the stage. Her loss looked heavy on her. Ruth couldn't take her eyes off the new widow. It was almost as if she was looking into a mirror. She saw her own pain in that woman, and somehow, for reasons she couldn't understand, Ruth felt better. It was almost as if Ruth's pain was a large, obsidian stone, dark and alien, that she carried around, inside. And seeing someone else with her pain, and the knowledge that Ruth had in some way played a part in that, made the sinister stone in Ruth's chest shrink. Like she had passed some of the poison from her system on to someone else.

A hot cramp splashed over the right side of her head and remained there for a few seconds. She often got these flashes, rippling across her skull. The beginnings of a migraine, she thought.

Another policeman stepped to the lectern. He wore a suit. NYPD media manager. Dan Puccini. Tall, with dark hair, a strong cut to his jawline, as if it had been chiseled out of a rock face.

Blue eyes.

Ruth moved forward to get a better look. Her eyes widened. Her body stiffened. That black stone in her chest swelled, the blood rushed to the surface of her skin and a searing flash broke over her head again, as if someone had set her brain on fire. And in that moment she saw him. The monster. His face staring at her. Reflected in a shard of broken glass in her kitchen door. It was fleeting. But it was there. Like a light burned into her retina, so that she saw him with her eyes open, and with them closed.

Dan Puccini looked up from the lectern, and the camera swooped tight to his face. His eyes locked on to Ruth's and she saw his lips move soundlessly, mouthing those words.

'*Hello, sweetheart . . .*'

She raised a hand, shot her finger at the screen and forced her voice through the pain to say, 'That's *him*.'

45
Amanda

Amanda walked into the diner first. Billy held the door open. She still had her fist round the little knife in her pocket. She had no clue who this man was, and until she was satisfied she would be ready to plant this thing in his neck. Public place or not.

They found a booth by the window and sat across from each other. The diner was a piece of retro Americana. Easy-clean red vinyl seats and high-gloss tables with ribbed chrome edging and a long counter with fixed, tall stools spaced out around it. The kind of place tourists like, and New Yorkers loathe.

Billy carried a small laptop with him, which he put on the seat beside him.

The waiter took an order for herbal tea for Billy – chamomile. Amanda ordered a glass of water and cup of coffee. The place was lined with booths, and a local radio station played rockabilly over their heads. There were enough people around to make a low-volume conversation pretty much private. Or as private as any conversation could be in the heart of Manhattan.

The waiter brought Amanda's coffee and water for both of them. It took another minute before he returned with Billy's tea. In that time, they said nothing. Billy stared out of the window, keenly alert whenever he heard a siren. In this town, on Thanksgiving Eve, people were partying, which meant a lot more sirens than usual. He also took the time to look around the diner. Giving every customer the once-over. Making sure they were sufficiently far away, or at least otherwise engaged, so he could talk safely.

Amanda poured sugar into her cup. She had given it up before Jess was born, but every now and again she needed a hit. Especially when the coffee had been sitting in a bun flask long enough to grow a skin. She didn't want to be here. Her thoughts flitted to her car, still parked a few blocks from Quinn's house, and how she wished she'd parked closer.

'Okay, you deserve some answers to your questions. I want to give you those answers because I need your help. I know we're both looking for the same woman. We have a common goal. If at the end of this conversation you want to walk away, that's fine. No hard feelings. Is that agreeable?' he asked.

There was a commanding tone in his voice, but only now and then. Like he was aware of it and so used it sparingly.

Amanda nodded. She wanted to keep her tongue behind her teeth for now.

'Good. I'll talk first. Then I need you to tell me what happened to you. I know some of it already, or I can guess, but you have specifics that might help me. Help *us*, I mean.'

Amanda said nothing.

'My wife was found dead in her office two years ago. Her name was Lucille, or Luce – that's what I called her. We'd been married fifteen years. We'd been together for another ten years before that, but she always said she could never marry a marine. Didn't want to be one of those wives wondering if some day she was going to be handed a folded flag as they lowered my coffin into the dirt. We married the same year I retired. That's why I got out of the service, really. By that time, it didn't matter if I got a pay check. Luce was always great with computers and money. She worked in investment-capital groups all over the city. Knew it all. I confess that most of that stuff went over my head, but it didn't matter. Luce earned good money of her own.

KILL FOR ME KILL FOR YOU

Everything was great, until one day she got a call from a guy about investing in an app. I didn't know what an app was – but she did. It was some kind of courier service for food. She left her job and went in with most of our savings. Six months later her partner, Jerry Gould, wanted to sell to one of the big tech firms. Luce said no – if they waited it out, they could make ten times that number in another twelve months.

'I never liked Jerry. He had gambling problems. Always broke. His behavior grew more erratic, and he got into debt with the wrong people. The kind of people who break your legs if you miss a payment. Luce told him she would help him with the money, but he needed to see a counselor and get his life together.'

A cop car flew past the window with its siren blaring. Billy paused, took a sip of tea and waited until the noise had died down, and the buzz of conversation started up again in the diner.

'He took the money, and a week later asked for more. Luce said no. The next night the cops found her body in the office. The place had been trashed. She was shot twice in the chest. Twice in the head. They tried to tell me it was a professional burglary gone wrong. Can you believe that bullshit? It wasn't a professional burglary – it was a professional hit. Jerry sold the company for six million dollars before Luce was even in the ground. He never came to see me to pay his respects – didn't go to the funeral. Never shared a dime of that money with me, like he was supposed to. I was her surviving spouse and entitled to her shares. I didn't want it, anyway. It was blood money. I knew it was him, but the cops said he had an alibi that held up, and there wasn't enough to charge him.'

Billy paused, picked up his cup.

'I'm sorry,' said Amanda.

His cup halted, inches from his lips as she spoke. As if those words had caught him off guard. It was the right thing to say, she was sure of it, but in the circumstances perhaps he had not expected common courtesy.

'Thank you,' he said, then cleared his throat and continued.

'I kind of went to pieces for a while. My doctor referred me to a psychiatrist who gave me pills, but I didn't take them. I've watched too many marines go down that road and they never came back. Counseling looked like an option. Group therapy. I tried it for a while. I found an online support group and that helped. Knowing that there are people who have been in your kind of situation and have come out the other side, well, it gives you some hope. Then I got talking to a new group member, Felicia. She joined a month after me. Her husband's killer had been acquitted on some kind of legal technicality. A faulty search warrant, or something. She wanted the man who killed her husband dead on a slab and said she couldn't find peace until that day.'

Amanda swallowed. Tried not to show any reaction. She took a long drink of water. Her grip on the pocket knife began to relax.

'We talked online, in a side chat. Privately. And we got to know each other. It felt like I was talking to someone who understood me. Someone going through the same kind of pain, with no resolution – no closure – no justice. After a month, she sent me a gift. A movie on DVD. *Strangers on a Train*. I'd never seen it. I watched it, and she called me afterward. She told me we should do what those guys did in the movie – exchange murders. She would kill Jerry, and I would kill the man who'd murdered her husband.'

He stopped talking and looked at Amanda. She felt as if he was staring right through her eyes, gazing all the way into the back of her skull. It wasn't uncomfortable. There was a kindness there. An easy, shared understanding of a wound they each had suffered.

'Felicia and I met the day after that phone call. And we talked. Got to know each other. And we discussed how it could be done – swapping the murders. Couple of days later, I got home from my regular Friday night bowling league and she called me and said to turn on the TV. Jerry was missing and there was an appeal on the local news. She said he wasn't missing – she had killed him. And now it was my turn.'

His brow furrowed and he took up his spoon and slowly stirred his tea, gazing into the dark liquid.

'She gave me the name and address of the man who'd killed her husband – said it had to be done that night, before the cops found Jerry Gould's body and hauled me in as a suspect. I still had my old service weapon, so her plan was I knocked on the man's front door, put two in his head soon as he opened it.'

Removing the spoon from the tea, he set it down on the table, wrapped both hands around the cup for warmth and brought it to his lips, but he didn't drink. He just held it there, looked out the window and said, 'I couldn't bring myself to knock on his door. I just stood outside his house, frozen.'

'You didn't kill him?' asked Amanda.

Shaking his head, Billy said, 'I've seen action in God knows how many countries. Pulling a trigger is not a big deal for me. In the military, it was different. It was combat. There was an enemy and I had my orders. This felt all wrong. I just turned and left.

'I called Felicia, to tell her I couldn't do it, but she didn't answer the phone. I went to her place and it was cleaned out. All the internet articles about her and the trial of her husband's killer vanished the same day. I didn't know what to think at first. Maybe she was just cutting ties, but I knew it was more than that. Then I saw a news report on Jerry Gould. He had been found alive, after being locked in a janitor's closet in his building with no cell phone for two days. A cleaner found him Monday morning. He was dehydrated, but otherwise alive and healthy. She'd only pretended to kill Jerry, to get me to kill someone for her.'

Amanda said nothing. She didn't want to give anything away that could get her into trouble. This could all be a set-up. Maybe this guy worked with Naomi. She was forcing herself to think like this – making sure she wasn't conned a second time. And while it was good to be skeptical, she knew, in her bones, that this man was telling the truth.

'Did you go to the police?' she asked.

He shook his head. 'I don't know much about criminal law, but I know if I went to the police and showed them our message history the first thing they would do is arrest me for conspiracy to murder. It wouldn't matter to them if they never found Felicia. Last contact I had with Felicia was when she gave me the name and address of the man she wanted me to kill. That was a month ago. I've been going slowly crazy trying to find her.'

'Did you find her?'

'Nope. Everything seemed to be a dead end. But I did know one thing. She wanted this man dead, and she had tried to con me into killing him. For whatever reason, this man was a target . . .'

His voice trailed off, and his face softened as he looked at Amanda.

She had a question she wanted to ask, but she was afraid of it. She already knew the answer, but it wasn't enough. It had to be said out loud. She had to face that fear, and meet it head on, no matter what the cost.

'What was the name of the man she told you to kill?' asked Amanda, her voice dry and cracked.

'Frank Quinn,' said Billy softly, 'but you already knew that.'

She nodded.

'I couldn't tell him. Too risky. He'd call the cops on me and then I'd be toast. I did the next best thing. I watched his house. Then I got an alert on my email. I'd been searching for anything I could find on the web for Frank Quinn, so I set up an alert to tell me if anything about him was published. I clicked on the link in the alert and I found new fake-news articles on Quinn. But this time he was accused of killing a girl named Rebecca Cotton. There were fake articles about that murder, and her mother – Naomi Cotton. I knew then that Felicia, or Naomi as she was now probably calling herself, was trying to con someone else. I knew someone was going to come for Quinn. Two nights ago, I was sitting in my car searching the internet on my laptop while I watched his house and I found something,' he said, lifting the laptop onto the table and opening it. He pressed a few keys, and Amanda saw the screen glare reflected in his glasses as he brought the thing to life. He pushed his finger around the track pad, typed, scrolled, then took hold of the laptop screen.

'I'd been searching for her online. There's nothing about Felicia Silver, only the fake Naomi Cotton stuff – all the websites about Felicia and her husband's murder had disappeared. Everything she told me was a lie, apart from one thing.'

'What was that?'

'She liked the movie *Strangers on a Train*. It's based on a book. I didn't know that either at the time. So I searched for fan pages, forums, news articles. Anything that might give me a lead on Felicia. That's when I found this . . .' he said, and turned the screen round.

Amanda leaned forward and saw a news article from the *New York Post*. The headline read *Killer Claims He Has a Copycat Accomplice*.

The piece was a year old.

Today a Manhattan court heard an extraordinary tale from Richard Kowalski, a thirty-nine-year-old librarian from Harlem, who pleaded guilty to the murder of Saul Benson. Mr. Kowalski's attorney claimed that his client entered a murderous pact with a woman named Deborah Mallory whom he met in an online support group. The victim, Mr. Benson, was unknown to the defendant prior to the murder. The defendant is claiming that he and Mallory copied the murder plot of the movie Strangers on a Train *– Mallory would murder the defendant's boss, and the defendant in turn would kill Mr. Benson for Mallory. The district attorney has confirmed that police have no information on the whereabouts, nor evidence of the existence of a person named Deborah Mallory matching the description provided by the defendant, and it is only the defendant who claims this woman exists at all. The hearing continues tomorrow.*

Amanda swallowed. She let go of the knife in her pocket and put both hands on the table.

'The cops found Kowalski's DNA at the murder scene in the victim's apartment. When they caught him, they couldn't find any connection between Kowalski and the victim. They didn't work together, had no friends in common, didn't know each other – probably never met before the night of the attack. I think this was Felicia. I think she's done this before.'

'Jesus,' said Amanda. 'What happened to Kowalski?'

'They never found Deborah Mallory and Kowalski is dead. Lasted a month in Sing Sing before somebody put a shank in his lung.'

Amanda leaned forward to reach for her glass, but her hands were shaking too much. She put them in her lap, tried to focus. She could have the exact same fate as Kowalski if she didn't find Naomi. She knew that much, but she wasn't completely convinced Naomi, Felicia and Deborah Mallory were all the same person.

'How do you know that's Felicia?' she asked.

'It would be one hell of a coincidence if two women were going around the city under false names, meeting men and women in online support groups and persuading them to swap murders.'

Billy made sense. He made a lot of sense in a situation that was way too fucked up to begin with.

'I was waiting for another poor idiot to show up and try to take out Quinn. I wasn't expecting a woman. No offense. When I saw you there that night, I thought you might be Felicia. You're the same height, same build and you were all covered up in that hood. That's why I tailed you,' he said.

Amanda shook off the thought. She had bigger concerns.

'If it is her, then what the hell is she doing? She's just killing people randomly?' she asked.

'I don't know. Far as I can tell there's no connection between Quinn and Benson, the man Kowalski killed. I've had a private investigator helping me with some pieces of this puzzle. He doesn't know the whole story, just for my own protection, you understand. He helps out with access to databases, credit-card information – deep background, that kind of stuff. The victims were not friends, not as far as we can tell. Quinn is kind of a mystery. He runs a lot of companies – every one of them seems to fail. But none of them are connected to the other victim.'

Amanda thought of the rolls of cash from Quinn's lockbox, now safely in her backpack.

'What do you want from me?' asked Amanda.

'I need you to tell me all about the woman you're looking for. That's why you went back to the house, right? To find out who Quinn really was and hope that it led you to her. That's a smart move. That's the logical move – the one I would've made. You want to know what the connection is between Quinn and the woman who told you to kill him. I'm not a detective, and I can't tell the private investigator the whole story because he would report me to the cops. I could've been you. I could've pulled the trigger on Quinn. We've both been conned, but we can help each other. Tell me everything you know about her. And maybe we can find her together.'

What Billy had told her felt like the truth. No one else could know those details unless they'd been one of Naomi's victims. And yet she'd just met this man. As kindly and as sad as he seemed, she didn't quite trust him yet. Maybe that was fair? Or maybe it was because she'd just been betrayed.

'Why should I trust you?' asked Amanda.

'Because I didn't have to grab you off the street. I could've left you for the cops. And you know I'm telling the truth. You and I have been through the same mill with this woman. She used your grief and your pain and made you do something terrible. That could've been me. I won't tell the cops what you did. I promise. This isn't the first time she's manipulated someone into murder and I think she'll do it again. It has to stop.'

'I couldn't do it,' said Amanda. 'I backed out at the last second.

But I'd hurt my knee and couldn't get away fast enough. Quinn attacked me and I defended myself.'

Billy nodded, said, 'I believe you. But you should never have been put in that situation. Help me stop her.'

Amanda drank some coffee, looked around and saw a sign on the counter that said – *We Never Close.*

She held out her hand across the table. 'My name is Amanda White.'

He took it gracefully. 'Nice to meet you.'

She scooched over, close to the window, said, 'Come on over here so we can look at the screen together. I'll help you, but if we find her then I need to talk to her.'

'Of course.'

'What are you going to do if we find her?'

'I don't know, exactly. She needs help. We have to find her before she persuades someone else to commit a murder. After that, we'll figure it out. That good enough?'

'For now, yeah. Show me everything you have on the other murder,' said Amanda, taking off her jacket. 'And you're buying the coffee.'

46
Scott

He stared at Ruth.

Her trembling finger pointed at the TV screen. At a cop. Her lips mouthing those words. Ragged breath giving them life, but only as a whisper.

'*That's him.*'

'Ruth, what are you talking about?'

'That's the man who attacked me,' she said.

The man she was pointing at was a cop – Puccini, it said, on the banner below.

Ruth turned to him, the fear washing her skin in sweat and making her body tremble. She looked at him now, in disbelief.

'Didn't you hear what he said?' she asked.

Scott shook his head. 'Something about the hotline?'

'No!' she screamed, and clenched her fist. 'He looked right into the camera and he said, clear as day, *Hello, sweetheart*. It's him. He wants me to know he's still alive – that we didn't get him. He's coming for me – don't you see?'

Scott had heard and felt every word of the press conference – every single one. Because each word was an evisceration – a nail driven through his skull – *he had killed an innocent man.*

'He didn't say that,' said Scott, his voice low, suddenly afraid.

'I heard him. I watched him say it,' she said.

Ruth's breath grew wild, her chest heaving.

'We have to kill him,' she said.

At first, he didn't register it. Ruth was clearly having some kind of breakdown. She was imagining things – hallucinating. Her wounds were deeper and more terrible than he'd first realized. In those first days after the attack, the focus had been on her physical health – the recovery from the internal damage. Then the fear, and the agoraphobia, and the nightmares, and now, this . . .

'Ruth, that's not him,' said Scott.

Her face contorted, repelled by Scott's tone. It only increased her anger.

'That's *him*. You killed the wrong man. You have to do it again. You have to kill him!'

Scott moved toward her, his arms open, as if to embrace her.

He knew what he had to do. There was only one choice now. Ruth needed help. She needed more than he could give her. Experts. Care. He couldn't do this alone. He engulfed her in his arms, her head on his chest. She gripped him tightly and he wept for her, and himself. His eyes flicked to the TV. The press conference was over. They were back in the studio and above the anchor's right shoulder they played images of Patrick Travers, and then footage of his tearful widow – broken, bereft and in terrible pain.

The weight of what he'd done in that hotel room sat like a brick in his chest. He couldn't stand it. He knew then if he left it there it would eat him alive, like a cancer.

'We have to do it, Scott,' said Ruth. 'We have to kill him. I can't breathe knowing he's out there. And he'll come for me. He'll come for us both.'

His thoughts drifted back to that day in school when he was lying on the shower floor, and the boots and fists rained down on him from every angle, sharp and hard, cutting his skin, bruising his ribs, splitting his lips, again and again and again, as if it would never stop. He could hear their voices, the bullies, laughing and shouting, and above it all the roar of the water on the tile. Getting louder in his head.

'This has to stop. Everything has to stop,' he said, and pushed Ruth away. Scott drew his cell phone out of his pocket, walked from the kitchen into the lounge.

The apartment was three floors up. He threw open the window, took a moment to close his eyes and listen. The cars on the street below, the sound of songbirds in the trees, and the faint smell of cut grass in the park across the street, and something else. Something sweet on the air. Moss or flowers. And with that sweetness, there was also the faint odor of decay.

His heart wouldn't stop pounding. He couldn't swallow. Mouth was too dry. Everything good in his life was gone. And it was all his own fault. Shame was a strange feeling. He felt disgust at himself, and his weakness, and his mistakes, and he couldn't stand another goddamn second of it. If there's enough guilt and shame, it becomes a fire. It consumes flesh like burning gasoline.

He stood there – immolated in shame.

He had to make the burning stop.

Scott dialed 911, told the operator he wanted police.

'What are you doing?' asked Ruth, coming behind him.

He held up a hand, a gesture to let her know to keep her distance.

'My name is Scott Gelman. I killed Patrick Travers in his room at the Paramount Hotel last night. I'm at 211 Parkview, Hartford. I-I'm unarmed. My wife is here too. I've taken her hostage. She knew nothing about the murder. She's innocent. And she's sick. Please help her . . .'

Scott threw the phone on the couch. He took a long look at Ruth, her mouth open, shaking her head, unable to process what he'd just done.

'I'm sorry. I fucked everything up. I love you,' said Scott.

Then he turned away from Ruth to the open window. He put one foot on the ledge, ducked his head under the glass, then swung his other leg out. He sat on the windowsill, his legs dangling over the edge. It was a long way down.

He could hear Ruth coming toward him, her feet on the wooden floor. He thought about his life, and of all the things that would end. His parents would be heartbroken, but nothing could stop that now. He had killed an innocent man – their hearts would break no matter what. The only thing he could do was spare them the shame of his trial.

Scott closed his eyes, pushed himself off the ledge and felt the wind in his hair one last time.

47

Amanda

She asked to see the message history between Billy and Felicia. He had screenshotted the conversation, and so Amanda flicked through a series of images of their texts on Billy's laptop.

To a casual eye, most of it looked like nothing more than a conversation between two lonely, damaged people. Some phrases from Felicia stuck out.

The pain changes, it dulls. It's always there, but it doesn't always rip your heart out . . .

It's only the first two years that are the hardest . . .

When I told you it gets easier – I lied. I feel exactly the same way as I did the day they found his body . . .

We're just talking right? Just you and me, hypothetically . . .

Did you get the movie I sent you? Strangers on a Train?

It was subtle, but Amanda could see the patterns. She'd been told the same thing by Naomi, in the same order. The manipulation was all there – practiced, and sure, and yet so light. Felicia never pressed. Neither did Naomi – but all the points were there that had played on Amanda's pain, twisting it, harnessing it, pointing it down a dark road. In Amanda's case, it was a road she was already halfway down. She hadn't needed any persuasion. And that hurt now more than ever.

Billy came back to the table with a Manila folder he'd fetched from the car. Moving aside Amanda's coffee cups, he opened it, took out about a hundred pages and left the stack on the table.

'She really knows how to work somebody,' said Amanda.

Billy sighed then pressed his lips together tightly. Nodded. He'd allowed his own pain to be used against him just like Amanda had. Naomi, or in his case Felicia, hadn't put the thought of murder in their heads – it was there already. All she did was use it.

Amanda flicked through the rest of the messages. There was certainly enough there to incriminate Billy in a conspiracy-to-murder charge.

'Is the fact that you didn't go through with the murder some kind of defense if the cops saw these messages?' asked Amanda.

'Maybe, maybe not. I looked it up. I'd taken active steps to murder. I'd loaded my gun, driven to his house, scoped it out. It's enough to convict me, even if I argue I pulled out. I don't want to take the risk.'

Amanda understood that. She thought if the cops came for her before she could find Naomi, Billy might be able to back up her story – but would he risk it if it put him in jeopardy of a criminal charge? – probably not.

She picked up the stack of pages on the table, started to flick through them. There was an address for Felicia, but it was different to the one used by Naomi. Different phone number too. The phone number and IP address for the private chat had been linked to Felicia's address – which of course had been abandoned.

The rest of the pages were internet articles and newspaper clippings on the murder of Saul Benson, and Richard Kowalski's arrest and trial for that murder where he blamed a woman named Deborah Mallory for manipulating him into killing Benson for her. Amanda took her time reading through them. She made sure the printouts from the internet were genuine by finding the news articles online and checking the website addresses were correct. It all looked legit, and after a while she stopped checking. Billy was on the level.

Billy got more coffee for her, and more tea for him. They'd been in the diner for coming up on two hours.

Amanda found a clipping from the *New York Post* on Quinn's attack. No picture, just the bare details in three column inches. She put it aside. Beneath it was a full color picture of Quinn. But a picture she'd never seen before. It had not been one of the pictures she presumed Naomi had taken, and it wasn't the one used by the TV news.

He was wearing a pale blue suit, white button-down shirt and a yellow tie, coming down the steps of what looked like a court building.

'Where did you get this picture of Quinn?' she asked.

'Huh?'

She picked up the picture – obviously printed from a news website and enlarged. Turning the photo round, she said, 'This picture. I looked him up online. I never found a picture of Quinn like this.'

He took the picture, stared at it.

'That's not Quinn, that's Saul Benson – Kowalski's victim.'

Amanda felt a chill wash the back of her neck. Beneath the picture of Benson was a news article with the same picture in the corner. Billy must've enlarged that picture and printed it separately. She looked at the headline, the date, and found the webpage from *The New York Times*.

She clicked on the image to enlarge it.

'What are you doing?'

'An image search. I've got a theory.'

She selected the picture of Benson, Kowalski's victim, typed in accompanying search terms – homicide – murder – police – and hit search.

Thousands of images. Most of them of male models. She refined the location of the search to US. Tried again.

The first page had nothing. Same with the second. On the third page, Billy said, 'Stop,' and pointed at the screen. 'Is that Quinn? Or maybe it's Benson?'

Amanda clicked on the image. A news report.

'It's neither of them,' she said.

She scrolled down the article, and midway there was another image. A woman. Amanda felt a surge in her stomach.

'That's Naomi,' she said.

Billy looked closer. 'Yes, that's Felicia,' he said. 'You found her.'

48
Ruth

It all happened as if it was in slow motion.

Her right hand reaching for him.

Her footsteps on the wooden floor.

Almost there.

Leaning forward.

The back of his checked shirt framed in the window. Almost within touching distance.

Reaching. Inches from grabbing him.

Her mouth open in a silent scream that suddenly erupted from her throat as . . .

His shirt disappeared as he fell from the window ledge, revealing a perfect blue sky over green trees in the distance.

Ruth's left hand grabbed the frame and she leaned out to grab the collar of his shirt.

She was too late.

Ruth closed her eyes right before he hit the concrete steps. She heard it, though. The smack of flesh, the crack of bone.

She forced herself to open her eyes.

He lay very still. On his left side. Right hand beneath his cheek, as if to cushion it while he slept. His legs were bleeding, one ankle pointing in the wrong direction.

She thought for a moment he'd somehow survived the three-story drop, that by some miracle he was still alive, but then she saw the pool of blood forming on the sidewalk beneath his head. Growing, as if someone was pouring it onto the ground from a watering can.

Ruth turned away from the window, covered her mouth with both hands and then ran. Out of the apartment, down the stairs, outside.

She knelt by his side, calling his name as she heard the sirens approaching.

Scott's eyes were closed. He seemed so peaceful. She whispered to him that he was going to be okay.

She stroked his forehead, taking no notice of the tremors in her fingers.

Then hands took hold of her, lifting her away. She only glanced at the police officers who then placed her on the ground. They spoke to her. Asked her what her name was. She couldn't answer. She couldn't speak. Her lips were moving. She could hear herself talking, but she knew they couldn't hear her. She felt as if she was behind glass.

What happened next seemed strange. Time seemed to move so fast. She was in the back of a police car, watching the paramedics take Scott away. She pounded on the door, but it wouldn't open. She was locked inside.

Then she was in a police precinct. There was a towel round her shoulders and a cup of coffee in front of her on a cheap gray table. She couldn't stop shaking. But now she could hear the buzz and voices of a busy police department. There was a man in a cell close by kicking at the steel doors. Cops were telling him to shut up. There were other faces of frightened people scattered around on wooden benches. She looked at her watch, but couldn't focus enough to tell what time it was.

She looked up at the TV on the wall.

CNN was playing to the crowd of people waiting to speak to a police officer. A woman with a child in her arms began to cry, and then the baby started crying.

Ruth looked up at the TV. President George W. Bush was giving a speech about his meeting with a foreign ambassador. Congratulating himself, and wishing for all Americans that tomorrow's holiday – Thanksgiving 2007 – would be their most prosperous yet.

49
Amanda

As they read the article, a news alert popped up onscreen for Billy.

New York Times – As President Trump gears up for the traditional Thanksgiving address tomorrow, commentators wonder if he might pardon more than just turkey this Thanksgiving, 2018.

Amanda swiped the pop-up away, and continued to read.

When she finished, she leaned back. Billy blew out his cheeks.

Wiping her face, Amanda tried to think. But she was too tired. She'd had too much information tonight. She read the article again. One last time. The article was from January 2008. It was about a murder trial. It was the picture of the man who had been killed which attracted Amanda to the story. Billy had already told her there was no link between Quinn and Benson, the victims targeted by Naomi, that is until you looked at pictures of them. They could've been brothers, separated at birth, they looked so strikingly similar. When Amanda found a picture of another man, a murder victim, who looked almost like a third twin of Benson and Quinn, she'd clicked on the link, and halfway down that article she'd seen Naomi's picture. And then it had all made sense.

Today, in the Manhattan Criminal Court Building, the trial began into the murder of mayoral campaign manager Patrick Travers. The defendant is forty-one-year-old Ruth Gelman, a former realtor from Manhattan. Mrs. Gelman stands accused of Murder in the First Degree, and Conspiracy to Murder. Assistant District Attorney David O. Rush opened the case for the prosecution, alleging that this was a misguided vigilante killing. It is alleged that Mrs. Gelman was, some months prior to the murder of Patrick Travers, a victim of a brutal attack in her own home, from which she was lucky to survive. It is believed Mrs. Gelman was a victim of an alleged serial killer, nicknamed by the New York Post *as the Prowler, but known in police circles as Mr. Blue-eyes.*

Mr. Rush explained to the jury that Mrs. Gelman identified Patrick Travers as her assailant and that together with her husband, Scott Gelman, they plotted and executed a plan to murder Mr. Travers in his hotel room, believing him to be the person who had attacked Mrs. Gelman. Evidence gathered during a separate investigation by the US attorney's office has ruled out Mr. Travers as being Mrs. Gelman's attacker, as he was in a different state at the time of the attack. Mr. Rush went on to say that the defendant is claiming to have been of unsound mind at the time of the murder. He urged the jury to be skeptical of such suggestions. The trial continues tomorrow . . .

Amanda opened a new tab, searched under the name Ruth Gelman, and scanned the articles. Patiently, silently, Amanda and Billy read them all.

A half hour later, she said, 'Can you take me back to my car? I need to go home, process this.'

'Sure,' said Billy.

Back in Billy's Escalade, on their way to Amanda's car, Billy broke the silence.

'Let me see if I understand this, because right now I'm still a little confused. Ruth Gelman is found not guilty by reason of temporary insanity; she spends seven years in the hospital and is released. And then what? She starts tracking down men with blue eyes? That doesn't make any sense.'

'You said it yourself – Benson and Quinn had nothing in common. Not on paper. They probably never met, and there was nothing to connect them. Apart from one thing – they looked practically identical. I knew that couldn't just be a coincidence. And it's not just the eyes. Travers, Saul Benson, Quinn – they all look so similar they could be family. Same hair color, same cheekbones, same chin, same kind of nose, lips and, yes, they all have blue eyes. I mistook Benson for Quinn when I saw the picture in your file, and I knew that couldn't just be a coincidence. She thinks she's found her attacker, and she manipulates someone vulnerable, like us, into killing them. Like she manipulated her husband into killing Travers.'

Amanda had read an article on Ruth's attack. She had been at home alone when a man broke in and almost stabbed her to death. That had been on the fourteenth of September 2007. Ruth had changed her appearance since. Amanda was living in Manhattan then, studying at night school and working in the care home during the day. Their paths could have crossed any time – standing in line for coffee, getting on the subway, passing each other on an escalator, or maybe not. Maybe they never came close to each other until a few weeks ago.

Billy turned right onto Bleeker Street from Sixth Avenue, taking the long way through the winding streets of Greenwich Village, making sure he wasn't being followed, and so he could drive past Amanda's car – make sure there were no cops around.

'Wait a minute,' said Billy. 'Surely she must know that Travers was innocent. And once she'd had Benson killed, why target Quinn? She must know she's killed innocent people. They can't all be – what did the police call him?'

'Mr. Blue-eyes,' said Amanda. 'Yeah, she must know. On some

level she has to know. Maybe she doesn't care, Billy. Sometimes people get too damaged. Trauma changes you. Losing a loved one to violence provokes a response. There are two common responses – either they don't want anyone to ever hurt like they do, or they want everyone to hurt like they do.'

Billy glanced over at Amanda.

'I don't want anyone to go through the pain I've experienced,' he said.

'Me either. That's why I want the man who killed my daughter. So he can never do that to another child. No parent should have to go through this. And I'm not the only one. The man who killed Jess murdered another little girl called Emily Dryer, about twelve years ago. The cop assigned to Jess's case has been hunting this monster for a long time,' she said.

'I'm sorry. I didn't ask about your loss. I didn't want to push you. Some people find it hard to talk about it.'

'That's okay. I'm getting used to it. I told Naomi all about the man who killed my little girl.'

'And did she tell you she had killed this man for you?'

Amanda nodded. 'Yeah, his name is Wallace Crone. He's a . . .'

'Henry Crone's son?'

'Do you know him?'

'No, I know of Henry Crone. Read about him in the papers. You can't absorb that much news about New York and not come across that name. He's a Wall Street guy, right? Billionaire?'

'Yeah, he's a powerful man. And he didn't spare any cash when it came to protecting his son. Wallace Crone killed my girl, Jess. She was six. Then my partner took his own life. He had been with Jess in the park. Turned around for like a second and . . .'

Her throat closed. That choking sensation. A cloying constriction right at the back of her gullet. If she let this grief build, it would sit in her stomach, making her feel sick and robbing her of all thought. She shut her eyes, bit down. Tried to fight it.

'I'm very sorry,' said Billy, and he reached out, placing a large palm gently on top of Amanda's hand. She looked at him and saw the pity and the sorrow in his eyes. It was a kindly gesture, and Amanda, who was often uncomfortable with close contact, welcomed it with a sad smile.

'No parent should have to bury a child. You've been through so much.'

They reached the intersection. On their right, Quinn's house. A blue-and-white parked outside. On their left, a quiet street, with Amanda's car parked halfway down it. No cops in sight. They sat silently for a time. The light changed to green and Billy turned left. He pulled up and parked at Amanda's car.

She unbuckled her seat belt, said, 'Well, can't say this has been fun.'

'I'll send everything we have on Ruth Gelman to my PI. Hopefully by tomorrow we should have an address for her,' he said. 'When I get one, I'll call you.'

'Thank you,' said Amanda, opening the passenger door. She stopped, hesitated, said, 'I never would've found her without you. Thank you. And thank you for helping me and not . . .'

'Not judging you? I could've *been* you, Amanda. In some ways, I was you. I was in your exact position only I backed out of it before Quinn saw me and attacked me. If that had happened, I would be sitting where you are now. I want to help you. I want to help us both come out of this. Now we just have to find her and stop her.'

Amanda watched Billy pull away as she opened the driver's door to her car and got in. It had been a long night.

She had been lucky to meet Billy. He seemed a sweet, generous man. Kind, but there was a toughness in him too. And a sadness. She had caught it now and then, in the corners of the light-brown eyes, or hanging at the end of one of his sentences like a dull echo. If she hadn't met Billy, she wouldn't have found Ruth Gelman. Maybe her luck was changing. Slipping the car into first, she pressed the accelerator and drove out onto the street.

A yawn grabbed her, and her knee shot through with pain every time she changed gear. She wanted nothing more than to climb into bed and go to sleep. And yet she knew it would be hard to get to sleep tonight. It was hard most nights. There was too much floating around in her brain – dealing with what she had done to Quinn – knowing he was an innocent man. Wallace Crone was in the back of her mind for now. Ruth Gelman was at the front. She suspected that their search for Ruth had only just started. And she was running out of time.

50

Ruth

Thanksgiving Eve

Ruth sat at a red light on Atlantic Avenue in a black Mercedes, a lit cigarette between the fingers of her left hand, the window cracked open an inch to let the smoke out. She checked her dye job in the mirror. Four hours in a salon and four hundred dollars later, she was now a redhead.

An Ed Sheeran track played on the radio. Ruth liked to keep up with new music, and she enjoyed the beat of this one. The fingers of her right hand tapped out the rhythm on the steering wheel. She took a drag from her cigarette, waited for an update on the news at the top of the hour.

Her thoughts drifted to Amanda. What she must be feeling right now. Cheated, conned, angry? All of those things. And none of it mattered. Amanda would not go to the police to give herself up and, even if she did, there was no evidence to back up her story. Naomi was gone. She'd never even existed.

She took another hit from her cigarette. The traffic light was still red against the night sky. The news came in at the top of the hour.

Quinn was still alive, but critical. With luck he would die soon. She had that feeling again – relief. She was reborn, free from fear.

She'd first experienced that feeling eleven years ago. That hour she'd spent walking along Park Terrace in Frog Hollow, Hartford, after Scott had told her he'd killed Travers. She remembered the smell from the grass. Going grocery shopping. Buying that coffee. Just walking the streets without fear. And the light. In her memory, that time had been during the golden hour, or what some called the magic hour. The period of time right before sunrise, when the sky, and the light, is a mix of burnished bronze and gold. It gives every surface a Midas touch. Puddles of rainwater on the sidewalk turn into pools of gold. Stop signs look like twenty-four-karat treasures lifted from a pharaoh's tomb.

And in the distance she could hear a brass bell ringing, softly.

It hadn't really looked like this that day, all those years ago. She knew that. It didn't matter. Not really. The warmth, the sheer relief and the sense of comfort she'd felt that morning had bled into her memory – painting it in shimmering gold.

The bad things that had happened later that day were not so clear in her mind. They had blurred and dulled with time and heavy medication.

She scanned the road ahead. A gas station, just beyond the intersection with Brooklyn Avenue. She would go there, fill up on gas and Lucky Strikes. A small thing. Something that people do every day. And she could do it tonight without fear. Mr. Blue-eyes, as she had come to know him, was gone. He lay fighting for his life in a New York hospital bed. He wouldn't be waiting, hiding in the back seat of her car when she returned from the gas station. He wouldn't be waiting for her later, while she lay awake in bed. His face would not haunt her dreams.

She could live and sleep in that golden haze again.

A horn blasted behind her.

She glanced in the rearview mirror. The driver in the car behind was gesticulating for Ruth to move on.

The light was green.

She put the car in gear and moved off slowly, turning into the gas station. She got out of the car, pumped gas into the tank and looked around while it filled. A rundown neighborhood in Brooklyn. The elevated train tracks ran down the center of Atlantic Avenue, carrying people in and out of Manhattan.

She went inside the gas station, bought four packs of Luckys and paid in cash for the cigarettes and gas. It felt good. The small things always did. To live an ordinary life without fear was something marvelous to her, and always would be. Back in the car, she checked her destination on the navigation system. She was close now.

Fifteen minutes later Ruth parked the car in the long-term parking lot, got her bag and her case from the trunk and took an Uber to her new apartment. The movers had been there yesterday, and when she entered the apartment the furniture had already been laid out, boxes opened, cutlery, plates and mugs put away and her bed made. It was an expensive service, but she could afford it.

The house sale gave her a lot of ready cash. She needed it. New York was an expensive place to live and it wasn't like she could work.

Not with everything else going on.

She showered and then got into bed, the fresh cotton sheets cool and welcoming. It was Thanksgiving tomorrow. She'd decided she would go to the parade. It would be safe.

Ruth closed her eyes and tried to empty her mind. Thoughts tended to cloud her peace. The certain knowledge of Quinn's incapacity allowed a sense of calm to flow through her entire body. She didn't need to think – she just felt it.

Thinking didn't help. It was all about feeling. *That* feeling.

Sometimes, in the dark, she would hear chains rattling. She knew it wasn't real. It was imagined. A box in Ruth's mind. A result of her EMDR therapy with Dr. Marin. He had told her it was the best way to deal with trauma – Eye Movement Desensitization and Reprocessing therapy at Kirby Forensic Psychiatric Center.

Dr. Marin was in his late fifties when they first met. He wore a beard and a ribbon of fluffy white hair surrounded his head, never encroaching on the shiny dome on top. They met in a sterile treatment room. Table and chairs bolted to the floor, and Marin in his white coat, a little yellowed with age at the cuffs, sat opposite her with his fingers clasped together over his belly. He had a kind voice. Soothing.

'Give me your hand,' he said.

Ruth held out her hand, over the table. Gently, Marin took it, and began to tap on the back of her wrist.

'I want you to imagine a box. A box you can open and close,' he said as he tapped softly on her wrist with his forefinger.

'It is strong, this box. Very strong. If you put something in there, and locked it, no one could open it but you. It is your box. See it now, clearly, in your mind.'

She closed her eyes.

Tap, tap.

He asked her to describe the box, and she did.

'We are going to put things in this box, Ruth. It is your box. For your things. We will talk about the things we put in the box. We can put anything in there. A person, a place, a dream . . .' He tailed off, tapped again and said, 'Even a face.'

Ruth saw him then. Reflected in the broken glass. The man who'd hurt her. His voice sounded in her head . . .

Hello, sweetheart . . .

She flinched, and Marin's grip on her hand tightened.

'Can we put a voice in the box?' asked Ruth.

'Yes. Anything you like. First, we make the box strong. Stronger than anything. Then, when you're ready, we will look at the things that frighten us the most. We will make them smaller. Shrink them. And we will put them all in your box. And then you will be safe from them. They won't be able to hurt you. And they will never be able to leave that box again.'

Tap, tap.

Ruth lay in bed, in her new apartment, Marin's voice in her head as she tapped her own wrist now and thought about the box.

Heavy chains were wrapped around the old oak chest in Ruth's mind. She could see the brass edging on the chest's corners, and the thick lock keeping its contents secure. The lock and the heavy anchor chains were not for keeping people out. They had a different purpose – they were in place to make sure what was in the chest did not escape. Now and again, in the dark, or the nightmare place between waking and sleep, she heard the chains groaning, rattling, as the things inside the box strained to get out.

She could hear them now. The noise was growing louder.

Ruth sat up in bed, tapped on her right wrist with her left forefinger. Rhythmically. Slowly. Every two seconds.

While she tapped, she looked at the metronome on the side table. Allowing her eyes to follow the ticking needle. Back and forth.

Tick, tock.

She tapped her wrist to that beat. She knew what was in the box, struggling to get out.

The blue-eyed man was in there.

All the blue-eyed men were in there.

She tapped. Breathed. And put more chains around the oak chest.

Twenty minutes later, the chains had stopped rattling. Ruth took a sip of water and shook her head.

She should not be feeling this way. This was different from the last time. The sense of calm and power that normally followed the kill was not there tonight. The warmth of peace had diminished. Already, she could feel a presence outside. Somewhere in the city, Mr. Blue-eyes was alive and hunting her. She could sense him. Those blue eyes, searching for her. A chill brushed her neck and shoulders, causing her to shiver.

Ruth got out of bed and checked the windows. One of them was open. She closed it and scanned the street below. No one there. She went to her bag. Emptied it onto the bed.

Five cell phones. All of them connected to remote chargers. All five phones held messages for her. Some on text, some on WhatsApp.

The messages were not for Ruth, of course. Not really.

They were for Jenny, Rachel, Simone, Amy and Sarah. Her current identities. Five in all. Most of them were members of two or three support groups. All of the identities looked like Ruth, and all of them were grieving and bitter and angry at a lost love who had been cruelly taken from them by a killer. To help organize her various live identities, Ruth had stuck name tags to the back of the phones. Otherwise she would lose track. Jenny, for example, was in two online support groups for bereaved parents. Rachel had a trauma group meeting on Thursday afternoons in Harlem. Simone in Queens on Tuesdays. Amy's groups were further apart, East Flatbush and Staten Island. Sarah was the busiest – four online groups and two physical – Wakefield in the Bronx and Bedford Stuyvesant, in Brooklyn. There were almost eight and a half million people in New York, and population density varied between twenty thousand and sixty thousand people per square mile. A perfect place for Ruth to hide. She was a red needle in a haystack of eight million. With all of the groups she sought out the same kind of person. A parent, a husband, a wife, a lover – who had lost a loved one to someone who had not paid the price. Sometimes they were hard to find. Other times, they were in the groups already – just waiting for her. All she had to do was tease them out.

Injustice and grief were her weapons, moulded from love, regret and sometimes even guilt. A few of her targets were already primed. Ready. Waiting. All she had to do was tell them the story of two strangers on a train.

She decided that in the morning she would go back into Manhattan. Into the streets she knew so well. Tomorrow was the parade. She could watch it, and try to enjoy it. The peace that came after the kill was fragile, and precious. She needed to grasp it, bask in it. While she could. It was dwindling already.

Ruth replied to the messages on the phones, turned them all off and went to sleep.

51
Farrow

It was getting late at the precinct. Two a.m. Early Thanksgiving Day.

The evening shift had clocked off two hours ago and the only light in the robbery homicide office was from Farrow's desk lamp. The night shift were out pounding the streets, running down leads or working calls. Farrow liked to work at night, when it was quiet. The dark suited his mood, boosted his thoughts. The lamp shone a single light on the notebook in front of him, creating a halo of concentration. He sipped at his cold coffee and made some more notes.

The Quinn case was starting to become a lot more intriguing. There were too many pieces of it that just didn't fit together.

Most murders were simple. The victims nearly always knew their attacker, and it doesn't take a genius to figure out the killer. It's usually blindingly obvious. The exceptions were the robberies, and the serial killers – like Mr. Blue-eyes. But they were few and far between.

Drugs, alcohol, money, sex. That's all there was to most murders.

He let the clicker on top of the pen sit on his lower lip as his mind wandered. Perhaps one of those motives was at work here and he didn't know it. Money didn't seem to be one of the factors, because whoever the limping woman was who had been in the house, she hadn't taken the two rolls of cash.

'What are you still doing here?' said a voice.

He recognized it instantly. Hernandez. She should've been home by now, cooking one of her famous paellas with a glass of something cool and white in one hand. He'd been to her place a few times for dinner and a couple of bottles of Sauvignon Blanc. Usually when Hernandez had a new man in her life. It was like an unspoken test. If her boyfriend could get along with Farrow, then he had a shot. Plus, it helped settle the boyfriend's nerves about Hernandez working with a male partner. Sometimes those evenings went well, with Farrow leaving in the small hours of the morning in a cab. Other times, the boyfriend got kicked out early and Farrow would leave shortly after. Farrow didn't mind. The wine and the paella were always good.

'I might ask you the same question,' said Farrow.

Hernandez approached his desk, looked down at his notebook.

'I might have guessed. This Quinn case is really bugging you,' she said.

He took off his reading glasses and set them down on the page.

'I took the case from Statler and Waldorf,' he said.

'Goddamn it, I knew you would. Actually, I don't mind. I want to find that woman. I hate it when I lose somebody on the street.'

'That why you're still here?'

Picking up his reading glasses, he cleaned them with the fat end of his tie, held them up to the light and then slipped them back on.

Hernandez put her hands on her hips, then threw her head back and sighed.

'It bothers me. You know it does. So how can I help?' she asked.

'No, it's okay. You go on. You got a life, Karen. It's not in this office. I called the lab earlier. They said they should have some DNA results from the scene within a few hours.'

He checked his watch, said, 'That should be any time now. There's not a whole lot to do until then.'

'Give me something,' she said, holding out her hand.

With a smile breaking on his lips, Farrow sorted through the pages of loose paper on his desk, found the one he was looking for and handed it to her.

'This is a list of shit jobs,' she said.

'Exactly right. There's a lot of ground to cover, but you know . . .'

Rolling her eyes, Hernandez said, 'Shit jobs clear cases.'

She knew it was pointless to argue with him when he had hold of a bone. Only thing to do was go with it. Farrow stood up now, stretched his back, let out a growl as the pain washed over him. He threw up his hands, leaned back until he heard a satisfying crack.

He reached out for his cell phone, which sat on his desk. Before he could touch it, the phone screen lit up and began to purr on the desk. Incoming call.

He picked it up, said, 'Farrow,' and listened. For another thirty seconds, Farrow said nothing. Then he thanked the person on the line and ended the call. He put his cell phone in his pocket, but didn't take his seat. Instead, he put on his crumpled suit jacket. Either the jacket or the call weighed heavy on him, because he leaned over, placed his hands on the back of his chair and hung his head.

'What's wrong? Where are you going?' asked Hernandez.

'That was the lab. They got the results back. I'm going to pick up Amanda White.'

52

Amanda

Dawn was a red promise in the sky as Amanda drained a glass of water that Thanksgiving morning. She wore a pair of shorts, sneakers and a tee.

It had been a late night. Cracking open her apartment door at three a.m., she had gone straight to bed. She'd slept fitfully, her mind racing. She felt tired and her knee ached. Sitting down at her kitchen table, Amanda counted the money she'd taken from Quinn's house the night before. Altogether it was close to seventy-five grand. Enough to solve her immediate problems.

Opening the cupboard, she found a box of cereal, but there was no milk. Amanda wasn't hungry, but she knew she had to eat. There had to be something in her stomach before she could take any more pain-killers for her knee. It had swollen again, and she'd taped a bag of ice to her leg.

Amanda filled the bowl of cereal with water from the faucet, sat down and ate what she could while she worked at the laptop. She'd only skim read most of the articles last night. There came a point when she was too tired to take them in. Her head was a little clearer now, and she took her time, looking through each one, making notes on a legal pad as she went. She read the piece on the original attack again – when Ruth had almost been murdered in her own home by a serial killer the police called Mr. Blue-eyes. The article contained a sketch artist's impression of the perpetrator. Looking at that sketch, and the pictures of Travers, Quinn and Benson – men who Ruth had arranged to be murdered – there was a definite resemblance. Now, in the daylight, feeling a little calmer, and in familiar surroundings, Amanda looked more closely at the pictures of Travers, Quinn and Benson.

From a distance, it would be hard to distinguish between them. But up close there were differences. Quinn was older than the other two, with deeper lines around the eyes. Benson had a higher hair line and a small scar on his cheek. Travers was paler than both.

She did another search against the images, scrolled through the irrelevant pages until she hit another image of a man, remarkably similar to Travers, Benson and Quinn. He'd been murdered in his home. Stabbed to death. No apparent motive, no suspects. Nothing taken from the property. This had occurred two years ago. There was no way to be sure this was Ruth's work, but it could well have been. His name was Sean Gardner. He'd lived in East Harlem. She saved that article, added the man's image to her search.

And found another.

Paul Beriano. Shot twice in the head at his front door in Queens. No motive. Nothing taken from him or the house. A hit, but Beriano had no connection to organized crime. He was an Uber driver.

Beriano had been murdered three months ago.

Adding his image to the search, she tried again.

Two more motiveless murders. Older crimes. Two more men with a striking similarity to the other victims. One was named Paul Anderson, an interior designer. The other was the earliest victim Amanda could identify – Dan Puccini, the media relations manager for the NYPD. Anderson died a year after Puccini. With all of the images of the victims together, side by side, it looked like one hell of an ID parade.

Six men murdered in different parts of New York since Ruth's release from Kirby Psychiatric Center. There would be six different police precincts working these crimes, and nothing to connect the victims other than their faces. Dan Puccini had been murdered six months after Ruth got released from Kirby. Then the next one about a year afterwards with Anderson, and then the murders had accelerated. Nine months later, eight months later, six months, and then just three months before Quinn.

There was no way to tell if these were all Ruth's victims. She knew there were definitely two, at least – Quinn and Benson – and the original victim Patrick Travers. And yet there was no way to prove or confirm any of them other than Travers because she'd probably had someone else carry out each of these murders. Each victim had another victim behind them – the bereaved, half-crazed person who was at the end of their rope when Ruth came into their lives with a plan for justice.

Amanda covered her mouth, swore under her breath. She had been one of Ruth Gelman's grim reapers – conned into killing for her.

At first, having read the article on Ruth's attack, she had felt sorry for her. Now, she felt afraid. Glancing up at the bookcase, she took down a thick volume she had read a few months ago. It was a book by a forensic psychologist on serial killers. She had read it trying to gain some insight into Wallace Crone. Perhaps she could learn something she could use against him. In the end she had not, but she knew more about how some of these freaks come to be, how they kill and, more importantly, how they get caught.

She had learned that most of them aren't insane, which was the first thing that surprised her. Some are disorganized. Some are highly organized. And they can hide in plain sight, just like any other normal member of society.

Flicking through the book, she found one of the pages where she had turned down the corner, to mark it as potentially important.

Serial killers are most vulnerable to apprehension by law enforcement when they are at the high point of a pattern of accelerating crisis, which we examine below. Yet these patterns of accelerating crisis are not present in all serial murderers. Expert opinion is divided, but some leading psychologists, law enforcement specialists and criminologists believe there is another type of killer who follows no pattern. They are highly organized, they have no innate psychological trauma, no hallucinations, no psychosis whatsoever. They do not fall into any category of the current or past DSM and therefore have no clinical mental illness of any kind. In short, they kill whomever they please, whenever they please, at random. They are the great white sharks of the human species . . .

Amanda shuddered, skipped two paragraphs and began reading again.

Often, with serial killers, there will come a time of crisis when they are most vulnerable to apprehension by law enforcement. These crimes often follow a pattern. Particularly with perpetrators who experience some form of psychosis, be it visual or auditory hallucinations. The pattern is cyclical for serial murder. First, the perpetrator fantasizes about the murder, sometimes for long periods of time. Then, a victim is selected and stalked. Again, the length of time involved can vary and this stalking period can take months or years. This builds up to the moment they take action, and gain fulfilment from the crime.

The memory and experience of the murder becomes a realization of the fantasy and that is enough for them in the beginning. Some killers never move on after this, but some do. As the heightened experience of the murder diminishes, the cycle begins again. What emerges is a continuous spiral of murder where, as the pattern continues, the cycle accelerates. And while every murder delivers a sense of pleasure and climax to the serial killer, it is also traumatizing, even though they don't experience it in this way – it actually deepens and heightens their psychosis, helping to create the state of crisis. This has been observed in numerous cases, Jeffrey Dahmer, for example. There was a break of nine years between his first and second victim. Then it accelerated to one a year and got faster still. At the time of his arrest, he had killed four men in the space of three weeks and was in a state of traumatic crisis . . .

Amanda put the book down. She was no psychologist, but, whichever way you looked at it, Ruth was doing this with greater frequency.

She picked up the phone to call Billy and walked into the bedroom to see if she had anything to wear.

That's when she remembered there was still a black garbage bag of clothes in the bathroom. They had bloodstains on them. Quinn's blood. And in among them was the second burner phone. She had to get rid of it, right now. Throwing on some sweats, she grabbed the bag and her smokes.

She took the elevator down, went through the small lobby and out onto the street. Fishing the pack out of her pocket, she lit one and smoked while she walked. Four blocks up and on the right was an alley with dumpsters.

It was a quiet morning, with few people on the streets. It would be a little busier later with the parade, she guessed. With any luck, no one would see her dump the bag. She made it to the alley, but the gate was drawn across it. Locked.

There was an alley beside her building. It wasn't ideal, but it would have to do. She couldn't walk the streets with the bag. Too many cameras.

She turned and headed back to her building, then stopped twenty feet from the entrance.

Detective Farrow exited her building. He took out his cell phone and began flicking his finger across the screen. Amanda slowly backed away. A twenty-four-hour laundromat was on her right. Those places never close, not even on Thanksgiving. She pushed the door and it opened. She went inside. Two people were in there, a little way from the door towards the back, staring at their phones. Amanda stayed by the window, keeping Farrow in sight. Then her cell phone began to vibrate in her pocket.

She took it out, stared at the screen.

Farrow was calling her.

He stood in the middle of the street, the phone at his ear.

Amanda held her cell in her hand. She'd known the cops would come for her once they'd connected her to the Quinn murder – probably with her DNA. She just hadn't expected it to be so soon. She'd been sure she'd have at least another day, maybe two. Farrow and Hernandez were working the Quinn case. She knew that all too well. He was here to arrest her. If he wanted to check in on her, he would pick up the phone. He never came to her apartment unannounced.

Her thumb hovered over the green circle with the picture of an old-style telephone in the center. She looked up at him, trying to read his body language. He was facing away from her so she couldn't see his expression.

It was a little noisy in the laundromat. A couple of the big industrial dryers were going, and the radio played over the top. If she answered, Farrow might hear the dryers. He might turn round and see her.

She let the call go to voicemail. Safer that way.

Farrow talked. She couldn't hear what he said, but she saw his jaw working. Then he looked at the phone, ended the call and put it back in his jacket. He made his way across the street to his car, got in.

He didn't drive away.

Amanda hunkered down in the window, making herself small in case he saw her. She had a bag of bloody clothes in her hand from the attempted murder case he was investigating. On no account could he see her.

She wondered if she could sneak out the front door and make it back to her apartment without him noticing. Moving closer to the front door, she kept her eyes on him as he sat behind the wheel of the car. He faced forward.

Taking hold of the door handle, she began to pull it down.

Farrow's head swung round, back in the direction of her building, and Amanda ducked, hiding behind a change dispenser. She waited, afraid to move. Glancing behind her, she saw the two people in the laundromat still on their phones, taking no notice.

She stepped back, took a seat on the end of the bench that divided the room, sat up straight. She could just see over the bank of coin machines and the small counter at the front of the window. The top of Farrow's car was visible. She inched off the seat, checked to make sure he was still behind the wheel.

And he was, thank God.

After ten minutes he still hadn't driven off. He was waiting for her. Watching the entrance.

Amanda knew then she had run out of time. She needed to make herself disappear and find Naomi as soon as possible. But the money she'd taken from Quinn's lockbox was in her apartment. With her laptop.

She needed all of it.

Amanda turned and looked to see if there was a rear exit to the laundromat. As she did, she took out her cell, dialed into her voicemail and put the phone to her ear.

53
Ruth

The crowds began to gather along the parade route in Manhattan at five a.m. By six thirty the streets were packed with families, five deep, waiting for the parade to begin at nine. Ruth didn't want to stand in the cold for that long. She had booked a window table at Stella 34 Trattoria.

She arrived at eight thirty and entered Macy's on 35th Street. The express elevators took her straight to the restaurant where she was seated with coffee and pastries as the parade began. The restaurant was full of kids, some in fancy dress – some of the parents too. There was face painting and a holiday atmosphere that gave Ruth a warm feeling.

Her early memories of Thanksgiving were getting up early to watch the parade on TV. Her family rarely went into the city on parade day. Her mom didn't like the crowds and her father complained about parking. After her parents divorced, Ruth didn't get to go to the parade until she was an adult. When she'd first moved to Manhattan, Ruth made a point of coming to Stella 34 to watch the parade. It was expensive – four-hundred dollars for a table, which she couldn't afford back then – but being so close to the sights and sounds and the floats and bands and cheerleaders . . . it was magical and worth living off instant noodles for a month afterwards.

The wonder on the faces of the children around her was more soothing than she cared to admit. Knowing she would never bring her own child to the parade somehow didn't matter in that moment. It would afterwards, but not now. She gazed at the excitement in the children's eyes as they pointed at the vast inflatables of their favorite cartoon characters. But, more than anything, Ruth just loved the spectacle of it all.

The highlight, for the kids, and for the grown-ups too, was the big guy. Macy's Santa closing the parade. It reminded her of sitting on her father's lap, watching *Miracle on 34th Street*.

Nostalgia was good for the soul.

As the parade wound down, Ruth made for the gift shop and saw snow globes on sale. One caught her eye. A miniature family, all in their winter clothes, standing on a snow-covered hill. A mother, father and two kids. She shook it, watched the white plastic particles dance in the liquid and then slowly descend on the hill. It was a plain souvenir, with no music box in the base, but still she couldn't resist. Ruth took the globe to the counter and paid for it. The assistant put it in a flimsy box for her and then Ruth went to the elevator. She was first in line.

Stepping inside as the doors opened, she moved to the rear of the elevator car, turned and leaned against the mirror on the back panel. Two children came inside. One was dressed as a bumblebee, a little boy, probably four or five years old with long blond baby curls. His sister was a little older. She was a fairy princess, in a pink sparkly dress with fine, plastic wings on her back covered in glitter. The fairy princess held her mom's hand – a woman with dark brown hair, chestnut. She wore an expensive navy cashmere coat and an equally expensive scent. The father was tall, with close-cut black hair, a square jaw and the most luminous, almost shimmering blue eyes. The family exuded the old wealth and privilege that was the dream of everyone who came to the city. The boy stood close to his father, who smiled at Ruth as he got in, then turned his back on her to face the door. Her heartbeat quickened. The big scar on her belly began to itch and burn, as if someone was swiping a blow torch over it.

Macy's department store was in an old building. A New York staple. With age came character and an accelerating demand on maintenance. The doors rattled and screeched closed, and the elevator descended with a metallic whine. The noise made her wince as it resounded in her head, painfully. For a moment, Ruth didn't know if it was the elevator making the noise for in her mind the old chest was vibrating – the wood was groaning, and the entire chest shook, rumbling on the floor. Something inside was trying to get out. The thick chains around it screamed with the strain as the lid threatened to break every link.

Instinctively, Ruth covered her ears.

It took half a second to register that she'd let go of the snow globe. She realized right before she heard it exploding on the floor of the elevator. It sounded like a shot. Ruth heard something else mingled with that noise – metal being torn asunder, wood splintering and the whine of heavy brass hinges turning.

The two kids jumped, and the girl let out a short squeal of surprise and hugged her mom, burying her face in the mother's coat. The globe had burst out of the box. Fragments of wet, curved glass sat in the puddle of liquid that had gushed from the globe.

Ruth bent down to pick up the box. As she did so, she must've stepped on a shard, because she heard a sound. *That* sound. The same sound she'd heard in the bedroom of her brownstone in Manhattan that night, all those years ago – the *crunch* of glass underfoot.

She saw her reflection in the broken arch of glass. Her image distorted from the curvature, but still brightly lit from the overhead light in the elevator.

That sound again.

Crunch.

Her flesh burned with fear. Her fingers began shaking as they reached down.

Crunch.

And then she froze. Her throat closed. Her body shut down as if someone had thrown a circuit breaker in her brain. She couldn't move. Couldn't breathe.

All she could do was see. Her eyes locked on the floor.

Because there was another face reflected in that elliptical shard of glass.

A man with dark hair and iridescent blue eyes. Gazing down upon her.

Ruth's head swam, and she was no longer in Macy's elevator. She was at home, in New York, in her hallway. Scott was out partying, and she was looking at her attacker's reflection in the broken pane clinging to the frame of her back door.

Her head tilted up. She didn't want to look. But she couldn't stop herself. As her gaze lifted, she saw them.

All of them.

Staring at her. In unison. The little boy, the girl, the mother and *him*. Cold grins on their faces. Their eyes were set in anger. Twin orbs of blue flame in each of their faces. All of them, looking *right* at her. And then she heard them.

They spoke as one. A stentorian choir of sibilant voices.

'*Hello, sweetheart . . .*' they said.

The elevator stopped suddenly with a booming *thunk*, taking Ruth to the floor. When she looked up, the father, the mother and the boy had turned away, staring at the doors, waiting patiently for them to open. The mother had a tight grip on her daughter's hand. She whispered to her to turn round – that she shouldn't stare.

But the little girl did not turn away. The fairy princess stared at Ruth over her shoulder, with large, blue, innocent eyes. Those eyes were so big, and so gentle. Her wings glistened in the light. Her child's lips parted into a smile.

'Happy Thanksgiving,' said the fairy princess sweetly.

Ruth, on her knees, was close enough to smell hot chocolate on the little girl's breath.

Another screech came as the doors parted. Ruth held her palm to the side of her head. She could feel a terrible pain pulsating in her skull. She stepped out of the lift, following the family as they weaved through the first floor back onto 35th Street. The headache began to ease, and she tapped at her wrist as she walked, keeping the family in sight and trying to keep the panic down.

She kept her distance along 35th Street – two blocks – watching the wings of the fairy princess fluttering in the wind that whipped round the corners. Then a right on 5th Avenue and they doubled back, up 34th Street, avoiding the crowds and the blockades as they were dismantled after the parade. They went into George Towers. The concierge held the glass entrance doors open for them. They walked past the reception desk, and straight to the elevators. Ruth stood in the recessed entrance, took her pack of cigarettes from her bag and pretended to fumble with the pack and her lighter. The concierge ignored her. He waited by the elevators, which were old and now considered positively chic in the city. A black iron gate had to be drawn away when the elevator arrived, and then closed again by the concierge before the elevator ascended. Like something from an old Hitchcock movie, thought Ruth.

The family got into the elevator, the concierge closed the gate and wished them a good day. Ruth opened the glass door and went inside. The concierge asked if he could help her.

'My lighter just went out – do you happen to have a light or a book of matches?'

'Sorry, ma'am,' he said.

'Thanks anyway,' she said, turning towards the doors. She took out her phone, stalling for time. She held it to her ear, said, 'Hello.'

She knew the concierge was watching her. She took another step towards the exit. Slow. There was a floor display above the elevator, art deco design, with a clock hand, like an arrow, that swiped from left to right, from floors one through ten. She watched the arrow on its arc, saw it stop at floor ten, the top floor, then she took another step.

'Ma'am, this is private property. Residents only,' said the concierge.

'Uh-huh,' she said into the phone, holding up an apologetic hand. She walked to the exit, turned again, one last time to mouth 'thank you' at the concierge and checked the readout above the elevator.

It was still on ten. That was their floor. The elevator hadn't moved for over a minute. No question that was their destination.

She glanced to the right. At the gold inlaid mailboxes. They were in numerical order.

1001, 1002, 1003.

Three apartments on the tenth floor. A brass nameplate beside each one.

1001 R. Walker

1002 R. Roman

1003 The Grangers

Ruth left the building, put her phone back in her pocket and headed through the crowds back to her car in the lot on 29th Street.

The Grangers. It wouldn't take long for her to find out more about them online. Instagram, Linked-In, Facebook, Twitter. She could have all the pictures she needed to create her fake web pages of news stories in a few hours.

This one would be more complicated than any before. She would need someone special for this. In the elevator at Macy's they had looked at her. They'd recognized her – and they'd all spoken those words – together. They all *knew*. The one who'd attacked her, the father, he must've told them. They were laughing at her.

She clutched her scarred stomach.

The man who did this to her needed to be punished. He should suffer. He should watch his children die. Then his wife should be killed in front of him, right before he was murdered.

Luckily, she had the perfect partner for the Grangers. Someone she had been working on for the last two months.

His name was Gary Childers.

When she got back to her car, she fished in her bag and found the burner phone with the label 'Gary' on the back. She turned it on, cycled through the messages.

Gary had been talking to her for two months now. Actually, he was talking to a woman he thought was called Amy. One of her current aliases. Gary had lost his entire family – wife and teenage daughter – when their house burned down in Jersey. A local boy from a troubled family, seventeen and full of spit and venom, well known to the police, had been out the night before, shooting fireworks around the neighborhood. Gary had caught him and told him to stop being an asshole or he would call the cops.

The next night Gary was on night duty. He was a security guard watching a warehouse in a nearby industrial park. He told Amy he saw a fire in the distance one night. He could see the flames burning over the rooftops of the houses a mile and a half away, lighting up the sky. When he got the call from the NYPD halfway through his shift, he collapsed.

According to the local kid's parents, he had been at home that night. All night.

The fire department said the fire had been caused deliberately. The front door had been nailed shut, his back porch soaked in gasoline. The fire had been ignited with a type of firework that spat out sparks like crazy.

Ruth scrolled through Gary's messages. Then found what she was looking for.

I can't move on. It's not right. There's no justice. I want to kill that fucking kid. Before I blow his brains out I want to kill his father, and his mother, and his kid brother and I want him to watch. Then I'll do him.

And, below that message, Amy's reply.

I know exactly how you feel.

Of all the men and women who had killed for Ruth, Gary was perhaps the most dangerous. The most seriously unhinged.

Avenging heroes don't kill children. She needed someone special, like Gary. To kill a fairy princess, a bumblebee, and mom and pop too, she needed a monster.

Gary was that monster.

She turned on the car, lighting up the dash. The purr of the engine soothed her. She tapped her thigh. Tried to control her breathing. She connected her phone to the car's Bluetooth and called him.

'Amy?' he said. His voice was thick and slow.

'The one and only,' said Ruth. 'I wanted to call and see how you're doing.'

He sighed, said, 'I'm not good, to be honest. It's always tougher around the holidays.'

She could tell from his voice he'd been drinking.

'You don't have your gun with you, do you?' she asked.

'Right here beside me on the kitchen table.'

'Is it loaded?'

'Not yet.'

'Do me a favor, Gary. Don't load it. Not today. Not yet. I know it's hard. It's so terribly fucking hard, but you're giving up on your family if you put that gun in your mouth. Don't quit on me. I need you. I've been thinking about Kirk and my little Sammy. It would've been our fifth Thanksgiving as a family. If that drunk driver hadn't ended it all . . .'

'I've been thinking about my family too. It's not fair, Amy. It shouldn't be this way.'

'I know exactly how you feel.'

'You always have,' he said.

'Gary, what I'm going to say may sound a little crazy . . .'

'Oh, don't worry. I'm all in favor of crazy these days.'

She pretended to laugh, then said, 'Well, I've been doing some thinking. Tell me, have you ever seen the movie *Strangers on a Train*?'

54
Amanda

The voicemail from Farrow made her want to throw up.

She listened as she watched him pull away in his car. He might come back. In fact, it was a certainty.

'Hi, Amanda, it's Detective Farrow. I called at your place late last night and again this morning – you didn't answer the com. We have to talk, urgently. You can get me on this number. We need you to come into the precinct. Call me back.'

The tone was formal. Not the same cop who'd held her while she wept, and whose heart had been broken by the loss of her family. Farrow had looked out for her. Stayed in touch. Kept her out of jail when she should've been arrested outside Crone's building. Made sure she went to group therapy and didn't violate her parole.

This didn't sound friendly any more.

She watched Farrow pull away in his car, but the relief didn't last long.

She left the laundromat, went round the side of the building to the line of dumpsters, lifted the lid on one that looked almost full and dumped the bag of clothes.

Her knee was beginning to bark again when she got back into her apartment, pleased and relieved that he hadn't hammered down her door. Don't cops need a warrant for that? Maybe that's where Farrow was headed. He might be on his way to get a warrant and then he would be back.

She packed a few things in a bag. Her laptop, the money, some clothes, Sparkles the unicorn and Luis's wedding ring. She couldn't leave those behind. Not ever. As she went into the bathroom to grab her toothbrush and personal items, she froze. Her hands full. Listening.

She thought she'd heard someone knocking.

She quickly stuffed everything she needed into her gym bag, zipped it up and then . . .

Knock, knock.

Jesus.

He couldn't have come back so soon, she thought. If he went out to get a warrant then there was no way he could have made it back that fast.

Knock, knock. And this time, the knocking came with a voice.

'Amanda White?'

She moved quietly to the front door. It was closed, but not bolted or locked. She carefully raised her eye to the peephole in the center of the door.

On the other side stood a man in a pale brown suit. White shirt. Yellow tie. Small, squat, balding and a shoulder bag on his arm. A man in his late fifties maybe. The skirt of hair that remained round the crown of his skull was almost completely gray, with only a few dark streaks here and there. His shirt buttons strained at his small, round belly.

A cop. A detective. They had come to arrest her.

The man's eye level rose, and a knowing smile curled his jelly cheeks.

'I know you're in there. I can see you blocking the light in the peephole. You need to open the door. There's no way around this, Miss White.'

She ducked, instinctively. It felt as if he was able to see through the peephole – as if he was looking her right in the eye.

Knock, knock.

'Come on. Let's not make a scene for the neighbors. Open up,' he said.

She swore. It was too late. She'd run out of time. With no Naomi, she would have to face the charges alone. And she would suffer for what she had done to Quinn. Her shoulders slumped, and she reached out for the door lock.

She turned it, opening the door.

The man still wore that sickly smile as he spoke. 'Amanda White?'

She nodded, her stomach tightening, bile in her throat.

He reached behind his back. Handcuffs, she thought. Amanda held out her hands, closed her eyes.

She awaited the sensation of cold steel snapping round her wrists. She had failed. And it was time to face up to what she had done.

She felt something in her hands. Paper. No handcuffs. She opened her eyes. A brown letter-sized envelope in her grip.

'You've been served, lady,' said the man before turning towards the elevator.

Every ounce of breath left Amanda's body. It was almost as if she'd been tensing herself in preparation for a physical blow. Her shoulders fell, the ache in her jaw subsided, her body uncoiled.

She stepped back into her apartment, shut the door and tore open the envelope.

It was Crone's lawsuit. His lawyers had filed it in court. Amanda had not answered any of their letters. They were now taking her to court for damages. They'd waited until Thanksgiving morning to serve the papers – knowing that it would be especially upsetting to get them today.

She almost laughed.

Amanda threw the papers on the floor, picked up her bag and shut the apartment door behind her. She thought she would never see the place again. All her memories were now behind a closed door. Soon, her life would be spent behind a steel door in a prison cell.

Part of Amanda accepted that fate. But she would be damned if she would be spending that time alone. She went back out on the street, made sure Farrow's vehicle wasn't around, just in case he'd made a loop of the block. It would be unwise to use her cell phone to make the next call. No point in making a road map for the cops. Instead, she found a payphone across the street and used it to call Billy.

'Hey, I know you were going to call me when you had something, but I need to see you. Whatever we're doing to find Ruth we have to do it faster. I think the cops are looking for me. I'm leaving my apartment; I can't stay here.'

'Oh no, oh God. Amanda, I'm so sorry. Look, let me know where you are and I'll come pick you up.'

'I need a place to stay,' she said.

'You can stay with me. It's fine. I'm just emailing my PI back. A lot has happened this morning. Good and bad,' said Billy. 'My PI contacted me to say there is nothing, anywhere, on Ruth Gelman.'

'What do you mean?'

'I mean she doesn't have a bank account, she doesn't have a credit card, there's no record of a current address, she's not registered with the usual utilities, no record of a cell phone in her name . . .'

'Jesus Christ, I thought we were getting somewhere,' said Amanda.

'She's using fake identities, so she can't be tracked. She dumps one ID then uses another. Unless we know which ID she's using right now, there's no way to find her.'

Amanda bit down, hard, grinding her teeth.

'But I think there's someone who might be able to help us find her,' said Billy.

'Who?'

'I've been talking to Dr. Marin at Kirby Psychiatric Center. He was the one who treated Ruth when she was inside. I told him I'd met Ruth and I believed she was experiencing hallucinations, delusions and accusing men of being her attacker.'

Smart, thought Amanda. 'What did he say?'

'He wants to evaluate her, and if she's become a danger to herself, or others, he can take her back into hospital. So at least we know what to do when we find her. But, more than that, Marin is helping set up a visit with someone tomorrow. Someone who might know how Ruth got those fake identities.'

'Who is it, and why can't we talk to him today?'

'He's in prison. Marin is going to help smooth things to get an urgent visit, but it can't be today. It'll have to be tomorrow. The man we need to talk to is Scott Gelman. Ruth's husband.'

55
Farrow

After he'd left Amanda's building, Farrow drove back to the precinct. The Thanksgiving Day shift varied. Sometimes it was busy – usually domestics. Sometimes it was quiet. Today was one of the quiet days. He had peace to think.

He called the hospital and they said Quinn hadn't improved. The bleeding and trauma to the chest had caused a cardiac arrest. He was deteriorating and remained unconscious.

Farrow glanced at the stack of files below his desk. All unsolved. Most cops kept their working files in the cabinets. When a case could not be closed, after a while, it got iced. It was supposed to be put away, marked as unsolved and relegated to a box in the basement. If new information came up, the case could be thawed and re-opened. Few, if any, were ever resurrected.

The stack below his desk all should've had a layer of ice on them. Instead, they had been saved from the freezing basement, and allowed to gather a little dust. Farrow could not bear to put them away. He had few unsolved for a veteran cop. Part of it was luck, maybe. But part of it was due to his stubbornness and tenacity.

At the top of that pile was a Manila folder. Actually, three Manila folders, held together with purple string. At some stage, probably more than five years ago, some joker in the homicide division had drawn a pair of blue eyes on top of the file in magic marker. Those eyes stared back at Farrow from below the desk.

Mr. Blue-eyes had not re-surfaced since the attack on Ruth Gelman, more than ten years ago. Farrow often wondered what had happened to him. Maybe he was in prison for something else? Maybe he was dead?

Farrow couldn't say what had happened to make the killings stop. The one possibility he feared the most was this – what if the killings hadn't stopped, and he was simply missing those victims, not connecting them to the first two murders and the failed attack on Ruth Gelman? He knew Mr. Blue-eyes had been interrupted during Ruth's attack – he'd heard sirens and fled the scene before finishing off the victim. Maybe he was too scared to do it again?

Or maybe he stepped up his game afterwards, and took pains to better hide his victims, change his MO.

That's why Farrow put out a standing order to all dispatchers. Any homicide or attempted homicides involving home invasion in the Manhattan area – Hernandez and Farrow got a courtesy call. Sometimes it was clear before they even went to the scene that it was unconnected – sometimes they got an incorrect call, like Quinn, where the victim was male; sometimes it wasn't exactly clear whether it was related to Mr. Blue-eyes or not. Out of the calls he and Hernandez had attended in the last ten years – maybe two could've been Mr. Blue-eyes, maybe none. Hernandez always complained about it – thought it was a waste of time, and an opportunity for Farrow to pick up more cases that they didn't need.

He knew that he took those additional cases because he could close them. And in doing so he could get some release. Some relief from the cold files that hung around his feet like ghosts.

He stared at the blue eyes on the cover for a while, shook his head. He had another old case gathering heat, and he somehow wanted that to start warming up Mr. Blue-eyes, melting that magic marker on the file.

He sighed, rubbed his temples and got back to work. He spent the shift with his head buried in reports, statements and then went home. He ate a turkey club, in honor of Thanksgiving, watched a game on TV, then went to bed.

Back pain woke Farrow the next morning just after four a.m. Slowly, he turned over on his side, clenching his teeth with the pain. His bladder was calling him to the bathroom, but it would have to wait. With great effort, Farrow swung his body over to lie on his front.

He panted, rhythmically, filling his lungs before his next move. Breathing hurt. Lying down hurt. Everything hurt. Swinging his feet clear of the bed, his toes found the floor. Then he began to push himself up into a standing position. Straightening up was a slow process. One he had to do in stages. Four minutes later, he stood by the bed, the pain manageable. It was two steps to the nightstand and his glass of water and a bottle of OxyContin. Those steps were halting and slow, as if each one brought a baseball bat across his spine.

He drank first to wet this throat, then again to swallow the pills.

They would take a half hour to kick in. About as long as it would take him to get downstairs and make coffee. They would take the edge off the pain and any dulling effect on his mind would have worn off by the time his shift began. He got into the shower, turned the water up as hot as he could bear and let the jet pound his back. It helped loosen him up. After that, he dressed in a clean blue shirt, and navy suit. He had a device he'd ordered from one of the shopping channels to help him put on his socks. His shoes were slip-ons, and he was able to work his feet into them. He unplugged his phone from the charger and put it in his pants pocket. Leaving the suit jacket and tie in the hallway at the bottom of the stairs, he went into the kitchen and started to grind coffee beans.

He'd just hit the plunger on the French press when his cell phone rang.

The time on the phone read five fifty a.m. Never a good sign when the phone rings at that time of the morning.

'Did I wake you?' said Hernandez.

'Nope, I was already awake and doing my hot yoga exercises.'

'I can't picture you in spandex. This is a good thing for me.'

'You're up early. Did you have a nice holiday yesterday?'

'It was boring as hell. I watched the parade on TV, ate dry turkey and harassed the forensic techs.'

'They find anything on Quinn's computer yet?'

'They're still looking. Apparently, he has state-of-the-art security.'

'His tax returns just say he's a consultant. Is he some kind of security specialist?'

'Could be, but we'll find out soon enough. I did get something back on the cell phone found in the tool shed, though,' said Hernandez.

'Something good, I hope.'

'It's a burner – disposable. The batch number was traced to an order from a smalltime store in midtown. I got the owner yesterday at home. She's got good records. She'd ordered five of those phones. She's got three in stock. Two were bought last week.'

'She remember the buyers?'

'We're not that lucky, but she did tell us that it wasn't two buyers, it was one. Both phones are recorded as sold in a single transaction. Are you coming in today?' asked Hernandez.

'I'm going to try to find Amanda. I didn't get her on Thanksgiving Eve and when I went by her apartment yesterday morning there was no answer. I left her a voicemail. Asked her to come in.'

'And you think she'll do that?'

'I think so. I didn't tell her what it was about. Not exactly the kind of thing you can lay out in a voicemail. She'll come in. She trusts me.'

'How do you think she'll react?'

'If I know Amanda, she'll put up a fight. Look, just keep on those computer techs. Quinn is a blank, and I think that laptop has some answers – maybe even a motive.'

He ended the call, pushed the plunger all the way down on his coffee and poured himself a cup.

It wasn't like Amanda not to return his calls, but it was Thanksgiving yesterday. Holidays were especially tough for the bereaved.

He tried calling again, but the call went straight to voicemail. He didn't leave another message. He'd been around lost and broken people for too long.

He knew it paid to be sensitive. And he knew Amanda was in trouble.

In the early days after Luis and Jess's funeral, Amanda would call Farrow every other day. When there was a development, or anything of note to report, he called her straight away. Farrow had never married. Didn't have kids. He'd realized early that the job and a fulfilled family life were not easy bedfellows. Some cops could do it. They could come home on time, switch that shit off and be with their kids, their wives or husbands. It was not something Farrow could do. The job demanded too much. It consumed his every waking moment. Even his dreams. He sometimes saw their faces in the dark – the ones whom he'd found. The dead victims. Crying out to him in the night. Reaching for him. Not to hurt him. They always wanted to touch his hand. Hold on to him.

And so he held on to them. Kept them close.

He owed the dead a debt. And he saw to it that it got paid.

He'd been the second cop on the scene when Jess's body had been found. That was one night he would never forget. A little girl in a dumpster surrounded by black garbage bags. Her small hands. Her toes. Cold. Dead. Unnatural.

That image took something from him that day. And replaced it with a fire. Something very human inside Farrow was brought alive. It burned in him. It flamed whenever he sat across the table from Wallace Crone in the precinct interview room. He knew the man had killed that little girl. He was certain of it. And while Crone had constantly denied it – in his black eyes Farrow saw the truth.

He'd seen not only that Crone had killed the girl, but that he had enjoyed it.

He would never forget that interview.

Crone had been questioned by police on multiple occasions. This time it was no different. He sat in the interrogation room with this lawyer, who told him not to say anything. Of course, Crone was too narcissistic to take the advice to heart. He didn't answer all of their questions, but he didn't mind riling them up.

'Where were you on the day Jess White was abducted?' asked Hernandez.

He didn't answer. He just looked at the shoulder of his tailormade suit and brushed some tiny speck of dust from it, then he smiled.

'We have a man on security footage leading Jess away from the park, and that man looks a lot like you. That's why you're here.'

Crone merely shrugged, said, 'It wasn't me.'

'Don't you care that a child was abducted, abused and murdered?' asked Hernandez. It was an open question – appealing to the side of Crone's personality that thought of himself as a victim of the police.

The answer he'd given to that question, in that room, that day, still made Farrow's heart beat faster.

'When you say abused, you mean, they had sex? That's not abuse. Some girls are more mature than you give them credit for. I treat them like the women they are. You know my history – my rap sheet. I like young girls, Officer Hernandez. I like to sleep with them. You wouldn't understand, but there's nothing wrong with that. They like it. I like it. I don't see a problem. I don't know this girl, but from what you've told me it sure sounds like someone had a good time with her.'

Hernandez had looked at Farrow then. They'd sat side by side. Her mouth was open.

'I knew you wouldn't understand. Society has created a false narrative. If you look at the Bible, this happened all the time,' said Crone.

Neither of them could speak. Farrow gritted his teeth.

'You're pretty cute,' said Crone, still staring at Hernandez. 'But you're too old for me. Do you have any kids?'

The lawyer told him, right then, to keep quiet, and Crone leaned back in his seat, folded his arms and put another smug grin on his face.

To this day, months later, Farrow still wasn't sure how he or Hernandez were able to hold their nerve in that room, and not reach over the table and strangle Crone to death. God knows he deserved it.

As well as a debt owed to the dead, Farrow owed something to those left behind. Amanda had been hit harder than most, and Farrow had watched her heart break, and yet what pulled at him was that she never gave up. She kept fighting. Even when it was hopeless.

He'd spent many late nights sitting on her couch, listening to her talk about Jess and Luis and the life that they'd had, and all the things that they would never have now. It was fuel for Farrow. The pain helped to keep him sharp. Ready. On the edge.

When the forensics team had called him and given him the news on their DNA results, he'd felt his heart trip out of rhythm.

Amanda didn't deserve what was coming to her. And he needed to be there, in person, to hold her hand once again.

56
Amanda

Amanda woke in a warm bed in an unfamiliar room.

Floral wallpaper, the scent of lavender on her pillow. The morning broke through the gaps in the shades, throwing rectangles of light onto the white sheets. Jess's toy unicorn lay on the pillow beside her.

She was in Billy's spare room, in his little house in Queens. She could hear music playing downstairs. Country music.

She showered, picked out some fresh clothes. The smell of fried bacon drifted up to her room as she was drying her hair with a towel. Amanda put on jeans and a white sweater, went downstairs.

The music she'd heard sounded more familiar as she reached the hallway. Dolly Parton. She didn't mind it.

The house was small, but well cared for. She passed the open door of his study on her way to the kitchen and paused. Stepped inside. Oak-stained floors and dark wood wall panels. Watercolors of Celtic landscapes hung below brass lamps that threw warm light on the pictures. On Billy's desk were notebooks, and a map of New York with red sharpie circles dotted around. Amanda tried to quickly count how many circles there were. A dozen, maybe more.

Last night, Amanda had told him about the other possible victims, and Billy had made notes. He must've mapped them out this morning.

'You hungry?' came a voice.

Amanda left the study, went into the kitchen.

'I am now. I could smell that bacon a mile away.'

The kitchen was larger than she'd expected. She guessed the house had been extended at the rear. Billy wore a cooking apron over his gray shirt and blue slacks. He had a frying pan in one hand, and a spatula in the other. He placed two fried eggs on a plate next to strips of crispy bacon.

He seemed more animated to Amanda. As if having someone around, someone to look after, had lifted his spirits. He brought two plates of bacon and eggs to the dining table and placed them next to a pot of coffee and a rack of warm toast.

'Thank you,' said Amanda.

As she ate, she watched him wash his hands, strip off his apron and hang it carefully on a hook behind the door. Then he came over and poured coffee for both of them.

'Good?' he asked.

'Amazing,' said Amanda as she crunched through the bacon.

'I'm not much of a cook, I'm afraid. Lucille, well, she did most of the cooking around the house.'

'Well, you've mastered breakfast at least.'

'How's the knee?'

'A lot better. The heat packs and gel are working.'

'Any more calls from the cops?' he asked.

She shook her head.

'Good. If the phone rings, don't answer. We've got an important meeting this morning. How do you feel about going to Sing Sing? You ever been there before?'

'No. What's it like?'

'I went there a few years ago to visit an old buddy of mine from the service. I won't lie – it's scary. I spent most of my life on dirt-floored marine bases and naval ships. Living with thirteen-hundred soldiers is no picnic. But that place, it's, well, it's not like the military. When you go through security, into the visitors' area, and you hear all those steel doors clanging shut behind you . . . it's unnerving. And I don't scare easy.'

Amanda took a sip of coffee, put her cup down and said, 'I'm sure it'll be okay. We just need to think about how we're going to handle it.'

Billy buttered his toast and said, 'It's not going to be a walk in the park.'

'What makes you think he'll talk to us in the first place?' asked Amanda.

He lifted a slice of toast to his mouth, paused and looked at Amanda.

'He might not. He'll need to trust us. Dr. Marin knows Scott. He visited him, to discuss Ruth – get a better insight into what happened to her so he could deliver the best treatment. He told me himself. So if the visit comes with an introduction from Marin I think we're halfway there. He's our last shot. If anyone knows how to find her, it's Scott.'

'And what if he won't help?'

Billy took a bite out of his toast, chewed it thoughtfully, swallowed and said, 'Then we'll probably never find her. We need a game plan. He's still her husband. His first instinct will be to protect her.'

'We could use that. Lean into it,' said Amanda. 'He has to trust that we've got her best interests at heart.'

She paused, took a moment to stare at Billy and asked, 'Do we have her best interests at heart?'

'I can only speak for myself. She's done terrible things, but maybe that's because terrible things have happened to her? Ruth is sick. She needs help. That's the way I see it. How about you?'

Amanda put down her fork, drank some coffee, thinking it over.

'I'm not a social worker and I'm not a cop,' she said. 'Part of me feels sorry for her, despite what she's done. When I get arrested, I'll need her. I don't want to hurt her. Not any more. I want to stop her from hurting anyone else. Scott just needs to believe we're trying to help her.'

'A lot will depend on who he is now. Before this, he was a young lawyer and an upstanding member of society. He has a conscience. Remember what it said in that article, Scott called the police, confessed to Travers's murder and then jumped out of a window. If there's still any of that man left, we have a shot.'

'What makes you think he's changed?' asked Amanda.

'The head injury and ten years in Sing Sing. If any two things could change somebody, those are at the top of the list.'

Amanda and Billy sat on a steel stool in front of a steel-framed booth in Sing Sing Correctional Facility. A thick pane of Perspex glass separated them from the prisoner area. It was one booth in a line of twenty. All occupied. The other visitors were already talking on the phone to the prisoners they'd come to see.

The stool on the other side of the glass was still empty.

The phone in the corner of the booth on their side remained in its cradle. There were large, fierce-looking corrections officers all around. The way Billy had described Sing Sing didn't do it justice. Amanda had left her phone and personal belongings in a locker at the visitors' entrance, then she had been searched, passed through a metal detector and even been sniffed by drug-enforcement canines. She brought three pieces of paper with her. No pens. And she was warned not to try to pass anything to the prisoner.

Zero chance of doing that when he was on the other side of a glass partition.

There was tension in the gray corridors. Almost a sound. As if a steel cable was being pulled taut and could break at any moment. And every time she heard a metal door slam behind her she jumped. When this happened, a half second later, she felt Billy's strong hand on hers. Just a light touch, and then he let go. It was reassuring, just to know he was with her.

She could be entering a place like this, maybe soon. Only this time it would be as a prisoner. Locked up for attempted murder.

Not if she could help it.

A thin man in an orange prison uniform, with a graying moustache, walked towards their booth from the other side of the glass. He stood before the stool on his side, eyeing Amanda and Billy before he sat down. She wasn't scared of him. He looked like he didn't belong with the rest of the prisoners, who all seemed large and imposing, with keen, shifty eyes.

He sat down, picked up the phone.

Amanda picked up the phone on her side.

'Scott?' she asked.

He nodded. Didn't say anything. He was close to her now. Not more than three feet away, behind the glass, and now she saw some resemblance to the picture of him she'd seen on the news sites. There were changes, of course. The moustache, and a long thin scar that started on the left side of his forehead and disappeared into his hair line, and behind his ear.

He'd fractured his skull when he tried to take his own life by jumping from a window.

'Thank you for seeing me,' she said. 'My name is Amanda White. This is my friend, Billy Cameron. We met your wife, Ruth. That's why we're here. We're worried about her and we want to know if you can help us to help her.'

'Are you reporters? Cops?' he asked.

It reminded her of the first conversation she'd had with Ruth. Back then she was Wendy. She'd told a convincing story about being wary of reporters delving into her life.

'Neither. We're just friends. We both met Ruth in a counseling group. We don't know where she is, and we're real worried.'

Scott's eyes narrowed. He looked confused.

'What do you mean you don't know where she is? She's in Kirby, right?'

Amanda and Billy exchanged a look.

'Scott, didn't Dr. Marin tell you Ruth got released?' asked Amanda.

'N-no, he didn't. He came to see me, years ago, just after I started my sentence. I haven't heard from him since. The message I got from the C.O. yesterday was that Marin wanted me to speak to some people about Ruth and it was important. That's it. That's . . . all,' said Scott, his voice just starting to break.

He wanted to say more. His lips moved, his chest puffed, but no words came. He sniffed, looked around at the other inmates and wiped the corner of his eye. Amanda guessed he didn't want the rest of the prison to see him displaying any emotion. Weakness can get you killed in Sing Sing. A single tear in this place was like a drop of blood in a shark tank.

He sat up in the chair, cleared his throat.

Amanda realized then the weight of betrayal that had just landed on Scott.

'How . . . how long has she been out?' he asked.

'A few years,' said Amanda. 'She didn't come visit you?'

'Aw, no, no, she didn't. It's okay. Maybe there were restrictions, you know? Maybe part of her parole was she couldn't have contact with me?'

Amanda knew there were no parole restrictions. His wife had been released because she was no longer deemed insane. Looking at Scott, slouched, empty in that chair, Amanda thought she could be looking at herself in ten years. In so many ways, Scott was Amanda – they had made the same mistakes.

'I don't know if there were restrictions – maybe,' said Amanda. 'Look, Scott, we don't have a lot of time. I'm going to tell you the truth. A lot of what I'm about to say may sound bizarre and I'm not in the business of opening up to strangers, but I don't have a choice right now. I met Ruth at a group counseling meeting. It was for trauma victims. I lost my little girl and my husband in April. Ruth and I got to know each other. We were close. At least I thought we were. She went missing from the group.'

'Missing? Like she just stopped going?'

Amanda took a breath, paused. She needed to level with Scott to get what she needed from him. It was the only way, but it came with a risk. One she needed to take.

'No, she asked me to kill someone. Same with Billy. He met her in an online group a few months before me, and she asked him to kill the same person.'

Scott folded one arm across his chest, then placed the other on top, like he was throwing up a barricade.

'I don't get many visitors here, Miss White. My parents are too old now. But I don't know who either of you are. You don't look like cops . . .'

'We're not cops. And we're not reporters. We're concerned . . .'

'If you were so worried about Ruth, why not go to the cops? I'm sure they can find her.'

Amanda glanced at Billy, took the phone away from her mouth.

'You're doing great,' said Billy. 'Keep going.'

She sighed, said, 'We don't want to get Ruth into trouble. That's the truth. We know what happened to her. We know all about the attack. At first she seemed fine, then she started acting a little crazy. She tried to talk us into killing someone, Scott. We don't want anyone else to get hurt and we don't want Ruth to get into trouble with the police. She's sick, and she needs help.'

Scott laughed, a quick burst, which died just as fast. There was no mirth in it, just incredulity.

'She hasn't come to see me since she's been out. Even if I did want to help you, which I'm not sure I do, I'm not exactly up to speed on her current whereabouts.'

'Why wouldn't you help? This isn't about us; this is about helping Ruth.'

Scott looked around. It seemed to be a pattern. He couldn't settle, couldn't focus for long without taking a time-out to check his surroundings. The lack of focus could've been something to do with the brain injury, but Amanda thought otherwise. You don't survive in a place like this without watching your back. Pretty soon, it would become second nature.

'I don't know you. I don't know your friend here. Dr. Marin passed a message to me that I should talk to you, but right now I don't see why. I don't trust you. Either of you. No offense.'

'I'm not asking you to take what we say on blind trust.'

Amanda took the first piece of paper from the small stack in front of her, slapped it up against the glass. It was a printout from the web.

'Recognize this guy?' she asked.

Scott leaned forward, momentarily, studied the picture and then recoiled as if the image burned him.

'Get that out of my face. I know why I'm here, lady. You don't need to show me a picture of the guy I killed. I see his face every night before I go to sleep.'

'That's not Patrick Travers, Scott. Look again.'

He blinked. Unsure for a moment. He moved closer to the picture, squinted.

'Who is it?'

'Read the article,' she said. 'The man in this picture is dead. His name was Saul Benson. He was murdered by a guy named Kowalski. Kowalski claimed a woman called Deborah Mallory convinced him of a plan to swap murders, like the movie *Strangers on a Train*. Only Deborah didn't kill anyone for Kowalski – she only pretended to. Kowalski believed the guy was dead and killed Mr. Benson for Deborah, right before Deborah disappeared. Benson looks a hell of a lot like Patrick Travers, doesn't he?'

She paused, studied Scott's eyes. He was leaning forward, reading the article. When he was done, he leaned back, said, 'That doesn't prove anything . . .'

'What about this man?' she said, throwing up another picture against the glass. 'Look familiar? This isn't Patrick Travers either. This is the man she wanted us to kill. Someone got conned into attacking this man at his home just a few days ago,' said Amanda, managing to hold her voice straight, not letting it waiver with emotion. 'We'll probably never know who did it, but we can't let this happen again.'

She could see Scott's eyes moving across the image, and, as they did so, his expression changed. He was making connections – finally.

'And this one.'

Slap, another picture.

This was the earliest victim Amanda had found. Dan . . .

'Puccini,' said Scott, his gaze locked to the picture.

'Did you know him?' asked Amanda.

He shook his head, but he looked as if he'd seen a ghost.

'Do you see a pattern here, Scott? If not, read the headlines above the pictures,' said Amanda.

Each one of them carried a headline about the attack.

'Do the math. You believe me now?'

He sat back, blew out his cheeks. His eyes were wet, glazed in tears. He quickly rubbed his face with both hands. Masking the emotional response.

Amanda had to make her play now.

'The last thing I want is for someone else to get hurt. For another wife or mother to have to grieve like I do. Ruth is dangerous and she needs help. We need to find her and get her that help before she finds another man she thinks should be killed. Look at me and tell me I'm lying.'

He had no choice but to hold her gaze.

'Am I lying?'

He paused, wet his lips, said, 'I don't want her to spend the rest of her life in jail, or in some hospital. She didn't hurt anyone. Not intentionally.'

'That was before. It's different now. *She's* different now. I think she has been hurt too much, Scott. I think what happened to Ruth at her home that night – the night she was attacked? I think those wounds were a hell of a lot deeper than anyone realized. Help me. Help me to find her and I'll get her help. She doesn't have to be in the hospital for the rest of her life. Just until she's better. Just until she gets well again.'

He swallowed, put his head back and stared at the ceiling.

'*Strangers on a Train* was her favorite book,' said Scott. 'She had an old paperback of that novel. Took it everywhere with her. Last time I saw it she was using it as a doorstopper while she went out to a vending machine in our hotel.'

'Do you believe me?' asked Amanda.

He nodded, said, 'I believe you. But I still don't see how or why I should help you.'

'Don't do it for me. Do it for yourself,' said Amanda. 'Before all this, you were a good man. A lawyer. You had a life and a future, and I know if you could, you would go back and change things. I know you would give anything to go back and change what happened with Patrick Travers. But you can do the next best thing. You can make sure there are no more Patrick Traverses, or Dan Puccinis lying on a cold slab in the morgue.'

In prisons across America, there is something rarely found. It's elusive, and it takes a long time to come along if it ever does at all. For some inmates, they'd have better odds finding a pink diamond hidden in their mashed potatoes. When it does come along, it is to be grabbed with both hands – redemption.

Scott saw his chance, and he could not let it pass.

'Okay,' he said. 'But I need you both to leave your cell phone numbers on my contact list. If anything happens to Ruth, if she is harmed in any—'

'We're trying to help her. Not hurt her,' said Amanda.

'If she does get hurt, I'll know it was you two. And I'll call the cops, and whoever else I can think of to come after you.'

'Fair enough. I'll call you when we find her. And let you know she's all right. I promise.'

He nodded.

'The main problem we have is locating her. She's been living under false identities. Moving around the city. Before all this happened, she was a real-estate agent. Normal middle-class family. She wasn't a criminal. She had no connections to that world. So where did she get multiple fake IDs to build all these different identities?'

'She doesn't know anyone. But I used to. An old school buddy. Jack. She never liked him. Jack was always plugged into some sort of scam. He's the only person she might have gone to who would have those kinds of connections.'

'Where do I find Jack?'

'You don't. He won't talk to you.'

'So what do we do?'

'Leave your numbers on my call sheet, like I asked. I'll call Jack. If he has anything, I'll call you.'

57
Ruth

Ruth pulled into the driveway of a detached suburban home deep in central New Jersey, around two in the afternoon. Gary had called her back last night, said he'd watched the movie she recommended. They talked for half an hour and Ruth told him she'd like to meet. In person. Today.

He'd given her this address.

After the fire, Gary's insurance company paid out a settlement that had allowed him to buy this house. The garage door was half open, and Ruth could see piles of boxes stacked just inside. He'd moved in a year ago, and he'd told her he was still unpacking. Most days he couldn't summon up the strength to eat, never mind decorate or unpack what few items he had left after the fire.

She pressed the buzzer, stood at the front door and waited.

No answer. This time she pressed the buzzer for longer. Then knocked on the door. A brown sedan was parked in the driveway, so she guessed he was home.

Two minutes passed by and a creeping unease swept through her. It wasn't her usual sensation of fear – this was different. She tried his cell.

He didn't pick up.

Ruth moved around to the garage, lifted the door up a little more and went through on her hands and knees. She got up, called out his name and listened.

She could hear voices in the background. And then music. A TV turned up loud. The dumbass probably couldn't hear her knocking on the door with the volume up so high. The garage was filled with boxes. Some opened, some empty, but most were still sealed. She could see a door at the far end. She tried the handle. It was open. She called out as she entered a utility room that led to the kitchen.

'Gary?'

No answer. The damn TV was so loud now it was almost unbearable. She followed the sound to the living room.

Gary Childers sat on the couch in front of the TV. ESPN was blasting out at what must've been maximum volume. She grabbed the remote, hit the mute button then swung around.

Gary hadn't moved.

His dead eyes stared at the screen. The top of his head was missing.

Ruth stumbled back, dropping the remote.

A gun lay on the floor by his feet along with an empty bottle of whiskey. He'd turned the TV way up to mask the sound of the shot. Gary had talked about ending it many times. Putting the barrel of his pistol in his mouth and pulling the trigger. Ruth had talked him down more than once, knowing how useful he could be to her. Ruth swore, angry now. Gary was the only one of her current group targets who could do the job.

With the sudden silence in the room, Ruth could hear her heartbeat, a thumping rhythm that grew faster, and faster and then she realized it wasn't her heart.

The chest in her mind was rattling, the chains screaming again. Sometimes things got out of the box even though she tried hard to keep it closed. The sound and images flooded her mind. She clamped her hands to the sides of her head, but the assault was so great it brought her to her knees.

It was getting worse.

The peace she enjoyed after the killing was growing shorter and shorter, and the chest was growing bigger and angrier and louder, no matter how many chains she wrapped around it, no matter how deep she tried to bury it.

She knew things had to change. She had to be more involved. The knowledge that her target was dead wasn't enough. She knew that she had to somehow make it more real – so that she would know he was dead this time.

They were all him. That family. They all knew – they were all part of it. The child of a monster is still a monster. They all had the look – they all had those eyes.

Ruth had thought of asking Gary to take pictures after he had killed the Grangers. Something she could look at, and hold, and use to stretch out that golden hour into a day, a week, a month.

The loss of Gary Childers was hard to take. She could manipulate the right people into killing, but this was different. No one, apart from Gary, would destroy a whole family. A man, a woman. And two kids. They just couldn't. Gary could have done it, gladly.

She needed the release. The fear was taking hold again, rooting her to the spot. She looked up, from her kneeling position, and saw the gun lying on the carpeted floor, bloodstains dotted around it.

It would be easy to pick it up. Take it with her. Any damn fool can pull a trigger.

The thought of it brought a wave of excitement. Her chest fluttered, and her fingers trembled as she reached for the gun.

She hesitated, her hand hovering over the butt of the pistol.

'*Pick it up*,' said a voice.

Her gaze flicked to the TV screen. There was a graphic in the bottom left corner, indicating the volume had been muted.

'*Pick it up*,' said the voice.

She recognized the voice. There was a slow, wet sound to each word. Ruth raised her gaze, even though she felt a strong urge not to.

A will from somewhere inside to keep looking at the carpet. Something old and primal in her brain was warning her not to look up.

She couldn't help it.

Gary was looking at her. His eyes were black eight-balls – swollen, filled with blood and quite dead. His lips moved, blood pouring from his mouth as he said, '*Pick it up. Kill them all.*'

Ruth picked up the handgun at Gary's feet, put the gun in the waistband of her jeans. She took the remote control too, and carefully wiped down the door handle of the garage as she made her way out through the garage.

She got into the car, reversed and drove away fast.

58

Amanda

In the half hour since they had left Scott, neither Amanda nor Billy had spoken. There was a pressure inside the prison, and Amanda felt as though any word that escaped her lips would stay there, suspended in the heavy air, and for all to hear forever. Billy must've sensed it too.

It wasn't until they'd left the complex and were strolling through the parking lot that Amanda started to feel the pressure ease. They reached Billy's Escalade, got inside, and as the doors closed Amanda let out a long sigh. Billy started the car. Dolly Parton played on the stereo.

Billy loved Dolly Parton.

'You did great,' said Billy.

'Don't get your hopes up yet. Let's wait and see if he comes through with anything. You were right – it's really scary going in there.'

'Yeah, but it feels good leaving the place.'

Amanda checked her phone. There was another missed call from Farrow. But nothing else. She'd had to turn it off when she put it in the locker in the visitors' center. Billy drove out of the lot, onto Correctional Facility Road and soon found Saw Mill River Parkway, which flows into the Henry Hudson Parkway that hugs the river all the way back to Manhattan and 79th Street.

Just the feeling of being able to walk out of that prison gave

Amanda a sense of accomplishment. She prayed she would never have to go back. If she had to spend the rest of her life in a place like that, she knew she wouldn't be able to cope. Her good knee bounced her heel off the floor of the car with nervous energy. Every second in there had been hard, and going outside, gazing at the river and watching New York fly by the window, it helped.

Billy talked a little, pointing out some local landmarks, or good sandwich joints across the river in New Jersey. All the while, Dolly begged Jolene not to take her man, and then made her living nine to five. Occasionally, Billy would sing along, low, just under his breath. He was out of tune, but that didn't matter. His enjoyment was enough. Amanda found herself relaxing into the leather seat, and for a time she forgot the police were looking for her, that she had been manipulated into almost killing a man, that she was getting sued, that her husband and little girl were gone and that the man responsible would never pay for what he'd done.

It was a short period of respite. Thirty minutes, by the time they got back into midtown. And, during that time, she was content to be in a car with a good man who was willing to help her. She was not alone with her troubles, and there was still music and life, despite everything.

'Thank you,' said Amanda.

'For what?' asked Billy.

'For being a good man.'

'I'm not that good. I'm cooking meatloaf for dinner tonight. I think it would be wise to reserve your judgment until then – you might want to report me to the cops after that one.'

'How bad could it be?'

'It's a crime against meatloaf. But I try.'

Amanda's phone rang. The display lit up a phone number she didn't recognize. For a second, she thought Farrow might be trying her on a number she didn't know. Just in case she was avoiding his calls. But she couldn't take the chance of missing a call from Scott's friend. She picked up.

'Is this Amanda White?' said a voice. It was male. And it wasn't Farrow.

'Yes, this is Amanda. Is this Jack?'

'I don't talk on cell phones, lady. Get to a payphone. Call me on this number in the next ten minutes.'

Billy had heard the conversation, and he was already pulling over into a parking space. They got out of the car, looked up and down the street.

'There,' said Billy, pointing to a bank of payphones on the corner. They were a lot scarcer these days. Amanda made for the payphone, and Billy started fishing in his pockets for change. He brought a newspaper with him from the back seat in case she needed to take notes. He set a small stack of quarters on top of the phone hood. Amanda inserted the change, dialed the number.

'Hello, Jack?'

'Look, lady, I don't know who you are so I'd prefer if you didn't use names, okay?'

'All right, sure. I'm sorry.'

'Look, if the cops ever ask you about me, don't tell them anything. I was helping out my buddy's wife when she came to me, looking for IDs. She had been through hell. So had her husband. Anything I could do to give her a fresh start? Well, I was gonna damn well do that. I didn't charge her any money – it was a favor for a friend. So there's no need to mention my name if any of this gets to the cops, agreed?'

'Agreed.'

'I'm making this call for the same friend. I'm doing this for him, not you. Look, I made some calls, got a list of IDs to give you. I'm gonna read them out. The names and dates of birth. Got a pen?'

Amanda made a sign to Billy that she needed to write something down. Billy reached into his shirt pocket for a pen and gave it to Amanda along with the folded newspaper.

She listened carefully, wrote down the names and dates of birth, checking the spelling of a few of the names. She wrote down ten.

'That's all I got. Those are the most recent. Don't call this number again.'

The line went dead.

'What do we do now?' asked Amanda.

'I'll get this to the private investigator. He has access to credit-check facilities, databases and all kinds of online records I don't know about.'

'Is that legal?'

'That's a question I've never asked, and I don't want to know the answer to. It's hard enough to sleep as it is.'

'That's fair,' said Amanda.

Billy made the call from his cell, read out the names and dates of birth and spelled out some of the surnames.

He hung up, said, 'My guy says give him three hours. I asked him to hurry, but that's the best he can do.'

Amanda checked the time on her phone. It was almost four in the afternoon. Billy looked around, pointed to a pizza parlor across the street.

'I'm going to show you some mercy tonight. Let's go get some pie while we wait. We'll take a rain check on the meatloaf.'

59
Ruth

She raged around the apartment, swearing, kicking over tables and panting.

Ruth had fucked up.

She'd left behind Gary's cell phone. It would have the text messages on it, and her phone-call records. She would need to ditch this ID, permanently. And she'd only just set it up. There was no way she could linger. She would have to go to George Towers tonight. And then get the hell out of the city until things cooled down.

That meant there was little time to plan.

She could go into the lobby of the building and bluff her way upstairs. There were any number of ways to do it. A gourmet fruit-and-cheese basket would be easiest. She'd picked one up from an artisanal store a half hour ago. It was a wicker basket, with a large hoop for a handle, piled high with exotic fruit and cheese wrapped in muslin. The whole basket was covered in cellophane and a thick silk ribbon, red, tied in a bow, finished off the presentation. A delivery of high-class goods that had to be signed for – in person. Rich people are lazy, and instead of coming down to the lobby to sign for it and hump a heavy package into the elevator, they would let her come up, deliver it and sign for it. The fact that she was a small, skinny female with an expensive gift basket would put the concierge at ease. If she was six feet tall and male, the concierge might think twice about letting her go up to the tenth floor on her own.

Once she was on the tenth-floor, things would be easier. She could shoot Granger as he stood in the doorway, then the wife. The kids last.

Back down in the elevator, and then take care of the concierge on her way out.

It was possible. It was messy, but it was the best she could think of in the time.

She picked out some dark clothing. Put it on, checked her watch.

Almost eight. She would need to leave soon.

Before she went anywhere, she knew she had to check the gun. Ruth sat at the small dining table in her apartment and placed the pistol flat in front of her. She turned the weapon over in her hands, examining it. There was a small button on one side, just above the grip. She pressed it, and the magazine popped out of the receiver. There were slots cut into the magazine to allow the load to be checked visually. The mag was almost full. She reloaded the gun, racked a round into the chamber.

Guns were not complicated.

Ruth stood, put the gun in her coat pocket and looked around for her car keys.

It was then that she felt the pressure in her head. Going through the motions of planning a kill – one that she would have to carry out this time – had been a great distraction. The feeling of nervous exhilaration had quieted the old chest, and all the voices it constrained.

She suddenly felt a little foolish that in all this time she'd never thought about doing this herself. In person. Watching the light die in those blue eyes. There was an electricity in her veins. She felt more alive now than she had done in years. And, more than that, she didn't feel afraid. She felt powerful.

This felt right.

Ruth saw her car keys on the kitchen counter, swept them up and went to the front door. She unlocked it, stepped out into the hallway with the gift basket and slammed the door closed.

60

Amanda

It was almost seven thirty.

They'd finished the pizza, had coffee, some ice cream and Billy had distracted her with his near encyclopedic knowledge of Dolly Parton.

'I've got a confession to make,' said Billy.

'What? You don't like meatloaf?' said Amanda.

He smiled, and then it faded quickly as he spoke. 'No, it's Dolly. I was never a fan. Not in the beginning. I was an Eagles man. It was Luce, my Lucille that is, she was the Dolly fan. Had her records playing in the house almost constantly. After she was murdered, the place was so quiet. I put on Luce's records. I never liked them before, not really. But now I can't be without them. It reminds me of her, standing at the sink, washing dishes, singing "Your Cheatin' Heart".'

He laughed then, and it was genuine and warm.

'Tell me about your daughter,' he said.

Amanda normally resisted talking about Jess. But not then. It seemed different somehow. The tidal wave of pain that normally accompanied her memories of her didn't hit so hard this time.

'She loved unicorns. She had a whole collection of soft toys – you know – teddy bears, penguins, that kind of thing. But she never slept with them. She put them up on her shelf and she'd stare at them at night. She only ever slept with one toy. A white, fluffy unicorn she called Sparkles. Jess couldn't go to sleep without it. I was sick, after Luis took his own life. He blamed himself for Jess being stolen. I was in the hospital when Luis's parents buried them both. They forgot to put Sparkles in the coffin with Jess. That still bothers me. Jess was just . . . I loved her more than anything in this world, you know?'

She gazed out the window of the pizzeria at the passers-by.

'How did you feel when you thought Crone was dead?' he asked.

'Relieved. Like a cancer had been cut out of me. You know, when they found Jess, she was in a dumpster. Her clothes were missing. It was like she had been used, and murdered, and then just thrown away. I can't ever get that out of my mind.'

'They'll get him some day, Amanda. Men like that never change. They . . .'

He stopped talking. His phone had started to ring.

'Hello?' he said.

Amanda couldn't hear the other end of the call. Instead, she leaned forward, put her elbows on the table and fixed Billy with expectant eyes.

He made notes on his newspaper, flipped it over to the list of names Amanda had written out and then circled one of them.

She didn't want to get her hopes up, but she knew they were close. They had to be. This was all that mattered for now. Billy thanked the man on the other end of the line and hung up.

'Let's go. One of those IDs showed up as having a credit check completed against it last week. It was a rental company. My guy called them and gave them a story about checking on the reason for the credit search, making sure it was necessary and the individual had consented, etcetera. The credit search was because the person had rented an apartment in Brooklyn. I've got the address. They also came back with a DMV check on a black Mercedes S Class. It's registered to a different ID and address, but that was two years ago. The rental in Brooklyn is our best bet. It's the most recent, and it fits with the timeline of her moving after Quinn's attack.'

'Let's go find her,' said Amanda.

61

Ruth

Ruth had parked the Mercedes outside her building. Didn't want to be carrying the heavy basket too far. She put it on the backseat. Got in, started the car and pulled into the street. George Towers was only fifteen or twenty minutes away. It wouldn't take long. Ruth made sure to keep the car under the speed limit, signal all her turns. Last thing she needed was to be pulled over. She would try to park as close to the building as possible. It would be important to get away fast. Her thoughts drifted to Gary, and she wondered if he really could have done this? His will and desire were there, but that wasn't all it took.

With the online group sessions, Ruth made a point of never meeting her accomplices in person. It was safer that way. She had made an exception for Gary, because he was special. He was already homicidal. Some are like that. Others only think they can kill someone, and Ruth had become adept at spotting them. Some, like Amanda, only needed to be pointed in the right direction. Gary, though, would kill anyone, and anything. She knew if Gary had been doing this job, he would likely turn the gun on himself afterwards. That was a price she had been willing to pay.

A space opened up when a truck pulled out on 33rd Street. She thought about pulling in, then moved on, hoping to find a closer spot. There was a space just thirty feet from the entrance to George

Towers. She turned in, killed the engine and sat behind the wheel. The rush was intense. She pulled in a few breaths, let them out, running down her system, before getting out of the car and retrieving the gift basket from the back.

She put on a cap, sunglasses, opened the glass doors of George Towers and stepped into the ornate lobby. There, behind the desk, the concierge looked up from his screen and said, 'May I help you?'

This was a different concierge from the man she'd seen here previously. This one was at least a hundred pounds heavier – none of it muscle. His uniform was stretched tight across his chest, which made his name badge stand proud. The badge said 'Raymond'. He wore a thin moustache and beard, not pencil thin, but not far off. It gave Raymond a comic appearance.

'Sure, I have a special delivery for the Grangers,' said Ruth.

'I'll take that,' said Raymond.

'It's gotta be signed for by the recipient, I'm afraid. I've gotta hand it over in person.'

Raymond stood, looked Ruth over. Top to bottom.

'That's against our policy. I'll have to call Mr. Granger,' he said.

'No need. I sure don't mind taking it to him,' she said.

Raymond picked up the phone, started scanning a list of phone numbers on his desk.

'Mind if I put these down for a second? They're kind of heavy,' said Ruth, placing the basket on the desk.

Bent over to check the numbers, Raymond then looked at the phone, started to dial. He didn't see Ruth come round the desk and approach him from behind. She raised the butt of the gun, high, her arm stretched toward the ceiling, and she brought it down hard on the top of Raymond's head. A hollow, metallic thud. Raymond slumped over the desk, grunting.

She hit him again, and again, until the blood splashed over the list of phone numbers and the phone, and Raymond slid off the desk, and onto the floor.

Moving quickly, Ruth tore the cellophane of the basket open, untied the silk bow and then wrapped it round Raymond's neck, tying it in a simple knot. She held both ends of the silk, put her foot on Raymond's back and pulled.

His thick arms flailed, and he tried to get up onto his knees, but Ruth pressed down harder on his back – putting her full weight on him. His arms stopped moving. Ruth let go of the ribbon, put the gun in her jacket pocket and picked up the basket.

She looked at the elevator. It was vintage, with a scissor gate. She didn't trust old elevators. Ruth took the stairs, carrying the basket by the handle. Ten flights. Concrete steps in a ten-story cinderblock stairwell. She couldn't help but make an echoey sound with every footfall. The rhythm of her feet on the stairs sounded like a drum. The beat from her boots melded with the sound of thumping as something inside the old chest began to hammer at the lid from the inside. Her heart beat faster, the higher she got. Three independent beats – urging her on, higher and higher. The closer she got to the top floor, the louder they became.

And then she heard something else. She looked around, thought for a second it might be coming from an apartment on one of the floors closest to her.

But she knew, after a moment, the sound was coming from the chest.

A man's voice. Gentle and kindly. He was whispering . . .

'*Stop. Stop. Stop.*'

'It's *him*, Scott. I know it,' said Ruth out loud. 'You can't protect me. Just shut up.'

In her mind, she draped a heavy cloth over the box, and Scott's voice quietened.

When she got to the tenth floor, she opened the door to the hall-way and the sounds in her head suddenly fell silent. Sweat dripped from her cheek.

She drew the gun.

Apartment 1003 was dead ahead.

62

Amanda

Billy and Amanda got up from their table and left the restaurant. As they walked to the car, Billy made a call.

'Dr. Marin, it's Billy Cameron. I've found Ruth. She's at an address in Brooklyn. I'm going to send you the address now via text. Can you meet me there right away? As I said, I think she's a danger to herself and others. Please, Doctor . . .'

They got into Billy's car. He put the key in the ignition and ended the call.

'The doctor is going to meet us there. If she has had a relapse, he needs her to be taken into custody, officially, before she is readmitted to Kirby so he's going to ask NYPD to accompany him.'

'He's bringing the cops?' asked Amanda.

'He has to. No choice. It's all part of the regulations – so he says. That's okay – I don't care. We just have to make sure he sees her.'

'What do you think she'll do when she sees the doctor?'

'Who the hell knows? She can pass in normal society, but we both know she's homicidal. I just hope the doc sees it too. Look, this could be dangerous. I think it would be better if I dropped you off somewhere . . .'

'Are you kidding me? I need this. I might be arrested at any moment, and if I'm going to spend my life in jail then I'm going to make sure the cops know her part in this. I don't have a choice. I'm coming with you.'

Billy hit the accelerator, turned the car out of the parking space and into traffic. Cars behind had to brake and some stood on their horns. Billy gunned the engine, handed the newspaper to Amanda.

'Put that address into the satellite navigation and buckle up.'

Amanda put on her seat belt, ran her hands over her face.

She knew this was her only chance to catch this woman. There was no avoiding Farrow forever. And now she had a story to tell him. One that could help explain her actions. Make sense of them. In the end, she'd just defended herself, but that was only half the story. She still had to tell the truth about why she'd been there in the first place. If anyone would believe her, it would be Farrow.

With trembling fingers, she typed the address into the navigation screen on the dash. It bleeped, then threw up a route.

'This says we'll be there in twenty minutes, just before eight o'clock,' said Amanda.

'I just hope we get there before she does something stupid. She could be lining up another victim as we speak,' said Billy.

The pitch of the engine increased as Billy depressed the accelerator further and started weaving in and out of traffic.

63

Farrow

Hernandez leaned against the wall, staring through the glass into the private room at Mount Sinai hospital.

Farrow stood beside her, watching the nurses as they removed tubes, needles and monitors from the recently deceased body of Frank Quinn.

'Now it's a homicide,' said Hernandez.

'Looks like it,' said Farrow. They'd got a call from the hospital that Quinn had suffered another major setback. One of his lungs had collapsed and the second one wouldn't hold on much longer. There was a chance, a small one, that he might wake before he died.

In the end, Quinn never woke. And he'd died five minutes ago.

Hernandez turned away and Farrow followed. There was nothing more to be done in the hospital.

'Did you get a hold of Amanda White yet?'

'Not yet.'

'Jesus, you got those lab results . . .'

'I know when I got them. I'll find her. What about the techs working on Quinn's computers?'

'Last I heard they'd broken through the security protocols. We should have the results any time.'

Farrow's phone vibrated in his pocket. The caller ID said it was from a man he hadn't heard from in a long time.

'Dr. Marin, how are you?' said Farrow.

'I'm all right, but I need your help with something right away. It's Ruth Gelman. Someone who knows her has contacted me and they're concerned she's had some kind of breakdown or relapse. I'm on my way to an address in Brooklyn. I may need to have her committed.'

'Committed? Is it that bad?'

'By the sounds of it, yes. Paranoid hallucinations, exactly like the ones she had when she first came into Kirby. Technically, I've discharged her. I would have to commit her involuntarily if she's not willing to consent to treatment, or if she's incapable of making that decision. I could've called the local precinct, but I know you visited her when she was here. She trusts you. It wouldn't hurt to have another familiar face when we show up at her apartment. Can you do it?'

'Give me the address,' said Farrow.

64
Amanda

It was five minutes to eight when Amanda and Billy pulled up outside the address in Brooklyn Heights.

'That's it. Eighth-floor penthouse,' said Billy.

Just as he spoke, the front door to the building opened and a woman wearing a cap and dark clothing left the building carrying a gift basket.

'Is that her?' asked Amanda.

'I don't know. I can't tell from here,' said Billy.

The woman carried the basket to a black car, opened it and put the basket in the rear seat.

'That's a black Mercedes she's getting into. Check the license plate – I wrote down the one they found,' said Billy.

Amanda used the light from her cell phone to find the newspaper at her feet. She read out the license-plate number Billy had written down.

'That's it. That's her,' he said, opening the driver's door.

He paused, one foot out of the car. The lights came on inside the Mercedes up ahead, and then the car pulled out into the street.

Billy closed his door. 'Dammit,' he said. 'Don't let that car out of your sight.'

He let the Mercedes move ahead, then followed it. As they got to the intersection, he hung back, maintaining a respectful distance between them.

He hit dial on the last number called from his cell. The phone linked up to the Bluetooth on the computer in the dash. Dr. Marin answered the phone.

'Dr. Marin, it's Billy. We found Ruth, but she's not at that address I gave you. She's in a black Mercedes. We're following her. When she stops, I'll text you the address.'

'Okay, I have to make a call too. Let me know when you have an address and I'll be right there. Be careful approaching her. If you have to, just keep her talking until I get there.'

Billy hung up, gripped the wheel as they sailed through the night streets of New York City behind the sleek black car.

For twenty minutes they followed the car in silence until it pulled in and stopped. Billy swung the Escalade behind the line of parked cars. He was too close to a corner, but Amanda guessed he didn't care if he got a ticket.

'She's getting out,' said Amanda, and they watched Ruth take the gift basket into a building.

Billy called Dr. Marin. At first the phone rang, and he didn't pick up. Billy dialed again, and this time he answered. Billy gave Dr. Marin the new address from his satellite navigation. It all seemed to take a long time, but Amanda knew it was only a few minutes. She wanted to get in there and find Ruth. Billy ended the call. They got out of the car and approached the building entrance.

Amanda glanced through the glass doors, but didn't see anyone in the lobby. There was a desk for a doorman, but there was no sign of one. Amanda pulled the door, it opened into a brightly lit marble lobby.

There was a single elevator. Old, with a manual sliding scissor-gate door. She didn't like that kind of elevator. Her first apartment in the city had had one just like it, and she hated being able to watch the floors go by through the gate as the elevator went up and down.

'Oh my God,' said Billy.

Amanda turned, but didn't see Billy anywhere. Then his head shot up from behind the reception desk.

'Help me,' he said.

Amanda ran round, saw a huge man lying on the ground, with red ribbon tied round his neck. Billy's hands were at the man's throat, pulling at the ribbon, trying to loosen it. He managed to get it free, then turned the man over and put his head on his chest. Billy then clasped his hands together and put them on the man's sternum.

The doorman coughed and spluttered before Billy could perform the first compression.

'Are you all right?' said Billy.

'She . . . she's . . . gone up. Mr. Granger . . .' said the doorman.

'What floor?' said Billy.

'Tenth floor,' said the man.

'Amanda, wait here for Dr. Marin and the police, and call a paramedic,' said Billy.

Amanda took out her cell phone, started dialing, stopped and said, 'What? No, I need to see her.'

'Not yet. Look, she's dangerous. Amanda, I've grown very fond of you. I don't want anything to happen to you – I'd never forgive myself.'

'It's okay. I'll just come with you, I promise . . .'

'No,' said Billy. 'Please. Let me go up there. Stay with the doorman in case she comes back down. You wait here for Dr. Marin and the cops. Okay? Tell them where I am and then you can come right up with them?'

Amanda nodded, dialed 911.

Billy helped the doorman back into his chair. He was gasping for air.

'Sir, my name is Billy Cameron. I'm going up to stop the woman who attacked you. Can you please call the people on the tenth floor, tell them not to open their doors for any reason? Okay?'

He nodded, and Billy said to Amanda, 'Can you help him with that?'

She nodded.

Amanda's 911 was answered, and she asked for paramedics and police. The doorman gave the address as George Towers.

Billy hauled open the elevator gate, stepped inside, closed it and hit the button for the tenth floor. Slowly, the elevator began to rise and with it came almighty clattering as the mechanism whined into life. There were no doors on the elevator. She could still see him through the scissor gate. The lift ascended, and as his face was gradually obscured, then his torso, his hands and his legs, and the light from the car disappeared altogether, Amanda was suddenly very afraid that this was the last time she would see Billy alive.

She heard the guard talking. He'd regained enough breath to call the residents, told them not to open their doors – there was a situation.

She stepped outside, checked the street for any passing cops.

Amanda hadn't prayed in a long time, but she muttered an oath to God on that doorstep asking him for protection for her friend.

Another sound drew her attention.

A silver Lexus pulled up across the street and the engine, which had been revving high, shut off. A man got out of it quickly. He was in his sixties, bald, but with a fulsome gray beard and delicate rimless glasses perched precariously on his nose. In his left hand he carried what looked like a leather medical bag. He looked around the street.

'Are you Dr. Marin?' called Amanda.

He waved at her, crossing the street just as another car pulled up. This was an old Ford with a dent in the chrome bumper. The windows were tinted, and she guessed this was the cops. Then she realized where she'd last seen that car.

Parked outside her building.

Farrow and Hernandez got out. Hernandez first, and then Farrow more stiffly.

Amanda's stomach lurched. She wanted to throw up. She was so

KILL FOR ME KILL FOR YOU

damn close now. She had Ruth upstairs, and she hadn't even had a chance to talk to her.

And it was too late.

Too damn late.

Farrow and Hernandez greeted Dr. Marin, as if they were expecting him, and suddenly Amanda felt unsure about what exactly was going on.

'Amanda? What are you doing here?' asked Farrow.

'You two know each other?' asked Dr. Marin.

'Yeah, ahm, we do,' said Amanda. 'I'm with Billy Cameron. We both knew Ruth – through our trauma therapy group. He just went up in the elevator. She's attacked the doorman. I think he's okay, but he's still winded.'

'Oh my God, what floor are they on?' asked Marin.

'Tenth,' said Amanda.

Marin, Farrow and Hernandez jogged inside. Amanda nodded, suddenly unable to say anything else and moved with them. Farrow checked on the doorman, who was clutching his throat, his breathing still heavy. Hernandez banged open the staircase door and started pounding up the stairs.

Farrow called out at Hernandez, 'Don't engage her until I get there. Wait for me. I'll take the elevator with Dr. Marin.' He punched the button to summon the elevator. 'I've been looking for you, Amanda,' said Farrow. 'Are you okay? I went to your apartment. I've been calling for days.'

'I know, I'm sorry. I'm okay, considering. We've got a lot to talk about. I have something to—'

'Look, ideally we would do this another time, but now I have you let me say this fast. The reason I wanted to talk to you is to give you an update on Wallace Crone.'

Amanda had taken a deep breath. Ready to unload. Ready to tell him she had hurt someone. She had gone to a house to kill this man, but backed out. Then he'd attacked her and she'd acted in self-defense.

She'd been manipulated into it by the woman upstairs, but she held her breath when Farrow mentioned Crone's name.

She said nothing. Her mind was suddenly wiped.

'We picked him up a couple of days ago on an anonymous tip. He's a registered sex offender so he's not allowed within a hundred feet of a school. We got a call saying he was talking to kids outside an elementary school and had persuaded one of them into his car. We checked with the school and they had no reports of missing kids or a kid getting into a strange vehicle. Even so, we held him for the day and questioned him relentlessly – got the lab to swab his vehicle. Turns out there were no fingerprints and no other DNA present in the passenger seat that he couldn't account for. I just got the word back from the lab the other night. Thought I should at least give you a call and let you know.'

Amanda's thoughts came rushing back to her, recalibrated, and yet too jumbled to allow her to express any of them. She let out her breath in a rush.

That's why Crone didn't get the subway to work that day. That's why he didn't show up for his psychiatrist appointment. Ruth had made the call to the cops, got him arrested and off the street, then told Amanda she'd killed him.

'Amanda? Are you okay?'

'Ah, yeah, I'm fine.'

'Good. I'm sorry it took so long to reach you. I know you always wanted to be updated first. I respect that. Look, we can talk later. This elevator isn't coming down any time soon. We'll take the stairs. Wait here.'

Amanda stood aside as Farrow and Dr. Marin stepped by her, opened the door to the stairwell.

Then she heard something. Loud and clear.

They all did.

It was unmistakable.

The sound of a gunshot.

65
Ruth

She tried the door to apartment 1003.

Locked.

Placing the basket on the floor, she took hold of the gun inside her pocket and was about to knock when she heard something.

The elevator. Someone was coming up. Maybe to this floor, maybe not. But she didn't want to take the risk of being seen going into the Granger's apartment.

As the elevator car got higher and higher, the noise from the mechanism grew louder.

It didn't stop.

Ruth saw a beam of light hit the carpeted floor from the elevator car. The beam grew wider as the car ascended, enough to see the pattern of shadows cast by the elevator gate. The light grew over the flooring, and up the wall. Ruth made her way back towards the elevator.

There was a man in the elevator car. She could see the top of his head through the gate, then his face. He was standing still, in the center of the lift. Something about his face drew her attention. It was hard to get a good look at him. Just when she thought she recognized him, part of his face was again obscured by the crisscross iron gate.

The elevator reached her floor and stopped with a sudden jerk.

Ruth peered through the gate. The man looked familiar, but out of place somehow. She knew his face, but couldn't place it.

'Don't you remember me, Ruth?' he said.

She knew that voice too.

'My name's Billy,' he said.

She stepped closer. The man who said his name was Billy placed his right hand on the handle of the gate, but didn't slide it open.

'You knew me as BillyCam2003, remember?'

Ruth's grip on the gun in her pocket tightened. Billy was one of her online targets from a bereavement forum. From her Felicia profile. A good candidate for Quinn, initially. He'd said he would kill him, but he'd wanted to meet Ruth first.

She never met her online targets.

Better to keep them at a distance. There were only so many support groups in the city, and she was taking enough chances by maintaining different identities in real support groups – so she never met the online people. And Billy had been adamant that he wanted a face-to-face. Too pushy, so she'd pulled out, burned the Felicia profile and found Amanda White for the job instead.

But he hadn't called her Felicia just now. He'd called her Ruth.

'I've been looking for you for a long time. All this would've been easier if you'd just agreed to meet me when you were targeting Frank Quinn,' he said.

She had never even spoken to him on the phone. Yet she knew that voice.

The man smiled at her.

Then, with his left hand he raised his thumb and forefinger to his eyes. They were the color of brown sugar. She thought he was going to close his eyes, and rub them clear, but he didn't.

He kept them open. His thumb and forefinger touched the eyeballs, and then gently pinched, sweeping out the contact lenses.

His brown eyes were gone. In their place, a pair of dead blue eyes stared through the gate at her.

Ruth's lips began to tremble, then her body followed, and a scream that began in her stomach erupted through her chest as she pointed at him and yelled . . .

'It's you! It's *you!*'

His voice echoed through the elevator shaft, into the hallway and deep into her frozen heart.

'That's right, Ruth. It's me. Hi there, *sweetheart.*'

She pulled the gun from her pocket, pointed the barrel through the gap in the gate, aimed straight at his chest.

She pulled the trigger, but she was half a second too late.

The man yanked the gate open, which caught the gun barrel, wrenching the pistol from her grip, but as it did so the gun went off, sending an explosion of splinters up around the man as the round hit the panel to his right.

Ruth fell backwards, her mouth open, unable to breathe, unable to scream, using her heels and elbows to back away toward the stairs as the man stepped out of the elevator and walked slowly toward her.

'I should have killed you that night all those years ago. I don't like loose ends. Because of you I had to leave New York. I continued my work elsewhere, of course. But it was not convenient. Fresh surroundings bring new risks. An old shark like me favors familiar waters for their feeding grounds. And now look at you. Look at what you've become.'

She backed away, unable to breathe or speak.

'I read about your husband killing Patrick Travers in that hotel, and when I saw Travers's picture and read about your case I knew what had happened. You thought I was Travers, didn't you? You killed an innocent man who looked just like me. You went away to Kirby hospital and I thought I was rid of you. Then I saw on the news one day, a picture of a man who looked just like me, just like Travers. His name was Saul Benson and the man who killed him said he'd been tricked into doing it. He'd agreed to swap murders with a woman named Deborah Mallory who he'd met in a support group. I looked online, found more men, killed in their home, with no motive. And they *all* looked just like me. Almost *exactly* like me. I knew then I had to find you. You were hunting me, Ruth. And that is not something I can tolerate. I am no one's prey.'

He was still coming towards her. Ruth glanced behind him, saw the gun on the floor. She couldn't get to it.

'I knew it was you. You'd made the same mistake. Just like Travers all over again. I searched the web, even went to a few support groups looking for you. Eventually we found each other, online. You should have just met me. I could have ended this weeks ago. When we talked online, I realized you were not making mistakes, Ruth. You were enjoying the kill. And you were killing again, and again and again, not in search of me. But for the pleasure. You know how it feels to end a life. You have tasted that sweetness. Still, I couldn't let you go. You might have accidentally targeted me one day. It's a pity all of this had to end. Oh, what a very fine monster you are . . .'

Ruth could hear footsteps on the stairs, coming up fast. Shouting. Different voices, all calling her name. And a female voice, calling out for Billy.

The man picked out fresh contact lenses from a dispenser and with practised precision he raised his head and slipped them onto each eye, blinking to let them settle.

He stared down at her then, just as she felt a hand grabbing her shoulder from behind.

'Ruth, Ruth, calm down, it's okay. It's Dr. Marin.'

She opened her mouth to scream, but no sound came. She shook her head, raised her hand and pointed at Billy and shouted again.

'*That's him! That's him! That's him!*'

She heard Dr. Marin's voice. 'My God, you were right, Billy. She is displaying precisely the same paranoid behavior as the day she was first admitted . . .'

Just then, she felt something sharp biting her upper arm. Turning, she saw Dr. Marin pull a needle out of her shoulder.

She felt tired, and she couldn't speak, and then she saw Detective Farrow and his partner, and Amanda. And she thought she was going mad, slipping into darkness, and she saw the chest, and the chains burst free, and she screamed again and felt as if she was falling.

Her fingers scrambled on the floor, her nails breaking, as the man called Billy stood over her again. His voice was the last thing she heard as darkness took her.

'You're going back to the hospital, Ruth. You're going to be okay. They'll take good care of you. Don't worry – I'll be sure to come by and visit . . .'

66

Amanda

TWO MONTHS LATER

Amanda stepped out of the elevator of her building into the lobby. It was almost seven in the morning and she only had a few minutes to get to 96th Street subway station.

She buttoned the coat of her business suit, and as she passed her mailbox she noticed the little flap on the side was sticking up. It was too early for the mailman. She stopped and quickly opened the box with her key. Inside was a letter in a small Manila envelope. There was no address on it. Just her name.

She placed it inside her jacket pocket and opened the front door to a cold January morning. Ice had compacted on the sidewalk. As she took her first step outside, her right foot slipped and she felt herself sliding, tilting. She was going to land in the dirty slush and ruin her suit.

And then she was no longer falling.

A strong hand had taken her elbow, and her heels skidded a few times before she regained her balance. She gazed up and saw the man who had caught her.

It was Farrow.

'Jesus, Amanda, you shouldn't be allowed out on your own,' he said with a smile.

'God, I'm sorry. Hi, I mean, thank you.'

'I was coming to see you. I heard you got a new job.'

'Yeah, I'm working in a new art gallery. I'm the manager, if you can believe it. I even get to display my own work from time to time.'

'That's great. Listen, I just wanted a quick word. Do you have time?'

Amanda checked her watch. 'I should be getting on the subway in like ten minutes.'

'Come for a cup of coffee and I'll drive you to work.'

'You can get to Tribeca from here faster than the subway?'

'I can if I put my siren on,' he said with a smile. 'Don't worry. I'll make sure you're not late.'

Amanda nodded and they walked a block to a Starbucks. Farrow paid for two coffees and they took the high stools at the window. Farrow said they were better for his back than low, hard chairs.

'I wanted to check in, see how you're doing?' said Farrow.

Amanda took a sip of coffee. It was burning hot all the way down her throat, but she needed that warmth on a morning like this.

'I'm okay. I've paid my back rent, got a new job. Things are looking up. Apart from Crone's lawsuit. That prick's still suing me.'

Farrow studied her closely for a moment, then said, 'Actually, there are a couple of things I wanted to clear up, if you don't mind?'

She swallowed, took another sip of coffee and said, 'What kind of things?'

'Well, we got a strange hit on a DNA search. You ever met a man named Frank Quinn?'

She shook her head.

'He was murdered around Thanksgiving. We think the perp got onto his property from the alley. One of our forensic teams found a spot of blood on Quinn's back wall. There were some fibers there too from black denim jeans. We could only get a partial DNA sample. The dried blood was degraded. Rain and God knows what else got on it. Not enough for scientific certainty, not enough to hold up in court, but the DNA from that blood was a partial match for your DNA. To me it looked like somebody might have cut themselves climbing the wall. I don't suppose *you* could offer an explanation?'

'I've no idea. I never heard of the guy.'

'It's just that the night we found Ruth after she had attacked that guard and was trying to get into Mr. Granger's apartment, when I arrived with Dr. Marin, I saw you were limping a little going up those stairs.'

'I fell that morning. Frosty sidewalk. Didn't have you around to save me,' she said.

'The guy, Quinn, was a money launderer for the mob. He had fat stacks of cash lying around and he was moving huge sums of money through different online accounts. He was a bad guy, Amanda. Also, he looked very similar to Patrick Travers, Ruth's first victim. And a lot like the guy Ruth was targeting that night we picked her up.'

Amanda said nothing. She held her breath, watched Farrow as he took a sip of coffee and stared out of the window at people passing by on the street. He said nothing for a time, and Amanda discreetly let out her breath, clasped her hands around her coffee cup to stop them shaking.

'Do you know what nickname they gave me at the precinct?' he asked, still not looking directly at her.

'Saint Jude. Hernandez told me once,' said Amanda, trying to keep her voice level, fighting down the sick feeling that was beginning in her stomach.

'Patron Saint of hopeless cases,' said Farrow, staring idly out the window. 'You know how I close most of my homicide files? I'm not any smarter than any other cop. I just don't give up. Ever. I feel like I owe something to those victims. And I carry it around with me. It's heavy. A burden. But I take it on and I keep going until I break the case. Hernandez thinks I'm obsessed. She says sometimes I have to let go.'

Amanda said nothing, her heart thumping in her chest.

Farrow stared out at the street, said, 'I think I might have to let this Quinn case go unsolved. He probably got caught skimming funds. The mob don't take kindly to be being cheated. Your DNA being on that wall? Like I said, it was a partial match. Could be a fuck up at the lab. I don't know . . .'

He shook his head, then turned toward her and asked, 'How's your knee?'

He knows it was me, thought Amanda. He just knows.

'It's fine now,' said Amanda finally.

'Good, because it's dangerous out there on those sidewalks,' he said, glancing out of the window, then fixing her with a dead-eyed stare. 'If you were to slip and fall again, I wouldn't be there to catch you next time.'

Amanda said, 'I'm going to stay home in future.'

He searched her face, making sure she was telling him the truth, then nodded, said, 'Come on, I'll drive you to work. There's one more piece of news. The press haven't got hold of it yet and I wanted to be first to tell you.' Farrow got to his feet slowly.

'Tell me what?' said Amanda, suddenly nervous again.

'Crone's dead.'

'He's what?'

'A garbage man found him at four a.m. He'd been stripped naked and tortured, then somebody had just thrown him into a dumpster.'

'Jesus Christ,' she said, her heart fluttering.

'There was a strong chemical smell off the body. Maybe chloroform. Looks like he was drugged before someone went to work on him.'

Amanda said nothing. She couldn't process it. Not yet.

'Just so I know, and I'm not for one second suggesting you're involved, but seeing as how his lawsuit against you is just as dead as he is, could you tell me where you were last night?' asked Farrow.

'I was at the Dolly Parton concert. A friend of mine sent me tickets.'

'Which friend?'

'Billy. You met him that night we found Ruth.'

'And was Billy with you at the concert?'

'Ah, no, he couldn't make it. I went with a new friend from work, Abbey.'

'Fair enough. Can't say it's a loss to the city. Hernandez found out about a half hour ago and she's already organized a party. Come on, I'll give you that lift.'

They walked a block and a half to Farrow's car. With each step, Amanda grew lighter. The air still felt cold, but no longer abrasive. It felt . . . clean. New. The sun split through a chestnut tree on the corner, and for a moment Amanda and Farrow were bathed in golden sunlight. The light turned orange, red and gold as if it was aflame.

Amanda got into the police cruiser. Farrow reached over to her side and opened the glove box. Inside were CD cases, most of them open, and some broken and cracked. He found a case that was still closed, opened it up and slotted the CD into the dash player. He handed the case to Ruth as the music started up.

Dolly Parton's Greatest Hits.

'You like Dolly?' she asked.

'Who doesn't?' said Farrow.

They listened to 'Islands in the Stream' and said nothing while Farrow drove her south through the city.

'Have you seen Ruth since that night?' she asked.

'No, I suppose I'll see her at her trial. Have you been asked to attend as a witness?'

'No, not yet anyway. I read about it in the paper. She really was dangerous if all of that is true.'

'It looks cut and dried to me,' said Farrow. 'The gun she had that night was registered to a former security guard named Gary Childers. Her fingerprints were on his garage door and from what I've seen of the phone messages between them she was coming to pay him a visit. Poor bastard. She shot him in the face with his own gun while he was watching TV.'

'She'll never get out again, will she?'

'No,' said Farrow, 'she sure won't.'

They fell into silence then. Amanda gazed at the track list on the back of the CD cover, and fast forwarded to one of her favorite songs.

'It's All Wrong, But It's All Right'.

They listened, and hummed along, and Amanda gave him directions to the gallery. He pulled up at the curb.

'Thank you for the lift,' said Amanda. 'Thank you for everything. You've been there for me more than anyone else. And you never gave up on Jess and Luis. I'll never forget what you've done for me.'

'I did what any cop would do,' he said.

'No, you did so much more. And you never gave up on me, either.'

'I think you're doing just fine, now. Keep it that way. I'm getting older and my back isn't going to hold up forever. I don't suppose we'll ever really know who killed Quinn, or Crone. I guess Hernandez is right. I just have to let some cases go. Take care of yourself, and enjoy the new job,' he said, before speeding away.

When his car had turned a corner, Amanda reached into her jacket pocket and took out the letter she'd found in her mailbox. She opened it, and read it.

Dear Amanda,

I hope you enjoyed the concert. My apologies, I couldn't be there, but as you will no doubt learn I was otherwise engaged. I wanted to thank you for all your help in finding Ruth, and I wanted to return the favor. I'm sorry I lied to you. I never had a wife, never mind one who was murdered. It is my hope that you might forgive me.

I already knew Ruth's real identity before I even met you, but I didn't want to draw attention to myself, you understand. I needed a buffer between me and the police. And a person that Scott would trust. Someone to help cover

up a few things. It was better that I had someone with me
for the ride. I would like you to burn this letter, if you
don't mind, after reading it. But I want you to know that
before Crone died, he admitted to killing your little girl. I
thought you deserved that closure. It's unlikely that we'll
meet again.

Good luck, and enjoy the rest of your life, sweetheart.

X

Amanda left work at five thirty, got home, picked something up and went right back out again. She hopped on the subway, changed to the N train at Atlantic Avenue and rode it until she hit the Stilwell Avenue station at Coney Island.

She loved seaside resorts in winter. There were always few, if any, people and there was a cold stillness to the place. As if it was sleeping. Waiting for the sun. It was dark when she stepped onto the boardwalk. Slippery too. Carefully, she made it to the beach and then removed her shoes. The sand was cool to the touch. Jess had loved this beach. They had come to this beach after Jess won Sparkles at the fairground. Luis had made sandcastles for Jess and they all ate ice cream together. There were no lights from the Ferris wheel behind her now as she walked out further toward the sound of the ocean – the Atlantic licking the beach. Both beach and sea were coal-black in the night.

Amanda sat down cross-legged, and using her hands she scooped out a small basin in the sand. The wind was picking up, and she had to cradle the flame from her Zippo as she lit Billy's letter, then placed it in the bottom of the sand pit. Amanda took Sparkles from her bag, and placed the toy on top of the burning letter. The flame ignited the toy almost instantly, turning the sand around it from slate gray to gold once more.

She sat for a time on the beach, warming her hands over the tiny flames, knowing she had finally crossed that great black sea.

There was no one else on the beach.

Amanda did not feel afraid.

And she did not feel alone.

The wind hurled the sea at her, but it could not touch her. It could not touch her fire, either. Whatever kind of stuffing was in that toy changed the color of the flames from time to time. The odors it gave off changed too. For a second, but only a second, she thought she caught the faint smell of oranges. The wind brought sounds to her ears. Waves curling into rolling hills and then smashing down into the water.

And something else.

She couldn't tell if it was the wind whispering over the boardwalk, or through the sand, but she thought that in the air she could hear a child's voice. Playing. Laughing. Happy.

At peace.

Acknowledgements

My first set of thanks is for my first reader, first editor, and first lady – my wife, Tracy. She's the best, in every way. I'm lucky to have her. And you are too, because she spots my mistakes, and with her suggestions she makes all of my books so much better.

A huge thank-you to my agent, Jon Wood. An incredible editor in his own right and a true friend. He's the reason you had the opportunity to read this book. In fact, he's the reason I got a start in this business when, in a different professional capacity, he published my first novel, *The Defence*. If you see him, or if you have the pleasure of meeting him – buy him a drink, or give him a cup of tea and a nice biscuit (depending upon the appropriate circumstances of your meeting, and the quality of biscuits to hand). All I can say is – he deserves all the drink, and all the biscuits you can spare. Huge thanks to Safae El-Ouahabi, for all her brilliant skills. And my enormous thanks go to the entire team at RCW Literary Agency. A lovely group of hard-working professionals who have so wonderfully sold my books all over the world. Thank you so much.

My thanks go to the incomparable Toby Jones, editor extraordinaire, and as lovely a chap as you could care to meet. Toby, Mari, Jennifer, Joe, Lucy, Patrick, Becky, Isabel and all at my new home at Headline Books, I thank you so very much for publishing me with such passion, creativity and professionalism. I hope to Christ we sell a lot of books.

A special thank-you to David Shelley. For his kindness.

My thanks go to my family, my dad, my friends, and supporters. And my dogs, Lolly and Muffin, who are terrible editors, but are very good at sleeping peacefully at my feet, and catching balls, respectively.

A final and most important thanks, goes to you.

Yes you, again.

If you have read this book, then I want to thank you for doing so. I really hope you enjoyed it. Even if you didn't like it all that much, I am enormously pleased that you took the time to read it. And I want you to know that I think about you a lot. I want you to have been entertained while you read, and for you to have forgotten whatever troubles you. At least for a while. For that's what reading is all about.

I hope all our troubles pass, and I wish us all peace and light.